Forces
of
Nature

BOOK ONE OF THE FAMILY BUSINESS SERIES

ELLE RIVERS

Cover Design by: Allie McGilbery

Edited by Kasey Kubica

Copyright © 2023 by Elle Rivers

CONTENTS

To...

To anyone who didn't win the lottery when it comes to their family. You are not alone, and you can choose a different one.

A NOTE FROM ELLE

This novel contains topics some might be sensitive to. Please note that this novel contains emotional abuse and manipulation from parents, as well as allusion to abuse. I've taken care to display these issues with as much care as possible. If there is another warning you feel should be added, please reach out to me on Instagram at @elleswrites and I will do my best to rectify the situation.

PROLOGUE

Ruth

"I bet he's *so* mad."

"Did she bribe someone?"

"She had to. There's no way Ruth Murray *beat* Knox Price."

Those were the whispers that broke out through the other graduating students as my name was announced as the valedictorian.

That's right. *Me.*

It took everything I had. Sleepless nights and constant studying. Kissing up to teachers and asking for extra credit.

But that work paid off because *I* was the valedictorian, the best in our graduating class.

And Knox Price wasn't.

I didn't think it could be done. He was always one step ahead of me. If I had a 100, he would somehow get a 101. If there was a mile run in gym class, he'd beat me by two seconds. He was insanely talented at everything he tried. He was a genius in the making.

I hadn't even tried to compete at first. I was only trying to make my parents proud. But then one day, he'd caught me at my locker and bragged about his stupid win, and I hated him from that moment on.

And for the last four years, he'd constantly driven me up a wall. He was always studying, always memorizing things in two seconds. He didn't seem to *sleep*. It was like the fun of beating me made him inhuman.

Not anymore.

I, at the very least, was proud of myself. But I wasn't the first in my family to get the coveted title of valedictorian. My older brother Tom had already done this, and my parents didn't hesitate to remind me of that.

But my brother had it easy. He'd skated to the top of the class with no one to stop him. I had Knox in my way the whole time. I rightfully won this.

And I'd won it from everyone's favorite. The perfect robot who got *everyone* to like him. Everyone except for me.

While I got called bossy and annoying, Knox floated through classrooms, always on the teachers' good side. When he got As on tests, people asked him how he did it, and if he could tutor them. I was asked if I cheated.

Or if I'd bribed someone, as I'd just overheard.

But I'd never see these people again, and in my adult life, I'd be surrounded by mature people who would treat me with respect. This kind of stuff didn't fly in the real world. People respected your work ethic and nothing else mattered.

The principal was still talking, but my mind was on my speech. This was my goodbye to all of these assholes, and rather than be a smug dick like all of my soon-to-be classmates expected, I had decided to take a higher road, as I always outwardly tried to.

Even if Knox's golden eyes were looking down on me in that very moment, as they always did.

He'd hit a ridiculous growth spurt in ninth grade that I could never fully forgive him for.

I'd always been made to feel inferior for my shorter stature. Tom had been tall, and when we were younger, he had a habit of stealing my homework and holding it above my head where I couldn't reach it.

My younger brother, Barry, had outgrown me when he was in eighth grade, and had reached six-foot-four in the time since.

Knox, thankfully, wasn't like my brothers. He didn't exactly make fun of my height, but the thought of seeing him crane his neck downward to look at me was the reminder of how much better he seemed to be at everything.

I started wearing platforms on my first day of high school because Barry had made fun of my short legs. I eventually moved to heels once Knox had mentioned how clunky my steps sounded during one of his brag sessions. I refused not to have my extra height because I already disliked that he had to tilt his head down at all to look at me. It made his subtle gloating all the more difficult to bear.

Unfortunately, my heels did no good sitting in the auditorium seat. Knox was looking down from his seat beside me, which had to be his favorite position to be in. I couldn't wait to be standing and walking toward this podium to get my damn graduation over with and finally tower over him for once.

I risked a glance at him and my eyes caught on his soft-looking, messy hair. If he were anyone else, I'd say he was cute in a nerdy sort of way. He had a nice jawline and cute, black-rimmed glasses. But even if I were interested—which I definitely was not—he never dated anyway. He was too focused on his studies.

On constantly *beating* me.

I thought that Knox would be mad that I'd stolen valedictorian from him, but he didn't take the news like I thought he would. Instead of trying to sneak ahead by completing one last project, he looked at me with the same expression he always did when I was annoying him. A sideways smile with narrowed eyes. One that looked kind but was also calculating.

There was always a hint of something else in his gaze, a fire that broke his polite exterior. Every smile was layered with an unsaid question: "When can I beat you next?" Sometimes he would even say it out loud, egging me on with a not-so-gentle reminder of my consistent standing in second place.

It was like he thrived off of my desire to beat him.

And that thrive turned into a phenomenal work ethic I couldn't compete with. I wasn't sure how he slept because he was always studying, always doing one more thing than I was. He couldn't be a fucking human. I was sure of it.

But it didn't matter, because all of it was ending tonight.

"I'd like to invite Ruth Murray to say a few words to all of you." Principal Avery gestured for me to come up on stage. I took a deep breath and stood.

When I got up to the podium, he muttered, "Be nice, Ruth."

My teeth ground together. I *was* nice to the people who were nice to me. I just wasn't *quiet* with the people who weren't.

The people in this place could never tell the difference.

"My fellow classmates," I greeted with a smile. I wanted it to be easygoing and proud, so I pointedly did *not* look at Knox. "Here we are. Graduation. The end of this chapter of our lives and the beginning of something new. Something big." In more ways than one for me. "I know I should say something inspiring here, but what we've done is already so powerful that I can't find the proper words. I've seen you, all of you, grow so much in the past four years. Sasha, your work in the science labs has been unparalleled, and I am so excited for your journey to Hawaii in their astronomy program. Jeff, I know you worked so hard to graduate with honors after such a difficult year. You're amazing." A few family members cheered for him. "And finally, I want to congratulate Knox Price on his stellar work being accepted into *five* Ivy League schools."

Parents cheered, but I could see my classmates whispering among themselves.

Everyone knew I despised Knox. No one thought I would be congratulating him. I glanced at him, finding his face to be in a similar state of shock. I wanted to laugh. Was he turning red? He never blushed. Did robots even have that ability?

I decided not to think too hard on it. I had a speech to get through, after all. I said more kind and cheerful words, telling everyone how I hoped they'd do great things with their lives. And I meant it. Sure, these people pissed me off, but this was a huge moment for us all. I wouldn't let my own anger over their doubts about me ruin this.

Except for maybe Knox. He could easily be a cryptid. Or maybe a vampire. Was there a ruder, more annoying version of Edward Cullen?

I concluded my speech with one last, kind word and a smile to the entire auditorium. After I thanked them for their time, they all cheered. A thrill ran through me at all the smiling, happy faces and the thunderous applause.

As the principal returned to the podium, I sat back down next to Knox, refusing once again to return his oddly intense gaze. Our story was done, but he didn't know that yet.

After this, I planned to *live*. While I didn't want to be like Tom, who was sleeping with a different person every night, I did hope I could find someone for myself once I was away from my high school title of *Ruth the Ruthless*. The name had followed me throughout high school, as did Knox's ability to constantly beat me.

And now I was valedictorian, and I was done with it all.

Including him.

Knox

My body buzzed with curious excitement. From the moment my name passed through Ruth Murray's lips, I knew she would have some snide little comment to make about finally beating me. I lived for it. I'd been up all night imagining what it could be.

Never in my dreams would *she* be congratulating *me*.

She was planning something. *She had to be.* If there was one thing I knew about Ruth Murray it was that she always had a trick up her sleeve.

I tried to remember what competitions we had running. School was over, but school was all we had. What else was there?

In the depths of my thoughts, I recalled her speech, and remembered *what* she'd congratulated me on.

College.

Had she gotten into more Ivy League schools than me? Was she going to the one I didn't apply to?

I knew her family had money, considering the car she'd been given for her sixteenth birthday. I bet she could afford more application fees than I could, since her family seemed to have more wealth than mine did.

But I *loved* fighting with her. She was the only one who made me try harder, and her expressions after my wins were priceless. The daggers she glared were softened only by how cute she looked when she tried to intimidate someone. I hoped that we would end up in the same college, but her speech made me wonder if that was in the cards for us. I didn't want this rivalry to end just yet.

My gaze returned to her as I tried to figure out what her plan was. The salutatorian was speaking now, but I couldn't bring myself to listen, just like I hadn't been able to before Ruth walked on stage.

She hadn't even stuttered. Her eyes roamed the crowd without a glimmer of nervousness, something I could never do. If there was one thing she would always beat me at, it was public speaking.

I was anxious about the impending walk across the stage to accept my own diploma. I bet she didn't feel the same.

She was the right person to be the valedictorian. I had no doubt about it.

Throughout the rest of the night, I kept my eyes on her, as if I could somehow memorize her sharp features and bright green eyes. I didn't know why, but I wanted to remember this moment for as long as I could.

Then the principal lined us all up, with Ruth and me in front. Everyone else was in alphabetical order, but because Ruth and I had both been vying for valedictorian, Principal Avery insisted we both remain in the front. I regretted agreeing to this arrangement, since all eyes would be on me as one of the first students to get our diplomas.

Despite Ruth's proximity, my nerves grew, and I busied myself with tracing the different colors of her hair in her bun. Once she had accepted her diploma and was no longer in front of me, I had to focus on not tripping over my own feet when I was finally called to get mine.

The noise in the room was almost deafening when my name was called. While I knew I was liked, I wasn't sure how I felt about all the attention.

"I can't wait to see what you become, Knox." Principal Avery shook my hand tightly, giving me her warmest smile. I could only manage a polite nod.

Once it was over, I took a few calming breaths, but then my mind instantly rounded back to Ruth. I needed to find her. I needed to know what she had planned.

As I made my way through the parking lot, a few people stopped to congratulate me, but I only had eyes for one person.

And that very person was already walking to her car.

I saw her quick walk. She was in her signature bun, but two pieces were pulled out and were curled against her face.

"Hey!" I called, and a few students looked on nervously. I was aware of three bets running on the two of us. One saying we would kill each other by graduation, another betting on who was going to be the most successful, and the last betting on if we would get married.

Ruth didn't know about any of these. Many of classmates were terrified of her in a way I wasn't, and there was an unsaid rule in the school not to include her for fear of her wrath. I thought about telling her, but I'd been begged not to.

She froze, and I could imagine her face scrunching up the way it always did when she thought I wasn't looking.

"What?" she asked, turning around.

"Thanks for the shoutout. I'm waiting for the other shoe to drop, though."

Ruth smiled, but her arms were crossed tightly over her chest. "Why would there be anything else?"

"Come on. There's always something else, Ruth."

"Maybe I'm being nice on our last day of high school."

"And what about college? Are you planning on being nice there?"

"To my new classmates, maybe."

"And to me?"

Her eyes narrowed. "And I hope *you* have a nice life."

"Come on, Ruth. You know I can go to whatever fancy Ivy League school you go to."

"I'm not going to an Ivy league school."

"What?"

"Did losing ruin your ears?"

"You're not going to an Ivy?" My heart stuttered in my chest.

"I decided to go a different route."

"Where?"

"I don't have to tell you."

"I'm going to find out."

"Why?" she asked. "Why does it matter? High school is *over*, Knox. We don't ever have to see each other again."

"What if I want to see you again?"

"You should have thought of that *before* you made up a question on the math final and then got extra credit for it. Or maybe before you wrote a ten-page essay instead of the required five to disprove my point that you read over my shoulder in class!"

"Hey, I couldn't control that Mrs. Absher read it for everyone. Maybe you could have tried harder."

There it was. That cute but angry expression on her face. "You really don't get it, do you?"

"I get that you don't like being beat, but we all have to be humbled sometimes."

"It wasn't sometimes for me. It was every damn day."

"It was in good fun!"

"Not for me, it wasn't. You have no idea how—" She cut herself off, pinching the bridge of her nose. "I don't owe you an explanation. We're done here."

I grabbed her arm. "No. We aren't."

"Let me go." Her voice was like ice.

"You can't just walk away."

"Yes, I can. You were the worst part of my life, Knox Price. I'm not giving you any more time. I'm going to go to college, and I am going to get a job at my dad's company and make something of myself. When you're an old man with no friends or no life, you can look at me and wonder how *I* did it. That's the only future we have."

The words hurt, like a betrayal I wasn't sure I deserved. There was something about her insistence that this was our last meeting that made everything sharper.

"Maybe I'll be the one to make something of myself," I said lowly. "You ever think of that?"

"No, I haven't. Because you're not a person, Knox. You're a robot who's good at pretending to be human."

I froze. Her cold words were true in a way I didn't want them to be. Sometimes during the late nights when I refused to stop working, I would look around and wonder what it must be like to go out with friends rather than study. What was it like to fall in love, or care about anything other than winning against one person. Some days, *smiles* were difficult.

What if she was *right*?

"And you're second best on a good day." If she was going for a low blow, then I was too.

She smiled, nodding her head as if this was exactly what she expected me to say.

"Not once I'm away from you."

She turned and walked away. I was left glaring in the direction of her retreating form. I stayed there until she'd driven off, my brain grinding over her parting words.

You're not a person, Knox. You're a robot who's good at pretending to be human.

Something hot and angry settled into my chest and I was determined to prove her wrong, even if I never saw her again.

CHAPTER ONE

Ruth

Ten Years Later

As I sat in endless lines of cars on the interstate, questioning every life decision I'd made up to this point, I realized that traffic was the bane of my existence.

It used to be a guy who always beat me in high school, but I tried not to let myself think about him all that much anymore. I could admit, however, that sometimes, having a human to focus all of your hatred on was better than inanimate traffic.

The roads in Nashville had only grown more congested as people moved to the state. New self-driving technology invented by a certain person I didn't like to name made things better, but nothing could fix the problem of too many people in one place.

I was sure others found the busy nature of the city charming, but as I got cut off by another sports car with a loud engine, I wondered if maybe I should have moved to the middle-of-nowhere Montana instead of staying in my hometown.

It didn't help that this Monday was already setting up to be a long, arduous day. My company had hired a new executive and there weren't even whispers of his name.

And a lack of a name more than likely meant controversy.

My notebook had been filled with ways on supporting another mediocre White man with a sense of entitlement and too large of a paycheck. It was the last thing I wanted to do, and I craved a month-long vacation.

But I never stopped, even if I sometimes felt like a hamster running at full speed on a wheel.

And then my mother called.

She could smell fear. Any whiff of one of her kids having anxiety and she would call to dial it up to ten. After all, anxious kids cared about their performance.

And an anxious kid had a hard time actually *living*.

"Hello?" I answered, wondering if I had any fast-food wrappers to crinkle in the speakers of my car to pretend I was going through a tunnel.

But I kept a spotless car. Curse my forethought.

"Hello, Ruth dear," my mother said in her smooth, practiced voice. She'd long since lost the southern farmer's daughter accent. Her voice now sounded like the esteemed mother of three—well, *one*, in her eyes—successful kids. "How are you today?"

Anxious. Angry. Tired.

Lonely.

"Fine as always," I replied, internally suppressing a scream as I got cut off in traffic *again*.

"How is work going?" she asked, going right for the point. "Any promotion opportunities?"

Definitely not. My boss was a timeworn turtle who I'd been hoping would retire for the last twelve months. So far, I'd had no luck.

"Maybe."

"You know the rule, one year and then up from there."

"Yes, I know," I said, my voice tight. I'd kept to that rule, either finding a new job that paid more or getting promoted once a year, up until now. And I was the only one who'd done so.

Tom was at my father's company, and literally could not be promoted any further. He was an executive. Barry did his own thing, somehow not caring about our parents' expectations.

As of today, I'd been a director for thirteen months. And despite being the youngest person ever in my company to hold the role, I was still failing by my parents' standards.

"Knox Price was a CEO five years ago," my mother said. "Take some notes from him."

And there it was. The mention of Knox *fucking* Price. Apparently, after I'd told him off at our graduation, he'd gone and started a tech company that revolutionized the way people drove. His company made billions patenting the software retrofitted into older cars to be able to drive themselves—the very one that had cut traffic congestion in half in most areas since computers supposedly solved most of the traffic-causing issues on highways, such as premature or late stops that clogged up the roads.

My last words to him were how *I* would be the one with the successful life and *he* would be nothing. The irony kept me awake at night.

But his product was revolutionary. He'd used his robot brain to design the almost-perfect system. A car retrofitted with PATH didn't cut people off, it didn't speed, and it never caused accidents.

I had one thing right in high school, apparently.

He was a genius.

I would bet money that none of the people cutting me off had his tech. Most of the problems on the road came from those who stubbornly refused to buy his surprisingly affordable package.

And that included me. It wasn't because I didn't believe in self-driving cars.

No, it was because of him.

I never imagined he'd do so much in the ten years since we graduated. For the first five years, he had disappeared. Then five years ago, people began whispering about PATH. Once it was out three years later, he was a household name, a multibillionaire who rarely made public appearances. Only a select few people even knew what the guy looked like, considering the grainy photographs of him were from a distance, and he *always* wore a disguise.

Maybe he grew up ugly. I doubted it, considering how he looked in high school, but at least losing his striking good looks would have been *something* bad to happen in the wake of all of his success.

He probably didn't remember me, and most days, I didn't mind it. Why would he give one shit about the annoying kid in his high school that picked fights with him? I was probably a blur of someone who once told him he would be nothing. I bet when he went to sleep at night, I was merely a whisper in his ear that had turned out to be wrong.

My only solace was that I wouldn't see him again. The distance should have been enough for me to move on from our rivalry, but I should have known my parents wouldn't let me forget my biggest motivator.

My parents, namely Mom, followed Knox's career like he was one of their own. She *cried* when he recently announced he was stepping down as CEO of his company for personal reasons.

Even though I had walked away from him ten years ago, I felt like I would always live in his shadow.

"Oh no," I said, fanning the area where my car's speaker was. "You're breaking up."

"I can hear you perfectly clear—"

Fuck my car's impeccable speakers. Couldn't they let me down this one time?

"Gotta go, bye!" I ended the call, knowing I was going to hear about this at our weekly family dinner, but in the moment, I felt relief. I needed to focus on work and get through this announcement in one piece. As always, work needed to have my full attention.

I worked in a ridiculous corporate high-rise in the center of Nashville. My company was a well-established banking company that made billions, and as marketing director, I was focused on ensuring our social media presence was larger than it had ever been. Our ancient CEO, Dave Stanford, was reluctant toward change. Convincing him and the other old-fashioned executives of my vision had always been a challenge and it was only getting more difficult the older they got and the fancier modern tech and social media became.

I arrived at the office at eight on the dot and had spent more than thirty minutes in the car. I only lived five miles away, but sitting in traffic made it feel so much longer.

I was tired before my day even began.

Stifling a yawn, I walked to the coffee pot in the break room, grateful the office manager and my only friend, Jenny, had brewed some for everyone. I poured a massive cup, added my favorite birthday cake creamer, and sipped on it before I returned to my office.

I had the smallest office in the corner of the building. Compared to the other directors, I was the farthest away from my employees and was the last to be called on in meetings. I strong-armed my way into this position, applying without my then-manager's approval, and followed up over twenty times with the CEO himself. I then blew everyone away with a prepared case study that wound up earning us over a hundred thousand dollars in revenue when I implemented it.

I was sure they hated me for it. I was qualified, but I wasn't their image of a perfect office woman.

But I made it my goal to be the best no matter how hard it was to get the job. And things weren't all bad. My boss, Caroline, the aforementioned turtle, had once told me I'd done a good job, which I'd heard was a rarity. My marketing team was getting more engagement than ever, and the greedy executives were happy with how much money we were making due to my campaign ideas.

I was doing a great job. I just wasn't liked, and I was used to that. When people saw my ambition, they were either threatened or jealous.

And that spilled over into my personal life too.

The few times I'd managed to score a date, they all questioned why I worked twelve-hour days. I didn't have many friends. I never connected with anyone in high school. Most people who met me at work were either my employees—who I wasn't sure if I could be friends with under the CEO's watchful eyes—or didn't like me. The only exception was Jenny.

"Knock knock," Jenny said, walking into my office. Her tightly coiled hair was piled on her head in a loose ponytail. She wore her trademark sweater and hoop earrings. I towered over her in the heels I wore every day. When we both started on the same day, I was sure she would be intimidated. Instead, she was friendly.

I smiled at her. "Your coffee is extra good today."

"Brewed it fresh just for you."

"My tired brain thanks you."

"We all need it, being stuck in this place," she said, rolling her eyes. She then leaned on my desk, smiling with interest. "So, any news on this new exec?"

I shook my head. "I know as much as you do. Worst case is it's some guy with an active harassment case on him."

"My bet's on Elon Musk."

I blinked in shock. "What? Why would a billionaire work here?"

"Maybe he owes Dave a favor. Our CEO has some serious connections."

"You're not wrong," I replied. Those very connections were why I thought it was a good idea to work here. "But you should probably say that quieter."

"Please, the man is so old he can barely hear. I have to yell when I talk to him."

"I'm always yelling, so maybe I don't know the difference."

"You don't always yell. It's only when people aren't being fair. You're nice, Ruth. Remember when Amber was sick with the flu, and you covered for her when Dave wanted you to write her up?"

"He shouldn't have even been worried about it."

Jenny rolled her eyes. "You know he's got control problems. The point still stands."

"You can't deny that I have a reputation."

"With the old executives, maybe. Anyone who's worked under you loves you."

I hoped that was true. I tried to be my best to my employees. I never expected them to work as much as I did. I always understood when they had to miss work for a legitimate reason, and I had no problem taking on extra work before I asked them to stay late to get something done.

"Thanks, Jenny," I said, smiling at her.

"No problem. I'll always talk you up because you're impressive. So impressive that I knew you got into that meeting about the new executive today."

A satisfied smile made its way onto my face. "Caroline asked me to email someone under her name since I know how Microsoft Outlook works. I may have also forwarded the meeting invite to myself."

"I love your brain. You'll have to tell me who it is." Jenny's phone jingled and she groaned when she pulled it out of her pocket. "I have to go. Dave sent me an email about setting up an executive lunch with the new guy."

I let out an annoyed sigh. The executives, mainly Dave and his smarmy underling Charles, always had lunch delivered using the company credit card. Sometimes the VPs were included. Anyone under them never got to partake in the feasts. As the marketing director, I probably should be a part of that group considering I'd be doing damage control, but I knew how Dave worked. He wanted Caroline to pass on the news, and when she didn't, it would somehow be my fault that I got it wrong.

But I'd figured out how to get around his methods.

"Maybe I could sneak a plate of whatever I order," Jenny said bringing me out of my thoughts. She was walking toward the door. "I'll see you later, Ruth. I need to go hunt down whatever restaurant we'll be spoiling the new guy with."

I gave her a pitying simper before I turned my attention to my work. I had to plan our next campaign for a new credit card program coming out. I could only hope this new addition to the executives didn't force me to do damage control rather than my actual job.

I buried myself in my work, and before I knew it, the clock was telling me it was eleven, and it was time to meet our newest hire.

As I walked into the largest meeting room in our office, I was greeted with a lavish layout of food from three of Nashville's most coveted restaurants. There were *steaks*, for crying out loud.

They must have really wanted to impress whoever was joining them.

I quietly retrieved one sandwich and sat in the back corner of the room. The last thing I needed was for Dave to see me and kick me out.

There was a podium set up in the front of the room, and I was pretty sure it was new.

Dave stood first, his bald head shining against the fluorescent lights. He was a large man who talked loudly and grew red in the face whenever someone challenged him. Today, he was all smiles and nearly bouncing on his feet. I'd never seen him so excited in my three years at this job.

He walked to the podium with purpose, chest puffed out like he'd won the lottery. The meeting room was filled with all the VPs, plus some other higher-ups from branches all around the company. I usually only saw them once a year when we had our end-of-year meetings. If they were here, then this was *big*.

"Well," Dave started, and everyone turned their attention to him, "as you may know, the market is ever-changing. Banking is quickly advancing into a technological arms race."

I had to keep my jaw from falling open. Since when did Dave give two shits about technology? One time, he described mobile banking as a millennial's way to be lazy.

"We have decided to expand our own stake in the technological market, which means adding a very experienced CTO to our roster, someone who's an inventor. We had a very impressive pool of applicants, but who we've chosen is so outstanding that I can't believe we even got him. Look at me, I'm glowing!"

Whispers broke out, and I glanced around, trying to see who it was.

"Now, we have worked hard to keep the press out of this. Every employee must sign an NDA to ensure his personal life does not get discussed. The goal is to not let this get out of our office walls. No one can say a *thing* yet."

I frowned. Just who was this guy, anyway?

"I expect you to have your teams' signatures by the end of the day," Dave added. I almost opened my mouth to say it left a very dangerous hole in our media defenses if someone talked before the NDA was signed, but I was interrupted by an opening door.

And when I saw who it was, all thoughts flew out the window.

I saw mussed brown hair, only slighter tamer than I remembered, golden eyes, and a damn-good jawline accented by a slight beard.

It had been ten years, but I knew exactly who this was.

And *dammit*, age had been kind to him.

A few people gasped. Others looked around curiously, since the man walking in tried his hardest to stay out of the spotlight.

"Now," Dave continued on, "please welcome Knox Price to Stanford Banking."

Knox

As I walked into a room of shocked people, I wondered if maybe I should have joined this company as an anonymous remote worker instead. When I'd arrived this morning, the CEO had talked to me like I was a perfect doll to add to his collection. "We're going to make sure you're respected here," he'd said. "You'll own these halls."

It wasn't exactly my idea of how I wanted to be treated. All the fixed-gaze shock put me on edge.

I hated this part of who I'd become. It was as Ruth had said all those years ago.

You're not a person, Knox.

How right she had been. And my success had made it even more so. If I wasn't a robot mechanically working on something I'd created, then I was a doll, dressed up for the people to gawk at. My only saving grace was that fewer people in this city knew who I was. No one was looking for me.

Until the news inevitably leaked. Then they would be out in droves.

Things weren't always this way.

I used to feel joy when I tested one of my inventions and it worked. Tearing apart a gadget and putting it back together again to make it function even better than before gave me an incredible high.

Then the paparazzi started following me and I started feeling annoyed. Then it turned to rage at how much of my life people felt entitled to. And now?

Any emotion I could ever feel felt like everything else did: just another bothersome part of my life that I had to deal with. The happiness I once felt was buried first. Then the anger and frustration was gone too.

The only emotion I barely experienced anymore was fear. My apathetic heart still managed to skip a beat at the thought of people's eyes following me, or the idea that I would be this robot forever.

I'd told my parents I stepped down as CEO of PATH, my tech company that sold my inventions, and wanted to return to my hometown to be closer to them. While that was partially true, I had another motive.

I was hoping returning to my childhood home would break this fog that had settled over everything in my life. My closest friend and business partner, Preston, had suggested that I find something to fix. Maybe I needed to feel *needed*.

Preston agreed to take over as acting CEO until I was able to figure myself out. In some ways, he was excellent in the role. People knew who he was since he gave all the speeches at galas and press conferences that I wasn't able to do due to my fear of public speaking. I knew that, on the surface, PATH would be fine.

But Preston didn't have the same crisis management skills that I did. He didn't create the technology like I did. We'd both agreed that this situation was temporary. He could be the talking head, making sure things continued to run smoothly while I went home to make my next move.

Thanks to his familial ties to Stanford Banking, Preston was also the one responsible for landing me this job. His father, Dave, the CEO, was currently looking at me like I was the moon *and* the stars from where I still stood near the side door.

And I knew why. Any tech I made could change the game for him.

Coding a better mobile app would be my first step, but I also had ideas regarding methods of catching fraud and suspicious purchases within that code that could innovate how the market ran. Customers wouldn't get the false alert that their own purchase was suspicious, but truly false items would be caught.

And while it didn't excite me like PATH once did, I would try anything to feel happiness again.

I nodded and waved to the people, holding on to my last emotion like a vice. I hated their prying eyes, but at least I felt *something* about it. It was a start.

As for my new boss, I hadn't gotten much of a read on Dave when I'd met him for my one and only interview. He was older than I expected, looking more like Preston's grandfather than his father. Preston rarely mentioned his dad to me, but he had given me a warning about what to do at Stanford.

"Change things slowly, Knox," Preston had said. *"Give it time."*

And that was about it, nothing about his father or what to expect.

Which is why my eyes widened when Dave waved me over. "Now I want to invite Knox to introduce himself to all of you," he said, still smiling as he continued to gesture for me to join him at the podium.

Shit.

I tried to shake my head, but Dave's movements became more pronounced. I knew I would make more of a fool of myself if I tried not to do this.

I wanted to hide and avoid speaking in front of so many people I didn't know. I could wait until I knew everyone by name, and address them individually. I didn't need to say anything at the moment.

The fear made my heart race. It could still do that, at least. I was thinking a mere skip of a beat would be all I got.

"I don't have much to say," I called out, ignoring my hammering heart. The podium was too daunting. If I had to speak, I preferred to do it not at the head of the class, as the center of attention. "I just look forward to working with you all."

People clapped.

"He's humble too!" Dave exclaimed.

I glanced back out at the people, wishing their eyes were on anyone other than me.

And that was when I saw her.

Fiery green eyes, sharp features, and hair tied into a bun. I would bet money that if she was standing in front of the audience, I would see heels on her feet.

To this day, I would see ghosts of her in random strangers on the street. I'd hear heels clack against the ground and think, if the beat was only a little faster, it would be her.

The fear in my chest made room for something else, something that made me stand straighter.

Was this . . . excitement?

Whatever it was, I could tell it was *not* what Ruth Murray was feeling. I hadn't seen her in years, but her pursed lips and narrowed eyes told me she was not happy about this reunion.

It was a shame she hated me so much. I loved being her rival. I still looked back on those high school days as the most fun I'd ever had. She was all fire, fighting back against everything I said and calling me out like I deserved for being a smug ass to her while everyone else looked up to me.

I caught myself desperately hoping nothing had changed despite my fame.

"Anything else to say before we get you started?" Dave urged.

Usually I would say no, but the look in Ruth's eyes drove me to get any kind of reaction of out her. "Actually, yes," I said. "I'm excited to get to know *each* and *every* one of you over the next few months."

Ruth rolled her eyes.

Perfect.

"All right!" Dave said. He walked up to me and clapped a hand on my shoulder.

I was too busy looking at the woman whose outward disdain for me was spread all over her face.

I hadn't seen someone look at me like that in years.

I had people who disliked my technology. There were entire Facebook groups devoted to people who hated self-driving cars. But no one dared to let their dislike show to me directly. They all waited until my back was turned.

But not with her. Never with her.

I counted the seconds until the meeting was over. When it finally concluded with one last round of applause, my eyes searched the sea of faces for Ruth. Many walked up to me, holding out their hands to shake, but I only engaged robotically, wondering where the hell Ruth had gotten off to.

By the time I was able to get through the doors of the meeting room, everyone had introduced themselves to me but her.

Dimly, I remembered Preston warning me that if anyone gave me trouble, he would send a security guard to make sure I was okay. I'd told him I doubted I would find trouble at a banking company.

But I had. If Ruth Murray was here, then there was no better trouble to be in.

CHAPTER TWO

Ruth

I grabbed Jenny and pulled her into the empty break room the moment I could get out of the meeting.

"Oh my God," Jenny said, and she pulled her arm out of my hand. "Girl, do you break wrists in your free time? Your grip is outrageous."

I took a shaky breath, running my hand over my pulled-back hair.

"No, I'm just freaking out." The words blew out of me.

"Did you find out who the CTO is?"

"Yes," I hissed. "And it's . . . bad. Well, not for the company. In fact, this is great for the company, but it's very bad for me personally."

"Why? Who is it?"

"Knox Price."

Jenny's eyes widened. *"What?"* she nearly screamed. "*The* Knox Price?"

I nodded.

"Holy shit! He's gonna turn the company around."

"I know," I said miserably.

"Wait, why is this bad for you?"

"Because I hate him."

Jenny frowned. "Why? What did he do to you?"

"He . . . we had a thing in high school."

"Like you dated him?" Jenny looked at me with wide, bright eyes.

And if there was that kind of history between us, then it would be big news. Knox was pretty quiet about his dating life. His longest relationship had been relatively private, but when it finally ended, everyone wanted to know why.

Knox Price—Bad at Love?

That was the headline. Mom had sent me the link. Apparently, he and his girlfriend, Gia, had broken it off amidst rumors of their engagement.

"No, we didn't have a thing, though I'm taking it as a compliment that you think I could land a man who's as hot as he is."

"He's hot?" she asked.

My face heated, but I refused to acknowledge the fact that Knox was attractive any more than I already had.

"Anyway, I didn't date him. Before he was rich and famous, we were rivals." It almost didn't feel right to say. Were we rivals if he always pulled ahead?

"If anyone could go toe to toe with Knox, it's you."

"More like toe to heel. I only won against him one time, which happened to be the last time we spoke. God, my last words to him was how he would be a failure and now look at him."

"I wish I knew you in high school."

"If you would have been in a high school with me and him, I promise you that you would have wanted to be his friend instead of mine. I was a pain in his ass. He probably doesn't even remember me."

Though the way his eyes lingered told me he definitely *did*.

"Don't think I didn't just hear you say I would choose Knox over some-one as awesome as you. Besides, high school was, what? Ten years ago for you? Whatever you said is probably forgotten."

"Not for me. I still don't like him for how many times he beat me."

"You hold grudges, though."

"What if he does too? Then I'll have another executive who hates me."

"What else is new? He can't be any worse than Charles."

That was true. Charles was a dick to me and a kiss ass to Dave.

"You've got this," she urged. "Just give him one chance before you go off on him."

"One chance. I can do that. Does him being annoying in the meeting count?"

"No," she said, her voice flat.

"Fine. I'll be polite. He said he was going to get to know each and every one of us anyway." I couldn't help but let my voice take on a mocking tone.

Jenny's eyebrows rose. "So, you're *very* bitter."

"Of course I am. Why did he come here? Why, of all the companies he could help, did he choose this one?"

"I mean, they could have offered him a lot of money."

"Maybe," I replied. "Maybe he owes Dave a favor."

She shrugged. "Or maybe, he's a nice guy."

"You didn't see his look when he saw me."

"What was it, then?"

I thought back to the meeting. He'd looked almost uninterested, some-thing I'd only seen during a long analysis of Shakespeare in English class. But then he saw me, and his golden eyes became impossibly brighter, and they stayed on me until I'd darted out of there.

"Like I was the only interesting thing in that room."

When I looked over at my friend, her eyebrows had risen high on her forehead.

"I know it sounds like I'm being dramatic."

"I'm not judging you. I'm just dying to see where this goes."

"It's going to go the direction of me getting my ass fired when I punch him in the face."

"If you do, let me watch the whole thing. I'll make popcorn."

Knox

"In here is the break room," Dave said as he led me through one of the most uninspired offices I'd ever seen. *Seriously.* They needed a decorator. "Executives have access to a secret snack closet. Here's your key."

"It's not for everyone?"

"We try to keep costs down by only providing snacks for key people. That would be us."

I had to suppress an annoyed glare. I wanted to tell him every employee was key. It wasn't like executives did every single thing in the office; most barely lifted a finger in the day-to-day.

But Preston's reminder to slowly change things echoed through my mind.

"Can we give the leftovers from the meeting to everyone?" I asked. "I'm sure they'd love it."

"Oh, they don't need anything."

"We had plenty."

Dave's face twisted, but he nodded. "Fine. They can have it. I was going to throw it in the trash anyway."

I took a deep breath. At least he'd said yes.

The words were a sore reminder that this wasn't my company. At PATH, I made a small, central office. Employees weren't forced to come in, but I did my part of making the space as accommodating as I could. I kept it brightly colored and stocked the fridges with snacks that everyone wanted. People were happy where I worked.

Some people here seemed happy, and there was free coffee and tea, but the office was a bland tan, and most of the people in it wore the same dull face of boredom.

I wondered what Ruth thought of it.

"Tell me about your employees," I said. "Who is your hardest worker?"

Unless Ruth had completely changed her personality, I knew it would be her.

"Oh, we hire good people. Wes from accounting is a hard worker. Also, Jim from IT is up there." Dave went through a list of employees, none of them Ruth, as we continued the tour through the beige landscape.

Had she developed a work-life balance in the last ten years?

Dave led me through IT, and then through accounting. Everyone had the same starry-eyed expression after Dave told them my name.

The last stop on our tour was the marketing department. The first thing I noticed was that it was the only department where the women outweighed the men.

Dave tapped one of the cubicle walls to get everyone's attention.

"Team, this is Knox Price. He's my newest CTO."

A few people did double-takes.

"I'm sure you saw the NDAs in your mailboxes," Dave added with a tight voice.

They all nodded.

"I'm Knox," I said, instead of intimidating them further. My heart skipped a beat at even *five* strangers looking at me, but this was better than being at the forefront of a meeting room. "I admit I'm very excited to meet you all. Your work for this company is incredible."

And it was. As much as Stanford's tech was behind the times, their advertising was not.

"It's all Ruth's doing," the woman in back said.

So this was Ruth's department. I should have known.

"Where is Ruth?" I asked, heart skipping a beat when I said her name. That excitement was back.

"Oh, Ruth?" Dave started. "Her office is down the hallway."

"She's that far from her team?" I eyed the empty office right next to the marketing department's cubicles.

"Yes, she needs some distance so she can spend less time talking and more time working."

The blonde woman, the same one who'd said this was all Ruth's doing, rolled her eyes.

"Ruth is difficult," Dave added. His loud voice echoed through the halls. "I wouldn't meet her on the first day."

"Why not?" I asked.

"She's got an attitude that leaves a . . . sour taste in people's mouths," he said, shaking his head.

The same employee glared before her eyes slowly drifted back to her computer.

I opened my mouth to argue with Dave, but his hand clapped on my shoulder.

"Our goal here," he continued, "is to keep you happy. If you have any problems with the people here, especially Ruth, I want to know about it."

I saw another one of Ruth's employees try to open a chat window discretely.

"I think I can handle it," I said. "I knew her in high school."

Another employee leaned over to hear what I would say. I could see the seeds of gossip spreading. *Shit.* This was going to be in the media by tomorrow.

"Really?" Dave asked.

"Yes. We were in the same graduating class."

"Was she always so . . ."

"Her nickname wasn't Ruth the Ruthless for nothing," I said with a smile.

Dave laughed, and I realized too late what my comment sounded like.

"I mean that she knew what she wanted and always went for it."

Dave rolled his eyes. "I know the type."

I had a feeling I hadn't done enough to walk back the use of her old nickname, but whatever thoughts I had were chased away by the sound of heels echoing through the hallway. It was in the exact tempo it always had been, even ten years later.

Ruth walked with quick, methodical strides, something anyone who walked in heels every day could manage, but she somehow made it her own.

When she came around the corner, I didn't see the girl who haunted my dreams. I saw the *woman* who'd taken her place.

While she had been sitting, I didn't see much more than her glare. Seeing that alone had given me a thrill I hadn't experienced in a very long time.

But being face-to-face with her? That was a different story altogether.

In this light, I could see that her cheeks slightly shimmered. Her hair, even pulled back into a bun, was wavier than I remembered. Her eyes were a shade of green I didn't realize I'd been looking for until now. Green had always been my favorite color. I now remembered why.

When she saw me, she froze for only one second. Then she put a hand on her hip and gave me a sardonic smile.

"Knox. Good to see you again."

Her voice was sultry. I'd forgotten how much I'd loved to hear it, even if it was while she was going off on me for beating her in class.

"Ah, yes," Dave piped in. "He told me you two knew each other in high school."

Her eyes didn't leave mine. "He was one of the top students in our graduating class."

"And you were the first, considering you were the valedictorian," I told her, but I knew she hadn't forgotten.

"Someone had to be."

"As you know," Dave interrupted, sounding nervous, "Ruth is our marketing *director*." He emphasized the last word to Ruth. "And Knox is our new CTO."

Ruth's smile dropped for half a second, and I wanted to strangle Dave. Instead, I said, "Don't think of me as an executive. I'm here to work together to make things better. That can't happen if we throw titles around."

"Good to know," Ruth said. "But I also know how useful titles are to those who need them. Nice to see you, Knox. I knew you'd be lurking somewhere."

She made to turn away, but I wasn't ready to let that happen yet.

"Why don't you tell me about your team, Ruth," I suggested, eager to hear her talk more.

I saw her gaze flick to Dave, and I could feel his glare even with my distance. She took a deep breath and her posture loosened slightly.

"Right. So this is John and Michael," she said, motioning to the two men sitting next to each other. "They manage the mailing lists and all communication goes through them. Christie and Elsa manage the social media page and posts. Amber here is our team lead. She also designed our website." She put her hand on the shoulder of the blonde who had mentioned Ruth to me first. Judging by her frown, she was defensive over Ruth.

"It's good to meet you all," I said. "I look forward to working with you closely through all the changes Stanford will be implementing."

"If you are making changes that will need to be marketed, please bring those up with me." Ruth's eyes were firmly on mine. "I design most of the marketing campaigns so I want to be aware of anything I might need to change with my existing plan."

"I'm sure someone else can handle it," Dave said.

"I don't mind working with an old high school friend," I said, and I held out my hand to her. Her gaze narrowed at me, but she slowly extended hers to meet me.

Her hand gripped mine tightly, and she gave me one of the firmest handshakes of my life. She had to have practiced that. It was better than Preston's.

"We've always worked together well," she said slowly. Both of us knew that was a lie. "I'm sure we can do it again."

I smiled in her direction. It was the first real smile I'd managed in years.

Ruth had been powerful in her high school years. I couldn't wait to see how much more impressive she had become over the last ten.

"We don't have to worry about new campaigns for a while," Dave said, interrupting my thoughts. Slowly and regretfully, I pulled my hand out of Ruth's. "Ruth, can you go check on that email Caroline sent you this morning? It's important."

"I answered it an hour ago."

"She might have something else for you."

At Dave's obvious dismissal, she nodded once and disappeared toward her office. I watched her go, my focus on her round ass as it moved in her pencil skirt.

Then I tore my eyes away before anyone could notice.

"See what I mean?" Dave said under his breath. "She's one of *those* women."

"Do you mean stubborn?"

"Don't worry about it. Let me show you the *better* parts of the office," he offered, grabbing me by the shoulder. "No need to hang around here."

A glare from Amber and Christie were tossed in our direction, and I realized I probably hadn't made a good impression. As I was led away by

Dave, my thoughts circled back to Ruth. I'd found something that made me feel an emotion other than fear, and I was desperate for more.

"Do you mind if I send a few emails?" I asked. "I want to introduce myself to the remote workers."

"We don't have too many of those, but that's fine. Send all the emails you need to. IT should have gotten your email set up."

I nodded, knowing I'd already added it to my phone. I made a quick stop to the break room to grab coffee and was surprised by an interesting find in the refrigerator. Alongside the drab decor of the office, I'd only expected plain and vanilla coffee creamer. The birthday cake variety was the sole interesting thing in there, however. Guess I would be having that.

With a cup of festive-smelling coffee in hand, I walked back to my desk, ready to get started on my task list.

It would only take me a few minutes to email the people who weren't working in office. But my real motive had to do with the very person who had just been sent to check her inbox.

I was buzzing with excitement I hadn't felt in years. It wasn't for work, as I had hoped it would be.

It was for the woman I never thought I'd see again.

CHAPTER THREE

Ruth

To: Ruth Murray

From: Knox Price

Subject: Saying Hello

Hello Ruth,

I wanted to extend an olive branch to you considering our past. I know you and I have fought, but considering my newest standing, I know this must be hard for you.

Attached is a gift card to Chuck E. Cheese for you to use at your leisure.

Respectfully, Knox

To: Knox Price
From: Ruth Murray
Subject: Saying Hello

Thanks. My husband and kids will love this.

Attached is a video presentation to familiarize yourself with the environment here at Stanford.

Have a GREAT day.

Disrespectfully, Ruth

Link: Never Gonna Give You Up *by Rick Astley*

To: Ruth Murray
From: Knox Price

I didn't realize you had a husband and kids.

Respectfully, Knox

To: Knox Price
From: Ruth Murray

Open the video. It will all make sense then.

Still disrespectfully, Ruth

From: Knox Price
To: Ruth Murray

Your video was incredibly helpful. I didn't know Stanford was so well versed in memes from the two thousands.

So, no husband then?

❦

I didn't bother with a reply. It was partially because he didn't need to know, but mostly because I was busy doing my actual job. Amber had come into my office to discuss our next marketing campaign.

About ten minutes into our conversation, I realized my employee was only half listening.

And I knew what she was thinking about instead.

Stopping in the middle of my sentence, I took a deep breath, and then said, "Go ahead. Ask what you want to ask."

"You went to high school with Knox?" Her eyes were bright with anticipation.

"I did."

"And *you* were the valedictorian?"

"I was."

"So, you were smarter than him?"

"I guess I had a higher average because of extra credit. He always pulled ahead of me by one point before that, though."

Even then I still didn't know how I'd gotten it. It must have been *so* close.

"Wow. I can't believe you know a celebrity."

"I don't," I reminded her.

"But you can admit he's cute though, right?"

"I definitely can't, considering he's one of our bosses."

But I had thought it, especially with the full force of his eyes and smile were on me while we'd talked just now.

Why couldn't he have been ugly or something? That would have made this so much easier.

"You're right. I'm seeing someone anyway, but those *eyes*. Were they always so gold?"

"Unfortunately," I muttered.

"I can't believe he hides out when he looks like *that*."

"It's probably to hide his shitty personality." I said it before I could stop myself.

Amber's eyes were wide, and a slow smile spread on her face. "So, he's a jerk?"

Yes was what I wanted to say.

"I don't know him."

"We overheard him say some stuff about you."

"What did you hear?"

"Well, Dave was his usual self. He was talking about how you were one of *those* women."

"Of course he was."

"And then after you walked off, Knox called you Ruth the Ruthless."

I dropped the pen in my hand.

Was he *fucking* serious? He'd been here one day, and he called me that cruel name?

Amber winced at my reaction. "I'm guessing that's a sore subject."

It was more than a sore subject. It was what everyone called me after I refused to let one of the football jocks look at my homework answers. I'd lost my temper at him when he called me a frigid bitch.

I knew Knox used that name, but it still hurt, even if it was ten years ago.

"He was good at making me mad in high school. Some of that is still festering."

"I'm sorry," Amber said sincerely. "None of us think that you're ruthless."

"Thank you, and I'm sorry they said that near your team."

"It's not the first time we've overheard stuff."

Dave had a bad habit of attempting to undermine my authority. I always thought letting my work speak for itself would be enough.

It wasn't.

"We should get back to talking about the campaign," Amber said, shaking her head. "I know you're busy and I've taken up enough of your time telling you things you don't want to hear."

I nodded, some of the tension easing in my shoulders as we moved away from talking about Knox.

I stayed in my office for the rest of the day, content to remain in the quiet rather than seeing him again.

Most people were already gone from the office when I left at five thirty. I only left this early once a week. My normal time to departure was after seven.

My *life* was work, but as the years ticked by, I found myself waiting for my parents to be proud of me.

But that had never come. Tom, who was four years my senior, beat me to all of this because of he was older. Before Knox stepped in as my rival, my parents had always compared me to Tom, who'd reached all the milestones first simply because he was born earlier. He was the one chosen to work with Dad at our family's company. I was denied within two days of applying.

Barry and I could never measure up.

But unlike me, however, Barry didn't even try. He was always the one who couldn't care less about our parents' expectations. He owned a bar downtown and never worked in an office in his life. He didn't even go to college.

I wasn't sure how he went about life letting our parents' words roll off his back. Because for me, they never did.

After being turned down by Murray and Sons, I was determined to prove my worth at a challenging company. I always thought that if I proved myself somewhere else, Dad would see how useful I could be to him.

And now I hadn't been promoted in a year.

When I joined Stanford three years ago, I was determined to rise through the ranks and make every naysayer regret ever questioning me.

I should have been working my ass off to do more—to prove myself.

But lately, I'd been spending my time thinking of all the things I'd missed instead. I wanted a boyfriend. I wanted a circle of friends. I wanted to be able to have conversations that had nothing to do with work.

And I didn't know how to go about getting those things.

According to my parents, those things weren't worth my time. They would never understand anything but life in the office. Dad was either networking or holed up in his executive suite. Mom meticulously checked in on us, always pushing Barry to go to school, or pushing me to get promoted. That was how it was. The one doing well, which was usually Tom, got attention from Dad. The rest of us had our mother trying to get us to do better.

She even went so far as to schedule family dinners once a week to discuss Barry's and my progress. Tom was invited too, but he was usually tied up talking shop while Barry and I received lectures.

Tonight was dinner night, despite the fact that Mom had already asked me about my career this morning. These dinners were regularly scheduled no matter how often we talked. I caught myself wishing that I didn't have to go, and then felt extremely guilty.

They were my parents, after all. I may not agree with their methods, but they only wanted us to be successful. What parent didn't want that for their kids?

I reminded myself of that every Monday night when I was trying to find the energy to go in and say hello.

Every week, I would sit in my car next to my parents' luxury vehicles. I would stare at their glamorous house and wonder why I dreaded this so much.

Both of my brothers were already inside, which meant I was already late, despite the clock telling me I was right on time.

When I finally walked in, I could hear Dad and Tom talking as they usually did at these events. I paused to see if I could glean any useful information.

"Use my method. Lay out their problems and have them begging for a solution," Dad said, his voice low. "That's how you'll win them over with this acquisition."

There was nothing new about that. Murray and Sons had been looking to increase revenue for years now. They weren't losing money by any means, they just wanted more of it. Dad thought everyone could be won over with his sales strategy.

That strategy worked very well in the eighties. It was how Murray and Sons became the biggest trucking company in the country. But these days, people weren't just concerned with how to solve problems. They also wanted to look good in front of the masses. Sometimes being bought out wasn't a good look.

Dad obviously didn't see it that way.

Tom was nodding along, but he looked bored. He'd probably heard this very talk every time they saw each other.

I paused only for a second to take in the two of them talking. God, I wanted to be welcomed into that conversation. I wanted to be whatever the hell Tom was.

Maybe I'd be able to do it without developing the drinking and anger problems Tom used to have. It had gotten so bad that Barry and I staged an intervention a few months ago.

"I've got it, Dad," Tom said, his voice tight. I hoped he would end up at the gym rather than a bar. "Don't worry."

"I always need to worry. You're my only successful child."

I rolled my eyes, taking that as my cue to walk away. I didn't need to hear any more reminders about how successful Tom was and nothing Barry or I could do would ever measure up.

As I walked into the living room, I saw Barry locked in conversation with Mom. "See, if you went to college now, you could finish your degree in four years and . . ."

I winced, sympathy filling me for my younger brother. I'd heard this conversation a hundred times too.

Barry had heard it more.

I couldn't imagine Barry ever wanting to go to school. His bar was well-known in Nashville, located right on Broadway. He obviously made enough to pay his bills. For some, that would be success, but not to the Murrays.

Dad had wanted him to be a businessman like Tom and join the famous Murray and Sons brand. He had dreams that Tom would be the CFO and Barry as whatever other executive he would be suited for. As for me? I was never sure what their plan was. It was evident it just wasn't at the family business, as the rejection proved.

Barry nodded along, but his eyes danced around the room. Once, he had told us that he didn't want to be at the family dinners. Mom had hassled us so much that Tom and I dragged him back.

"Ah, Ruth," Mom said. "You've finally arrived."

"It's before six," I said.

"Your brothers had the time management skills to show up earlier than you. You should too."

I glanced over at Barry, both of us sharing an exhausted glance.

"Besides," she continued, "don't think I'm not aware of the fact you hung up on me this morning."

I closed my eyes, taking a deep breath. "I was on my way to work, and I needed to focus on my tasks for the day."

"Tasks for getting promoted?"

I opened my mouth to respond, but thankfully, Tom strode into the room. Sometimes it was easier to divert the conversation when the three of us were together. Either Tom or Barry would speak up when one of us was getting hounded. It was the only way to survive our weekly dinners.

"Ah, Ruth," Dad said, belatedly acknowledging me. "You're finally here. I was just talking business with Tom."

"I heard. Still trying to boost revenue?" I asked.

"It's nothing you need to concern yourself with. What we need to be concerned with is this delicious dinner."

I glanced over at Mom, wondering if we would be blessed with the almost-mythical presence of her cooking. But she brought out plated food that was obviously from a local steakhouse.

When Dad met her, she was a southern farmer's daughter. One of my earliest memories was in our grandparents' fields, playing in mud with Barry.

But our dad always wanted her to be *proper*. She barely spoke to our grandparents, and she'd pushed them to sell the farm a long time ago. She didn't even serve us her own food anymore since Dad hated how southern her cooking was. He'd always said being able to eat out all the time was an obvious sign of wealth and success.

"Ruth," he said slowly. "Any good news from work?"

I thought about Knox, but I couldn't talk about him even if I wanted to.

And I definitely didn't.

"No," I said. "Nothing new."

He frowned. "You've been in your role for how long now?"

"Thirteen months."

He shook his head. "That's too long. You're getting complacent."

"It's really hard to move up in the company I'm at. It was a challenge even getting this role, and with a recession looming—"

"All I hear are excuses."

Barry rolled his eyes. "What do you make now?" he asked. "Like 100k or something?"

"Yeah, pretty close to that."

"That's a huge salary."

"But it's not enough in the long term," Dad added. "Especially if you stay single forever. Your old classmate Knox Price was a CEO by the time you started at this company of yours."

I clenched my teeth at the mention of his name. It was exactly what Mom had told me this morning, before I saw him again.

I hated him.

Or at least, I hated how my parents idolized him, but it was hard to tell the difference.

"You know," Mom said, "I heard he moved back to Nashville."

"Don't let Ruth see him." A slow smile spread over Barry's face.

"Oh, that's right. You had that little rivalry with him," she added.

"There isn't much of one anymore." Dad looked me square in the eyes. "Considering his career has been far superior to yours."

My fork clanked against the table loudly. It was exactly what I'd been thinking, but hearing it hurt more than I expected.

"Dad," Tom said. "She's still very high in her career. You weren't a director until you were thirty."

I silently thanked him.

"Ruth needs to be pushed," our mother said, frowning. "Just like you did."

"There's been some hierarchal changes at my company," I said, before someone could turn things around on Tom. "I'm hoping to see some organization changes from there. Waiting is my best option for a good promotion."

It was a lie. My only option for promotion was if Caroline retired, and I had no clue when that would be.

But it wasn't like I could leave.

Most high-level positions like mine were few and far between. I'd started looking casually once I hit twelve months in my position. Nothing at my level and at a respectable company had been posted in months.

I should probably put more effort into it, but I didn't know if I had the energy to try.

"I heard that Knox Price is starting at a banking company as a CTO now. Rumors say he's made his own company and wants to help others find the success he did."

A pleased smile crossed Dad's face.

But I froze. No one was supposed to know. Did someone leak it?

"Do you know which company?" I asked. I silently begged for them to say no.

"Stanford Bank and Trust." Mom looked at me pointedly, like she knew I was sitting on information useful to her.

"Why does that name sound familiar?" Dad asked.

"Ruth? Do you know?"

"You must have some personal connection," I said flatly. Even if the NDA was broken, I couldn't mention Knox at all to anyone at this table.

Tom looked at me, as if he knew exactly what personal connection they had with the company. I shook my head at him, and he thankfully kept his mouth shut. My mother frowned but thankfully didn't say anything else.

"It must be a bank we have funds in," Dad mused. "Maybe Ruth should go and work for them. With Knox Price there, it will be booming soon."

"I'll add it to my list of places to check out." I was torn between being relieved that I didn't have to mention Knox, and pissed off that my own father told me to go work for my own damn company.

Mom *had* to know. I could tell by the way her forehead was creased that she was trying to work out why I didn't say anything about my job at Stanford.

Tom looked to be having a similar thought, but I kept any information to myself. I was not about to get myself fired for talking. And even if I could, I wouldn't want to talk about Knox anyway.

The conversation turned to Barry and his bar. As much as I hated them zeroing in on him, I was relieved to be out of the hot seat for a bit.

By the time dinner was over, Barry had been told his career wasn't good enough three times. I was told to get promoted twice. Tom was reminded to use Dad's favorite sales method four times.

As much as I was grateful that my brothers and I could steer the conversations and successfully distract, it only did so much. When I finally walked out of the house, I was torn between screaming and throwing something.

If only Knox were here. Maybe whatever I threw could hit his beautifully angular head.

I drove to my apartment in silence. My day was so draining I couldn't even enjoy a good Lila Wilde pop song. I needed pure, uninterrupted silence.

My place was dark, and as always, empty. I didn't even have a pet since I could never be home to take care of it. I never had the time to decorate my walls with anything I enjoyed. My apartment felt like a hotel room, not a home.

I flopped on the couch and yelled into a pillow. When I was done, I rolled over and tried to calm down.

But in the silence of a lonely twentysomething's apartment, it didn't work. I needed a distraction, and there was only one thing that was easy enough to access while exhausted.

Social media.

Sometimes, I liked to look at other people's lives. My feed was all people who were happy. I could see my high school acquaintances getting married and having kids and pretend I was a part of that.

Even people I worked with had more of a life than I did. I tried to stay away from my employees' pages for their own privacy, but every now and again, I would look at others that weren't directly under me. I may not have been friends with them, but I could see their public posts.

One I went to quite frequently was Simon Pace's profile. He was in IT. He was quiet, reserved, and apparently, a photographer in his free time. While I never had time to develop a proper crush, he was someone I could possibly like. I wasn't his boss in any shape, form, or fashion, and as far as I knew, he was single.

I scrolled down his profile to photos that were about a month old. Once I did that, I scrolled back up quickly, not wanting to be a stalker.

That was when I hit the friend button.

"Shit," I muttered, sitting up. I wasn't even sure how to unfollow him, and I panicked for a moment, wondering if I had made a massive mistake.

Then he accepted my request.

My profile only had my name on it. I didn't have any photos because I hadn't lived a life worth sharing.

But apparently it was enough for Simon.

This was my chance to finally solve the loneliness that was plaguing me. He was the perfect candidate. He was attentive with his job and had a respectable reputation. He smiled at me as I walked past him in the hallway, and always asked how my day was.

I wanted someone sweet and caring. Someone who had a job but wasn't so invested that he'd be there all night.

I could love him if he fit the bill. At least, I thought I could. Some people thought love meant passion. The only passion I'd ever felt for a man I wasn't related to was toward Knox, but those were fiery, angry *"I want to kill you"* emotions.

For me, love meant finding someone who made sense. Simon was a little like my ex. He'd been a nice guy too. Our lives were just going in different directions.

Maybe things would go differently with Simon.

I had only a moment to ponder my good luck before I heard the first rumble of thunder.

My body tightened, and I checked my weather app to see that, *of course*, there was a pop-up storm.

This was why I hated summer.

I could handle nearly anything. Give me an asshole CEO. Give me Knox Price. Give me my parents pushing me to get a promotion.

But the one thing I couldn't handle was a damn thunderstorm. It was my kryptonite.

Taking a shaky breath, I made my way over to the closet in my bedroom. It was near no exterior walls and had no windows.

I was aware it was overkill to climb in a closet every time I heard thunder, but it was the only method that kept me safe in case there was a tornado.

Because once I'd heard the rumbling sky, my entire body would lock up.

I wish I was exaggerating. Fear would render me immobile, because any sound reminiscent of the night I'd developed a fear of storms made me leave reality and go back to the worst night of my life. Thankfully, I'd seen no warnings of a tornado. Nashville had quite the robust alert system for those who lived in the city. The sound of that added a panic attack to my already miserable state.

Most of the time, the weather was calm here. We were out of Tornado Alley, so it was somewhat rare for the devastating force of nature to hit town.

But when I was six, one not only hit Nashville, but the neighborhood I lived in. The night had been loud, with thunder erupting through the sky every second. The alarm started minutes into the storm. Then there was the rush of air circling around itself, followed by a sick silence that I would never get out of my head.

The tornado had demolished the alarm system in my neighborhood, leaving us all in silence after the chaos. Our house's roof was ripped off, but the neighbor's home had been completely demolished. When I peeked outside, I saw dust, splintered wood, and brick tossed around like it was nothing.

That night changed me in ways I wish it hadn't. It rendered me useless during a storm because all I could do was relive the night I couldn't get out of my head.

I could still recall every part it. Tom had screamed and tucked Barry and me under him as a way of trying to protect us from the very air around us. I could hear the sound of siding blowing off of our house, and then the cracking sound of our neighbor's home falling to pieces. And even to this day, I could hear the way our neighbor sobbed the next morning as she couldn't find her husband.

A therapist told me to try to anchor to the current moment to avoid reliving the night, but I couldn't, not when each rumble of thunder replayed the night like a tape of horror.

Everyone else moved on, even my brothers. But I stayed there in my mind, unable to move on from the fear I felt.

Time was lost as I relived the worst night of my life over and over again.

Then the voices started, reminding me how weak this was.

Get over it, Ruth. A thunderstorm is nothing. Mom.

Oh, here she goes again. There's not even a tornado warning this time. That was a younger version of Tom.

Of course she's scared of something so small. Just like every girl is. Dad.

These words played on a loop as I hid. Even when alone, I was ashamed of my fear, but helpless to stop it.

And I stayed in that damn closet until the sun came up the following morning.

Knox

There was the distant sound of thunder as I stepped over the threshold of my parents' humble home.

I hadn't been here in years. Gia had taken one look at the place and told me she wanted to invite my parents out to San Francisco instead of visiting in Nashville. The old wallpaper and well-loved carpet had been too much for her.

Once my parents had figured out that she didn't like it, they only came to visit me. At the time, I'd hoped they enjoyed visiting a new state. Now I realized that they had been embarrassed about their small, shabby house.

My parents weren't rich. They'd spent their savings just to have me, since infertility ran in Mom's family, and ever since then, they'd done everything they could to support me through their hard work and small paychecks.

Their little house barely had enough room for me and them, but they'd loved it. These four walls were where Dad proposed to Mom, where they brought me home, and where I'd grown up.

"Not much has changed," I said, glancing around to see all of my baby pictures on the wall. It still smelled like home, even after all these years. My mechanical heart skipped a beat at the familiarity of it. Then I sank back into the familiar feeling of nothing.

"Knox!" Mom called, racing over to give me a hug. "So glad you made it!"

"We could have done this at your fancy place, kid," Dad said, slowly walking around the corner. He was still in his electrician's uniform. I'd told him he could quit his job a long time ago, but he'd refused, saying he enjoyed working to fill his time.

"I wanted to be here. What's the point of being in Nashville if I can't come home?"

"I bet he's bought a dozen new plants," Mom teased. "He just doesn't want us to see his addiction."

"I've only bought four," I said, shaking my head. When I moved, Preston had told me to find a hobby. The only thing remotely interesting was collecting plants. My new home was essentially a greenhouse. I found the closest thing I could to peace when I watered them on schedule.

Besides, plants were a living thing. Maybe if I was around more of them, I could feel like the human I obviously wasn't.

Dad shook his head. "You and those plants, kiddo." He walked over to turn on the ancient ceiling fan. It was the same one he and my aunt had struggled to put up fifteen years ago. "Do you hear a funny noise from this thing?"

"No," I said, frowning. Was it causing them problems? Maybe I could have someone come look at it.

"I hear something. It's telling me it's *your biggest fan*."

I should have seen the terrible joke coming.

"Benji!" Mom exclaimed, struggling to conceal a laugh. "You're going to make him move back to San Francisco with jokes like that."

Dad cackled, and even I cracked a smile at seeing his amusement.

"That's my best one! Knox always loved that joke."

I used to laugh at every single joke he'd made, but these days, a chuckle was all this robotic heart of mine could muster.

"You've still got it, Dad." I forced a smile onto my face. "What's for dinner?"

"Twice-baked spaghetti," she replied.

I cringed. Mom had many talents. Cooking wasn't one of them. If she didn't burn the food, then she forgot a key ingredient.

"You should check on it. Just to be sure it doesn't burn," Dad said. Mom nodded and disappeared to the kitchen.

"Pizza for takeout?" I asked.

"I was hoping you'd say that."

I nodded, glad to have a backup.

But I couldn't even dread the impending doom of Mom's dinner. Even though I still felt numb, I'd missed this.

Moving to California had been a great idea, up until it meant I left my family too.

"Dang it!" Mom said loudly. That was when the smell of burnt food wafted through my nose. "I burnt the food again. I blame your bad joke, Benji!"

"I'll order in a pizza," I said.

"How do you burn pasta, Knox?" Dad asked as I was getting my phone.

I tilted my head at him.

"You cook it *al-done-te*."

That did get a genuine chuckle.

"I haven't heard that before."

"You can thank my book of *1,000 Best Dad Puns*. I'm gonna get you to laugh, kid. I mean a full-on, loud laugh."

"You might have to get a new pun book," I said, but I felt the guilt I always did when someone asked why I didn't laugh.

He grumbled something about how he was banned from buying more pun books by Mom and walked off to the other room. I took the time to order dinner.

About thirty minutes later, the food was on the table, and Dad had brought out his book, and was reading his favorite ones to me.

I faked a laugh for half of them to humor him.

"How is work?" I asked Mom after faking another laugh. I wasn't sure how many more I could manage. "Any new clients?"

"Well," she said, blushing. "Fake Dolly Parton came in."

"Who?" I asked.

"We have this woman who insists she's Dolly Parton. She tried to do the accent and everything. None of us have the heart to tell her we know it's not her."

"Tell him why you know it's not her."

"Benji, you are the worst." Mom rolled her eyes.

"Now I have to know," I said. I hadn't been this interested in anything since I'd seen Ruth earlier.

"Her boobs just aren't big enough."

I stared at Mom, who was turning red.

"Don't you look at me like that! I know exactly what Dolly's boobs look like and those are just not it!"

A genuine smile made its way onto my face. I almost laughed, even.

"Besides," Mom continued, "I've heard that Dolly doesn't wear her wigs out. It's how she's not recognized. Maybe you should try it."

"I don't think I'd look good in a wig," I said. "My ball cap mostly works."

"Didn't someone catch you out and about shopping for rings with that ex of yours?"

"I bet you were pissed," Dad said, shaking his head. "You always wanted your privacy. As you should."

I nodded along, but I knew I hadn't cared when I was caught ring shopping for Gia. It just felt like another fact of life.

"How's Preston?" Mom asked. "I hope he's doing okay under all this pressure. Oh, he was so sweet when we met him."

My parents loved most people, and usually people loved them back. Preston wasn't close with his parents, and rarely talked to them after he moved across the country. My parents' warm smiles and receptive demeanor had made him open up to Mom immediately.

She had the strangest talent for that.

Well, except with me. She would be sick with worry if she knew how I felt nothing. I couldn't do it to her.

"He's good," I said. "Busy. I can tell being the CEO is going to be challenging for him."

I hadn't told them I was working with Preston's dad. While Preston had been fine with it, my parents would be suspicious. After being a product of selfish parents, Mom could sniff out a parent who only cared about themselves.

And she was probably right about Dave. Even I could see it, and I'd only worked with him for one day.

But Preston had insisted I needed to work for Stanford. So much so that even I couldn't say no.

"He needs to visit," Mom declared. "You better tell me when he comes around."

"I will. I bet he'd love to hear about your fake Dolly Parton."

"And I have so many other fun stories," she said, smiling. "Oh, let me tell you about the one-hundred-year-old woman who comes in once a month."

As she delved into another story from her hair salon, I listened as intently as I could. Dad, however, was more engaged than I could ever be. He hung on each word she said, eyes shining as he looked at his wife of thirty years.

It served as a painful reminder that I wasn't like them. I would never be able to love someone like he could. Everything, even love, faded into nothing when one was a robot.

As Mom laughed at a joke Dad made, I could feel myself chuckle along, but only because it was what was expected of me. I loved my parents, but when had I made someone laugh like that? When had I done anything but push out updates to one of my inventions?

Life had become a series of problems to be solved, and the biggest one was myself.

You're not a person, Knox. Ruth's words played in my head like a tape I couldn't stop. *You're just a robot good at pretending to be human.*

I wanted so desperately to prove her wrong.

But I didn't know where to begin.

CHAPTER FOUR

Ruth

I found myself dreading work the next day. Not only was I exhausted after dealing with the storm the night before, but I knew I would more than likely be walking into a shitstorm if someone had told the press that Knox was at Stanford.

I refused to look at the news so I didn't send myself into a panic attack right after the storm. I didn't know if Knox was a forgiving man, but I didn't want to find out.

After getting out of the shower, I tried the breathing exercises that my college therapist had told me to do when feeling nervous. They usually worked during times when there wasn't a storm breaking my concentration.

Once my heart rate slowed, I took in my appearance.

My wavy hair fell down my back, still damp from the shower. My face, bare of any makeup, stared back at me. I took one last deep breath before beginning my morning routine.

I tried my best to look like the businesswoman I wanted to be. I wore a variation of the same outfit every single day—a blazer and a pencil skirt. My hair was always tucked into a neat bun, free from my face. Wearing the same thing gave me enough confidence to face whoever my adversary was. It had worked ever since high school.

As I saw a poised woman stare back at me in the mirror, I felt my shoulders relax. I could do this. Sure, I had told Knox he would never make anything of himself in high school. Sure, someone at my company had possibly leaked his location to the press.

I, as the person who would inevitably be deemed the one to fix it, was probably fucked.

But at least I would be self-assured about it.

As I drove in, I listened to a podcast on confidence, which boosted my mood even further. By the time I was in the elevator, I was feeling better than ever.

I even walked past Simon by the copier. Seeing my possible love interest reminded me that he'd followed me back. I had hope for a less-than-lonely life.

But then I reached for my favorite creamer and found it emptier than I left it. Since I had to ration it between Jenny's orders for the office, I was careful not to drink too much of it. What was worse, the lid was left open, which was something I didn't do.

"What the fuck?" I muttered to myself.

No one in this office had the same taste in creamer as me. Most preferred the basic half-and-half or vanilla. Jenny specifically ordered this for me because I loved it and had it at home. In the year that I'd been here, everyone knew this was my flavor and left it alone.

But maybe I was losing it.

I must have had an extra cup and left the cap open. Knox's arrival must have rattled me more than I realized and I was all out of sorts.

Once my coffee was made, the smell was too tempting. I took a sip of it next to the coffee pot. It was cheap coffee, but the creamer made it so much better.

"Must be a good drink," a voice said.

I froze. For a moment, I hoped I was imagining that voice, because it belonged to none other than *him*.

I slowly turned in his direction, acutely aware of the fact that we were alone in the break room. Yesterday, we'd had the buffer of Dave and my whole team. Now that it was just us alone, I had no idea what could happen.

His messy hair was only a touch more styled than it had been yesterday, but his eyes remained as intense as ever.

"I do love my coffee," I said and walked to the door. "Excuse me."

My heels clicked against the linoleum. Knox's eyes trailed down to my feet.

"I hear it's bad for the feet to wear heels. You've been in them for about fourteen years now." It wasn't even a question.

"Most people in this office don't comment on footwear."

"Maybe I'm interested in foot health."

"Maybe you have a foot fetish."

A slow, irritatingly handsome smile made its way to his face.

Goddamn it. He was *enjoying* this.

"You never lost your snark."

"You never stopped being annoying."

"Most people would be intimidated by me now that I'm a successful billionaire."

"Most people didn't know you when you were a beanpole with glasses in high school."

"A beanpole. I don't think I've heard that one before."

"How about a smug flagstaff? I know I called you that one."

"Right to my face too."

"I don't do things behind people's back. I call it like I see it."

"And what do you see now?"

I could tell him I saw the man who loomed over me, like a ghost I couldn't escape. I could say that he was the person I dreamed of beating, or perhaps that all I saw were those eyes that could pierce right though me.

"I see the man who's standing in my way." It was the safest option.

"What am I in the way of?"

"The doorframe, Knox. I need to get to my office."

He blinked, as if he'd forgotten where we were. "Right. Well, there was a reason I came to find you."

"I thought annoying me was your only job. Mission complete," I said, voice flat. "What is it?"

He smiled, but got right back to business. "We have a meeting at ten to go over the changes I'm making and how you can market them."

"Okay," I said, and I expected him to move. He stayed put, his eyes locked on mine. My skin prickled, but I refused to let him see that he affected me. I gritted my teeth and crossed my arms over my chest. "This is the part where you move, Knox."

"What would you do if I didn't?"

"I could make your very nice shirt stained with boiling coffee."

He stared at me and I wondered if I would have to make true to my threat, but he slowly sidestepped. As I walked past him, I got a whiff of rosewood cologne.

Damn him for smelling good. It made my body heat in ways I wasn't ready to acknowledge.

I'd rather lie and say it was my coffee.

I took one shaky breath, determined not to let this muscular, tall, and annoyingly handsome version of the boy I once knew get to me. He would absolutely use it against me if he could.

I sat at my desk, determined not to think about him. I'd all but forgotten that someone might have leaked his whereabouts to the press.

When I turned on my computer, however, it was impossible to ignore.

I had tons of messages from reporters asking for me to comment on Knox's new role at the company.

Damn it. My dreams of it just being something Mom miraculously knew were dashed.

Not only was it leaked, but it was a headline story. Everyone was talking about his new job, and everyone had emailed whoever they could find at Stanford to get information. This blew up way more than I expected it to.

"I'm sure you've seen the emails," a gravelly voice said. I glanced up to see Caroline standing in my doorway.

"I have. Do we know who did it?"

"Not the problem. The problem is keeping Knox happy and getting on top of this. Do you have media training?"

"I got some in college."

"Then you deal with this. I'm too old to have to talk to reporters."

While I was used to Caroline's hands-off nature, this was too much freedom, even for me.

"Caroline, if I do this wrong, Dave will kill me."

"Then don't do it wrong." She shrugged as she walked away. I gaped at the empty doorway after she left. Then I sank back into my chair and rubbed my temples.

It looked like I was going to be thinking a lot more about Knox Price than I wanted to.

Knox

"We really didn't want this to happen," Dave explained. He and Charles were in my office. The CFO had his arms crossed over his chest, looking one step away from snapping at someone.

Dave hadn't stood still for a single moment. He paced the room, fists clenched at his sides, keeping his gaze on me, waiting for me to explode.

"I expected this," I said. "Even if it wasn't an employee here, it could have been someone who saw me walk into the building. I'm not all that worried about it."

I hadn't even blinked an eye when my phone blew up this morning. I just wanted to get here and see what Ruth had to say to me when we could manage time one-on-one.

And it was had been exactly what I needed.

"We said you would have what you wanted here," Dave reminded, bringing me out of my thoughts.

"If it is someone on our team, then we will ensure they are fired," Charles said, his voice tight.

"That's not necessary. We just need a good statement, and this will die down. Who is overseeing the media statements? I might be able to give them some pointers."

"Caroline. She's got the most media experience, but you might want to check in. *Ruth* might try and take it over." Dave said her name like a curse.

For a moment, I froze. Maybe egging her on had been a bad idea. It wasn't hard to think of all the ways she could use this as a revenge tactic to get back at me for this morning. She had an in, and the Ruth I knew would use it to her advantage.

"I'll do just that then," I said, standing. "Excuse me."

"Do you know where her office is?"

"I memorized the layout yesterday. I know where everything is."

I gave them a single goodbye wave before striding toward Caroline's office, hoping to see her working on the press release statement.

Instead, she had her head down at her desk, snoring loudly.

For a moment, I could only stare. What the hell was the VP of marketing doing sleeping on the job?

But then I narrowed my eyes at a Post-it on her desk, visible through her glass door.

Media statement—assign to Ruth.

Fuck. It wasn't hard to think of all the ways Ruth could use this opportunity as a revenge tactic to get back at me for poking fun at her this morning. The last thing I needed was her sending out a scathing statement that would have Preston asking what the hell happened on my second day at my new job. He had enough on his plate.

I followed my mind's view of the building to where I knew Ruth's office would be. It was tucked in the back corner of the building. I knew it was small, but nothing prepared me for how small it was. A woman like Ruth deserved an office as fancy as mine or anyone else's.

"Why is your office so small?"

"Oh, for fuck's sake," she responded, rolling her eyes. "Can't you find anything else to do?"

"Are you working on the statement from Stanford about my hire?"

Her eyes widened for a second, but then she took a breath. "I am. Caroline dumped it on me and is probably napping in her office."

"That's exactly what she's doing," I confirmed.

"Sounds about right."

"So, what are you going to say about me?" I asked, leaning against her office door in an effort to play off my own nervous energy. "That I'm a troll working as an executive? That I'm planning on eating the CEO?"

"While those things might be true, I value my job more than being petty. I'm planning on saying that Stanford is incredibly lucky to have you and we are excited to see what you bring to the future of our business."

I hesitated. I thought having her verbally spar with me was interesting, but a compliment, even an indirect one, was a totally different ball game. I was unable to come up with a reply for her, and I found myself gazing at those forest green eyes.

My heart fluttered in my chest and I had no idea what to do about it.

Eventually, her eyes narrowed.

"What?" she asked.

"Nothing," I said, shaking myself out of my daze.

"It's definitely something," she said. "Are you mad this got leaked?"

"No, I knew it would."

"Really? You're not going to demand that whoever did this get fired or anything?"

"It's fine. It really is."

She lowered her eyebrows, now practically squinting at me, and the heat of her gaze made the hair on my neck stand up straight. "What if it was me?"

"You leaked it?" I asked. "I didn't know you had it in you."

She scoffed. "Of course I didn't leak it. But I've known since last night that it was a possibility."

"You've known since last night?"

"Unfortunately."

"It wasn't a big news story then. Only people who followed my name very closely would know."

She crossed her arms. "And?"

"Do *you* follow me closely?"

"Absolutely not."

"Then who does?"

"You're zeroing in on me pretty hard here, Knox."

I hadn't taken my eyes off of her since I came into the room. Usually, I had to fight to stay engaged with anyone past pleasantries. By the time they asked anything deeper, I was thinking about work.

"Is being interested in an old friend a crime?"

"It is in my book. And we weren't ever friends. Rivals is the more appropriate term."

"You never answered my question on how closely you follow me."

"It's none of your business," she said. "Are we done here? I'd prefer not talk to you anymore."

"We have a meeting in today."

"Fuck," she muttered. "I forgot about that. Can we move it?"

"Why?"

"Because, honestly, I'd rather eat a pile of garbage than be in the same room as you."

The phrase was so shocking that I did the one thing I hadn't done in forever.

I burst into laughter.

"I forgot how brazen you can be," I said, wiping at my eyes.

She glowered at my reaction, unaware that she was the first person to get a genuine laugh out of me in years.

"As much as I enjoy being laughed at by a billionaire who I used to dream of squishing under my heels, I have work to do."

So did I, but I couldn't find it in me to care.

I felt joy lifting me up, a relief I'd desperately needed. The smile on my face wasn't forced, and it was the sole reminder that I didn't have to force my lips upward.

My gaze hadn't so much as left hers, and I caught her annoyed sigh. "Is this how you get people on your good side? By giving them that smile?"

"No," I replied. "This one is just for you."

For a second, her tough exterior fell. She blinked, jaw opening slightly as my words caught her off guard. Then, her frown returned. "Don't say things that you don't mean." I started to argue with her, but she stood, interrupting me. "Out of my office, Knox. Or I will throw something at you."

"You don't have anything in here that will hurt me."

"Anything is a weapon if you throw it hard enough. Bye."

Her eyes flitted back to her desk, and I caught my shoulders sinking at our conversation being over. I could have stayed in her office all day, if she would have let me.

But once I was in the hallway, I returned my attention to the word I had to do.

And I still hadn't found out if she was married or not.

I paused in my stride as my thoughts slipped to her again. Usually, work invaded all my thoughts.

But she seemed to be the exception.

The emotions she brought out of me today alone was more than I'd felt in years. I was relieved, but also exhausted. I had no idea they could feel so . . . intense.

All I knew was that I needed more caffeine. I grabbed a cup on my drive in, but it obviously wasn't doing enough. I made a stop in the break room, reaching for the birthday cake creamer that I was now addicted to.

I'd downed half of my cup by the time I reached my desk.

"Knox!" a voice called. I turned to see Dave hurrying toward me. "Did you see the press release? It *just* went out."

"I haven't, but I have no doubts it was well done."

"It was. Caroline went above and beyond for once."

"I think Ruth sent it out."

"Of course not. That's why I warned you. If she sent it out, then it would have been crass. She's one of those women who hates men."

"I think she only hates people who disrespect her."

"You won't say that when she loses it on you for no reason." He shuddered.

I took a long drink of my coffee, nearly finishing it.

"I'll take my chances on that," I said.

Dave shook his head. He glanced around when he heard heels clicking, but luckily for him, it was someone else. I could have told him in an instant that it wasn't her, just by the tempo of the gait.

I realized in that moment that he was scared of her.

And rightfully so. If I had met her with how she looked these days, I'd have been scared too. She'd only perfected that withering stare, and the heels made her tower above half of the men in the office.

I went to take another sip of my coffee, only to find it was gone. I sighed, knowing these feelings might be more draining than my job as a CEO.

"I need to get more coffee," I said. "Mind if I talk to you later?"

"Of course," he said. "Let me know if you have any *problems* here, namely with her."

"I will," I lied, and made my way to the break room. With the rate I was going, I was going to use all of this creamer by the end of the day.

⚜

To: Knox Price

   From: Ruth Murray

   Subject: Media Release – Please review and advise

> *Attached is the media release that has gone out. Since you were incapable of forming a complete thought regarding my intentions for the media release, I decided to take the liberty and decide for you. Hope it meets your expectations.*

Regretfully, Ruth

*2 Attachments: One is a photo of a crying clown. The other is
the media release.*

To: Ruth Murray
From: Knox Price
Subject: Media Release – Please review and advise

*The media release looks as good as the attached photo of you
from high school. Great work.*

Sincerely, Knox

To: Knox Price
From: Ruth Murray
Subject: Coffee Creamer

*Are you the one drinking ALL the birthday cake creamer?
Almost the entire bottle is gone.*

Suspiciously, Ruth

To: Ruth Murray
From: Knox Price
Subject: Coffee Creamer

> *I thought that creamer was for everyone.*

To: Knox Price
From: Ruth Murray

> *That's still most of a bottle of creamer. Did you drink it like milk?*

> *Still suspiciously, Ruth*

To: Ruth Murray
From: Knox Price

> *I have been drinking an appropriate ratio of creamer to coffee, thank you. It's just been multiple cups of coffee.*

> *Besides, who's drinking milk right from the bottle? Gross.*

> *No judgment if you do though.*

Sincerely (but a little grossed out), Knox Price

To. Knox Price
From: Ruth Murray

> *Didn't you see all those ads about needing milk to be a big, strong man? You had to have at least a couple of glasses . . .*

To: Knox Price
From: Ruth Murray

> *I'd like to retract my previous email.*

Regretfully, Ruth

CHAPTER FIVE

Ruth

"I think he's playing mind games. Maybe he's one of those billionaires that manipulates people for fun because money no can no longer buy him joy."

Jenny stared at me wide-eyed. I was at her desk in the front of the office, and thankfully, no one else was around. I'd just spent the last ten minutes telling her about my weird conversation with Knox.

"That's . . . a lot."

"The first thing he did was be all weirdly flirty in my office. Then he murdered my creamer."

"Wait, how does one murder coffee creamer?"

"By drinking it all in one day."

"The whole bottle? Is that possible?"

"There's maybe one serving left. When can you make another order?"

"Two weeks from now."

"No," I moaned. "Now I have to drink the basic bitch creamer. Why did he have to do this to me? He calls me Ruth the Ruthless on his first day, then he comes into my office and knocks me off guard. Then he drinks my damn creamer. This is torture. Was it not already hard enough dealing with Dave every day? He's a billionaire, Jenny. He doesn't have to be here."

"Oh, you are *really* going through it. I've never seen you like this."

"I've never felt like this."

"Would it help to hear me say I know you can handle his pompous ass and still get promoted like you want?"

"Maybe," I said.

"You're also amazing at your job."

"Sometimes I'm so tired of it, though. This place sucks."

Jenny definitely knew it. In the last three months, she had become more of a glorified assistant than an office manager.

"It does," Jenny said. "But it's not our life. You need to go do whatever it is outside of work that you love. What hobbies do you have?"

"Does working count?"

"No," she said, her voice flat. "Do you seriously not do anything else but work?"

I sighed. "You're going to think I'm so boring."

"I won't judge. I'm just shocked. Is work really all you do?"

"Work is my life. I haven't had a relationship since college. I don't have any friends, and I don't even know how to live a life. For as long as I can remember, my life revolved around what I can do and not what I enjoy and I . . . I don't know how to break that."

Jenny stared at me, eyebrows twitching like she was trying to process the most unbelievable statement she'd ever heard. I had never admitted any of this to anyone, and I wondered if she would be scared off. I wondered if she would break her promise and judge me for it. I deserved it, if she did.

But she did neither of those things.

"Work is not life," she said slowly. "How about we work on finding you one?"

"We?"

"You're my friend."

"I mean, yeah, but like a work one."

"A real one. What if we went out soon? Do you like bars?"

"I've only been to one. My brother owns Movers and Shakers."

Her jaw dropped. "Are you *serious*? That place is so hard to get into! The owner only lets so many people in."

"Does he? That explains why it's never too crowded when I meet him there."

"Yeah, his bar is amazing. He showcases some of the best singer-song-writers in the city. And he does a dance night."

"Dancing sounds fun," I admitted. "I might be bad at it, though."

"Can you get us in to one of the dance parties?"

"Yeah, probably. Let me text him." I took out my phone and shot Barry a message. He responded a minute later.

"He can't get us in for two weeks," I muttered. "How fucking busy is his bar?"

"That's *so* fast. Say yes! It'll be so much fun. We can dress up and have nice drinks. And we can be each other's wing-woman, if you know what I mean."

"I can be yours, but I don't know if it will work the other way around," I said, my cheeks growing hot. "I'm not really good with strangers."

Jenny looked me up and down. "With your figure? You'd be good with anyone for a one-night stand."

I glanced down at myself. I wasn't bad looking, but I certainly wasn't conventionally attractive. My dress size had only gone up since high school. I tried not to worry about it, since my focus was my job, and body type did not dictate ability, but I did sometimes wonder what people thought of my curves.

My thoughts were interrupted when Simon walked by, giving me a friendly smile. I returned it, but my eyes lingered on him for longer than I should have allowed them to.

He was cute, I'd give him that. Not Knox-level attractive, but still cute.

I then cursed myself for even *thinking* of Knox.

"Oh, does someone have a crush?"

"No!" I hissed. Had she read my mind as I let it slip to myself that I found Knox attractive?

"You were looking at Simon for a good minute there."

"Oh, right. You were talking about Simon."

"Who else would I be talking about?"

"No one," I blurted. "Besides, I think Simon is nice. There could be something there."

She gave me a narrow-eyed, suspicious look that told me she was onto my diversion tactic. I zipped my mouth shut, refusing to crack. After a moment, she let it go.

"He's not a bad choice, but he doesn't seem ambitious. Not like you are."

I thought of Knox. *Again.* "I don't think I can handle more ambition. I want something simple with a guy not involved with anything huge like work. I need a non-workaholic to balance me out."

"Seems like a logical point, but you do realize feelings never really follow that, right?"

Fear tightened my shoulders. "Logic works for me. I think Simon is a good candidate, but it might not go anywhere. He's *only* polite to me."

"Candidate?" Jenny asked. "Are you interviewing someone for a job or looking for a boyfriend?"

"It's kind of the same thing."

"It's definitely not. Do you even like this guy?"

"Of course I do." Or I *would*, once I knew more.

"If you want to talk to him, he gets a snack around this time every day. That's where he's heading now."

"How do you know?"

"I see everything. And he does the same thing every day."

"Wow, that's kind of a perk."

"I wish you the best, but not *too* much luck, because it would be very fun to have a single night out."

"I haven't even talked to him about anything outside of work, so I'll definitely be single in two weeks. I still want to try to talk to him, though."

"You have about five minutes. You've got this!"

I smiled at her encouragement before heading for the break room.

Simon was there, as promised, getting something out of his lunch box.

When I walked into the room, he turned and smiled at me.

"Hey," he said.

"Hey," I replied. "Midday snack time?"

"Yeah, I schedule when I eat," he replied. "It's my nut time."

I blinked. "What?"

He held up a bag of mixed nuts. "I always eat them at this time of day."

I wanted to laugh, but I didn't know if he would take it well.

"You like routines?"

"It keeps me from forgetting," he said, shrugging.

The conversation immediately died, and I was left wondering if this was it, if this was all we would talk about.

"So," I started. "Any fun plans this week?"

"No," he said, putting away his lunch box, snack in hand. "I'm going to play video games with some friends. Not much else."

I nodded, trying to think of my own weekend plans. I had . . . nothing.

"Have a nice day," Simon called as he walked out of the break room. I nodded, trying and failing to not feel disappointed.

This was how conversations went with most people when I tried to talk about anything other than my job. My parents had only prepared me for a life of toiling and that's all I knew how to do.

Someone else walked in. I turned to leave, ready to wallow in my disappointment on my own, but that disappointment turned into annoyance when I saw who it was.

Knox.

He was looking right at me, probably plotting my demise. I rolled my eyes and went to brush past him.

"Want a snack?"

I turned, somewhere between offended and curious. "Is that a euphemism?"

Considering what he'd said earlier, I wouldn't be surprised.

"No," he said. He pulled a key out of his pocket and walked to the always-locked door. He turned it once, and it opened. "I do feel bad for using all the creamer. The least I can do is offer you something from in here."

My jaw dropped. That closet was reserved for Dave and the executives. Most thought it was an ordinary supply closet, but it was actually filled with some of the most expensive snacks Dave could want, and only those close to him knew about it.

Jenny did, and in turn, so did I.

"It's your second day and you have access to the snack closet?"

"I *am* an executive."

I shook my head. "It's for Dave's favorites. I could own the company and I'd never get my way in there." I thought about taking him up on the offer, but then remembered what he called me in front of my employees. I needed to remember *not* to trust him.

"So, that's a no then? Our meeting might run long, and I'd hate for you to get hungry."

I turned to him slowly. "I don't want your pity snacks."

I *was* hungry, though. I hadn't eaten yet today. I peered in, seeing full-size boxes of Oreos. Damn. Those were my favorite.

And, of course, Knox reached for those. They were even the kind with extra filling.

Then he did the last thing I was expecting. He handed me the whole container.

"What is this?"

"They used to be your favorite in high school."

My face burst into flame. How the hell did he remember that? It must have been that robotic brain of his.

"But maybe your favorite changed?" he added at my silence.

"No," I said quietly, and I took the package from him. "I still like them."

"They're good," he said.

"Why do you know that?"

He smiled. "I watched, and I noticed."

"Why?"

"You were the only one who challenged me."

"Not much of a challenge now—not when you're so much higher up than me."

"You'll find a way," he said. "And I'll enjoy it every time."

"Are you some sort of masochist?" I asked, blushing at the way he remembered so much about high school. "Why would you enjoy me bothering at you?"

He laughed. "I ask myself the same thing. Glad you accepted my olive branch."

"I thought your olive branch was a gift card to Chuck E. Cheese."

"That was a funny joke. You already got me back for making me think you have a husband and kids."

"Their names are 'got,' 'you,' and 'good.'"

He laughed, but his eyes trailed down to my finger, which definitely didn't have a ring. I hid my hand, unsure what to do with his attention.

"Anyway," I said, "I'm still mad about the creamer."

"I doubt you will be," he said. "Check the fridge."

"If there's a bottle of birthday cake creamer in there with your name on it, I'm going to throw it at you." I turned to the office fridge, opening it with suspicion.

When I saw three bottles in there, I wondered if I was about to have to make true to my promise.

But then I saw they had *my* name on them.

"You replaced the creamer? With three bottles?"

"There are actually six, and three were for me. They're in the back. I figured if you saw those first I'd get something thrown at me."

Damn. He'd be exactly right.

My already hot cheeks grew impossibly warmer. "T-thank you," I stammered. "You didn't have to."

"It's one less thing for you to hate me about, and it's a good flavor. You have me hooked."

I stared at him. The Knox I remembered wouldn't have cared about drinking all of my favorite creamer. But maybe the Knox in front me wasn't the person from back then.

"Ruth?" he asked.

I blinked out of my thoughts. "What?"

He was standing near the door, watching me with a curious expression. "It's time for our meeting."

Knox

The Oreos were a good idea.

Ruth's eyes were considerably *less* narrowed in my direction, and she'd already eaten two of them by the time we arrived at my office.

And I'd gotten confirmation that she wasn't married with kids.

That was a win. Kids, I would be fine with. Her being married would be a major problem, however.

"Enjoying yourself?"

"Just tell me whatever the hell I need to market so I can go back to my desk. I'm still dealing with the consequences of your hire."

"My usual PR person is also putting out a statement. It usually dies down within forty-eight hours."

"You sound used to this."

"I have to be. People want to know all about my life."

"I don't know why," she said, shaking her head. "You're not *that* interesting."

"I'm not sure whether to be offended by that or not."

"If you'd asked me that before giving me Oreos, I'd have told you to be offended. But now I'm in a better mood, so . . . take your pick."

"Then it's nice to not have someone pry."

Her lips twisted into a sardonic smile. "Glad to be of service."

Ruth leaned back in her seat and motioned for me to begin.

I started in about my plan to code a new app, one that was easier to log into and could do more than just show balances.

Five minutes into the conversation, she stopped me by shaking her head.

"Dave isn't going to like that. He says those apps are going to ruin in-person banking."

"There would still be limitations to what it could do. I'm aware Dave doesn't want to crowd out in-person banking, which would lead to tellers being let go. I don't want that either."

Ruth took a bite of her cookie, eyes focused on my face as if she could read my mind. "I thought big tech companies love automating what they call easy jobs."

"Not when people still have to feed their families. I'm not a fan of getting rid of jobs when they are the only way people can afford to exist."

"That's surprisingly empathetic for a billionaire."

"I tried not to let it cloud my judgment." Her eyes were still on me, and I had to look at my computer to avoid saying something dumb like, *Do you think better of me now?* "This is the app I want to move us to."

She took one look and shook her head again. "It's too much change."

"What?"

"You can't completely overhaul things here. A lot of people *like* Stanford because it's steady. They know what to expect. You have to slowly integrate these features."

"The app Stanford is using now is ten years old. It's a security liability at this point."

"Then focus on the security and build off that. I'm telling you that the customers who use the app are going to have a problem with this."

At PATH, we were all about innovation. We cared about having top-of-the-line tech. I was surprised at how frustrated I was that she was telling me not to do what I was wired to do.

But I also appreciated being told no so plainly. Ruth didn't care about placating me. She cared about saying what she truly thought. Her honesty brought forth true emotion from me.

"The Stanford app is a mess. I don't even want to look at the coding."

"And I don't want to be in this office, but we both don't get what we want."

I blew out an annoyed breath. "I thought the Oreos were an olive branch."

It was surprising how much I wanted her to continue being friendly with me. I'd only gotten small tastes of it, and I wanted more.

Ruth, however, was as stubborn as they came. I doubted she would do anything I wanted her to.

But then she surprised me. Her eyes trailed to the cookies and she bit her red lips. She let out a long breath, her shoulders falling by an inch. "Okay, I'm being too snippy. The app you have looks nice, Knox. It's worlds better than what we have. And if I was the only person whose opinion mattered, then I would say yours is the one we should go for. But I'm not the customer base, and I'm not Dave. You know he won't go for a complete overhaul. Our personal feelings don't matter. Things here need to be done *slowly*."

"That's not the first time I've heard that."

"Whoever said it was right. This isn't PATH."

Her kinder demeanor unnerved me as it had before, but I refused to let it show this time. We were talking business, after all. "You're right. You know the market, so you'll know if I'm headed in the right direction."

"Glad you agree," she said with a coy smile.

"So, in the interest of doing this job well, I need you test the app for me."

The smile fell. "Why me?"

"You know what the customer wants better than I do. And I can pay you in expensive snacks."

"You could ask Dave to."

"I absolutely will not."

"Why not? He's your buddy, right?"

"I don't like the way he talked about you yesterday."

"Really? Because that's not what I heard."

"What did you hear?" I raised an eyebrow, waiting for what she had to say.

"I believe you called me Ruth the Ruthless."

I let out a huff of breath. "I didn't mean that like it sounded."

"There's no other way you could have meant it."

"Yes, there *is* another way. A lot of people here look at your drive and see a threat. I don't. I always loved that you were ruthless. You called it like you saw it, no matter who it was. You never diminished yourself for anyone else. And I love that you're still that way, even if it would mean pleasing the CEO of this company."

She stared at me, emerald eyes wide, but her expression otherwise blank.

"I bet no one else has told you that," I said.

"No, they haven't." Her voice was low. "I guess I owe you a thank you."

"You don't, because it's just the truth."

"So, you're really not intimidated by how I act?"

"Never have been. Are you intimidated by me?"

She laughed. "No."

"I thought so."

Her eyes met mine, and I found myself attempting to memorize the curve of her eyelashes and the arch of her eyebrows. Silence stretched on, but I could not think of one single thing to say.

"Well, if that's everything, I'm going to get back to work," she said, standing. "I'll see you later, I guess."

I nodded, still feeling unnerved by how much I enjoyed looking at her. I'd never focused on a person like this before—not even when I was with Gia. My attention was only ever held by an invention I couldn't wait to finish. And now, Ruth seemed to garner the same response.

For a while after she was gone, I stared toward the doorway, feeling a smile trying to make its way across my lips.

The only thing that brought me out of it was my phone ringing. When I saw Preston's name on the screen, I answered it immediately.

Technically, I was still part owner of PATH. I'd told Preston that if there was ever a problem that he couldn't solve, he could call me, and I'd help with it. I'd told him he could call for personal problems too. As my best friend since freshman year of college, I would always be there for him.

I'd been worried that taking over as acting CEO would be too much for him. So much so that I put off stepping down for too long, forcing myself to function while numb.

"Hey," I said. "What's up?"

"Just checking in. PATH isn't the same without you."

"Is everything okay?"

"Mostly. There've been a few questions from the research and development team that I've had to figure out. I'm not the scientist you are, but it worked out okay. I didn't call about work, though. I wanted to see how my dad's treating you."

"He's been fine to me. Not so much with some of his other employees."

"He always played favorites," Preston mused. "I bet you're busier than ever working on fixing things there."

"Somewhat. I wanted to code an app that was too new for them. So I'm using the one they had."

"The ten-year-old one?" He laughed. "Good luck."

"You said to go slow, and someone told me very firmly that I should stick to that."

"Who had the balls the say that?"

"Did I ever mention a Ruth Murray to you?"

Preston was silent for a moment. I almost wondered if the call had dropped. "You did. You said she was the only person who ever challenged you."

"She's here," I said. "And nothing has changed. She tells me what I need to hear."

"Sounds like your kind of woman."

"Maybe. She said she would rather eat a pile of garbage than be in the same room as me."

Preston laughed. "That's the best thing I've heard all day."

"It definitely made me laugh," I added, still smiling at the idea.

"She seems good for you. You sound better already."

I sighed. "It's too bad she hates me."

"You'll wear her down. I give it two weeks and she'll be coming home with you."

"She's far more stubborn than that. Maybe make it two years."

"I'm willing to take that bet," he said, a smile in his voice. "It's good to hear this is helping, though. I've missed the real Knox. PATH did too. It'll be great when you're running it again."

My shoulders fell. The idea of returning to San Francisco and to my company was one that made me sink right back to where I was. I didn't know why. I loved work, I loved my company. It gave me purpose. But that had turned into nothingness over time.

I knew the allure of work would return eventually, so I pushed back the dread and turned the conversation to focus on Preston and how his day was going.

CHAPTER SIX

Ruth

I'd not made any headway on finding an outfit to wear to Barry's bar.

But then again, I hadn't had the time to try all that much. Between working with Knox on redesigning the existing app—which I could tell he hated by the way he complained about every detail of it—and my weekly dinner with my parents, I was too tired to get out of the apartment to go shopping.

The night of, I changed my hair into a ponytail rather than its usual tight bun. As I waited for Jenny to come over, I took off my heels to rub my feet and get dressed.

When I was done, I both looked and felt underdressed, so I texted her to see if she would be okay with coming early to help me with my outfit. As she arrived, I slipped my heels back on.

But when she walked in, her eyes weren't on my outfit.

"Wow," Jenny said. She gazed at my white walls and lack of decoration. "Your place is . . ."

"You can say it's boring. I don't have time or energy to decorate."

"I was going to say like a bachelor pad."

"It's fine. I don't spend much time here anyway. What should I wear?"

"I brought you something. I have a habit of collecting clothes and I'm pretty sure we're the same size."

She pulled out a bag and dug through it. As she did, I took in her outfit. She was wearing a tight dress with pink lace. It was long sleeved, and went up to her neck, but there was a keyhole cutout over her cleavage.

That was when she held up a gold dress that caught my eye. My first thought was that it was the same color as Knox's eyes.

It was shorter than my usual pencil skirts. I knew before even trying it on that it was lower cut than anything I'd worn in years.

It was so beautiful that it was impossible to look away from.

"I'll try it on," I said slowly.

She smiled excitedly and handed it over to me. I grabbed the one strapless bra I owned and stepped into the bathroom attached to my bedroom.

The gold fabric stretched over my wide hips and ass, and I wondered if maybe I would get a ticket for public indecency.

"I think this is a no," I said as I threw the door open.

Jenny's jaw dropped. "What the fuck do you *mean*? That is gorgeous on you!"

"My tits are out there. They have their own zip code."

"You're used to seeing yourself in work outfits, Ruth. This is perfect for a night out."

"To my *brother's* bar. He's gonna kick me out when he sees me."

"Is he one of those weirdly protective types or something?"

I tilted my head as I considered it. "I don't actually know. He's only ever seen me in work clothes and pajamas."

"Then I think it will be fine, but I won't push you to wear something you don't like. You can change if you really are uncomfortable."

I glanced in the full-length mirror one last time. My not-so-flat belly was the first thing I saw, but even that was shiny and beautiful in light of the dress. My legs looked long due to the shorter hem and tall heels. For once, instead of seeing a businesswoman looking back at me, I saw a twenty-eight-year-old woman about to have a fun night out.

"I'll wear it," I muttered.

"Yes!" Jenny said. "Now let's go. We have a bar to get to."

We wound up taking a cab to the bar so neither of us would have to drive home if we were drunk. My plan was not to drink much, considering we had work the next day, but Jenny didn't seem to share the same concern as she talked about just how much alcohol she planned to consume.

When we got in line, I saw many of the excited partygoers in front of us get turned away. When I presented my ID, I wondered if even we would be allowed in the door.

The bouncer saw my last name and nodded, letting us in. I heard people behind us gasp.

"This is unreal," Jenny said. "We got in!"

"Barry put us on the list," I said. "I was a little worried he'd forgotten."

Dance music was growing louder as we approached the bar and dance floor.

Jenny's jaw dropped. "Look at all the lights!"

I hadn't ever seen it from the inside. I usually talked with Barry in his apartment upstairs the rare few times he would want to meet here.

Now that it was in full swing, I could see why so many people loved the place.

"Ruth?" Barry asked, coming around the corner, voice raised over the music playing. "Is that you?"

"Yes," I replied.

"You look . . ."

"Finish that sentence and I will throw something at you."

"Hi," Jenny said, holding out her hand. "I'm her friend and the reason she's out tonight. We're getting her a life."

"It's about time."

"The threat still stands," I said, glaring at him. He only laughed.

"Whatever. I'm not Tom and I'm not going to tell you what you can wear. I just thought when you said you were visiting that you'd come in your work clothes."

"Who's Tom?" Jenny asked.

"Our brother who used to spend most of his time under the influence," Barry said, shaking his head. "Be careful out there, Ruth."

"I'll be fine," I said. "I don't drink every night. This is a onetime thing."

"Don't have too many. The bartender on staff tonight makes them strong."

"I'll have one, maybe two."

Barry nodded, smiling over at me. "You always were the responsible one. You two take care. I'll kick out anyone who bothers you."

I nodded, and Barry returned to whatever he had been doing.

"I thought you said he wasn't overprotective," Jenny said.

"He's usually not like that. But it was kind of sweet."

"And hot."

"Oh, gross. I don't want to even think about that."

"But he *is*. That long hair? The beard? He looks like he belongs on the stage, not running it."

"I think he plays guitar from time to time," I said. "Maybe he takes the stage of the bar."

"I'd pay to see that," she said. "But for now, I want a drink and to dance!"

As she grabbed me and pulled me to the bar, I took notice of the music. Pop played through the loudspeakers, and a DJ was having the time of his life in front of the dance floor. For a weekday night, the bar was full, but thankfully not so much that we couldn't move.

It didn't take long to get our drinks. Jenny gulped down hers. I took one sip and nearly gagged.

"Barry wasn't kidding."

"I love it!" Jenny said. She gazed out over the people who were dancing without a care in the world. I took another sip of my drink before she was pulling me into the crowd.

"Um, I'm not good at dancing!" I yelled in her direction.

"You don't have to be. Just have *fun*!"

I glanced around. Some people were swaying their hips to the music. Some were very into the whole scene, swaying their hips with their arms raised. A few couples were grinding in the corner. No one seemed to give me a second glance.

One of the bars had a mirror behind it and the woman staring back at me was not the poised businesswoman who had never danced in her life.

She was someone else.

I took a deep breath and decided to say fuck it and follow Jenny's lead. I downed my drunk and joined her on the dance floor where I let the music take me over.

To: Ruth Murray
   From: Knox Price
   Subject: App Changes

   Please see the report on what changes I've made to the app so far. It's been slow, but I'm making it work.

Sincerely, Knox Price

To: Knox Price
From: Ruth Murray
Subject: App Changes

> *Hwy are you woking? It's nighttume. Go DANCE. Go to a*
> *brar. Get a life!*

To: Ruth Murray
From: Knox Price

> *Are you drunk?*

To: Knox Price
From: Ruth Murray

> *Myabe. But I'm hvng FUNE!*

To: Ruth Murray
From: Knox Price

> *Where are you?*

To: Knox Price
From: Ruth Murray

I'm at Movers and Shkers, having the tme of my LEIF! BYE KNOX!

Knox

After a moment of shocked staring at the email, I looked up the bar she was talking about.

Movers and Shakers was apparently famous. It prided itself in showcasing all kind of talent. A few very famous stars had been seen there.

Judging by her emails, she was more than enjoying herself, but she wouldn't be the next morning if anyone else saw she'd emailed me while drunk.

I quickly logged into the admin email monitoring software to delete the emails from existence. I then stood from my desk, legs tired from sitting for too long.

The right thing to do was to go home. I shouldn't care if Ruth was at a bar having fun. I needed rest and to water a few of my plants.

Was this normal for her? Had she gotten into partying since high school? There was nothing wrong with it, but she had to be extremely drunk to have that many typos in her emails. I didn't know what she would be like, but I knew what other men could do in a busy club.

Maybe I would check in, make sure she was fine, and then leave.

My self-driving car took me to the bar and parked at the curb. I couldn't help but wonder what she was going to do when she saw me. I'd never seen Ruth drunk, and I was dying to know what she would be like.

When the bouncer at the door asked who I was, I showed him my ID and he let me in without another word. He did, however, raise his eyebrow. I wasn't a frequent flyer of bars, but my name had done me well to get in just about anywhere I wanted.

I adjusted the ball cap on my head and looked around the dance floor. My dark sunglasses slightly obstructed my vision, but the bright lights illuminated things just enough so I could see her.

And I was not prepared for what I saw.

She was in a shiny gold dress, swaying her hips and flailing her arms in the center of the dance floor. She looked completely different than she did at the office. The dress clung to her hips as they swayed to the music. I was struck with just how beautiful she was in the flashing light of the bar. My heart raced; I had never felt this sort of shock in my life.

She was obviously okay and having fun. It seemed a drunk Ruth was a fun Ruth. I hadn't been invited here, so it would be best if I left before she saw me.

It should have been easy to leave, but my feet propelled me toward her instead of in the other direction.

I stopped right in her field of vision, eagerly awaiting whatever reaction she would have to my presence.

"What the fuck?" she asked, jaw falling open. "Are you real or are you a figment of my imagination?"

"You have quite the vocabulary for someone who just emailed me in a drunken stupor." My voice was loud in the chaos of the bar.

"First of all," she said, and she swayed on her feet, "I'm having fun. Second off, why are you here?"

"I won't stay long. I wanted to make sure you were okay."

"Why wouldn't I be okay?"

"It's a bar and you are very drunk."

She stared, as if her brain wasn't able to process my words. "I'm here with Jenny." She gestured behind her where the office manager was currently making out with someone. "Ugh, I'm so—whoa!" She was cut off as someone knocked into her on their own way to the bar. She fell forward, right against my chest.

In a cruel twist of fate, the music tempo slowed. She asked, "Why do you always smell so fucking good?"

"You must be incredibly drunk if you're complimenting me."

"I am very drunk," she agreed, and then she leaned into me. I froze. "Don't you ever dance?"

"I do, but I would like it if you were sober."

"I'm fine," she said, winding her arms around me. "I just think I'm so drunk even *you* seem nice."

"I *am* nice," I huffed.

"You're annoying." Her cheek came to rest on my chest. "You should think *I'm* annoying."

"You should go home."

I should too, but the heat of her was doing more to my brain than drinking ever could. I needed to step away to put distance between us, but every cell in my body begged for me to bring her even closer.

"Do you have friends, Knox?"

"I have one."

"I bet in the friendship competition, you're like . . . *the best*. Like you always are." Her eyes moved to the bar. "I kinda want another drink."

"I think you're done."

"But I only had one!"

"Really?"

"They're *strong* and get someone drunk fast. Just like I am." She made a clumsy attempt to get around me, but all I had to do was step in front of her. "How fast are you? Do you have superpowers?"

"Yes, It's called being sober."

"Fine, *fine*. I guess you win. *Again*."

"It wasn't that difficult."

She rolled her eyes and nearly lost her balance. Apparently her heels worked against her while she was drunk. That, or she'd rolled her eyes so hard that it nearly knocked her over.

"I'm going to take you home," I announced.

"Is that code for you're going to take me into your backyard and kill me?"

"Definitely not. You'd be a screamer."

"I'm definitely a screamer," she said. My mind went to dark places at those words, but I shook them away. I needed to get her home and get away from her before I made a mistake she would murder me for.

"Hang on!" another voice yelled as we were getting close to the door. "You're not taking my drunk friend home to—"

Jenny had run over, holding her purse like a weapon. I slid my sunglasses down my nose.

"It's just me."

"What the fuck?" Jenny asked.

"She drunkenly answered my email and told me where she was."

"Ruth! This was supposed to be a fun night!"

"I did have fun! I had fun telling him to get a life!"

Jenny shook her head. "No working when we're out. Rule number one!"

"But he was working too."

Jenny raised an eyebrow at me. "Seriously? It's like nine."

"I had stuff to do," I insisted. "Don't worry about it. Let me get her home. You're, uh, *friend* is waiting on you."

Jenny looked back at the man she had been making out with, and then to Ruth. "I have no attachment to him no matter how good of a kisser he is."

"I think he's going to take me home to kill me," Ruth said.

Jenny's nostrils flared.

"I am not!" I insisted. "She's obviously tired. She's stumbling in her heels."

"My feet are working just fine!"

"I don't want anyone taking advantage of this situation."

"How do I know *you* aren't taking advantage of that?" Jenny asked with narrowed eyes.

"Because you could call any reporter and ruin my life," I said.

"Ooh, do it!" Ruth said.

"Oh, wow, she's *really* drunk," Jenny said. She then looked at me. "I don't know if I trust you."

"You probably can," Ruth muttered. "He's, like, *nice.*"

"So do you want to go with him or not?" she asked Ruth.

"I want to see a bed. And it would take a cab forever to get here."

"Share your location with Jenny," I urged. "That way she can check on you."

"Ugh, I hate how smart you are." Ruth clumsily handed her phone to Jenny.

"You're going to hate this in the morning," Jenny muttered, taking the phone and sharing Ruth's location. She only had time to give me Ruth's address before the man she had been making out with walked over to us and kissed on her neck. "Ooh, that feels nice," Jenny said. "You two go, but I will be watching you, Knox!"

"I'm not going to hurt her." I put an arm around Ruth's shoulders to lead her to the car. She didn't say anything, even as I reached over to buckle her in.

"Ruth? Are you okay?"

I was still leaning over her, and she was dangerously close to me.

"I hate you," she muttered.

"Still?"

"I will always hate you after everything you've put me through."

"What did I do?"

"You were just . . . *you*."

"But what exactly did I do?"

"I'll never tell."

"Then how am I supposed to fix it?"

"You don't," she muttered.

"That's a shame."

"I know." Her voice was quiet. "And I guess I'll be alone."

I shook my head, thinking that she had me.

But did she? My time here was limited, after all.

"I was supposed to meet someone tonight," she added. "Someone who would take me home."

"Someone *is* taking you home."

"I mean someone who would also take me out on a date after. Or maybe not. I don't know one-night-stand etiquette."

"I'll take you out for coffee at least. The other thing is probably a bad idea."

I wished that it wasn't.

Ruth turned to look at me, not immediately rejecting my offer.

"That sounds nice," she said so softly I wasn't sure if I'd heard it right.

"Really?"

"Yeah," she said. I couldn't help but smile. Then her eyes went to my head. "Is your hair soft? It's always looks soft."

"I don't know," I said. "I barely mess with it."

"Can I take this off?" she asked, touching the ball cap on my head.

"Why?"

"For funsies."

"For *what*?"

"Please?"

"Fine."

The hat came off and she dropped it into her lap while her hands ran though my hair. Her nails grazed my scalp and I found myself leaning into the touch.

"Damn it," she muttered. "It *is* super soft."

Her hands tilted my head up to where I was looking deep into her eyes. A compliment from her was much harder to take in comparison to an insult. Getting to see past her tough exterior and glimpse the softer side underneath was something I would never forget.

"I knew it," she whispered.

"You knew what?"

"Two things, actually. One. Your hair is as soft as it looks. And two," she licked her lips, "your eyes are the same color as my dress."

"Ruth, let me go," I said lowly.

"What are you gonna do? Kill me?"

"No, but it's something you'll regret in the morning."

"I'm on the top of the *world*. I can't regret anything." Her breath whispered over my skin, and it smelled like cherries and alcohol.

"Then I don't kiss drunk woman." My eyes trailed down to her dress. "No matter how much I might want to."

Her hands slowly let go of my hair, and my eyes slid back up to look at her expression. Her lips were parted, eyes still on me.

Then, she laughed. "I'm definitely dreaming. There's no way you just said that to me."

I slowly stood, keeping my mouth shut. Some distance would do us both good.

Even if it was the last thing I wanted.

I walked over to my seat and punched her address into the car. Ruth watched with great attention as it pulled away from the curb.

"So how do we know this thing isn't going to crash?"

I was both relieved and devastated that we were no longer talking about kissing.

"Magic," I said. "And I'm here as a backup."

"Magic is a cop-out answer. I know that you know exactly how it works."

"I think you're too drunk to hear that."

Her lips scrunched. "You're right. Ugh, it's hard to bicker with you about anything that's not work. I just wind up talking to you instead."

"And let me guess, that's a bad thing?"

The car pulled into Ruth's apartment complex, parking in a parallel spot on the road. She blew out a breath. "Of course you're one of the few people that's easy to talk to."

"What does that mean?"

"I think I'm no longer fun-drunk," she muttered. "Just sad-drunk."

"Then it's time for bed. I'll help you inside."

She nodded and I got out of the car to open the door for her. When she stood, she leaned against me. I took her weight easily, wondering if I'd ever be lucky enough to have her do this sober.

Her apartment was clean but barren. There were no decorations anywhere.

"I hate how boring this place is," she moaned. "I was so embarrassed when Jenny came over, but I have no time to decorate. Is your place decorated?"

"It is."

"I bet it's with posters of models or something."

"Nice guess," I said, leading her to her bedroom. I gently put her in bed. "But no."

"Is it with neon signs?"

"Nope."

"Then what is it?"

"Houseplants, mostly."

"That's *so* cool."

"Pretty interesting for a man you once called a robot, right?"

Her face scrunched up. "You work like a robot, but you're not one. You're too warm to be one." Her hand was still on my chest and I wondered if she could feel how my heart hammered. The hand drifted up and touched my face. "Your face is too squishy too."

I laughed shakily. My entire equilibrium was off at her evaluation of me. I didn't realize I'd always wanted Ruth Murray to tell me how human I was until that moment.

"Are you alive enough to remember your phone number? I'll text you about the coffee shop." All I could think about was seeing her again to-morrow.

Her eyes closed, but she recited her the number. I committed it to memory, hoping she wouldn't regret everything that transpired tonight when she woke up.

I used to think only annoying Ruth would be fun, but I had a feeling being her friend would be even more so.

Chapter Seven

Ruth

When I woke up, my head *pounded*.

I groaned and considered calling Jenny to ask why I'd gotten so drunk on a weeknight. I didn't even remember anything after finishing my drink. Anxiety hit me at my lack of memory. I didn't even know how I'd gotten into my apartment. Maybe I'd somehow stumbled back.

I slowly rolled over to check my phone. There was a message from an unknown number, however, that drew doubt to that theory.

Unknown number: Drink some water when you get up. Meet me at this coffee shop at 7.

My eyes widened at the message and I flipped over to Jenny's and my text chain.

Ruth: Did I go home with someone last night?

Jenny: Someone took you home.

Ruth: Did I sleep with them?

Jenny: Are there signs you did?

Ruth: No. I'm still in my clothes. I even have my shoes on.

Jenny: Then the man that took you home had pure intentions like he said he did.

Ruth: I have a message from an unknown number about getting coffee this morning, plus a reminder to drink some water. It's gotta be him. Do you remember who it was?

Jenny: You don't remember what went down?

Ruth: No. I drank way too much.

Jenny: He's safe, if that's what you're worried about.

Ruth: Who is it?

Jenny: If you knew, you wouldn't go. Your stubbornness will cost you free coffee.

Ruth: Okay. Fine, but if this goes sideways, I blame you.

Jenny: Sure . . . See you in a few hours. *eye emoji*

It was early in the morning, and I had an hour to make myself presentable and meet this mystery person at the coffee shop.

The place he had chosen had good ratings. As I took off the shimmery dress and redid my makeup, my heart pounded with anticipation. Had I finally met someone?

It took me a few minutes to park, and when I did, I glanced at myself in the mirror. I looked as I usually did, except today, I opted for thicker foundation to cover the dark circles under my eyes. My bun was perfect, and I looked better than I felt.

Before I climbed out, I took a sip from the water bottle I'd brought from my apartment. It only helped a little. I walked into the coffee shop, excited to meet this mystery person.

That excitement dropped when I spotted Knox waiting by the door.

He was wearing a ball cap that looked vaguely familiar.

"You've gotta be fucking kidding me," I grumbled.

"Hi, Ruth. Did you drink any water?"

It all made sense in that moment. Why Jenny said I wouldn't come if I knew who it was, and why I'd woken up with a distinct feeling I'd done something I would regret.

Because Knox was the one who took me home the night before.

"What did I do last night?" I asked, dread filling my chest.

"You mainly danced in that dress of yours and asked me if I was a good friend."

Shame made my cheeks hot. "Goddamn it," I muttered. "Okay then, get it over with."

"Get what over with?"

"Just make fun of me so I can get to work and not think about the huge embarrassment I am."

"I'm not going to make fun of you. I'm going to get you coffee and then we'll go to work."

My eyes jerked up to his. "No way. You saw me drunk and in a dress that should have been illegal. This is too perfect to pass up."

"I'm not the asshole you think I am. We're just here for coffee."

"That's it?"

"That's it."

I stared at him, and my pounding head was the only reason I said, "Okay. Fine."

He pushed off the wall he had been leaning on and led me to the line. I watched him carefully in case he turned on me.

"Ruth, it's fine. I'm not going to make fun of you," he assured me, his eyes firmly fixated on mine.

"So, you took me home last night?" I asked.

"I did. Jenny was preoccupied."

"That was very . . . nice of you."

"I was worried when you emailed me drunk."

"I *what*?"

"Don't worry. They're purged from the system. No one will know."

"I am never drinking again." I now felt even better about intervening about Tom's drinking.

"I don't regret it, not when it got you to talk to me like a human being."

"You're not a human being."

He narrowed his eyes at me, which made me lean away from him. With his mouth flat and the way his fists clenched, what I'd just said struck a chord.

And I felt bad about it. Here he was getting me coffee, and I was pissing him off. Maybe this was why I didn't have any friends.

"I was hoping we were past you saying things like that."

"Sorry," I said. "I didn't mean to hit a nerve."

His eyes widened. "You're apologizing? While sober?"

"I'm not heartless," I said. "You're taking me out to coffee and not making fun of whatever I did while drunk. I shouldn't be rude to you."

"Does this have to do with why you hate me so much?"

I froze. "You . . . know why?"

Did I tell him about my parents last night? Was he being so nice out of pity? My heart raced at the thought.

"No," he said, and I let out a breath of relief. "But you did say you hated me. Was I really that bad back to you in high school?"

He was annoying, but by far, the worst thing about high school was my own failure to ever beat him. It's why my parents seemed to care more about him than me.

That wasn't his fault, though. And sure, he'd irritated me a few times, but even I could admit he didn't deserve how defensive I'd been.

Especially after he'd gotten me home last night.

"It wasn't that bad," I said slowly. "Don't worry about it. I'm just good at holding grudges."

"You're the best at it. Maybe even better than me."

"What a great thing to be number one in," I said, smiling deprecatingly despite my lingering headache.

His eyes caught on mine, and I found myself staring into his amber irises, thinking of the dress I'd worn the night before.

I tore my eyes away and focused on the menu. "What are you getting?"

"So, we're letting this go?"

"I'm far too hungover for this." It was a lie. The hangover was not why I didn't want to talk about it. I would never be ready to let anyone hear about how many opportunities my parents had given me, only for me to be stuck as a measly director at twenty-eight.

"Fine," he said, slowly turning to the menu. "I'm not sure what I'm getting. What do you want?"

"Coffee with cream and sugar," I said blandly.

"Really? Not a latte?"

I had no clue what that was. A twenty-eight-year-old woman probably should, however.

"It's not my taste."

"Even the Oreo one?"

"Oreo makes a latte?" I asked, turning to him.

"The actual brand doesn't, but coffee shops often add the cookies and cream flavor."

"How?" I asked. "Is it all powder or something?"

"Kind of. It's mostly the syrup."

"Syrup goes into these things?"

He stared at me, then a smile crept onto his face. "You have no what a latte is, do you?"

"I'm not answering that."

He laughed. "You don't need to. I can see it on your face."

"Awesome. You now have another thing to use against me."

"How would I find a way to use your lack of latte knowledge against you?"

I didn't know, but I was embarrassed all the same. "You can make fun of me with Dave."

"I highly doubt Dave knows anything about coffee. Besides, your lack of coffee knowledge is far from the worst thing I know about you."

"Thanks for bringing that back up. Why would I need to know about coffee anyway? I need to know marketing tactics and how to make my company look good. If you would ask me about the coffee *brands*, I could tell you which one had a commercial that made people think a brother and sister were a romantic couple, but I couldn't tell you the quality of their product."

"Hang on, I must have missed this commercial."

"It was an Internet joke for years and an example of what not to do in advertising."

He laughed again and covered his mouth to stifle it. "Well, I can tell you that the coffee here is roasted in the back, and it's delicious. I can also tell you that a latte is espresso with equal parts milk and foam."

"Foam?" I asked.

There was that smile again. "It's what happens when the milk is steamed. It's really good. You've been missing out."

I bitterly turned to face the front. I was aware I had been missing out on a lot in my life, but I didn't need him knowing anymore about that. I was sure he got to live a full life in a way I hadn't. While I was working my ass off and trying to find my footing in the corporate world, he was on top of everything. I wished I could hang on to my bitterness forever, because it was comfortable.

But he was being far too nice for it.

"Um, I'll have a large cookies and cream latte please?" I found myself asking as we got to the front of the line.

"Nice," he said quietly.

I glared over at him, but he was smiling at the barista and giving her his order—an Americano on ice.

He handed her his card before I could jump in and say I could pay for my own. I glanced in his direction, but he put a hand on my back and led me away.

I eyed his hand, and he removed it immediately. "Sorry. After last night I thought . . . never mind."

"What happened?"

"You're just . . . *open* when drunk. You touched my hair."

My jaw dropped and my face erupted in flame. This was the last thing I wanted, and besides, if my parents had any idea that I was sitting in a coffee shop with him, they would be telling me to use him for a promotion.

And then they'd credit him with anything I got.

He was perfect to them, and while that wasn't his fault, my heart couldn't take what being close with him would mean for my relationship with my family. I needed distance, and I needed it fast.

When our names were called, I grabbed my drink, determined to do just that.

"Aren't you going to try it?" he asked. "We could grab a table and—"

"I need to go," I said firmly. "Thank you for the coffee, but I have a lot of work to do."

And I ran outside.

I didn't even try my drink until I was in the privacy of my office. A part of me didn't want to, because it served as a reminder of Knox's kindness, but the smell of coffee and Oreos was too strong for me to resist.

After one sip, I knew why people liked lattes. It was light and airy in a way coffee wasn't, but it still had the slight bitterness to it that I loved. The syrup they'd used captured the flavor of Oreos perfectly. I'd definitely have to go back.

"Ah, Ruth, there you are." Caroline's raspy voice brought me out of my thoughts. "I need you to do something for me."

"I've already refused to comment on the lone reporter still asking questions about Knox."

"They're *still* after him?" she asked. "I haven't checked my email in a week. That's what I have you for."

I clasped my hands tightly in front of me. She wasn't even hiding it at this point.

"What can I do for you?" I asked slowly.

"I need you to send out an email announcing my retirement." She smiled for the first time in months. "I'm getting out of this hellhole."

Knox

From: Caroline Fitzpatrick
   To: Stanford Corporate
   Subject: Retirement Announcement

> *Caroline is happy to announce her retirement, effective immediately. After working at Stanford for twenty long years, she will be moving to Florida with her husband to enjoy time by the sea.*

> *Any questions can be directed to the executive team. Ruth Murray will be taking on some of the day-to-day tasks for the foreseeable future.*

To: Ruth Murray
From: Knox Price
Subject: Caroline's Retirement

> *I'm assuming you're applying for her job, especially since you'll already be doing part of it.*

> *Sincerely, Knox*

To: Knox Price
From: Ruth Murray
Subject: Caroline's Retirement

> *Of course I am. Are you going to try to stop me or something?*

> *Suspiciously, Ruth*

To: Ruth Murray
From: Knox Price

> *I could put in a good word with Dave. You ARE the best person for the job.*

> *Truly, Knox Price*

To: Knox Price
From: Ruth Murray

> *I don't want to use your weird friendship with Dave to get this job. Thanks, but no thanks. I've got this.*

> *Independently, Ruth Murray*

To: Knox Price
From: Ruth Murray

> *Thanks so much for your help! You're the best.*

> *Sincerely, Ruth*

To: Ruth Murray
From: Knox Price

> *???*

To: Knox Price
From: Ruth Murray

> *That wasn't supposed to go to you.*

Apologetically, Ruth

To: Ruth Murray
From: Knox Price

Who are you THAT nice to?

Sadly, Knox Price

To: Knox Price
From: Ruth Murray

Sadness (Jealousy) isn't a good look on you.

Knox

It wasn't even noon, yet the swirl of emotions I'd already felt had me so exhausted I was downing a third cup of coffee.

When Caroline's email made its way to my inbox, I instantly formulated a plan in my mind on how to help Ruth get the job. I knew it was going to be a hard sell. The jump from director to VP was a huge one, and it meant she would be involved in more decision-making than Dave was ready to give her.

He needed to see that Ruth was the best person for the job, and as much as I disliked the man, I could use our working relationship as an in.

Dave wanted her to be nicer, and if I could just get her to listen to me, she could play the part until the job offer was in her hands, and then she would have the job she deserved.

It was a rushed plan, and I still needed to work on how to keep her in the job once she was promoted. Then, I'd gotten the email that was obviously meant for someone else.

I thought maybe it was for Jenny, but that seemed too formal for the friend she got drunk at a bar with.

My curiosity got the better of me, and I walked to her office to see if I could catch her in person. When I arrived, she was sitting at her desk, but gazing at something underneath it. She was smiling at whatever it was.

"Do you have a kitten underneath your desk?" I asked as I approached her.

The last thing I expected was to see Simon from IT's head pop out.

I froze, taking in the sight from an all too different angle.

It was probably innocent. She was pushed back from her desk, and Simon had a wire in his hand. He was probably working on something.

But he could have turned and seen *right* up her skirt.

Shock morphed into annoyance, which then turned into something else I didn't like. I hadn't thought about the idea of Ruth being interested in someone else. Now I was struggling to keep my composure.

"Simon?" I asked, my voice taking on a harder edge than it had a minute ago.

"Oh, hey," he said. He was possibly the least intimidating guy I'd ever met, and I didn't want to be angry at *him* for his proximity to her, but I felt angry in general. I was used to it from having my privacy invaded, but this felt more intense somehow.

Maybe because it was her.

"What, Knox?" Ruth asked impatiently. "I'm a little busy."

"Simon," I repeated, not taking my eyes off her. "Can you go take charge of organizing the stock room closet? I will help Ruth with her problem."

"Sure," he said, not at all bothered by my lack of eye contact. He stood and walked out of the office, content to go complete the task I'd given him. It was going to take a while, considering the IT stock closet was filled to the brim with computers and cables that people had just thrown in there.

"Really?" Ruth complained as she stood. "He hadn't even replaced my charger yet."

"Do you know how that looked?"

"He was just changing the charging cord to my laptop," she said.

"Isn't that something you could do?"

"He was also testing the power strip since there was a power outage recently. I'm good at a lot of things, but electrical is not my thing."

"But that looked . . ."

"No one comes back here anyway, and even if it *was* like that, I'm not breaking any rules. He's not my employee. If I want to date him, I absolutely can."

I stared at her. "Date him?"

"Why do you even care?"

Because I want it to be me.

Nope. No. I wasn't going there.

"I . . . guess I don't," I said, slowly. "He seems nice."

"Exactly. He's a great candidate." At my disbelieving look, she rolled her eyes. "Don't say anything. I *know* interviewing a boyfriend isn't the same as interviewing a potential employee."

"I don't know if interviewing is the right word to use at all."

"Okay, I already got this from Jenny, and I actually *like* her. I don't need this from you too. Let's just talk about whatever the hell you came in here for."

I should change the subject like she asked, but I was struggling to.

"So you are looking for a candidate then? You're hiring?"

"I'm not *hiring*. I'm in the market, and I don't appreciate you making fun of me."

"I'm not." I only wanted to speak her language.

"Don't we have business to talk about?"

My eyes trailed down her neck, where I could see her turning red. Was this conversation affecting her like it was me?

My entire world felt flipped upside down because suddenly dating was on the table. At least possibly.

But maybe not for me.

"Knox," she warned. "What did you really come in here to talk about?"

"It was . . ." It was hard to remember anything other than what she'd just said. "It was about that very nice email that wasn't meant for me. I was going to ask how I could get you to talk to me like that."

"You should try being Simon."

That was not the answer I was hoping for. "And that's the only way?"

"Yep. We've never liked each other."

"More like you never liked *me*." The words came out harsher than I meant them to.

"What is wrong with you?" she snapped. "Why are you in such a bad mood?"

"It was just a bit shocking to see someone from IT under your desk like that."

"And we're back to this. I have other things to do, like get a damn charging cord, since you rushed Simon off before he could finish his goddamn *job*."

She made her way to the door where I was.

My eyes met hers, and I tried to think of ways to extend my time in her office. I could ask if I could see her résumé so I could help her use it to get promoted. I could talk to her about the app and get her feedback on what I needed to change.

But she was now in my personal space, looking at me expectantly. "That was your cue to leave, by the way."

"I . . . don't want to."

"Why not?"

I should have mentioned one of the things that were job related. Instead, I said, "I don't exactly know. But somehow *this* is better than going back to my office."

"Of course. Because you like this. You like annoying me. You always have."

"Ruth, I—" I wanted to say that I liked more than annoying her. I liked being near her, something I didn't think possible for me.

"Get out of my way, Knox," she said firmly. "Or I will move you myself."

She was so close. I could smell her lily perfume. I could see the flecks of blue in her green irises, and the way one single piece of hair fell out of her perfect bun.

Fuck, she was beautiful.

Her eyes met mine steadily, and I saw her breath hitch as she stood close to me. But her lips pursed, and she didn't waver.

Ruth's hand came to rest on my chest, and for a moment, I forgot every word of what she said. Her touch was electric, and all I could do was focus on where her hand rested against my shirt.

Then she shoved me out of the way.

"I warned you," she said, and continued down the hall. I was left staring after her, heart hammering in my chest.

My body was thrumming from one single touch from her. I was warm all over, breathing hard.

Was I . . . hard from that? From just her pushing me out of the way?

It took a long time for the feeling to recede and I was grateful for the distance of Ruth's office from everyone else. I walked back to my desk, glancing at the IT closet where Ruth met with Simon to acquire a new charger.

I had to resist the urge to interrupt them, to kick him out of there and lock myself in with her.

And that was when I realized I was in an all-new sort of trouble.

CHAPTER EIGHT

Ruth

To: Ruth Murray
   From: Knox Price
   Subject: The App

   *I have another version of the app ready for you to test. Let's
   set up another meeting.*

   Sincerely, Knox

To: Knox Price
From: Ruth Murray
Subject: The App

   Are you going to act normal this time?

Suspiciously, Ruth

To: Ruth Murray
From: Knox Price

> *I'm sorry I was weird earlier. I was worried someone else would catch you in that position and say something.*

Sincerely, Knox

To: Knox Price
From: Ruth Murray

> *It was innocent, but whatever. I'll set up a meeting. I will leave if you get all weird again.*

Seriously, Ruth

"So, adding the features works well enough," I said, sliding my report across the desk to Knox. "I think we should move forward with development of this."

I watched him closely. His eyes were not on the sheet of paper.

"Do not mention earlier," I told him. "We're here to talk about work and nothing else."

He took in a deep breath, leaning back against his chair. "Fine." He ran a hand through his hair and I caught myself following the movement. "If we're talking about this app, then I hate this version of it. It's subpar as best."

"We can add more later. This works."

"I want to redesign the whole thing. It took me way too long to make the old one work, and it still only barely functions. I can do way more with a new platform."

I rubbed my temples. "Too much change will scare customers away."

"I can make it look like the old one. It will take me a while, but it shouldn't be too difficult, considering I've been working on the old one for weeks."

I took a moment to think about it. "If it looks very close to the original, I highly doubt Dave would even know the difference."

"Thank God," he said. "I couldn't put my name on this. It's not my best work."

I didn't say anything else. After he'd admitted that he was jealous earlier, my mind wouldn't stop thinking about how he'd smelled up close.

Knox was *not* the kind of guy I wanted, anyway. I needed someone to loosen me up, to get me *away* from work, even if only in the evenings. Knox's work ethic was the only one more intense than mine.

My best option was to stay away from him.

"So, are we done here?" I asked as I stood.

"No, there's one other thing," he said. I tensed. "We need to talk about that promotion."

"I don't want help."

"I understand, but you *need* it."

"Don't tell me what I need."

"Dave isn't going to consider you because of his own prejudices. If we work together—"

"No," I said forcefully. Working with him felt like an admission that I *needed* him in order to get the promotion.

I could hear Mom now. *Knox was so kind to get you this job. It's really a testament to how powerful he is.*

I refused to give my parents any more ammunition. It was why I'd left the coffee shop so suddenly.

"You know I'm your best option," he added. "You need me."

Now I was getting angry. "I *don't* need you. I barely even like you."

"Really? I thought we were friends."

"Friends don't get jealous when another guy was helping them with a surge protector and a charger."

"Under your *desk*."

"The point still stands."

"Fine. Maybe friends don't get jealous. But you know what friends also do? Help each other get promotions."

"Not all friends. You don't see Jenny up my ass about this."

"It's the kind of friend *I* am."

"Then we don't have to be friends. You can be the new executive that's a pain in my ass. You'll fit right in."

"Don't do this."

"I think I will. I don't want anything from you, Knox. I don't need you to get me this job. I've been doing fine without your help these last ten years, and my work speaks for itself."

"Not here it doesn't."

I opened my mouth to tell him to fuck off, but there was a knock at the door.

"Hey, Knox," Simon said, popping his head inside the office. "That closet is a mess. Mind if I take a few days to focus on it?" Simon's eyes trailed over to me. "Oh, hi, Ruth. Am I interrupting something?"

"No." I forced my voice to be kinder than I felt since I didn't want to scare Simon away.

"We're not done," Knox said to me.

"I think we are," I replied. I turned to Simon. "Thanks for the new cord. Maybe it'll last better than the old one."

"Yeah, I need to order more of them. You're not the first person to ask for a new one."

"Ruth," Knox started, but I refused to look at him.

"See you around, Simon," I said to the one person I could tolerate in that moment and left Knox's office to get back to my job. The more I proved to Dave that I could handle Caroline's responsibilities, then the more I could strong-arm my way into the position.

I didn't need Knox. I refused to believe that.

After two hours of attempting to work, only for my annoyance to get in the way, I realized I needed to vent.

I glanced at the time. Jenny would be stocking the break room. Maybe we could chat while everyone else was working. No one was ever in there past two.

Jealousy was a much more powerful emotion than I was used to.

It sat in my chest, making me want to pick a fight with anyone in my vicinity.

Now that I was alone, I needed to focus on work, which usually was never a problem. I always wanted to work.

Now I wanted her.

I sighed and pushed away from my desk. I was frustrated at my own distraction, but I was hoping it wasn't anything coffee couldn't fix.

Even if the birthday cake creamer reminded me of her.

I made my way to the break room, but as I got closer, I heard voices. The first was Jenny's.

"So, you've decided *not* to be friends with Knox?"

"No," Ruth's voice answered. "Fuck him."

I wasn't one to eavesdrop on conversations, but I also couldn't bring myself to move once I heard my name, and her voice.

"I'm starting to think you're going to. Your neck is red."

"Jenny!" she hissed. "No. He's being all weird right now anyway."

"How so?"

"He's . . . acting angry when I'm around Simon. Earlier, Simon was under my desk and—"

"Hang on, under your desk or *under your desk*?"

"He was changing out my charging cord, nothing else. But Knox thought the same thing. He was so jealous about it."

"Jealous, huh?"

"Don't make it into something it's not."

"I'm only saying what it sounds like. He could be into you."

Jenny was correct. I couldn't remember a time when I wasn't around Ruth and didn't want her, even when I was a nerdy, lanky high schooler.

"No," Ruth said. "I refuse to believe it's that."

"Then you're refusing to believe what's extremely obvious. He was *on* you at the bar."

If anyone had managed to photograph us, I was well aware of what they would assume.

"I thought he didn't touch me."

"He didn't, but his eyes were on *you*."

"No, we are not discussing that."

"Why not?"

"Because he's not what I need. I need a guy who will get me out of work, not the one who spends all their time here."

So *that* was what she wanted. My heart sank at the words. I was the wrong candidate then.

"Then you need to start talking to Simon about something that's *not* work."

"And say what? How's the weather?"

"That's a good start. Just *try*, Ruth."

"I did at his last snack break. We only talked about *nuts*."

"Trying to talk to men about anything other than work is new to you," Jenny reminded her. "It may take some time for you to figure out how to do it. He brews tea at ten a.m. Try to talk to him tomorrow."

"You know his tea schedule too?"

"He works like a clock. It's kind of weird, but he's not the only one. Amber goes to the IT closet every day at eleven."

"Why?"

"Probably to chill for a bit. We all have a favorite dark closet to sit in when we need a break."

"Oh, Knox, is that you?" Dave's loud voice gave me away. I turned to him, chest tight at being caught.

"Yes, what do you need?"

"How is that app coming?" He put an arm around my shoulder and led me to his office. I caught one glance of Ruth as we walked by.

Her eyes locked on to mine, and I caught myself wishing she had been talking about me like she had with Simon.

Jenny's eyes darted between us.

I nodded in her direction, but I could see her gaze follow me as I walked with Dave.

My brain was buzzing with all the new information I'd gathered. As Dave questioned me on what I was doing, I answered robotically, my mind somewhere else.

She was going to talk to Simon tomorrow. She wanted a man whose life wasn't all work, and I was definitely not that man. The only thing not work related that I did was water my damn plants. She wouldn't find that interesting.

But damn it, I wanted to be.

CHAPTER NINE

Ruth

The next day, I was determined to focus on one person: Simon.

Not Knox.

I refused to even think of him.

Did he slip in a few times? Sure, but I ignored that. My short-lived friendship with him was over, anyway. I was okay with that.

In an effort to look my best, I wore the one blouse I owned that showed off just a hint of cleavage. I set my hair in a ponytail instead of my tight bun, and I wore just enough highlighter to make my cheeks shimmer.

And I knew the one thing that would make my good mood better was getting a damn latte.

I doubted Knox would happen to be there two days in a row.

The line was as long as it had been yesterday. As I stepped into it, I surveyed the menu, trying to take in each name. Maybe one day I would try an Americano or a cappuccino.

Then I felt someone walk up behind me. They were tall and stood too close for my liking. I clenched my fist, prepared to physically push them away.

"Ruth," a deep voice said. I recognized it instantly.

"Oh, come on. Knox, what are you doing here?"

"I could ask you the same thing. I thought your pride would stop you from coming here again."

"You thought wrong," I said. My lack of caffeine was dangerous for his well-being.

"Are you getting the cookies and cream latte again?"

"I'm going to try the lavender one, actually."

I waited for him to make a comment about my choice. My shoulders tensed as I imagined him laughing and saying I would hate it.

"It's good," he said. "I think you'll like it."

I nodded, thinking the conversation was over.

After a long moment, and only a few movements in line, he sighed.

"Are we still not friends?"

"We can be friends when you stop being a pain in my ass, which by my calculations is going to be never."

His sharp breath of air ghosted the back of my neck, and I had to resist the urge to shiver.

Not now, body.

"I can be more than a pain in the ass, you know." The words were spoken quietly.

I turned to him, and his eyes immediately fell to my outfit. I immediately tugged my blazer tighter around myself.

"You look beautiful today."

My brain shut off for a moment. That was *not* what I expected him to say.

"R-really?"

"Yes. You always do, but this is even more so."

And somehow, despite all odds, I was beginning to forget why I was even mad at him.

"Thanks."

My skin felt hot, and I was now considering ordering an iced drink to cool off. My eyes searched the menu for the answer, but all that was listed on the chalkboard menu were the types of lattes.

"Hey," I said to Knox, "this might be an incredibly stupid question, but can lattes be iced?"

"Yes, they can."

I let out a sigh of relief.

"This place has a more descript menu online if you ever come here on your own."

"I feel like a fucking idiot when it comes to coffee."

"To be fair, most people don't know what they're doing at coffee shops. They often don't know what they're ordering."

"Like me with the lavender latte. Is it actually good?"

"It's not as sweet as some others."

"That sounds perfect then. I had my fill of Oreos."

"That's a shame. Jenny ordered more."

My body temperature rose impossibly higher. Why was it so easy to talk to him? In high school, he wouldn't hesitate to make fun of me for anything he could find. And I would have done the same, if there had been anything to harass him about.

Maybe he'd figured out a way to disarm people. It worked on almost everyone I'd ever seen him interact with.

It must have finally been working on me too.

"Speaking of the Oreos, how many people have you shared the executive closet with? Be honest."

"Just you."

"Why just me?" I asked, turning to him.

"I could easily get caught if I did it with too many people. And you work harder than some of the executives. Anyone with sense can see that."

"Sure, but it doesn't come without sacrifices. I don't have much of a life."

"Neither do I."

"Come on, you have to have a hobby."

"Okay, I *do* have a hobby."

"What is it?" I asked. "Wait, why am I thinking it's something to do with plants?"

"Because I told you my home decor was houseplants the night you were drunk."

"Well, that's one thing I remembered then. I've never even tried taking care of plants. I'm not home enough to." I muttered the last sentence, the words more for me than him.

"Being a workaholic isn't exactly good for you. There's a reason I stepped down, you know."

"That's why you stepped down?" I asked. *Oh, if only Mom could be a fly on the wall.*

"I realized I was a robot," he said after a moment of deliberation.

Well, shit. "Is that why you were so hurt when I said you weren't human?"

"Those words have haunted me ever since graduation. For a long time, I thought you were right. I'm still not convinced you were wrong."

I looked at my feet, shame heating my cheeks as I thought back to that night. I may have been eighteen on paper, but I was still only a kid, and I regretted the things I'd said. I'd been so hurt that my parents weren't excited about my achievement.

"I shouldn't have said that back then," I said slowly. "I'm sorry my words stuck with you."

His wide eyes met mine. "Really?"

"Yeah, I am. I was upset at how some people reacted and I didn't know how you managed to work all the time."

"I was determined. I always have been, and then I stopped feeling anything once I'd done it for too long."

"And that's when you stepped down," I added. "Did it help?"

"Something did," he said lowly, almost like he didn't want anyone to overhear.

"Is fixing the dumpster fire that is Stanford's tech the something? You can admit it, I won't tell."

"Stanford definitely has something that's gotten my interest."

I wanted to call him out on his cryptic words and see if I could annoy him into admitting whatever *really* was at Stanford.

But I was next in line, so I didn't get my chance.

"I'll have an iced lavender latte," I told the barista.

"And I'll get an Americano. Her drink's on me."

I paused at Knox's voice.

"I don't need to you to pay for me," I muttered as he handed his card over. Again.

"No," he said, and he turned to me. His eyes fixated on mine. "I'd imagine you don't. But I like to buy coffee for people I'd like to be friends with."

Damn. He was good.

"Okay, then. We can maybe be friends again, as long as you don't get weird when I ask this next question."

"What is it?"

"What do you think of Simon?"

He blinked. "You really want me to answer?"

"Yes," I said. "But I'm talking about him as a person. Sometimes men will be nice to a woman's face and then awful when in a room with only men. Has he done anything like that?"

"From what I've seen over these last few weeks, I gather that he's perfectly nice."

"So then he's perfect."

"If that's what you want."

"He's nice. That's what matters. Feelings can come later."

He glanced over at me, his lips pursed. Then he gave me a stiff nod.

"What?" I asked. "You're thinking something."

"I'm not trying to start a fight with you but . . . I don't know if that's how romantic feelings work."

I wasn't sure how to respond to that, but thankfully, our drinks were ready. I had a much-needed moment to think about my next question before he was back, both of our drinks in his hands.

"Then how *do* they work, Mr. Know-it-all?"

He handed me my drink, but his eyes remained focused on mine.

"It hits you like a train, Ruth. It keeps you up at night and is always on your mind. You could be a robot like me and feel your heart start beating again."

For a moment, I couldn't move. He *had* to be talking about Gia. There was no way it was anything else.

"And how did it end?" I looked up at him. It couldn't have been well, considering he was now single, and she was the only person he'd had a long-term relationship with.

"I'm not sure. I'm still waiting to see what happens. And if I can manage to get an interview." His eyes drifted down to my lips, and then back up to my eyes. I took in a shaky breath as I realized he might have been talking about *me*. "Enjoy your coffee, Ruth."

For once, my brain failed me. I couldn't come up with words. I could only feel my heart race in my chest. Knox walked out but not before shooting one last smile in my direction.

My body thrummed, telling me to go after him. I wanted to run my fingers through his messy hair and press his lips to mine.

But I stayed rooted to the spot, determined to follow through with my plans with Simon, even if I now questioned them.

Knox

The smile stayed on my face until I got to the office and saw Simon. I wondered if my words had changed her mind.

I was distracted and couldn't focus on work. I tried, but I kept glancing in the direction of where he sat. I now knew he had tea at ten but I was hoping what I'd said would make Ruth forget about his like-clockwork schedule.

But then Dave walked into my office.

"I want you to interview these people today for the VP role," he said, dropping a pile of papers in front of me.

"Me?"

"I'm locked into meetings with the shareholders about our newfound success now that you're here." He gave me a smile. "And I trust whoever you pick."

"Charles might have more experience."

"He scares whoever he interviews. You're the best person for the job."

"All right," I said, unable to think of any other way to get out of it. "I'll do it." I took a look at the résumés. They were messy and unprofessional, and I noticed one similar trait.

"Are you related to these people?" I asked. "They all have the same last name as you."

"It doesn't matter as long as they can do the job. Oh, ignore the degree on my cousin Steve's. It was technically considered null since the government broke up his school."

"Ruth is not going to like this," I warned. "And I don't know if this is—"

"Ruth won't know. It's why I put her in the office I did. And she's taken on about half of Caroline's work, so she's busy."

"Are you interviewing her since she's currently doing the job?"

Dave laughed. "Of course not. She should know she's not getting the job. Someone better will."

"She should be compensated for her time then."

Dave laughed. "Good one, Knox. I like your sense of humor."

"I'm not joking."

"You got the deadpan down and everything." He continued to laugh, clutching at his chest. "My doctor will have to have a word with you. You're going to give me a heart attack."

Dave walked out before I could say another word. My fists clenched; I knew I was about to be the bearer of bad news.

But I was not going to let Dave screw her over like that. I made my way over to Ruth's office, knocking on her door as I approached.

"Come in," Ruth called. When I entered, her eyes widened. "What? Is the app giving you a hard time? Why do you look so pissed?"

I put the résumés on her desk.

"Look at these."

She picked up the papers and her jaw dropped. "Are you fucking kidding me? He's interviewing his family members?"

"Yep."

"Awesome. I should have seen this coming. I bet they all are going to be as incompetent as he is."

"You could find out for yourself. Join the interviews."

"Dave will kill you if he finds out."

"He's in meetings all day, but if you're there, you can tell me the exact reasons why they won't work. I don't know the job requirements like you do."

"And you'll use that to convince him?"

"I'll do my best."

"When do they start?"

"Ten minutes."

She looked at her calendar, and then her lips pursed. "Well, so much for talking to Simon."

Damn. So she was still going to talk to him then.

"You can skip the interviews if you want, if he's more important than the promotion."

"You know I'm not going to. I'll see you in ten."

"None of these people are even worth our time," Ruth said, standing abruptly after the last person left. "The first one had a degree from a scam institution."

"I don't disagree," I replied thoughtfully.

She slid a piece of paper at me. "Here're all the reasons why they won't work for the job."

I glanced down at her swirling handwriting. There were detailed reasons listed out, such as lack of proven email software experience all the way down to personality traits that could potentially cause problems with existing employees.

"This is impressive."

"I know what the job needs," she said.

"I'll tell him these reasons then." I tucked the paper into the stack in front of me. "And then I'll mention you for the job."

"No," she said.

"It's the best chance you have. You know it."

She crossed her arms. "Maybe it is, but my answer is still no."

Ruth made her way toward the door.

"Where are you going?"

"I'm going to go make up a reason to talk to Simon. I can still catch his nut time."

"You can catch *what*?"

"He means it for *mixed* nuts."

"Then why did you say it like that?"

"Because he did."

"That's . . . kind of funny."

A smile played on her lips. "It is, isn't it? I didn't know if I could laugh or not. He might take his nut time very seriously."

A laugh escaped me. "Ruth, that is the funniest and most unprofessional thing I've ever heard you say."

"I'm full of surprises." She grinned before walking out the door. My feet propelled me to follow her before I could stop them.

"Ruth, wait," I called.

"What? We don't have anything else to talk about."

We walked into the break room, only to find no one there. She checked her watch. "Oh, I'm a little early."

Thank God. I had a little bit of time.

"You had to feel what I did in the coffee shop this morning. Unless my eyes are playing tricks on me."

She glanced over at me, eyes wide. Then she looked away. "It doesn't matter."

"I just want to know one thing," I said. "Why not me? Give me an honest answer and I'll leave you alone."

"I—" Her eyes moved from me to the hallway, where people were walking past. "I am *not* talking about this out in the open."

I doubted she would leave, considering she still wanted to talk to Simon. But there was one place we could get some privacy.

"Fine," I said, opening the executive supply closet. "Then we can chat in here."

"In a *closet*?" she asked.

"It's private," I said. "I just want an answer to my question. And you want to hear if Simon comes in."

"Fine," she said, walking into it. I shut the door behind us. "If Charles comes in here, this is your fault."

"Dave is in meetings all day, and Charles already raided it. The beef jerky is gone."

"What if he wants something else?"

"He *only* eats the jerky."

"Probably because he needs to chew on something other than his anger problems." She turned to me and her eyes widened as she registered just how close we were. I saw her breath hitch in her throat, and then she shook herself out of it.

"You're very stubborn, Ruth," I said. "But I can still see this affects you."

"I don't even know if you meant me earlier. You could have been talking about your ex."

"Then I'll make it clear. *You* were the one who hit me like a train. *You* are the one that I'm still hoping will look past her stubbornness. It's you."

Her eyes were locked onto mine. It was too dark to trace the colors of her irises, but I remembered them from the day before.

"Why?"

"Because it's always been you."

I sighed as I heard Simon's voice say goodbye to someone as his footsteps shuffled into the break room. I expected her to make a break for him, ignoring what could be igniting between us.

But she didn't move. Her gaze was still on me.

Simon didn't linger long, rustling around in the refrigerator for a moment before leaving just as quickly as he'd arrived.

"You just missed your chance."

"I . . . don't know that I did." The words were whispered. I had her so close, and her lily scent clouded my thoughts. "For once, I think my stubbornness is losing."

"Good," I said.

"So, what is this?"

"I don't know," I replied, because I truly didn't think words could describe how I felt when she was this close to me. "But I do know that I'm going to be thinking about this for a very long time. This closet will be burned in my memory. And . . ." I closed my eyes as I remembered the other person that had her attention.

"And what?"

"I wonder if you'd rather be in this closet with *him*."

Her eyes tore away from mine as she thought about it. "I don't think I'd want to be with him. But I'm not sure what that means."

"I've been in this situation before."

"In a closet with your former rival?"

"No, choosing someone who fit the bill. The right *candidate*, if you will."

"And what's the alternative?"

"You find someone you're passionate about."

"I don't even know how that feels."

"Do you want a demonstration?" I moved my hand so I was now holding hers. Ruth's eyes fell to them clasped together, and her chest filled with a held breath—but she didn't pull away.

"If you're about to lead me to the Oreos, then I'm sorry to say I'm still too tired of them to feel passion."

"No. I was going to lead you here." I pulled her hand to my neck. "Feel my heartbeat."

Her hand pressed into my skin, gently feeling the pounding rhythm.

"I think you should see a doctor," she eventually said.

"I'd rather see the woman in front of me."

"Fuck," she muttered and rubbed at her neck. "Maybe *I* need to see a doctor."

"Is your heart beating as fast as mine?"

"It's because we're in a closet."

"Is it? Or is it because right now, it's just you and me?"

"It's . . . not *not* that." That was as close to a yes as I was going to get.

"Is your skin hot? Are you breathless? Because I am."

"Fine," she hissed. "I'm all of those things, but it's miserable, Knox. I don't like it."

"Neither do I. It's miserable because we both want *more*." I couldn't take my eyes off her lips. She was *so* close. I could see the light glint off her cheeks.

"Honestly," she began, "I don't see how any good can come from this."

"You can leave," I said. "Or I could prove you wrong."

"You think you know everything."

"I'll give you one chance to push me away," I whispered, inching toward her. "And I'll stop. But if you don't, I will prove to you how good passion can feel."

One breath.

Two.

She leaned in too. "Do your worst, Knox."

My hands moved to cup her face and I finally closed the distance between us. My lips slotted over hers, and my body came alive in ways I didn't know it could. Electricity shot from my lips straight to my chest, sending my heart into overdrive.

I was hers. There was nothing else to it. One kiss proved that there was nothing else for me.

There was a sharp intake of breath, and I wasn't sure who it belonged to. Her head tipped back, and I pushed her against the shelf of the supply closet, desperate to touch more of her.

Her lips tasted like coffee creamer, and I swiped my tongue over one, desperate to take in more.

Her fingers ran through my hair, nails scraping against my scalp. Her fingers pulled me into her while her body simultaneously pushed to get closer.

Her body was soft yet rigid against mine, and a swell of emotions swirled inside me, none of which I could name.

I could feel her glorious breasts pressed against my shirt. I reached my hand down to grab her ass through her ridiculously tight skirt. Her mouth opened, and a moan escaped out of her. I used the opportunity to slip my tongue into her mouth.

I had never experienced a kiss like this. This was in our place of work. We were breaking all the rules by doing this, but I couldn't justify pulling away.

The sound of someone's laughter as they walked past was enough to remind us of where we were. Ruth's hands disappeared from my hair and she leaned away.

Before I could think of a single thing to say in response to what just happened, she ran from the closet, leaving me behind in her wake.

CHAPTER TEN

Ruth

Fuck. Fuck. *Fuck.*

My body was hot all over. I could barely breathe. And yet, I felt more alive than I had in years.

I had just . . . kissed Knox Price.

And I *liked* it.

Beyond that, even that kiss was . . . the best of my life. His lips were unwavering against mine. His body was hard and solid.

My body begged me to go find him again.

I was in my office, sitting at my desk, horrified. I didn't dare look at anyone because I knew my neck was so beyond flushed that they would know something had happened.

When I closed my eyes, I only saw flashes of him.

It had broken something in me. I wasn't used to feeling attracted to, well, anyone. While I thought I could have something with Simon, he had never given me anything to think about, to fantasize of, let alone the heat I felt now.

My thighs clenched as I remembered the kiss. If just lips felt like that, then what would something more do to me?

Maybe . . . maybe he was right. Maybe I should reconsider trying anything with Simon. Maybe I should try following passion instead of logic for once.

But I knew one thing: I couldn't leave my office until I cooled down.

When I tried to fan myself, my hands shook. When I tried to take deep breaths, all I could think about was how his exhales brushed my cheek as we kissed.

I needed to focus on something else. Work usually did the trick. I had a mountain of emails to answer. I struggled to get started on them, but eventually, I was able to force myself to get things done.

My cheeks had finally cooled, right as my laptop flashed with a low battery warning. I frowned and checked the charger, only to find it not working.

Again.

Simon had warned me that the cord he'd given me when I went to find him might be a bad one, since they were all in a pile in the mess of the supply closet.

Maybe Knox had a point in assigning him to cleanup duty.

With one thought about Knox, my body reminded me of exactly what I'd just done with him.

But I shook it off. I needed a new laptop charger.

I glanced at myself in my phone's camera to ensure I looked all right. Then I made the trek to the supply closet to get a new cord.

And that was when I walked right into Knox.

"Ruth." His voice was low, and I wondered if I could drag him away for a moment alone. "Why are you over here?"

I blinked, bringing my attention back to the problem at hand. "I need another cord."

"Me too," he said, raising his hand to show off the adapter he was holding.

"Glad we have someone organizing that closet. Simon gave me a bad cord."

"About earlier . . ."

I held up my hand. "It's fine. It's more than fine actually. It's great. Thank you for helping me clean out the old food from that closet. It was very helpful."

"You're . . . welcome?"

"We should do it again sometime."

His eyes widened for one second before he nodded in acknowledgment. I took in a shaky breath, trying to keep my cool since we were out in the open.

He reached for the supply closet doorknob right when I did. Our hands brushed, only for me to jerk mine away before I jumped him in front of everyone.

Knox opened the door and both of us turned to see the last thing we were expecting.

I saw the bright, blonde hair of Amber, nestled close to someone else. They were kissing, and when I squinted my eyes, I could see it was Simon.

My jaw dropped, and I heard gasps behind me. I slowly turned to see a few people who had frozen mid stride at the sight of two employees kissing in the supply closet.

Others were standing from their desks to see the commotion, and their eyes widened when they looked in our direction. By the time I'd turned back to them, Simon and Amber had sprung apart.

Whispers broke out around us, and I dimly realized this could have been Knox and me had any of the executives come to the snack closet.

And I was suddenly reminded why kissing your coworkers was a bad fucking idea.

Knox

"I want detailed records of their messages and emails. I want them both fired and banned from ever working again!"

I rubbed my temples, losing the battle to keep my anger at bay.

Ruth did not do the same.

"You do realize that we can't control if they work again, right?" she asked, eyes narrowed at Dave. "Besides, Amber was on her break."

"Of course you'd stick up for that—" Charles's tone was harsh.

"Choose your words wisely, sir," Dina, the HR rep in the room, snapped.

"They definitely broke rules," I said, and it reminded me that Ruth and I were guilty of the same thing. "But we can't go about this the wrong way."

"*You* found them. This is an embarrassment for our newest executive to catch something like this! Especially one of *your* candor."

"Seriously?" Ruth asked. "He's that special?"

"They're human," I said. "It's not a huge deal."

"If they did no other romantic activity on company property, then it would only be their first strike," Dina added. "A write-up would be far more appropriate."

"We can't let them get away with this!" Charles snapped.

"They're not," I said. "They'll get a write-up, and we can install cameras in the closets. But it's not uncommon for employees to develop feelings for people they interact with on a daily basis."

I glanced at Ruth, only to find she was looking back at me. She averted her eyes immediately.

"You're really okay with this?" Charles asked. "If it were me, I'd be demanding proper recourse."

"It's not a great situation. They should have had better . . . impulse control, I'll say that. But they're valued members of the team. Neither had any seniority over the other."

"Exactly," Dina added. "It isn't like one of the executives was caught with an employee."

Charles and Dave nodded.

"Out of curiosity . . . what if that did happen?" I asked.

"That would be a lawsuit waiting to happen."

Fuck. I was in trouble.

Ruth had gone still, and I had no doubt she was realizing how bad this could have gone for us.

"I can write them up for their actions on company property," Dina said.

"I think we need to make a new rule for the future," Dave said. "No work relationships. At all."

"Even if it's on their own time?" Dina asked. "I don't know how we can enforce that."

"It's not that hard to know what your employees are doing. *Watch* them. If we have any other embarrassing stunts like this, people will be fired."

I clenched my fist. Adding in a rule too? That was just giving Ruth another reason to never touch me again.

And she'd definitely hinted at wanting to do it again.

"Does anyone know of any other relationships they want to come clean about?" Dave asked, looking at us all.

I could feel Ruth's eyes snap to mine, but I kept my mouth shut. If she wanted to say it, then I wouldn't deny it, but there was no doubt the consequences would be severe.

Silence rang out.

"Fine. Dismissed." As the meeting attendees filtered from the room, Dave walked over to me. "Sorry about this. I can't believe the gall of my employees."

"It's fine," I said. "I'm more worried about—"

He cut me off. "Let me take you out for drinks as an apology."

"I'm not sure that it's—"

"Nonsense. You've had a rough day. We can go now. You need a break from the office."

I let him take me, dreading the fact that I needed to tell him none of his relatives would work out for the VP job.

He drove us with wild abandon to an elite bar in downtown. Each drink was near a hundred dollars, and while I didn't care about the money, I cared that he used the company card to pay for our drinks.

"It's for team building," he insisted when I raised an eyebrow at him. "Charles is staying behind to watch everyone. He's going to inform them all about the new rule too."

"I don't know that even he can catch everything that goes on in the office."

"But he can scare people into submission. That is what always works."

I was starting to see why Preston had moved all the way to San Francisco for college. How many times had Dave done this exact same thing to him, his own son?

I was about to tell him off and quit. But quitting would mean leaving Ruth, and I already knew I couldn't bear that just yet.

"How did my relatives do today?"

"I don't think any of them will be a good fit."

Dave frowned. "Really? Why?"

I listed out the reasons I remembered from Ruth's handwritten notes.

He groaned when I was done. "You got all of that? One of them has to work. They'd be better than Caroline by a long shot. They're boys like *us*. We need more of those in the office."

"Actually, I think we need less."

"Why in the world would we need less?"

"I hear discriminatory hiring practices lead to very expensive lawsuits."

"No one will mention anything."

"Really? No one?" I leaned in. "I think you and I both know there are people with interest in this hiring process that will have no problem fighting you."

Dave's eyes widened. "Ruth."

I meant me, but that was close enough.

"Then what the hell should I do?" he asked. "I can't hire *her* for the job."

Ruth didn't want me interfering, but I couldn't keep my mouth shut.

"You easily could. She's running the department in Caroline's place."

"There's no way."

"You know Caroline didn't know how to answer an email."

"Her and me *both*." He shook his head. "I hate all this technology."

I raised an eyebrow. "Really?"

"I mean not *your* technology. Just the useless stuff." It was a bad lie. "A-anyway," Dave said, chuckling awkwardly, "Ruth is too . . . gruff for the job."

"I'm aware you don't like her, but don't bring personal feelings into it. If you expect your employees to stay professional and not have workplace relationships, the least you can do is keep your own feelings out of your hiring decisions. Besides, other male employees in high positions are gruff. Why can't she be that way too?"

His lips pressed together. "This is *my* company."

"And it's also yours if someone sues you."

Dave let out a long, whiny sigh. "I see why you're the leader at PATH. Preston could never stare people down like you do."

"Preston is good at handling the public."

"If he was a little more like you, he'd be *my* protégé." Dave frowned and looked at his hands. "How's he doing at PATH, anyway?"

"He's fine. He's acting CEO right now."

"I bet he's begging you to come back. Too bad *I* have you now."

I glared over at him. "Preston was the one who recommended your company to me. He wanted me to help you."

"Oh. Well, I suppose that somewhat makes up for him abandoning me."

I put my foot down. "I'm not going to be in the middle of your problems with Preston. If you need to talk this out with your son, then call him."

"I'll wait for him to call me."

He would be waiting a long time, then. I shook my head and looked out the window. This was the last place I wanted to be. I'd rather be back in that snack closet with Ruth.

"But . . ." Dave admitted slowly. "I'm glad he made something of himself instead of doing nothing. At least I have that."

I looked back over. "So, you're proud of him."

"I am in a way." Dave took another drink. "You're a smart man, Knox, and I know I need to trust your judgment. Just your name being attached to my company made our stocks *double*. You've made me a lot of money in such a short period of time. I have half a mind to let *you* present at the next board meeting."

"I don't do well with public speaking."

"Really? Why? It's so easy. Everyone must want to hear what you have to say."

I shook my head, eager to move on from the idea. "What were you saying?"

"Oh, yes," he continued. "I was saying that I'll *consider* Ruth for the job, if it makes you happy."

"I want her to have the job."

"One step at a time," he replied. "We'll see where we get with that."

It reminded me of a parent telling their child "maybe" when they meant "no," but I would make him change his mind. I just had to do it as he said—one step at a time.

"Fine. Consider it. And when you do decide to hire her, I'll be the first to tell you congratulations on promoting the hardest working employee at your company."

CHAPTER ELEVEN

Ruth

"I'm so sorry," Amber said, teary-eyed. "I didn't think we would get caught. No one goes in there."

I nodded, biting my tongue. She didn't need to know how close she was to losing her job. I hated even having to give her the write-up in the first place.

"With Knox being here, Dave is very concerned about how things look. We need to stay professional."

"I will. I promise I will. I am so embarrassed." Her voice cracked, and I felt for her. After all, I was guilty of the same thing—I imagined I'd be acting the same way had I been caught.

"We're all human," I said. "We all have feelings. It's okay."

She nodded, face still red from the events of the day.

"Should I break it off with Simon?" she asked quietly. "Will it help my job?"

I hesitated. I was aware of how delicate the situation was. Technically, I was going to ask Simon out one day, but I wasn't even jealous that he was with Amber. That told me exactly how I'd felt about him.

If it had been *Knox*, then I knew it was a different story.

After taking a deep breath, I answered, "Do you like him?"

"I do, but no relationship is worth getting fired over."

"Then don't break it off with someone you like because of this job. It's not like he's your boss or anything."

"But Charles said we couldn't have any relationships with coworkers . . ."

"Yeah, I know. It's an unfair rule."

She looked at her hands, and I wished I could do more. There was a knock at the door.

"Hey," Simon said, poking his head in. "I just wanted to let you know that I quit."

His eyes weren't on me; they were on Amber.

"What? Why?"

"Because I love you too much to let them tell me I can't be with you."

My eyes widened. No wonder he barely wanted to talk to me.

"B-but—"

"It's fine. I think their new rule is bullshit anyway. No offense, Ruth."

I put up both my hands. "No need to apologize, it's not my rule."

Simon turned back to Amber. "I can find another job. I can't find another you."

"Aw, babe . . ." Amber's smile was wide, but then she turned to me. "Sorry, Ruth. Do you mind if I walk him out?"

"Go for it," I said, and I waited until they left my office hand in hand before my face fell.

I had a lot to consider. The biggest thing being Knox.

One thing was for sure, I wasn't like Simon. I couldn't give up my career for anyone—no matter how much I enjoyed that kiss.

No matter how much I wanted more.

I'd already broken a rule by making out with Knox in the executive closet, but this new rule promised termination if I even had a relationship with him. While Knox wasn't my immediate boss, he was still in a position of power over me. I'd do well to forget him in any romantic sense and move on.

But I was not prepared for the wave that would hit me as I came to that conclusion.

By the next beginning of the next week, I could somewhat manage the crushing feeling. I had no romantic prospects but the one man who could get me fired, but I'd be fine. I was used to being alone.

I'd just forgotten one tiny detail about Knox.

He was famous, and I had been outside the office with him.

I should have considered it the moment I'd talked to him in public. People had always been desperate to know what he was up to, especially now that he wasn't the head of the one of the most profitable companies in America. His silence was enough to drive the media wild.

When I woke up to a ton of messages from various people, I knew I was *fucked*.

Someone had seen us in the café and snapped photographs of us together. They noted how close he stood to me and the way we'd talked—like we were old friends.

Knox Price—In Love Once More? the headline to one article read.

Tom had sent it to me along with a question mark. My jaw had gone slack as I read the juicy gossip. The journalist had done some digging on me, finding out that Knox and I went to the same high school, and that we worked in the same place.

This was some cruel fucking timing.

Not only was Dave going to murder me for being seen with Knox, people were assuming I had a relationship with him, which I was strictly forbidden to do. Dina had said it would be bad if someone in mine and Knox's positions were together.

And Dave had a permanent bullseye on my back.

I didn't have time to answer my brother because my email notified me of something much worse than my family's curiosity. It was a meeting invitation from Dave and Charles.

And it started in forty minutes.

I had to rush to get ready and I barely arrived in time. My heart was racing with the anticipation of what was to come. Knox wasn't in this meeting, and while I knew I shouldn't be the one to get in trouble for this since I was technically under him, I also knew that in Dave's eyes, Knox could do no wrong.

When I got in, I only had time to dump my stuff in my office and race to the conference room Dave had booked for us.

He and Charles sat at one end of the table. At the other end was a stack of papers labeled "immediate termination."

I was definitely getting fired.

"Welcome, Ruth," Dave said, his loud voice hitting my ears like knives.

"I want to start this off by saying this news isn't real."

"Oh, we know," Charles sneered. "Knox Price would never be seen stooping to *your* level."

I bit my tongue to prevent myself from blurting out that he *had*, in fact, stooped to my level. We'd made out in front of their precious snacks.

"The issue is that you've stained the reputation of one of our most esteemed executives," Dave added.

"Actually," another male voice chimed in, "the real issue is that you're trying to fire your best employee."

I knew that voice all too well. So did my body. I slowly turned to find that the door was open and Knox was leaning against the frame.

As casual as he looked, his narrowed eyes promised fire.

And it was *hot*.

"Knox?" Dave asked. "What are you doing here?"

"I was trying to talk to Ruth and apologize for the articles. And I heard someone mentioning your little plan, so I investigated. Did you really email Dina to fire Ruth because she was photographed with me?"

There was a stony silence that stretched on forever. I could only look at Knox, who was technically my savior, and wonder what the fuck was about to go down.

Knox

I'd found a point when all politeness was lost to anger.

And that point was when someone messed with Ruth.

I could see the redness on her neck and the shakiness of her hands. I could see how hard she breathed.

And I was about to fucking kill Dave.

The older man stared at me, jaw slack for a long, annoying moment. "W-we weren't aware you would care so much."

Through my anger, I knew I was in a tight spot. I couldn't explain away my rage by stating just how unfair this was. I also needed to explain why we were in the coffee shop together. A quick plan formulated in my mind.

I glanced at Ruth and hoped that, for just once, she would go with something she wouldn't understand.

"Of course I care. She's been my closest friend since high school."

Ruth's jaw dropped.

"You are?" Dave asked.

"Her?" Charles parroted.

"Don't," I hissed. "Do not question anything about my friendship with her."

"You never told us."

"I wanted to give her space to showcase what she could do without my name influencing how she's seen, but I can see that neither of you are capable of giving her the respect she deserves."

Dave's eyes went from me to Ruth and then to me again. It was obvious he wasn't sure how to proceed.

"Ruth?" Dave asked. "Is this true?"

I silently begged her to go with it.

"It . . . is," she said slowly. "I'm good friends with Knox."

She looked over at me, and I gave her a nod as a thanks.

"From now on," I said, focusing back on Dave, "you will treat her with respect. No more calling her names behind her back. No more refusing to give her an interview for the job she deserves. One more sexist comment and it'll be *me* you're up against. Am I clear?"

Dave was red in the face, but he slowly nodded. Now that he told me how much money he'd made off my name, I was aware that he couldn't afford to piss me off.

"Why didn't you say anything the first time you saw her?" Charles asked. "None of this makes sense!"

"When I got the job here, she asked me not to. She wanted to be herself without the weight of my name. But I refuse to let her get fired over some pictures and assumptions from reporters."

"So you only care about *her*, then?" Charles asked.

"The way both of you treat Ruth isn't appropriate for anyone in this company."

"But—"

"Charles, don't." Dave's voice was strangled. "We've already done enough."

Charles looked at him like he'd grown a second head.

"That's right. You don't want your stocks to fall," I said. "Come on, Ruth. Let's go take a minute to calm down. I'm sure this meeting was stressful enough for you."

Ruth nodded, but her fists were clenched.

I gestured for her to leave the meeting room first, choosing to shield her in case Dave and Charles tried to say anything else to her. I shut the door behind me, and when we were all the way to the elevator, I let out the breath I was holding.

"What the fuck was that?" Ruth ground out. Her voice was low, as if she was worried anyone could possibly overhear us even though we were making our way out of the office.

"It was the best lie I could come up with to get them to back off of you." Besides, I'd been itching to go off on Dave since I started.

There was a Starbucks near the office. While it wasn't my favorite place, it was somewhere easy to get to for a break from everything.

She dug her nails into the palms of her hands. "I'm getting the worst stress headache, and it's not even noon!"

I could feel it rolling off of her.

"You job is safe," I told her.

"Sure, it worked on them. But everyone else thinks we're dating!"

"I'm sorry the media photographed us. I should have done a better job of hiding myself."

"And it was with *me*. That just makes it worse."

"What does that mean?"

"It means that I'm aware that I'm a step down from your last girlfriend."

"Do not tell me *you* think you're a downgrade for me."

"I don't *think* I am. I know I am."

I stared at her, taking in her curvy, beautiful body. I was mad at her for even thinking it, but even angrier that I couldn't show her exactly what I thought of her.

"Believe me when I say," I began, "you are the most exquisite woman I have ever fucking seen. Do not even try to say anything else because this is the one thing you are entirely wrong about."

She froze, eyes wide.

"You . . . you can't save my ass and then say things like that. We *have* to be friends because of the stupid rule."

There was a tiny bit of hope that she'd say screw it all and break that rule, but I didn't blame her for not taking that risk.

"I know."

She let out a long breath. "You passed the interview though. With flying colors."

Those words lifted the disappointment, even if only slightly. "Good to know."

My eyes were reluctant to leave her, but I needed to step into line. I was eager to get her a cup of coffee for her troubles.

"You don't have to get me coffee."

"But I am."

"Do you think I'm broke or something? I can get my own drink."

"Maybe my love language is gifts."

"I think you might mean friend language."

"Fine."

"My point still stands."

"Hasn't anyone bought things for you before?"

"Not in a strictly platonic friendship. My last boyfriend did, but that was in college."

"I refuse to believe you haven't dated anyone since college."

"Don't act surprised that I don't have men lined up. I'm difficult, and I know that."

"Then you're around the wrong men." My voice was rough as sheer *need* coursed through my veins. "Because I know some would love how difficult you are."

"Maybe a masochist."

We were at the front of the line, and instead of declaring myself a masochist like I wanted to, I ordered my drink. Ruth surprised me by ordering hers without complaint. After I paid, I expected her to follow me to the pickup window, but she stayed behind, grabbing and paying for two yogurts before I could step in.

"I can't let you pay for everything." She handed me one of the cups.

"What would you have done if I didn't like yogurt?"

"You strike me as a yogurt guy."

"I suppose I could be if you were offering."

A smile crossed her face, but then our drinks were called. We grabbed a table in the back of the space in order to get more privacy.

"So, what are we going to do about this article?" she asked as she opened her yogurt.

"We release a statement that says the same thing we told Dave, that we're old friends."

"Right." She nodded "There are a few people in my life who aren't exactly going to believe that."

"Who?"

"Just people."

"I think a friend should know who it is."

"A friend also wouldn't pry into my life."

I frowned at her. I was hoping she would give me more to go off of. She'd been so open lately, and I wondered if it was a result of the events of the day, or if this was something deeper.

"One day, I will find out all your secrets, Ruth Murray."

She rolled her eyes. "They're not as interesting as you think. So, how do we get a statement out there? I assume we can't release a company statement like we did with your hire at Stanford."

"I'll get my publicist on it."

"Sounds good." She checked her watch. "Come on, let's get back to work. Dave's tolerance of me not being in my office will only last for so long."

I wanted more time with her, but the longer I looked at her, the closer I wanted to be to her.

And judging by the news that was out right now, that didn't work in our favor.

CHAPTER TWELVE

Ruth

Knox and I parted ways at the door.

When he was gone, the fear hit me. What if they'd only let this go because he was looking? What if they found a way to make my life a living hell when Knox wasn't around?

It was what my parents did when my brothers and I banded together.

And to make matters worse, I had to walk past Dave's office to get to my own. My goal was to make a break for it and get so much work done that even he would be impressed; there would be no time for him to scrutinize me or the situation.

But he was looking for me.

"Ruth," he called, his loud voice echoing in the office hallway. "Come here a second."

Fuck. Couldn't he wait until I had something impressive to throw in his face if he tried to be mean?

I hesitantly walked in, hands behind my back. I didn't want him to see them shaking.

"You needed me?"

"I feel the need to apologize about earlier."

"What?" I croaked inelegantly.

"I believe you heard me." There was a hint of disdain in his voice, but he cleared his throat. "Our main goal is to ensure Knox is happy. You have to understand how important he is to the success of our company."

My fear turned sour. *He* was important to the company, not me, not anyone else.

"I understand," I lied.

He nodded, and then looked back to his work. "Let me know if there is anything I can do to make up for it." It was possibly the quietest he'd ever talked, and I bet he hoped I hadn't heard him.

"I heard that your interviews for the VP position didn't work out."

He stopped. "Knox told you?"

I shrugged noncommittally.

He sighed. "I am . . . aware you are taking on some of Caroline's responsibility."

"Yes, I am."

"Then I suppose I can schedule an interview."

"I look forward to the that then." I turned away, hoping to feel pride at getting an interview for a promotion.

But it felt rotten. I'd used Knox to get this chance, and the moment my parents found out, the promotion wouldn't be mine. It would be his.

When I arrived in the safe haven that was my office, all I wanted to do was sit in silence.

Unfortunately, I was not alone.

"You better be ready to tell me everything," Jenny said. She was sitting in the extra chair in my office. "Because I will force it out of you."

"Um, hi to you too."

"You're literally in the news as Knox's new girlfriend. Last I checked, you didn't even want to be friends with him. You don't get a hello until I know what the hell happened."

I sighed and set down my purse. I plugged my laptop into its docking station and cringed at how many messages and emails I'd missed due to my late morning.

"Fine," I said. "But it's not that dramatic. Knox and I aren't dating."

"I thought you'd say that," she said, crossing her arms. "It still doesn't explain the way he was looking at you in the photos. That was *longing*, Ruth."

For one second, I thought about lying, but I remembered that visit to the coffee shop. There had been longing on both sides.

"I can't exactly act on it after what happened yesterday."

"Yeah, true. But you can admit it."

Saying it out loud, especially within the walls of the office, seemed like a risky move. But at the same time, I wanted my friend's input. I'd already gone out for coffee, so I knew I couldn't leave again today.

I took a deep breath. It looked like I would be taking a risk.

"You're right. There was longing. And it turned into a kiss yesterday."

Jenny's jaw dropped. "Yesterday? As in the same day Amber and Simon got caught?"

"Like literally right before. And he's an *executive*, Jenny. That's pretty much my boss. Just now when Dave even thought I was dating him, he tried to fire me!"

"You?" she asked. "That's very illegal."

"Knox saved my ass. If anyone asks, we've been best friends since high school."

Jenny stared at me for a long time, then she slowly rubbed her temples. "That is a *lot* of information. And here I was about to ask you about Simon."

"Simon's obviously off the table. I wasn't even sure I had real feelings for him."

"But Knox?"

"It doesn't matter how I feel. I'm not losing my job for this. I'm not letting any feelings for him ruin things. God, why couldn't it have been anyone else?"

"I don't know, you tell me."

"I should hate him, you know. He indirectly has tortured me for years."

"How?"

My parents were the answer, but I couldn't bring myself to say the words.

"It's not important."

"There's no way it's not." Jenny shook her head. "When he first started, I thought maybe he bullied you or something, but I don't get that vibe from him. What makes you hate him, Ruth? What did he do to you?"

"It's complicated."

"Ruth, I love you, but you've gotta stop keeping everything in a locked box."

"I don't . . . I mean . . ."

"Something happened and that's okay, but I'm here to help. I know you may not trust me—"

"It's not that. I do trust you. I told you about the kiss."

"Then why not tell me about your past? You didn't even tell me what high school you went to. I only figured it out when I Googled it after you finally mentioned you went to school with him. I'm not going to tell anyone, nor will I use it against you. I just want to help."

I looked away, hating that it was so hard to talk about my past, but once she knew how much my parents wanted me to succeed, she would say their disappointment was warranted. I'd been given everything, only to not make anything of myself. I wasn't Tom or Knox. I was Ruth, and that was never enough.

But she looked like she really wanted to know.

"It has to do with my parents," I said slowly. The words felt weird in my mouth. "They want me to be to be successful."

"You *are* successful."

"Not by their standards. My brother is the CFO of my family's trucking company, and Knox was a CEO five years ago."

"What do they have to do with anything?"

"Because they're what I'm measured against."

Jenny's lips turned downward. "That's not a fair comparison. Knox was the CEO of his *own* company and invents things. Your brother works for the family business which could easily afford him special privileges."

"Tom worked hard. He did it all first—"

"He's also a man in the workplace. Statistically, women get promoted less yet shoulder more expectations. But besides all of that, you're a fucking director, Ruth. The first of your age to do so at this company, and you did it within two years of starting."

"But I've been stuck in this job for fourteen months. That's longer than my family allows."

"That is not a feasible goal, Ruth. There's not always a position open in that amount of time."

"There is at another company."

"Not right now there isn't. Is this why you work so hard? To meet your parents' expectations?"

"Of course. They've given everything to help me succeed. My college was paid for, and I grew up in a nice house as a result of my father's and his father's hard work. I should be as good as they were."

"So they gave you everything, huh? How about some grace and understanding when things didn't go to their plan? Did they give that to you?"

"Well, no, but that's because I didn't deserve it."

"You're a human being, Ruth. Of course you deserve that."

I blinked. This was not how I expected this conversation to go. "You're not . . . on their side?"

"No!" She shook her head and leaned forward. "Why do you think I would be?"

"Because they're right."

"They're definitely not. This is not normal behavior, Ruth."

"Then what is normal behavior?"

"There's no single answer to that, but my parents check in to see if I'm eating, for example. They ask if I'm feeling okay, or when they can see me because they miss me."

"Maybe you have unique parents."

"Okay, then. Maybe I do. But if it's so weird, why do you offer so much grace to your own employees?"

"Because I *care* about them and how they feel."

And that was when it hit me. My heart skipped a beat as I took in what I'd just said.

"Exactly. And it's what your parents would do if they cared about more than your success."

"Oh, *fuck*," I said, horror clawing its way into my stomach. "You mean weekly dinner to discuss our progress with work isn't normal?"

"No," Jenny said, eyes wide. "They do that?"

"Yeah, and my poor younger brother gets the worst of it because he owns the bar. They're always on him to do something better."

"I'm sorry, he owns one of the most popular bars in the state and they want him to do *better*?"

"Because it's not what they pictured for him."

"My God, Ruth. Are the three of you okay?"

"I don't think we are," I said, thinking of Tom's drinking problem and Barry's distance from all of us. I didn't even know if my younger brother was seeing anyone.

"I'm an idiot. How did I not see this?"

"No," Jenny said forcefully, reaching out to grab my shoulder. "You're not dumb for not realizing. They're your parents and you thought they cared about you. That's not your fault."

"They measure our success solely on our careers. I have this . . . fear, and they used to tell me I was weak for having it."

"I have a feeling the more you tell me the more I'm going to repeat 'that's not okay,' because none of this is."

"My parents bring up Knox every time we talk. They have for years. That's how he tortured me from afar."

"More like *they* tortured you."

She was right. When I first saw Knox again, I blamed him for their comparisons. Then I blamed myself.

But maybe it wasn't me.

"I have dinner with them tonight." I put my head in my hands. "How am I supposed to face them when I not only have this news about Knox, but when I feel like I'm suddenly seeing everything differently?"

"You could not go."

"No, my brothers are going, and I don't want them to go through it alone."

"That's . . . really sweet actually."

"When one of us isn't there, our parents take it out on the other two."

"That's less sweet."

"I don't know what to do," I moaned.

"You could tell your parents to shove their expectations up their asses."

I blinked over at her.

"T-they won't listen."

"You can at least try. Then you leave if they don't listen and get your brothers to go with you."

"Then they'll just be mad at me and I'm not getting what I want."

"What do you want?"

"For them to be proud." The words made my chest ache. "I'm still waiting for that."

"Okay, so tell them about this VP thing. Then see what they do. Most parents would be amazed that their child is so dedicated, but if they tell you it isn't good enough, then it goes to show you may *never* be good enough."

"What if my brothers step in and side with our parents?"

"Then fuck them too."

"But that would mean I have *no one*."

"That's not true. You'll have me."

"Really?" I asked, daring to be hopeful.

"Yes! You can talk to me about anything at any time. You're not alone."

"Thank you," I said, a warmth settling into my chest at the thought of having a real friend. The idea of going against my parents' expectations was terrifying, but it was a little less so now that I knew I wouldn't be alone if it all blew up in my face.

"No, thank you for listening. You're so smart, Ruth. And you deserve people who see that."

"I just thought I was never good enough."

"You don't have to be good enough to be respected. But I think you already know that. You just didn't know it applies to you too."

Knox

I let out a long breath as I tried and failed to focus on the Stanford app. Coding was second nature to me, as was anything to do with making something from scratch.

But this wasn't something I cared about. I didn't understand why people were so resistant to change when it was done for good, and that lack of understanding killed what little motivation I had.

What I wanted to do was see Ruth, to make sure that she was truly okay. Getting coffee wasn't long enough to figure that out. I wanted to be there for every part of her emotions, not sitting in this office wondering about her.

But my musings were interrupted by a knock at the door.

"Come in," I said, and I hoped it was Ruth.

But instead of the woman I saw in my dreams, it was Jenny.

"Hi, Knox," she said, shutting the door behind her. "I have some questions for you."

"That's ominous."

"It's meant to be. Did you know that Ruth is the sweetest thing on this planet, and I will shank anyone who hurts her?"

"I didn't, but it certainly makes me respect you more."

"Good answer," she said. "What are your intentions with Ruth?"

"I don't have any."

She raised an eyebrow. "Really? Because you're in a position of power and she's not. You stood up for her today, but I want to know if you're going to start *asking things* of her in return."

I immediately shook my head. "I will *never* do that. I'm not that kind of man."

"I didn't think so, but after hearing what Ruth's been through, I refuse to let anything else happen to her."

"She told you what she's been through?"

"After years of being her friend, yes."

"Then I'm jealous. I notice how guarded she is around me. I'd love to know what I did to hurt her."

"And what if it's not you? What if someone else made her this way?"

"I don't think I should answer that question."

"Why not?"

"Because I've been quietly threatening Dave with a lawsuit if he doesn't treat her better, and I worry about what I would do if I knew who hurt her worse than I could have."

A slow smile spread on Jenny's face. "Oh, you've got it *bad*."

"I do, but I can't do anything about it. You know the new rule. Everyone has heard about it."

"Heard, yes. But it's not in writing."

"Ruth won't risk her job. Her career means a lot to her."

"Almost too much, if you ask me."

"The same could be said for me. I overheard you guys talking in the break room. I know she wants someone who will get her out of the office. That's . . . not going to be me."

"Something tells me that you both need a *reason* to be out of office, because I know you'd be out that door in a second if she asked you to be."

I opened my mouth, and then closed it. I had no argument because she was right.

"You guys will figure it out soon. I give it a month." She flashed a smirk at me before she walked out of my office.

I stared at the door, pondering Jenny's words. Maybe I could get out of the office more. Maybe I could take Ruth plant shopping.

Then my phone rang, and Preston's name flashed on the screen. All thoughts fell away as I was reminded of PATH.

I answered the call immediately. "Preston. What's up?"

"So, you and your high school rival?" he asked. He sounded . . . smug.

I took a deep breath to calm my nerves. "It's not like that. I have nothing to report other than we're friends. And that I'll be lying and saying we've been friends for many years."

"How did that happen?"

"Dave doesn't like her. It's the closest thing I can do to get her at least a little bit of respect."

"She does seem like the kind of woman that would make my dad shit his pants. I saw her glare in the photos. If she hadn't smiled in one of them, I would be worried for your well-being."

"I love that about her. She's intense."

"I haven't heard you say anything like that about a person in years."

"She's interesting."

"She is? Enough that you're smiling again?"

"Yes. I've . . . I've been smiling a lot recently."

"Good. I'm glad you're finally feeling better. We miss you around here."

"I miss PATH."

"Are you thinking about coming back soon?"

My heart sank; I was hoping he wouldn't go there so quickly. "I don't know. Do you need me to be back?"

"Nothing is dire, but this whole CEO thing is not for me. I don't like decision-making. I like decision-announcing. People are asking me a lot of questions about the PATH-branded car and the safety tech project, ones I don't know the answers to."

I pinched my nose. We knew this was going to happen. I had a strict idea of what I wanted things to look like. While I'd handed off some of the responsibility to the research and development team, a lot of the decision-making went to me as the CEO. It was how PATH always functioned. And now that task fell to Preston.

"What do you need me to figure out?"

"Do you have any testing reports on the PATH prototype? Especially on long distances?"

"Nothing other than the drive from San Francisco. It had no problems."

"The most recent update caused some bugs. Maybe it's time for you to take a road trip. If something comes up, you can figure it out faster than anyone here."

"Okay, I can do that."

I didn't know when I had the time, but I added it to my mental to-do list anyway.

"Anything else?"

"Nothing that can't wait," Preston said, sighing. "I'll keep making the decisions for now. Thank you for offering to help."

"It's still our company."

"I know. It'll just be nice to have you fully back. The real you."

All I felt was dread at the idea of returning, and I didn't know why. I still loved PATH. I was excited to look at whatever bug this was, but the thought of going back to my old life in San Francisco inspired nothing but panic. My life there would just end up being a series of days where it was the same routine surrounded by an emptiness with no escape.

I'd have to work on figuring out how to tell Preston that at some point.

To: Ruth Murray
From: Knox Price
Subject: Media Statement

> *Please see attached media statement. Once I have your approval, I will send it out.*

Sincerely, Knox

To: Knox Price
From: Ruth Murray
Subject: Media Statement

> *Yikes. That's a stiff reply for someone you're apparently dating.*

> *Sadly, Ruth*

To: Ruth Murray
From: Knox Price

> *Sorry, Ruth. It's the standard thing I send out.*

> *I am respectfully asking you to personally read it over and let me know if it sounds good.*

> *Is that a better way to ask?*

> *Apologetically, Knox*

To: Knox Price
From: Ruth Murray

All right, all right. I'll forgive you this time.

The statement looks good. Go ahead and send it out.

To: Ruth Murray
From: Knox Price

No snarky email sign-off?

Curiously, Knox

To: Knox Price
From: Ruth Murray

I don't have anything to be snarky about.

Please see the attached Chuck E. Cheese gift card as my apology.

To: Ruth Murray
From: Knox Price

Good one. I can't WAIT to take you there for dinner to relive our childhood friendship.

Somewhat sincerely, Knox.

CHAPTER THIRTEEN

Ruth

Walking into my parents', as usual, felt like a death march.

But now I told myself not to feel guilty about it.

This dinner was setting up to be a huge dumpster fire. I had good news about an interview, but I also was supposedly close friends with Knox Price, and that was going to be the harder sell.

I knew my parents had seen the news story. I knew they were waiting for this very dinner to bombard me with any and all questions they could come up with.

This dinner was not going to be about the three of us. It was going to be about *me*.

Jenny's words played on a loop, along with some of my own. I'd been thinking about this all day.

I knew that I didn't have to take this. I could tell them no. I didn't owe them an explanation. Especially about Knox.

I knew that I also needed to tell them to butt out of my business with my job, but I wasn't sure I was ready for that.

When I pulled up, everyone's cars were already in the driveway. I wasn't late, but I was sure they all had come early to witness the impending interrogation.

Barry must have been thrilled it wasn't him in the hot seat for once.

The house was silent. I knew better than to think they had forgotten, but rather, they were at the table, all seated to one side to get a view of whoever was to be questioned.

And as I arrived in the dining room, I saw just that.

Dad was at the head of the table, Mom to his right. Barry and Tom were seated on either side of them. There was a lone chair on the other end of the table for me.

For a moment, I wondered what Jenny would think of this. Would she say this was ridiculous? Because I was beginning to think it was just that.

"Ruth," Dad said slowly, "do you have something to tell us?"

My mind unhelpfully flashed back to the one time I'd gotten a B on a test.

"I-I do."

"Have a seat." He gestured to the lone chair.

I took a shaky breath and sat.

"I *knew* you worked at Stanford," Mom said first. "I *knew* you'd seen him!" Her country accent slipped into her voice.

"Dear," Dad started. "That's no way for a lady to talk."

Mom blushed and closed her mouth.

Hang on. That was a really fucked up thing to say.

"You've been keeping secrets." His attention was back on me.

My heart hammered.

Should I be this terrified of my what my own Dad thought?

"Yes, I have. I didn't want my long-term friendship with him to be a big deal." The lie felt weird, but it matched the statement Knox had sent out. "We've always kept it a secret."

"Then why are you still a director?" Mom snapped. "He could change your life."

"You need him," Dad added.

"To do what?" I asked. "Get a job that I should be able to get on my own?"

"He obviously has the better connections."

"We're done talking about him," I decided, feeling my skin prickle at Dad's probing.

"I wonder if you've earned any of your promotions, Ruth. How much of your success has been due to his influence?"

I stared with tears clouding my vision.

God, what a cruel thing to say. I could see Jenny's jaw drop in my mind.

"I don't like what you're insinuating," I said slowly. Out of the corner of my eye, I saw Barry glaring at Dad.

"Then don't make it true."

"It isn't true. I don't need to prove it to you." I stood. "We're done talking about Knox."

Dad shook his head. "I'm not—"

"We're done," I snapped.

The room was silent for a moment.

"Excuse me?" Mom said.

"You don't get to speak to me like that," Dad added. "I decide what we discuss."

"And I get to choose what I answer, and I get to choose if I stay. If you continue to push me to talk about something I don't want to discuss, I will leave."

"Ruth Anne Murray," Mom hissed.

"Have you forgotten who we are?" Dad's voice boomed, and my instinctual flinch told me what I needed to know.

"I haven't. But my boundary still stands."

Barry looked over at me, eyes wide. I didn't blame him for his shock; I usually didn't speak to our Dad like this.

"What is this about boundaries?" He raised his voice, standing to meet my eyes. "We are in control."

"I hate to break it you, but I'm a grown woman. You're not in control."

I clenched my fists to prevent anyone from seeing my shaking hands. I looked past the angry gaze of my father, choosing to imagine it was Dave instead. It was the only way I would make it through this conversation.

"Ruth Murray," Dad said.

"She's right," Barry cut in. "She doesn't have to explain anything to us."

I looked over at my brother, giving him a grateful smile.

"The two of you are the worst of my kids."

"Let's get on with dinner," Tom insisted. His voice was firm. "Just let it go, Dad."

"I don't let go of insolence."

"Neither do I," I said. "I'm leaving."

"I am too," Barry added. "I'll follow you, Ruth."

I spun on my heel, ignoring the indignant cries of my parents, and left the room. I made it as far as my car before my eyes grew wet.

"Ruth, that was amazing."

I took a moment to will away the inevitable tears.

"Thank you," I said. "But I think I'm going to cry now."

"Oh," he said, rubbing the back of his neck. "Then you go do that."

Barry wasn't much for emotional support; he never had been. I gave him a watery smile and a nod, which he returned. Then I got into my car.

Tears fell as I pulled out of the driveway. As much as I wished that I felt right in my decision to leave, I didn't. I still felt like a bad daughter, despite the fact that I also knew I was allowed to tell them no.

It should have been simple, but it wasn't. Logic didn't win over emotion, and I was stuck with a heartache I couldn't shake. If I was still a little girl, I'd crawl into Mom's bed, but the woman I knew then was long gone, ripped apart and stitched back together by Dad. And I had no one else in her place.

But I did have a friend.

As I sat on my couch, I reached for my phone.

Ruth: I set a boundary with my parents. Please tell me why I feel like it was the wrong decision.

She answered within minutes.

Jenny: Because you feel guilty, and it's okay to feel that way. You did something hard, so it's normal to feel bad about it. What boundary did you set?

Ruth: I told them I wouldn't answer any questions about Knox. And left when they pushed me.

Jenny: WOW. That's exactly what you should have done. You catch on fast.

Ruth: Don't be too impressed. I cried for like two hours after.

Jenny: Doesn't matter. YOU DID IT!

I slowly smiled, rereading the messages when the guilt ate at me again. It was enough to let me sleep that night, at least.

The next day, I felt worse than I had when I was hungover. But instead of an alcohol-induced hangover, it was an emotional one. For the first time in a very long time, I considered calling out of work.

But I was not about to get my ass in trouble right after Knox had saved it.

As I dressed, I could feel the weight of what I'd done yesterday sinking in. Barry had sent me a thumbs-up text, but there was only silence from Tom. I bet he was pissed at what I did.

The urge to give in and apologize was strong, so I replayed Jenny's messages in my mind again and again as I drove to work.

The moment she saw me, she told me it was okay and handed me a cup of warm coffee. I nearly cried as I thanked her.

Unfortunately, Knox walked by, took one look at me, and stopped in his tracks.

"What's wrong?" he asked.

"Nothi—"

He tilted his head at me with raised eyebrows, and I knew he didn't believe me.

"Ruth, what happened?" His voice was low and made my cheeks heat.

Jenny looked at her watch. "Wow, I need to go stock the break room. You two have fun."

"Traitor," I hissed.

"Ruth," Knox said, bringing my attention back to him.

I wanted to say no one hurt me, but that wasn't exactly true. "It's not a huge deal."

It was the safest answer I could come up with.

"Is this about Simon?"

"Why would this be about him?"

"You liked him. I figured you would be sad he quit to be with Amber."

I shook my head. "No, it's not that. I really am fine. Don't worry about me."

Knox sighed. "I want to help."

"I know you do, but this isn't something I exactly trust you with."

"What did I do to make you not trust me?"

I looked at my feet. Once again, *he* wasn't the one who did anything. I let out a long breath.

"It . . . it's not you, okay? You didn't do anything."

"Now or back then?"

"Both," I admitted.

"Okay, then who hurt you? Now *and* then."

"I'll tell you why I'm sad now, okay? I don't want to get into my past at work."

Just doing it with Jenny had made me miserable all day. I still had far too many entangled feelings about Knox and my parents. Telling him might put me out of commission for a week.

"I can work with that."

I nodded, grateful that he wasn't pushing me.

"I told someone that I didn't want to talk about a specific something. They didn't take it well."

"Did you say it in a particularly mean way?"

"I was firm at first, and then I cut them off when they continued."

"That sounds like you stopped them when they tried to push. They should have respected your boundary."

"Apparently boundaries are 'New Age shit' to this person, and what's worse is that I feel terrible for even telling them no in the first place."

"Some people like to push their guilt onto whoever is closest. It means they don't have to feel it."

His words hit harder than I expected them to. My mind played back the night, and how Dad had made it seem like *I* was in the wrong.

Just like they both had my whole life.

"It was just hard."

"You ask for very basic things, Ruth. But the people around you love to make it seem like you're asking them to move a mountain."

"I-I've noticed that too," I said softly.

"It's not like that with me," he added. "I would be happy to give you every little thing you wanted."

My heartbeat picked up, and some of my sadness melted away. His bright eyes lit up the darkness I'd been feeling.

He glanced at my lips once before he stepped away. "Can I get you more coffee?" he asked.

I looked down at my almost empty cup. "That would be great."

He nodded, eyes lingering as he grabbed the mug from my hands. Our fingers brushed, and I found myself wanting more.

But I couldn't have it. We were at work, and there were rules we shouldn't break again.

"Is your morning free?" he asked. "I'd like to do some more work on that app."

"Sounds good."

By the time Knox led me to his office, I was feeling more alive. Being near him, even to talk about work, was the exact distraction I needed.

But then, when I finally sat to eat lunch, I noticed a text.

Tom: Sibling meeting at Ruth's apartment tonight.

I cursed. Either Tom was going to yell at me, or worse, stage an intervention like Barry and I had with him. I could see it now. He'd tell me I was being unreasonable and bring Mom and Dad there to ambush me.

But I didn't think Barry would let it happen. He'd stuck up for me last night. I'd never missed a meeting, because my brothers were still important to me, even after everything.

Ruth: Fine. But if you tell Mom and Dad and they show up, I'm stabbing you.

Knox

To: Ruth Murray
  From: Knox Price
  Subject: Dinner

  Ruth, fancy reliving our childhood at Chuck E. Cheese (or anywhere else of your choice)?

Hopefully, Knox

To: Knox Price
From: Ruth Murray
Subject: Dinner

Why?

Curiously, Ruth

To: Ruth Murray
From: Knox Price

Sometimes when friends want to cheer each other up, they hang out. I felt like being a good friend today.

To: Knox Price
From: Ruth Murray

That's actually very sweet of you. But I can't. I'm meeting up with my brothers tonight.

To: Ruth Murray
From: Knox Price

Were they the ones who made you sad this morning?

To: Knox Price
From: Ruth Murray

Thankfully, no. But if they do then I'll take you up on your dinner offer.

⚓

I didn't want to have to look at the Stanford app for another moment and was in the mood to socialize. Since Ruth was busy, I decided to call my parents and see if they had any plans for the night. I'd been so busy with Stanford, I felt like I didn't have any time devoted to them. They were more than happy to have me come over.

I walked into the house carrying plenty of food for all of us. "I'm here!" I called, eager to see Mom and Dad. "And I brought food!"

"Is that why you never answered my text on what I should cook?" Mom shook her head, but a smile was on her face. "Hi, sweetie."

"No offense, but I wanted something edible. Surprise?" I held up the food with a smile.

"I suppose I can let it go since you seem to be in such a good mood."

"Do I? It wasn't a great day."

"But you smiled. You weren't like that a few weeks ago."

"Maybe I'm glad to be back in town," I said.

"Or it's that I'm not cooking. You can admit it."

I shrugged, not wanting to hurt her feelings.

"Is that my kid I see?" Dad asked as he walked up me.

"He's in a good mood tonight," Mom said with raised eyebrows.

"I wouldn't say good. I've just smiled."

"Then I'm going to make him smile even bigger," he replied. "I've been saving this one."

"Here we go," I muttered in mock exasperation.

"No, no, let me tell my joke! What's orange and sounds like a parrot?"

"Um, an orange parrot?"

"A carrot."

I snickered. "Come on. That was terrible."

"You're still smiling though! Look, Lynn, he's still smiling."

I shook my head, but the smile stayed firmly in place.

"Good timing on that joke, because I brought orange chicken. I'm sure there is a pun in there somewhere."

"I bet it will be *im-peck-able*."

"Oh, don't start lining up chicken jokes," Mom warned.

"But I'm *egg-cellent* at making them!"

"Look at what you've done."

"I'm sorry me being in a good mood sent him on a roll."

"An *egg roll*," he added.

"I can't." Mom shook her head despite the smile on her face. "I will divorce you."

"Can I divorce him too?" I asked.

"Okay, I'm all out of puns. Can I not be divorced out of my own family now?"

"We'll think about it," Dom said, winking as she handed him a plate.

My mind drifted, but instead of feeling nothing, I was suddenly thinking about Ruth.

"What has you in a decent mood?" Mom asked. "I'm so happy to see that smile again. We were hoping you'd be more like yourself once you came back."

"I'm not in that great of a mood, I promise." I was just feeling alive. "I was thinking about a . . . friend of mine."

"Preston?"

I shook my head. "No, she works with me."

"She?" Mom's eyebrows were impossibly high on her forehead.

"It's not like that," I said.

"We *did* hear about you being seen with a woman."

"Yes, that was her, but we're not dating."

"I haven't seen you so interested in someone since . . ." Mom trailed off. "Oh, Benji, what was her name?"

"Who?"

"Do you mean Gia?" I asked.

"No, you didn't seem all that interested in her. There was this girl he used to compete with in high school. Oh, it's on the tip of my tongue."

"Ruth," I said, my mouth dry.

"That's it! I only saw her in passing, but you followed her around like she had you on a leash." Mom laughed and my face heated.

"Um, I don't know if it was quite like *that*."

"Oh, you had a crush on her," she insisted. "It's been ten years. You can admit it."

"Maybe he still does!" Dad added, chuckling.

I couldn't think of anything to say because my brain was still reeling from the shock that my parents remembered her.

"I wonder where she is," Mom mused. "If she still lives in Nashville, maybe we can set them up!"

I sighed, rubbing my face. "I guess you didn't read too far into the articles about me then."

"We never do. Why?"

"Because Ruth is the woman I was seen with."

"That explains everything then!" Mom exclaimed. "It's no wonder you're in such a good mood."

I rolled my eyes. But as embarrassed as I was, I was more grateful to be able to feel any emotion at all. I missed this. I missed being a person around them.

"Can we meet her?" Dad asked.

"We're not *that* close," I said, shaking my head. "And I can promise you we're *not* like that."

"Okay . . ." The tone in Mom's voice told me that she didn't quite believe me. And I didn't blame either of them because what I felt for Ruth didn't stop at friendship. It teetered dangerously close to how Dad felt about Mom.

But my newly revived heart burned for the one person I couldn't have.

CHAPTER FOURTEEN

Ruth

"I regret giving you two keys," I muttered as I stepped into my apartment. My brothers sat on my barely used couch. They made my five hundred square foot place seem even smaller. My feet were starting to protest at being in heels, as they usually did at this hour, but I refused to take them off with them in my space.

"So, are you gonna start this off?" Barry asked, looking at Tom.

"If it has anything to do with me not following through with my boundary in order to keep the peace, then I don't want to hear it."

Barry put up his hands. "I'm on your side. That was badass. It reminded me of the time when I tried to do the same thing."

My shoulders fell as I remembered when Barry had said he was done with our parents.

"You were right to set that boundary back then. I'm sorry I didn't respect that."

Barry's hands fell to his side and he looked at me with wide, gray eyes. "Who are you and what have you done with my sister?"

"I *am* your sister. I'm just realizing how bad our parents treat us."

All three of us sat in silence.

"Tom?" Barry asked. "Isn't this where you chime in and say that we should deal with it and stick together?"

"No."

It was now my turn to be shocked. "Really?"

"I've known this was wrong for a while."

"And you never did anything?" Barry retorted.

"I've been a little busy trying to stay sober at the request of you and Ruth."

Barry sighed and looked away. He couldn't argue with that logic.

"So, what's the plan?" he asked instead. "Because they're not going to let this go."

"If they aren't going to respect what I say, then I'm done. No more family dinners. No more pressure." My words were firm, even though my heart skipped a beat as I uttered them. "They get one more chance from me. Then I'm done."

"Then I'm out too," Barry added. "I've wanted out for a long time. I function better alone."

We both looked at our older brother.

"Tom?" I asked. "Any thoughts?"

"So we have a week?" he asked. "Then both of you are done?"

"I'm still surprised you're not giving your usual spiel that they only want what's best for us and if we followed their instructions, we would be fine."

"I've never said it like that," Tom hissed. "And besides, I'm seeing things a little differently now that I'm not drunk all the time. I'm fine with you two being done with these stupid dinners, because I am too."

"Really?" I asked again.

"Yes. I'm tired of Dad's stupid business plan and how he corners me every time I'm there. But I can't just walk away. I work for him."

"So when you do this, Dad's going to make your life hell," I said matter-of-factly.

"Of course he is. God forbid one of his kids does something for themselves." Barry's voice was bitter.

"I have a work-around. But I need a week. I'm asking that neither of you hint at leaving until next week's dinner. Can you do that?"

"Easy for me," Barry said. "I don't talk to them about anything."

I glanced at my younger brother. When had he become so . . . grumpy? He used to be the light of the room, always joking and having a good time.

"Ruth?" Tom asked, pulling me out of my thoughts. "Will you be able to wait a week?"

"Sure," I said. "I don't exactly talk to them either, not about my life."

"That much is obvious," Barry said. "You've really been friends with Knox this whole time?"

"She said she didn't want to answer questions about him," Tom reminded.

"It's fine," I said, picking up on the tension in the air between them. "I'll answer it to you guys. No, we're not friends. We weren't until recently, but there was a whole debacle with my boss, and we decided lying was easiest."

"Now I have more questions," Barry said. "First and foremost, how have you not killed him?"

"He's a decent guy," I muttered.

"Excuse me?" Barry said.

"Don't make me repeat it."

"Can you stop antagonizing her so we can make it through this conversation without a fight?" Tom snapped.

"Hey, we were fine," Barry said, his glare returning.

Tom rubbed his brow, and his shoulders sank. "Sorry. I'm still prone to bursts of frustration."

"An apology?" Barry asked. "Being sober must be agreeing with you."

"I still don't know why you were so for sobriety considering drinking is your business."

Barry's face darkened and I rubbed my temples. These two always found a way to get on each other's nerves.

"My bar is more than a place where people drink. I'm responsible for the people that walk through the door, and I know when someone has a problem, just like I knew you did."

"Guys," I said. "Don't fight. Tom, Barry was complimenting you. And Tom, Barry's bar is really successful. We should be more respectful about his career."

Barry turned to me so fast that he probably pulled a muscle. "What?"

"I said your bar is successful. A friend told me how famous it is."

"Even I know," Tom added. "People talk about it at the office even though Dad tried to ban it. I didn't mean to insult the bar, Barry. I'm just still struggling, and it's easy to take it out on those around me."

"Kind of like Dad does," Barry added. I glared at him. "I don't mean it as an insult! It's just what he does, but he doesn't even have a drinking problem as a reason. He's just an ass."

"I'm trying," Tom said, sighing. "Some days I don't know why, but I'm trying. Every one of my employees looks at me like I'm a monster."

"It'll get better," I said softly.

Tom looked away and didn't answer me.

Barry checked his watch. "I need to get to the bar. We have a celebrity coming in tonight and I need to be sure no one tries anything."

"Who?"

"I'm not at liberty to discuss it." Barry stood. "Are we all good?"

"Yeah, mostly." I glanced at Tom, who was still silent.

Barry nodded and then walked toward the door. As he got near it, he turned. "Thank you, guys . . . for the compliment about the bar. It really means a lot."

"You're welcome," I said, smiling at him as he walked out. I then turned my attention to Tom, wondering what I could say to get the distant look out of his eyes.

"I'm heading out too," he said, standing abruptly. "I have some things to get settled before next week."

"Are you okay?" I asked.

"No," he replied. "But that's not your problem to worry about."

He walked out without another word, and I was left staring at the space he once occupied. Tom was always stable when we were kids, and before he'd started drinking, but now I was seeing how much things had taken a toll on him.

And I'd been too worried about a promotion to see it.

I laid awake most of the night thinking about Tom but found no answers. I'd texted him to check in, but he didn't respond.

If I asked Barry what to do, he'd tell me to give him space, and as much as I hated focusing on anything else when my brothers were obviously hurting, I knew that I wouldn't get anything out of him until he was ready to talk to me.

Instead, I focused on the next thing on my calendar—the annual marketing conference.

With everything going on, I'd almost forgotten, but once I saw that it was coming up, I knew it was the perfect distraction. This event was huge. All of the greatest minds in marketing would be there talking upcoming trends and strategies for the next year.

I'd gone with Caroline last year after much pleading. I was still new to my position, and I was well aware I would never be able to present, then or now, considering I'd need a company to sponsor me.

I was fine with simply attending. I'd at least gotten Caroline to approve that many months ago.

But with her retirement, I wasn't sure if her approval stood.

Technically, Charles or Dave were the point of contact in the VP's absence. Between the two, I figured Dave would be easier to convince.

And yet, the man frowned at me when I brought it up to him.

"You want to go to this . . . AMC?"

"I went last year," I said. "It's where I got the idea for the campaign that boosted revenue."

"And we've already paid for the tickets?"

"Yes," I said. "And we have hotel reservations."

Dave frowned. "And Caroline was fine with this? We're tight on money, Ruth."

Were we? Knox's presence had made over a thousand new customers sign up for services. The snack closet was still fully stocked.

"We only paid for the first day of the conference to save money. It's important for me to go if you want me to keep revenue up."

"It's not *you* who is keeping it up."

"It's Knox, *and* my marketing plan," I reminded.

"You're right about one of those things," he muttered. "Fine, you can go."

"Thank you, I'm so—"

"But you need supervision." Dave's eyes moved to the hallway. "Knox!" he called. I turned to see Knox had been walking past the door, probably en route either to his own office or to the break room. I wondered how many times he'd been pulled into Dave's office this exact way.

"Yes?" he asked. His eyes lingered on mine, as if he was trying to work out how this conversation was going by my facial expression alone.

"There's this . . . marketing conference. Has Ruth told you about it?"

"Of course," he said, smiling as if I'd actually told him. "It's really important to her."

I'd never admit it out loud, but Knox Price was my favorite person in that moment.

"Here's the thing," Dave added, "I want to be sure Ruth makes us look good."

"I can assure you she will."

"Yeah, yeah, professionally and all, but *you* would add even more to the event. We have a second ticket anyway. Why don't you go? Hell, you can even present!"

"No."

"Come on. I bet you can get over your little fear and show everyone how well Stanford is treating you."

He shook his head again.

"I could do it," I offered, hopeful.

"No, there's no need for that. Knox, how about you just go to the conference, then? I want people to *see* you."

"I don't know that Knox wants to give up part of his weekend to go to this convention," I said as Knox shook his head.

"Nonsense. He can go. Besides," Dave lowered his voice and looked at Knox, "I've heard there are some very pretty girls in marketing."

I blinked in shock. Was Dave trying to set up Knox?

"I'm not too worried about that," he said slowly.

"Okay, maybe you don't want to find a date." Dave shook his head. "Don't say I didn't try."

"I would never." Knox's voice was strangled and his clenched fists told me he was not a fan of Dave's set-up attempt.

Neither was I.

"But I do want you there to showcase what our company has under our belt," he continued. "That being *you*. If you don't go, then I'll cancel the whole thing. There's no point in Stanford being there if you won't be there."

Motherfucker.

"Plus," Dave continued, "the next big marketing campaign will be about this new tech, so there is an actual business need to you going."

"I'll go," he said, obviously annoyed at more or less being forced to go.

"Great. I look forward to hearing about your adventures over drinks."

I was fuming when Knox and I finally walked out of Dave's office.

"Sorry," Knox apologized. "I figured you'd want me to go rather than him canceling the whole trip."

"We would have lost money if he did," I said, crossing my arms. "Guess we need you to make Stanford look good."

"At least I got out of presenting."

"Why are you so against it?"

"I don't like public speaking."

"But you're basically famous."

"It's why I stay out of the spotlight."

"Interesting," I mused. "Have you always hated public speaking?"

"Yep. It's why Preston does the press briefings and new tech events."

"I always wondered why you didn't show off your inventions."

"I don't need to show them off. They speak for themselves."

"As work should," I added. "Hope you didn't have plans. We have to drive down to Atlanta on Friday night."

"Wait, it's *this* weekend?"

"Yep. We're only going for the one night, though since Caroline and I knew Dave would balk at the cost of the hotel."

He nodded, looking at his phone. "I can make it happen on one condition."

"What's that?"

"We take my car. I need to test the system on long trips."

"Test it for what?"

"There's a bug in the programming after my research and development team pushed an update."

"*Your* research and development team?"

"I meant PATH's." His rubbed his neck and looked around, as if making sure no one overheard him. I knew PATH had to still mean a lot to him, but his slipup made me wonder why he'd even joined Stanford in the first place. His heart was obviously not in it. "So, do we have a deal?"

"I guess so, but if we crash, I'm suing the shit out of you."

"I wouldn't expect anything different."

⁂

To: Caroline Fitzpatrick
   From: Opulence Hotel in Atlanta
   Subject: Your Room Reservation
   (Forwarded to Dave Stanford, redirected to Spam folder)

   Hi, Caroline,

   Since we were not able to reach you via phone, we have can-
   celed your reservation for the second room tonight. The other
   reservation made under Ruth Murray remains.

   Have a great day!

Knox

Friday night, I picked up Ruth from her apartment. It was past sunset and both of us had been stuck at work later than we'd hoped to be.

She came out in the same clothes she'd worked in. Her heels were still on. I frowned, wondering why she hadn't opted for something more casual. Even I had changed into a T-shirt and jeans.

"You're in heels for a three-and-a-half-hour drive?" I asked as I got out of the car to help get her luggage into the trunk.

"I live in them." Her flat tone left no room for argument, but I wondered how she could stand to be in those things for so long. "Are you sure—"

She cut me off. "Let's get going. I want to get there as soon as we can. The weather is supposed to be bad."

"I heard there were some storms forecasted," I said.

Ruth stiffly nodded and hustled to the passenger seat. My frown deepened. She must not have been in a talking mood.

I didn't waste time in getting our destination input into the car. Ruth's eyes watched the wheel closely.

"I guess you don't remember much from the last time you were in here."

"I don't. I thought PATH made technology for cars already on the road. Are you guys making your own now?"

"We're trying to. We want a good car that's affordable for the average person."

"You could have just stuck to making products that fit on other car brands."

"We still do, but I got the idea for a self-charging vehicle. I had to make it then."

"You don't have to plug this in?"

"Not for about six hundred miles or so."

"Wow, that's a lot, considering the top-of-the-line electric car can only go half of that."

"We're trying to innovate."

"It's cool," she admitted. "Even when the wheel turns itself like that. It almost makes me wish I hadn't purposefully gotten one without the self-driving feature."

"You did? Do you have something against self-driving cars?"

"I'm not against them," she replied. "It was mostly because you invented it."

"How could I forget? You really don't let a grudge go, huh?"

"The grudge wasn't your fault. So, I'm working on it."

"Wait, it wasn't me? I didn't cause this?"

"Nope, not you. I'm sorry I held onto it for so long."

"Who hurt you then?" I asked slowly, careful not to let slip how much I despised the idea of anyone hurting her.

She bit her lip, hesitating to say anything further.

"My parents," she finally said after a long minute. "I'm only now coming to terms with it, though."

"What did they do?"

She sighed. "Can we maybe not talk about this? It's not that I don't trust you, but I've been thinking about it for days, and now there's a storm and—" She cut herself off and closed her eyes. "I want to enjoy this weekend away, Knox. I don't want to think about all the shitty things my parents did to me."

"Okay," I said quietly. "But I want to know eventually."

"I'll tell you. I promise. God, I'm just so tired. And no matter how much I sleep, it doesn't go away."

"Sounds like burnout."

"Yeah, probably. It's not like anyone at Stanford would care though. Can you imagine what Dave would say if anyone told him they were burnt out?"

"He'd laugh in their face."

"God, he's such an asshole."

"He is. Some days I don't know why my best friend insisted I work here."

"Your best friend?"

"Preston. He's also my business partner. He said this would make me feel better, and I do, but not because of the work."

"Because of . . . someone."

"Yes." I risked a glance at her. "I guess I like to be challenged."

She rolled her eyes, but a smile was on her lips. "By an old high school rival?"

"You're more than that now."

"But not that much more. I can't be."

"I know," I replied. I once again cursed Dave for his stupid rule.

Ruth looked over at me and cleared her throat. "By the way, about what Dave said, about you finding someone at this convention. If you did, then I'd . . . I'd understand." Her voice was tight, and when I looked over at her, her gaze was on her hands.

"Why the hell would I do that?"

"We're not a thing, and we can't be a thing because of work. So, if you're lonely or wanting a night of fun, you could find that."

"No."

"Really?" she asked, looking back up. "You don't have to stay celibate or anything. We're *not* a couple. And I can't believe I'm saying this, but you're a really nice guy and I don't want you to feel like you have to wait for me. Some of the women here are really cute and—"

"Ruth, stop talking."

"I'm trying to be nice. You don't have to get defensive with me when I just want you to be happy."

"I wouldn't be happy, Ruth, because none of them would be *you*."

"Knox, I'm not that special."

"You are to me," I said, one of my fists clenching. "You're driven, and stubborn, but in the best ways. You could be climbing over everyone to get your promotions, and yet every single one of your employees glared at me my first day when they thought I was talking negatively about you. You're funny and smart, and in the ten years I was away, I never met one person who even came close to you."

"I thought . . . I thought you forgot about me."

"Forgot about you?" I laughed. "Your ghost followed me everywhere. I would hear heels clicking and hope it was you. I still, to this day, prefer green eyes because of *you*. There is going to be no one else, Ruth, because you're the only one that I want."

She was silent, and when I looked to her, she was staring back at me with wide eyes.

"B-but we *can't*," she said, her voice shaking. "And if you find someone else—"

"I'd rather imagine a night with you, risking our jobs, than spend it with anyone else."

Ruth shook her head, and I waited for her to say something, but she stayed silent.

"Do you have no other rebuttal?"

"I'm . . . I'm in shock. I don't know *what* to say."

"You could say fuck this rule and do it anyway."

"How good are you at keeping secrets?" she asked.

"I'm great at it. It's the photographers who follow me who are bad at it."

"Right," she said, sighing. "If it weren't for that, I'd break Dave's rule in a heartbeat."

"Let me know if you decide to anyway."

She nodded. We lapsed into another silence. For a long while, the car drove, and I was content to glance over at her when I could.

But as we neared our destination, thick clouds crept over the moon, blocking out its light. Soon after, rain pattered against the windshield.

Ruth's leg jiggled nervously.

"The car does fine in rain," I said. "That's not the bug I'm watching for."

"Okay," she said, eyes on the sky. "Rain isn't too bad."

She was quiet, but a different kind. She wasn't pensively rubbing her neck as she thought about my words. She was thinking of something else.

As the car finally pulled in to the hotel parking lot, there was a distant rumble of thunder.

"Motherfucker," she muttered.

"What?"

"Let's just go inside and get our rooms," she said, hurrying out of the car without another word. She moved quickly, grabbing her suitcase so tightly her knuckles turned white.

She sped off to the front desk and I had to jog to keep up with her. When I arrived inside, I threw on my ball cap and sunglasses, just so no one would see me.

The lobby was ornate and loud. Atlanta was busy this weekend. Despite all the people congregating, I could hear the rain pouring on the pavement outside.

Ruth was already chatting with the front desk clerk by the time I reached her. I wondered what the hell had caused her mood to shift. Had I somehow upset her in the car?

"We have two reservations under Stanford Bank and Trust," Ruth said. "Mine is under Ruth Murray and there should be another one under Caroline Fitzpatrick."

They clerk nodded warmly and looked up the reservations. However, when her eyes scanned the screen, she froze.

"Is everything okay?" Ruth asked. I watched her grip on her suitcase grow impossibly tighter.

"Um, well . . ." The clerk laughed awkwardly. "There's actually only one room here."

CHAPTER FIFTEEN

Ruth

I stared at the hotel clerk in pure, unfiltered shock.

I'd stayed in many hotels in my life, and this was a first.

"I'm sorry," she said, her face tomato red with embarrassment. "The bookings were made a long time ago, and this one was canceled when it wasn't confirmed by the number on file."

I asked her what number it was and groaned when she read out Caroline's. Of course she didn't answer. She was retired.

"Ruth, if it's a double queen room, it's fine." Knox sounded much calmer than I felt.

"It's a king room," the receptionist replied.

I remembered requesting that room. The last thing I wanted to do was share a room with Caroline again, because last year she'd snored so loudly the neighbors complained to the front desk. And I'd figured if I wasn't presenting, then I could at least have a king-sized bed to myself.

Now it appeared my forethought was biting me in the ass.

"We can get you a room at one of our partner hotels," the receptionist said. "The nearest one is about ten miles away."

Maybe I could ask Knox to take that one. I didn't have it in me to try to get anywhere else. I could feel the fear of the storm settling in, and I needed to get to privacy *fast*.

"Oh no," the clerk said. She looked up at me like I was a bomb about to go off. "That one is booked too."

"What?" I asked. "How?"

"We have six major events happening this weekend. Lila Wilde is in town doing three shows, then we have four conventions as well as a flower festival in one of the parks."

"We'll check in to the one room." Knox's voice was firm. "We'll figure it out from there."

Knox handled the rest of the transaction while I stared at the wall, panicking.

My heart was already racing. I'd heard one rumble of thunder, and it was only going to get closer. I was on borrowed time.

Knox pulled me away and I broke out of my one-woman wall-staring contest to glance out of the glass front doors in the lobby. Maybe if I silently begged hard enough whatever god out there would spare me a storm. Maybe I could get out of this with my pride intact.

"Damn it," Knox said, and I glanced over to see him glaring at his phone. "There is literally nothing available around here."

"Great," I said, my voice shaky.

Knox's eyes met mine and I knew he was picking up on my weird mood. "We could share the room."

"No," I hissed.

"It's our best option."

"I can't."

"Is this because of the rule? I'm not going to touch you without permission. We can share the bed and pretend it never happened. I won't tell a soul."

That was the furthest thing from my mind. I only cared about finding a safe space before I fucking lost it.

"This is a nightmare."

"Do you have a different idea?" he asked.

Another clap of thunder made me jump, a grim reminder of the impending sleepless night.

"Can you just kill me right now?" I asked.

"Ruth, what is going on with you?"

I shook my head. "I just need to get out of this fucking lobby."

I power walked to the elevator, thinking of ways I could go through my usual storm panic alone. Maybe I could run the shower for a few hours while I worked through the terror. Maybe the warm water would help.

Then I remembered the possibility of electrocution in water during a storm.

Not only was my former-rival-now-friend about to share a bed with me, but he'd also be around while my irrational fear took root. Whatever respect he had for me was about to be *gone*.

My hand gripped the metal bar of the elevator tightly, and I squeezed my eyes shut, begging for the thunder to hold off long enough for us to get in the room.

His hand came to rest over mine. "It's going to be okay, Ruth."

"You don't even know what's going on."

"That's true, but trust me when I say that I will do everything in my power to make sure you're okay."

There wasn't much he could do for the storms, but his words did help a little. I slowly nodded and my heart calmed slightly.

I managed to take out my phone to check the weather and the forecast had shifted to rain only. This was backed by the absence of the sound of thunder as we made our way into our room; only rain pounded on the windows.

My shoulders sagged in relief. Maybe I would get lucky after all.

"I know something isn't right. What can I do to help you?" he asked.

"I'm fine," I said, and my voice sounded somewhat normal. "Everything is good now."

"What was wrong?"

"I had an upset stomach, but it's resolved now." I set my bag in the closet, feeling assured that I wouldn't need the small space for the night.

"Are you sure?"

"Yep. Very sure."

I turned to go sit on the bed and give my angry feet some time to rest, but the moment I tried to walk, my ankle rolled.

"Ow!"

I didn't usually do this in heels. I'd mastered them on any hard surface years ago, but the carpet of the hotel room was inexplicably soft. It also didn't help that I'd been in them for over fifteen hours at this point.

That was when it hit me that Knox would also have to see me without my heels, unless I slept in them again. My feet ached at the mere thought.

My earlier panic had made it impossible to think this room-sharing thing through.

"Take off the heels," he urged. "You've been wearing those things all day."

"I'm good."

"You are definitely not good."

"What do you mean? I always wear these right until I get into bed."

"Are you serious?"

"Yes." Even though it sounded horrible.

"Take them off," he repeated slowly as he walked over to me. I looked at him, opening my mouth to fight his command, but he spoke before I could. "You wore those on the entire car ride over. We're in the room now."

"I'm *fine*."

"You're a smart woman, Ruth. One of these days you're going to figure out that I see right through you when you're not okay."

Fuck. What the hell was I supposed to say to that?

"Fine. My feet hurt, but I like being tall."

"So it's just a height thing?" He smiled when I nodded. "Then I have a very easy solution."

My lips pursed as I tried to think of what it could be, but then he fell to his knees in front of me. My breathing stuttered as my heart kicked into overdrive at the mere sight.

His messy hair looked so soft in the light, and his eyes gazed up at me. This might have been my favorite view. The Atlanta city skyline out of the window paled in comparison.

He held out a hand. "May I?"

"What are you doing?"

"Taking off your heels for you." His hand trailed the skin of my leg. "But only if you say yes."

There was not a woman on earth who could say no to him. I once thought I was the exception.

I was wrong.

"Y-yes," I said, my answer catching in my throat.

His grip moved to coax me to lift one shoe. His other slid around the back of my calf before grazing down to my heel.

For a man who'd probably never worn heels in his life, he was good at taking them off. He knew the way to gently slide them without any tugging. I stepped down on my newly free foot as he worked on the other one.

My feet were singing from relief, but I was caught on how, even while kneeling, Knox came up to my chest. I still looked down on him, but only barely.

I was hyperaware of his touch, including his hand still on my calf. What would it feel like if it drifted up to the skin under my skirt?

"I don't care what angle I see you in," he said, his voice low. "You're fucking beautiful in every single one."

I couldn't take him looking up at me like that any longer. I was dangerously close to risking everything and bringing his mouth to mine.

"You can stand," I said softly.

He slowly obliged, eyes never leaving mine.

And *fuck*. His eyes were just as intense as he gazed down at me.

His head tilted to the side. "I was right. Perfect in every angle."

Knox

My mind dimly noted that I needed to step away from her. But I was busy calculating the perfect angle to lean down and press my lips to hers. I wanted to carry her to that bed and make her scream my name.

But I'd told her I wouldn't touch her, and I was a man of my word.

My chest ached as I stepped back.

"See? Not so bad."

"Speak for yourself. I'm going to get neck pain from looking up at you."

"You're not that short," I reassured her. "And while we're on a roll here, are you ever going to change out of your work clothes?"

"What if I slept in this?"

"No," I said. "You're not sleeping in a pencil skirt."

She blew out a breath. "Fine, but if you say *one* thing about how I look, you're sleeping in the tub."

"What if it's a nice thing?"

"Then maybe you get to use the bed." She turned to grab clothes out of her bag in the closet, and then disappeared into the bathroom.

My thoughts turned to the sight of her legs when I'd bent down to take off her shoes. I could have run my hands up and down her silky skin forever.

Moments later, the door to the bathroom clicked open.

And I couldn't look away.

Her black hair was long, falling down her back in waves. She was wearing an old T-shirt from our high school, as well as striped pajama bottoms.

She looked perfect like this too.

"I hate every second of this," she muttered.

"I'm not going to say anything negative."

"I appreciate your discretion."

"Let me rephrase that. I *couldn't* say anything negative, even if I wanted to." I walked over to her, taking in every inch of her face, scrubbed free of makeup. My hand twitched as I resisted the urge to bring my hand up to feel her soft skin for myself.

But I knew, without a shadow of a doubt, if I started touching her now, I wouldn't stop.

"It's your turn to go get comfortable," she said, but her voice shook. "If I'm not sleeping in a pencil skirt, then you're not sleeping in jeans."

My jeans were the only thing somewhat concealing how hard I'd grown at the sight of her, but I knew I needed a moment away from her so I could take a deep breath and calm down.

When I'd finally gotten my thoughts under control, I walked back into the room to see Ruth was adjusting something on the bed.

She glanced up at me, and then her eyes trailed down my body. It made my still half-hard member try to jump back to life.

I needed to get my mind off of that, and desperately. That was when I noticed what she was doing.

"Is that a wall of pillows?"

"We need a line to not cross. I also have no clue if I'm a kicker. This is for your benefit."

"Okay," I said, already regretting my promise not to touch her. "I won't cross it."

Ruth gave me a firm nod and then laid down on the bed, back away from me. "Night."

"Night," I muttered back, still staring at her long, dark hair.

I wished I could touch it and feel the silky strands between my fingers. I wished I could gently brush it to the side and plant my lips on her shoulder to taste the skin there.

But Ruth had made it clear she didn't want that, so I would respect it, but my desires never waned.

CHAPTER SIXTEEN

Ruth

Thunder boomed in the hotel room, shattering the peace that I'd fallen asleep to.

I screamed in shock, nearly catapulting myself out of the bed as I realized the storm that I thought had broken up was now in fact, *not*. I had no idea what time it was, only that the room was pitch-black.

My eyes scanned the room, desperate for a closet to climb into to hide. Panic clawed its way into my chest as I realized I'd put my damn suitcase in there. I could already feel myself locking up.

"Ruth?" Knox asked, his voice bleary. "Was that you?"

I couldn't even answer him. Thunder rumbled again, and I curled tighter around myself.

If there *was* a tornado, I was out in the open.

My fear was so strong that I didn't have a moment to feel embarrassed; all I knew was that I was the scared child again, hearing the very air I breathed rip through houses next to me. I wasn't Ruth the Ruthless any longer.

"Hey, what's wrong?" Knox asked, his hand on my back. "Bad dream?"

I could only shake my head.

"Are you sick?"

Another shake.

"Then what's going on?" His voice was sharp with urgency.

More lighting, followed my loud claps of thunder shook everything around us. I whimpered helplessly against the force of nature.

"Is it the storm?"

I didn't want to answer him, but I nodded anyway.

My fear was irrational. I knew this, but I couldn't calm my racing heart or shaking hands. I expected him to laugh, or to ask why someone like me was scared of something so insignificant.

His hand moved up and down my spine, a comforting reminder that he was next to me.

"We're safe here," he said, his voice so soft I didn't even think it was him. "It's okay."

I wished I could believe him, but my fear was winning.

I was back in that closet. I could hear the wind, feel Tom grabbing me. I was just as helpless then as I was that night.

"All right, that's enough of this."

I heard shuffling, and I knew his patience had run dry, just as everyone else's always did.

"Come here." I felt his solid leg press against mine.

Knox pulled me to him as if I weighed nothing. Both of his arms enveloped me, creating a cocoon of safety I hadn't felt in years. Another rumble of thunder made its way to my ears, but I barely noticed because he covered one with his hand, and the other was pressed to his chest, listening to the steady beat of his heart.

"You're okay," he whispered. "You'll always be okay when you're with me."

Lightning flashed, but he protected me once more. The thrumming of his heart overrode the sounds of a memory now long gone. Instead of seeing that night play on a loop, I only saw him.

With every flash, his hand muted the sounds of the impending crash. Second by second, my heart rate slowed. I thought it impossible, but Knox found a way to protect me from the thunder.

"I-I'm sorry," I said, as my voice came back to me.

"Never apologize for being scared."

"It's stupid."

"Nothing is stupid about you. Not to me."

Tears clouded my vision, which didn't make sense. I wasn't scared anymore.

But it was because of *him*.

I clung to him desperately, as if he would vanish into thin air at any point moving forward. Even as the storm dissipated, I found that I could not let him go.

"Please don't leave me," I whispered. *You're the only one who helps.*

"As if I ever could."

I hoped he meant it, because if he didn't, then this would be the cruelest moment of my life.

"Go back to sleep, Ruth," he murmured. "I'll be here."

My eyes fluttered closed, his heartbeat soothing me to sleep while I was in the safest embrace I'd ever known.

As the sun woke me from my unexpected slumber, I'd hoped it had all been a nightmare, but I knew immediately that what had happened was *very* real. I wasn't on the edge of the bed where I should be. Rather, I was in the middle, practically clinging to Knox like an octopus to a rock. My legs were haphazardly thrown over his, my face pressed against his shoulder. My hand was lingering on the edge of his shirt, but my pinky brushed against the warm skin of his stomach.

And my body refused to move.

"No more storms for today." Knox's voice made me jump. My instinctual reaction was to clamber away from him to the other side of the bed. But his arm, which was wrapped around my waist, kept me from moving. "You don't get to move away until I know you're okay."

"I'd honestly like to find the nearest cliff to jump off of."

He looked over at me and then the calm weather outside.

"Are you embarrassed about last night?"

"I'm fucking mortified."

"It's okay," Knox said. "Your secret is safe with me. I just need to know that you're okay now."

"I'm fine. This happens during every storm. Summers are miserable because of it."

He hummed, and I peeked at his face—his brow was creased.

"It's a dumb fear," I said. "I know you're thinking it."

"I meant what I said last night. Nothing about you is dumb. You were terrified."

"I know," I said. "And it's just thunder. "

"Every fear has a reason. What happened?"

I looked away from him, but I was still pressed into his side, so I wound up staring at his shirt instead.

"Do you remember the tornadoes that hit Nashville twenty years ago?"

"Sure."

"I was in one of them. Not *in* it, but next to it. All I remember was hiding in our basement, hearing thunder, and then the loudest noise I'd ever heard. It tore apart my neighbor's house. Her husband died."

"Ruth. That's terrible."

"It was, and what makes it worse is that it didn't affect *anyone* else. Tom was his usual, stoic self afterward and Barry didn't seem to need anyone. And I'm happy it *didn't* tear their lives apart, but my parents saw me as weak because I wasn't okay. That's when I started to hide it."

"No." His voice was hard. "You're not weak because you had a reaction to something traumatizing. You're human."

"I don't think my parents wanted human kids. They wanted trophies." My voice cracked and I could feel tears welling up. He was silent for a long moment. "Are you judging me?"

"No," he muttered. "I'm just realizing why you work yourself to death. It was your parents, wasn't it?"

"A lot of my problems started with them. Namely, my dad. He always told me to stop crying over stupid things."

"You can cry anytime with me. As long as I get to wipe away every tear."

As one escaped down my cheek, he made true to his promise.

"Why are you being so *nice*?"

"Why wouldn't I be?"

I didn't have an answer for that, mostly because I was wondering when I'd began expecting cruelty instead of kindness.

"Thank you," I said. I moved only slightly, but then stopped. "You're going to have to let go of me, though. I need to pee. Bad."

"Are you being serious or are you using the bathroom as a way to hide something?"

"I'm serious. Now move before I piss on you."

He laughed and moved his arm. I darted to the bathroom to do my business, but then took a second to think.

The moment Knox crossed my mind, my entire body flushed. *Fuck.* What I had been feeling the night before had only grown tenfold, and now I wanted to climb him like a damn tree, both to cling to him for comfort again *and* to soothe other *needs*.

I was in danger.

When I came out of the bathroom, I was evaluating everything I knew and unexpectedly ran face-first into Knox's chest.

"That's like a brick wall," I muttered, rubbing my nose.

"Thank you for the roundabout compliment," he said. I looked up at him; both of his hands were on the doorframe.

I took in a shaky breath. I wanted to feel those lips on mine again, and after last night, the threat of losing my job was not enough to stop me.

And we were so close to each other.

"Ruth," he said, his voice low. "I could kiss you right now." He then shook his head. "But I don't want to risk—"

I grabbed him by the shirt and pulled him to me.

He let out an abrupt breath, but it didn't take him long to return the kiss.

His lips were soft, unlike most men I'd kissed. The slight scratch of his beard against my cheek was something I hadn't felt in the snack closet. His scent of rosewood filled my nose.

It wasn't harried like the last one we'd shared. This was slow and deliberate. Instead of shock coursing through my veins, there was a different kind of heat racing inside.

Feeling bold, I dragged my tongue over his bottom lip, getting only a small taste of him. His groan in response was something I'd remember for the rest of my life. I ran my fingers through his soft hair, and it felt just like I imagined it would.

I lost track of how much time our lips were pressed together. I felt like a teenager experiencing their first kiss, and I wondered if he would have tasted like this if I'd kissed him then. As he pressed his body to mine, I could feel his hardness against my lower stomach, and I wanted him to fuck me right then and there.

That was when my phone's alarm went off.

I pulled away from him, both relieved and annoyed that I'd set a reminder of when to get ready. I looked at him again, wondering if we would spend the day together, and being afraid of how much I wanted that to happen.

"We should get ready," I said. "The event starts in an hour, and we still need to get the luggage into the car."

"That last thing I want to do is go to a marketing event when I have you willing to kiss me." His voice was rough and low. It did unfair things to my spine.

"We have tonight."

"We have to drive back."

"I don't have to go home," I said playfully. For a moment, I wondered if I was being too bold. Maybe I needed to back off and let him have some space.

"That is exactly what I wanted to hear."

I nodded, catching my breath as I let him use the bathroom. I grabbed my clothes for the day and worked on my makeup at the table.

Despite me still wanting to kiss him more, I also felt myself grow excited for the reason we were even in Atlanta. I couldn't wait to see all the people from the year before and talk about one of my favorite things.

After the both of us were ready, Knox continued watching me.

"What?" I asked him as I slid on my heels.

"You look nice."

"I look like I always do."

"There isn't a side of you I don't like."

"Nice line. Who all have you used it on?"

"Only you."

Ugh. That did nothing to quell how much I *wanted* him.

"We have time for a quickie," Knox said. I swiveled to him, eyes wide. *Is he suggesting . . .* "I meant a quick date. B-breakfast, not a date."

I stared at him for a moment longer, then I burst into laughter. "Your face!"

"It's . . . I . . ." He rubbed a hand over his face.

"Oh, Knox. You have such a way with words."

"It's a true talent," he said, still touching his red cheek. "Shall we?"

"I think we shall."

Knox

"The hat clashes with your suit," Ruth said.

I'd dressed up for the convention after looking at the dress code. But for breakfast, I didn't want anyone to know it was me.

No one knew I was in Atlanta, but I was always on the lookout for people snapping photographs of me. I was worried we'd have another incident where I'd be caught with Ruth. Once was more than enough to get people speculating. And now that I knew what her lips felt like on mine, I realized my face would spill our whole story.

"It's either that or we get questioned if someone recognizes me."

"The only people I've seen are hungover Lila Wilde fans. I don't think they know who you are."

"Let's be safe," I said. "I can handle clashing for just a bit. I'll take everything off when we go to the convention."

She raised an eyebrow. "Everything?"

"That's for tonight," I reminded, opening the door to the café. "So, what do you normally eat for breakfast?"

I desperately had to get my mind off the idea of *tonight*. Small talk would have to do.

"Usually I skip it," she answered. "But at this moment? I want French toast."

"I'll get you whatever you want."

"Maybe I should be the one to pay. I was the one who was a baby about the storms."

"Scared," I corrected. "You deserve to be taken care of after that." With my hand at the small of her back, I led her to the hostess's stand. Even though I was concerned someone might recognize me and put us in the news again, I was finding it difficult to resist my desire to always be touching her. When she didn't answer, I said, "So, it's settled. I'll get the bill."

I then told the hostess there would only be two of us. I looked back to see Ruth staring at me.

"What?"

"I'm just . . . not used to being taken care of."

"You'll get used to it."

"At least it wasn't a tornado warning."

"Is it worse?"

"Much worse. I cower in fear with storms, but tornadoes cause literal panic attacks. The last one actually made me pass out."

My heart clenched. I'd had an idea this morning to help her with her fear, and now that she'd told me more about just how debilitating it was, I knew I'd be up every night designing it until it was complete.

But for now, we were at our table and I needed to get some food in her before the event.

Ruth ordered the French toast she wanted and I got a simple breakfast plate.

As we ate, we talked about the convention. I didn't have much of an interest in marketing, but seeing the way her eyes lit up as she talked about trends and how to sell products made me rethink my alliances.

It also made me see why Dad always listened intently whenever Mom talked about hair care. Time was lost as I listened to her, but she'd thought ahead and set timers to remind us when to leave.

By the time we got to the convention center, the doors to the event had just opened.

At first, there was a presentation for marketing trends. Ruth pulled out a notepad from her purse and scribbled down every word. I barely listened to the presentation, choosing to focus on the way her eyebrows furrowed when she concentrated. Every now and then, she would make an out loud comment to herself on the information, correcting it with data she'd previously gathered.

She should have been the one presenting; it was obvious she knew her stuff. She would have been stellar.

I'd noticed a few people turning to look at us, and I knew I'd been spotted. I expected to have to deal with a swarm by the time the presentation was over.

But I didn't. Attendees flocked to *Ruth*. She answered questions about me, but they were mostly directed at her, ranging from people asking how she was doing to why she wasn't presenting. Apparently, she had left a fantastic impression from the year before.

She gave smart, superficial answers, but I could see the way her smile fell every time someone asked why it wasn't her on stage. She'd wanted to present, and Dave had turned her down. If she were at PATH, I'd have let her do it in a heartbeat.

But she took it all with grace, answering questions as the day went on. By the time of the networking dinner, however, I could see she was getting tired. I couldn't blame her, she'd been talking all day.

"Do you need some more water?" I asked into her ear as she talked with someone else. The waitress was very busy, and I'd seen a vending machine outside of the interior door to the catered part of the event space. When she nodded vigorously, I stepped away to get her a drink.

I made my way back inside to get to our table, but I ran into one of my employees.

Well, one of PATH's employees.

I froze. I had no idea the company even planned to be at this event.

And I hated that I didn't know.

Jimmy, a man dressed in a three-piece suit with a height nearly matching mine, was the closest thing PATH had to Ruth's job. He had only started a year prior, and proved himself to be decent at the job; I remembered him saying he wished there was someone within the company he could learn more from, being a recent college graduate and there being no mentor sort for the role at PATH.

"Is that Knox Price?" he asked in his low voice, jaw on the floor. "I didn't know you'd be here."

"It's me," I confirmed.

"I can't believe I didn't see you until now. Why didn't you present?"

"I figured I would leave space for others to shine." It was the excuse I always told my employees when they asked why I didn't get on stage. "Besides, my partner definitely deserved to present, if anyone from Stanford would have had the honor."

I was still mad at Dave for that one.

"Does that person happen to be Ruth Murray?"

"You know her?"

"She's a bit of a legend in the marketing world. None of us know how she keeps Stanford afloat." His eyes widened as he realized what he said. "Not that it's a *bad* company, but—"

"It's okay. I'm aware it's not run well."

Jimmy laughed, and I was struck with how much I missed the environment at PATH. I couldn't think of one person who laughed with Dave like Jimmy was with me.

"We're all hoping you'll come back. Poor Preston is stressed out."

"Maybe one day," I said noncommittally. I glanced over at Ruth, feeling like my heart was in two different places. I wanted to be in Nashville with her, always by her side.

But I missed my company.

Ruth's eyes met mine, and she seemed to excuse herself from who she was talking to so she could walk over.

"Oh, shit, that's her," Jimmy said, almost panicked. "What do I say to her? Is she nice?"

I opened my mouth to respond, but Ruth was already near us. She grabbed the bottle out of my hand and took a long drink. Then her eyes caught PATH's logo on Jimmy's shirt.

"I should have known this is where you'd be lingering," she mused. She turned to Jimmy. "Hi, I'm Ruth Murray."

"I know of you. Everyone says how much of a badass you are at marketing."

"Oh, really? That's really nice of you to say."

"The marketing campaign you came up with from this last year was so impressive. I was hoping to have the same inspiration here."

"Any luck?"

"No," he said, sighing. "I'm very lucky to work for a company that basically markets itself, but I wanted to make some sort of splash with my job here."

"I think you're doing fine," I reminded him. "The last I heard, sales were still steady."

"Yeah, but I want a good marketing campaign. Especially with your newest thing coming out."

"Newest thing?" Ruth asked.

"Oh, maybe I shouldn't have said anything."

"It's fine," I said. "She can know."

"It was the last thing he invented before he stepped down. It's this amazing safety package that provides protection for classic cars that don't have airbags installed."

Ruth's eyebrows raised. "Really?" She turned to me. "What made you think of that?"

"People shouldn't have to get new cars just to be protected in a crash. PATH is all about working with what we have, but the older models have always been a danger for drivers."

"Oh, I know. My brother drives an old truck."

"What model?" I asked.

"I have no clue, but it's certainly an antique." She turned to Jimmy. "I think you should focus on Knox's noble efforts to stop overconsumption and advertise based on that."

Both of us blinked.

"W-what?" Jimmy stuttered as he reached into his bag to grab a notebook.

"PATH is one of the few companies that focuses on improving what we already have rather than pushing for the newest version of everything. I've seen your advertising model. You focus on the safety, which is a great feature, but also, you can speak to people who don't want to upgrade every few years, especially the people who can't afford to."

Jimmy scribbled furiously.

"It's going to lead right into your next product announcement, which will have the public primed to hear about it. Oh, you could start polls on your social medias about people's favorite classic car."

Jimmy's eyes never left the page.

I stared at her, amazed at her quick thinking. I had no doubts Jimmy would get there eventually, but even I hadn't thought of ways to connect our products like that.

Thinking of the other invention I had brewing in the back of my mind, I wondered what she could make out of that one.

"If only you worked for PATH," Jimmy said, echoing my thoughts. "You could probably have my job."

"I don't want to take you from Knox," she said politely. "Plus, there's no way I could move to California. I've got family in town."

A weight settled on my chest. Of course she wouldn't want to move. She had her brothers and her life here. *I* didn't even want to go back.

But I would have to. I would never be done with the company I built.

"Understandable," Jimmy said. "Mind if I use these ideas, though?"

"They're all yours," she said.

Another person came up to me, eager to learn about PATH, but I diverted them to Jimmy, who excused himself to go speak with them. Ruth walked back over to our table and I followed her loyally.

But my mind was on the future.

I needed to be with my team, especially research and development. Even now, I was answering questions about the PATH prototype and the safety technology from afar. I knew some of them would be figured out more quickly if I was there with them.

I wanted to be there *and* here, but until I figured out how to split myself in two, I couldn't do that.

"What are you thinking about so hard?" Ruth asked as I followed her through the mass of people.

"Nothing," I lied.

She raised an eyebrow and I decided to give her at least part of the truth of my thoughts.

"You *would* be good at PATH."

"I'm not in the market of job stealing."

"But you would be. Imagine what you could do with a product that actually works. You're amazing at what you do, Ruth. You should have been running this thing."

"You might be right," she muttered. "I wish I had pushed harder to present. People expected me to."

"You shouldn't have to push at all. Bosses aren't supposed to stand in your way. They're supposed to help you achieve your goal."

"Maybe they do that at PATH," she said softly. "Not at Stanford."

"You deserve that and more. You're incredible."

"Be careful, or I'm going to have a head as big as yours."

"My head is perfectly proportional."

She rolled her eyes but was distracted as someone else came to talk to her. I listened to her dutifully, unable to get the idea of her and PATH out of my mind.

CHAPTER SEVENTEEN

Ruth

After four more people asked me why I hadn't presented, the bitterness in me was rising.

And my feet were hurting. Thankfully, people were leaving, so I felt less bad about grabbing Knox and making a break for it before anyone else could stop me to chat.

But walking was miserable.

I was used to long days in heels, but at the office, I could sit and rest. Here, I'd been going for hours. The damn dinner was at bar-height tables with no stools, which meant I was continuing to stand. All that on top of the long day I'd had yesterday meant my feet were not happy.

But I was the one who refused to let people be taller than me. So, I would suffer in silence until we returned to Knox's car. I'd have to soak my feet for hours after this.

"Are you limping?"

"My feet are killing me."

"I thought you could live in heels."

"I thought I already told you not to question my footwear. I'll be fine. We just need to get back to the car and then I'll take them off."

"Why don't you sit for a minute?"

I shook my head and walked for the door. "I want to get this over with. Plus, I need to make my escape. I love networking, but I've done too much of it for the day."

As he followed me through the doors, I heard him mutter, "Stubborn as always" under his breath. I didn't get to call him out on it because he stopped me.

"Hold on tight," he said and then he picked me up.

"What the hell!" I yelled, angling away from him in a desperate attempt to get down. "Someone could see!"

"And I'd tell them my *friend* was being too hardheaded for her own good." He walked me over to a nearby bench and set me down.

"I'd rather get back to the car so I can sit for the rest of the evening."

He sighed and turned; his eyes trained on the road. I opened my mouth to demand he look at me, but I was too distracted by the sight of the very car we were supposed to be walking to pulling up to the curb.

Self-driving cars. *Right.*

"I thought those weren't approved to drive without a human in the car."

"It's approved in select cities for shorter distances. Atlanta is one of them." He walked around the edge of the vehicle, inspecting it for any damage from its driverless adventure. When he knelt down to check the bumper, I could only stare at the press of his ass against his slacks.

"Get in the car, Ruth," he said, turning to me from where he was. His hand slid across the bumper. "Or I'll carry you again."

I was tempted to let him do it.

But that was a bad idea. We didn't need to draw any more attention to ourselves than we already had. A few people had taken photos of Knox in the venue. More cameras were definitely on the way.

He opened my door. "How are your feet?"

"They're fine." I wrenched off the heels and threw them in the back.

"If I promise you a foot massage, can you be the one behind the wheel for a bit? I need to send a report to someone at PATH."

"Me? Doesn't that break some rule or something?"

"I made the company, and I made the rules."

Right. Of course.

But I'd do it anyway. Now that I was off of my feet, I wouldn't mind driving. And with this thing, I didn't need to worry about using my feet at all.

It was scary for different reasons, though.

I slid over very inelegantly. Thankfully, Knox didn't comment on it.

"How the hell do I operate this thing?" I muttered.

Knox pulled up a map. "I've set it to go to its destination. You just need to be sure it doesn't veer off the road."

Having a car move without pushing the gas made my heart race, but I let go for just a moment. Slowly, the car pulled onto the highway. The steering wheel moved of its own accord, driving us square in the middle of the lane. To my right, a 3D version of the car in front of us was displayed.

Knox reached behind me to pull out a laptop and immediately started typing a mile a minute.

"Since you're new to self-driving technology, tell me if you see anything that throws you off."

"O-okay," I stuttered.

As we drove, I noticed how *safe* the car felt. It didn't go over the speed limit. It obeyed the laws of the highway, staying to the right for faster cars in the left, and it slowed down with an appropriate distance between it and the car in front of us. It was one thing to hear what these cars could do. It was another to experience it.

The car even knew to stay out of the blind spot of an eighteen-wheeler. Knox must have spent ages programming this thing.

At the sight of a big rig, I instantly thought of my parents' business. Technology like this would revolutionize the trucking world, but as far as I knew, nothing was in the works.

"Have you thought about implementing this into bigger vehicles?" I asked.

Knox looked up. "We have, but no company we work with will guarantee to not lay off or dock the paid employees if we produce and sell the products for eighteen-wheelers. The vehicles *are* safe, but they still need a human's eye. I don't want my company to be the reason people lose their jobs."

"They wanted to lay off drivers? That doesn't make sense."

"They think they can make do with just PATH installed. Every company we spoke to says the drivers would be useless."

"But they're not."

Drivers were needed for all sorts of things. They needed to be there to assure the load was kept safe. They needed to be there to assure the item could fit. There were so many things to so many businesses that would always need a human eye. Dad had tried to cut corners to justify lowering new hires' pay.

It didn't work.

"This technology will save people and make their lives easier, but it shouldn't come at a cost of jobs. Not when people have to support themselves or their families."

I wanted to glance over at him, every fiber of my being begging me to let my eyes drift to that handsome face. His soft lips spoke such considerate works. It made me all the more attracted to him.

It was unfair.

But I kept my eyes straight ahead.

"That's noble of you."

"It isn't noble to do the right thing."

I knew Dad wouldn't do the right thing either. It would be a tough sell to make him not fire drivers if PATH was in his trucks.

I wondered if his own tried-and-true method had been used against him. If I had a pen and paper, I could dream up something that not even he could refuse. Before I could think too hard on it, I pushed it out of my mind. I didn't need to be thinking of my family when our next scheduled dinner loomed over me like a storm cloud.

"Out of curiosity," I started, eager to change subjects, "what's our destination?"

"My place." He said it as if it were obvious. "Unless you want to go somewhere else."

My throat was dry just thinking about it, but I still wanted to go. He'd seen me at my worst, and I knew next to nothing about him. Seeing where he lived was a decent start.

I imagined that he lived in an upscale penthouse in downtown. I could picture him looking over the city skyline. I bet it had a lot of windows for his plants.

"We can go there," I said. "But I'll need to get my car."

"I can drop you there in the morning."

In the morning?

He'd assumed I was staying the night, but what was even more concerning was that he had guessed exactly right.

The drive was easy. Every now and again, the car would put control to me if it didn't have a good view of the road. He would look up and at the screen, noting each time it did it.

"Okay," I said as we finally entered Nashville. "You've been working in a moving vehicle for three hours now. You need a break."

"I'm fine," he said.

"You should save your work at least."

"Okay, fine." He pressed a few buttons.

I then shut his laptop.

"Now you're done."

"Wha—"

"Take a break," I urged. "You can work later, but you need to look at something else."

He glared over at me, but I could see from a quick glance that his eyes were red. Then the three hours of staring at the screen seemed to hit him.

"Maybe I do need a break," he said, rubbing at his face. "Thank you."

"You're one of those people who works until they pass out, aren't you?"

"Of course. You called me a robot for a reason."

"Unfortunately, you're not a robot. You're a human, and you have needs. So, look at some nature for a bit."

"Fine," he said. "We only have twenty minutes until we arrive anyway."

I couldn't bring myself to regret making him stop. I wondered how many nights he'd stayed awake far too late, or skipping sleep altogether, to focus on work.

It was easy to picture a life where I would come grab his hands and drag him to bed with me. There were many things that were too easy to picture with him.

My thoughts were on that idea until we pulled into a quaint two-story house with a wraparound porch covered in potted plants.

"Are we in the right place?" I asked.

"Yep. This is it."

"This is . . . not what I pictured." My eyes slowly dragged over the brick exterior. It was nice, and probably cost a lot in the city, but I expected something flashier.

"I don't need the nicest of things. I wanted something with a lot of windows. Come on." We grabbed our luggage from the car, and he put a hand on my back as he led me inside.

The lights flipped on automatically and I was greeted with a modern open floor plan. And plants.

A lot of plants.

"It's a jungle in here," I said. They were on every surface and sitting in every window. The air smelled fresh. It took me a moment to see past them and notice the inviting blue on the walls, and the warm-toned hardwoods.

"I need to water some of them." He walked into the kitchen and I followed, watching him with fascination as he watered whichever ones he needed with intense focus.

His kitchen was larger than any I'd seen. It was all state-of-the-art and pristine, like it had never been used. The kitchen in my apartment was tiny compared to this, and the very few times I'd attempted to cook, I found myself immediately cramped.

"Sorry," he said. "I know it's a lot."

"It's what you like, so it's never a lot. They're beautiful."

"My parents want to stage an intervention, but I think they're happy I'm doing something that's not work."

"The office could use some of this."

"The office could use a lot of things."

I nodded, letting my eyes drift to each plant. Maybe I needed more greenery in my life too. The different patterns of the leaves were calming in a way I didn't expect.

This was a place I could spread out.

Knox cleared his throat. "Want a tour?"

I gave him an eager smile.

He showed me the upstairs, which held a quiet office and guest room. Each room housed more plants, and he made sure to tell me what each kind was.

We made our way back downstairs, ending up in his bedroom.

I caught a glimpse of a neatly made bed, two nightstands, and a dresser against the wall. There were more plants sitting near the two windows in the room.

I gulped as an unwelcome thought crossed my mind. "Have you had the time to bring . . . you know, a *night guest* here?"

"With my work schedule?" he asked with a grin. "It's only you, Ruth."

"Seems like a waste. A house like this that's well-kept? Anyone would kill for the chance to be in my shoes."

"You know I don't want anyone else."

"What about when I was bothering you? You can't have wanted me then."

He walked close to me, enveloping me in the scent I was quickly becoming accustomed to. He reached a hand up and traced my temple.

"These eyes, full of so much fire, are the only ones I ever want to look into." His hand moved down to my lips. "Your lips are the place I want to call home."

"Isn't that from a Taylor Swift song?"

His hand covered my mouth.

"I have a feeling you're making a joke because you're still somehow not seeing how beautiful you are."

I'd been read like a book.

He spoke to me in a whisper. "I didn't even let myself dream of this moment." Knox's hand trailed down to my shirt. "Not even as a teenager. I never thought this would happen." He looked up at me, gripping the hem of the fabric. "Can I take this off?"

"Y-yes."

"Are you sure?" he asked again. "I am not interested in doing anything you don't want me to."

"I want this. I'm just nervous."

"You have nothing to be nervous about. You're beautiful, Ruth. Every inch of you."

Knox gently lifted the fabric over my head and I felt the cool air hit my belly and my chest. I had to fight the urge to ask him to turn off the lights. I didn't want to be seen.

But I also refused to look away from him. I wanted to see if his eyes would narrow in judgment. If they did, I could push him away before he could even dare to make a comment about me going to the gym.

"Jesus *fucking* Christ. I think I'm dreaming."

"You don't have to play it up."

"I'm not," he said. "Your skin is as beautiful as the rest of you." He leaned down, kissing my neck and down my chest. My skin burned from his lip's touch. "These are even better with fewer layers." He cupped my breasts, and my nipples begged for more friction. The thin padding of my bra was only in the way.

"You can take it off," I said, but my voice didn't sound like my own. It was too breathy to be me.

In a single, impressive motion, he unhooked my bra. With one more motion, it was across the room.

His mouth covered my nipple, teasing it with his tongue. My knees grew weak, and he let go only for a second to guide us onto his bed. The second we were lying down, his mouth was back to torturing me in the best way.

"You are perfect, Ruth," he said when he let go.

"The flab on my stomach disagrees with you."

"I don't fucking care about that. I like every single part of you. I like how you're yourself even if you're nervous. I like how your hips look in those skirts, and how you move when you wear those damn heels."

My heart was going to give out at this rate, especially when his mouth moved back to my skin. He kissed his way down my body, stopping when he got to where my skirt sat on my hips. "Can I take this off?"

"I give you express permission to do whatever you want to me," I said. I trusted him, possibly more than I'd trusted anyone else. One stormy night could change a person.

His lips curled into a grin. "You might regret that."

I somehow doubted I would. Despite him only having his mouth on a few parts of me, this was the most sensual experience of my entire life.

He slid off my skirt, only leaving me in my underwear. The cool air did nothing to tame the heat growing inside.

"I knew it. Every single part of you is perfect."

When he said it in that husky tone of his, I started to believe him. He made his way back up my body. When his mouth finally slotted over mine, I leaned into it, desperate to touch him in the way he touched me.

One of his hands trailed back down and stopped on my hip, right where my underwear rested.

"Now tell me," he said, pulling away from my lips to whisper in my ear. "How do I make you come?"

What a loaded question. "I won't."

"Excuse me?" He pulled away, eyes narrowed.

"I don't . . . come with other people. I never have."

"Then what do you do when you're by yourself?"

"I'm not talking to you about masturbation."

"I want to do what you *like*. So tell me what it is."

Fuck. "I like . . . I like the vibrator I have in my suitcase."

His lip curled into another smile. "You took it to Atlanta."

"I *thought* I would have a room to myself. It's fine, though. I know how men are about vibrators, so don't worry about it. I'll still enjoy it even if I don't come."

"I'll go get it,"

"What? Why?"

"Because I am making you come, and I'll use every tool in my arsenal to do it."

I stared at him. I'd never told a man I even *had* a vibrator, much less had him use one on me. I couldn't imagine why they ever would. What would they get out of it?

When he rolled my suitcase into the room, I sat up, biting my lip.

"You don't have to do this."

"I know I don't," he said. "But I want to. Where is it?"

"Tucked in the front pocket," I muttered. When he grabbed it, shame colored my cheeks. It was a small, simple thing that I often used when alone. It provided a feeling that no partner had managed to create, but I often heard women on social media say to 'detox' from these things, which made me feel like I was broken somehow.

"How do you use it?" he asked, lying back down next to me.

"Well, there's a button—"

"I know how to turn it on. I meant what do you *like* to do with it?"

I was never going to live this down. "I . . . I usually move it up and down."

"Show me, Ruth." His words ghosted over my ear.

My hands shook as I guided his hand. I had serious doubts this would work, but he seemed so determined. His lips latched to my neck as he moved my underwear aside and pressed it against my center.

I gasped, the contact shooting up me in ways I didn't expect. Knox's mouth closed over my lips, and his tongue dipped in to touch mine.

It took time for my body to get used to someone else making the moves. Every now and again, I paused, telling him to move in a different way, or to adjust his grip. He did so without complaint.

Eventually, the familiarity of the vibrator I always used, coupled with his scent and mouth, quieted my doubts about what my body could do. I lost myself to the feel of the pulsing of the vibrator, as well as the taste of Knox's tongue.

I didn't even realize I was building to something, but I gasped, pulling away from the kiss.

"Oh my God, I'm gonna—"

"Move how you need."

I jerked my hips, all embarrassment gone as I chased the orgasm I usually never got. When my body finally shattered, it was mind-altering. A broken moan escaped me as my head fell back against his bed.

I moved his hand away gently as pleasure turned to sensitivity. "I can't believe I . . . That took a while. You must be—"

"I enjoyed every fucking second, Ruth."

"Fuck me," I groaned, body lost in a state of post-orgasm haze.

"I would love to, but only if you want me to."

I was hit with a new desire, one to make him feel just as good as I had. I slid off my underwear and moved my hands under his shirt.

"What are you doing?"

"Getting you as naked as I am."

As I took off his layers, my eyes trailed over his skin, taking in his toned chest. But then my eyes were drawn to his cock springing free from his underwear. I'd never been *this* excited about sex. While it always felt good, it wasn't something I wanted all the time.

"Do you have a condom?"

He nodded, reaching into his nightstand. When it was rolled onto him, I straddled him, bringing him to my center.

"Fuck," he groaned. "You somehow look even better on top of me."

"You look pretty good under me."

The tip of him pressed against my entrance. I took a deep breath, preparing for the pain this often caused. Usually, people didn't take their time with preparation.

"Go slow," he murmured, hands on my hips. "I don't want this to hurt."

"I know you have to be ready for this by now. You've been so patient."

"And I will continue to be. I only enjoy it if you do."

I nodded, slowly moving my hips down. The tip of his cock pressed in, but I was wetter than I'd ever been. I could feel myself stretching around him. I moved down, taking him in inch by inch until he was fully inside me.

"Ruth," he said, his voice choked. "Are you okay?"

"I'm fine," I said, leaning over him. "I promise."

"Then I'm going to fuck you now. And I don't think I can hold back anymore."

I nodded, and that was when he jerked his hips, pushing even deeper into me. He thrust quickly, bouncing me on top of him in a rhythm I didn't think possible.

And it felt *amazing*. My breaths were hasty and I desperately found myself wishing I could come again.

That was when I felt the vibrator move in between us. Knox had paused in his movements, grabbing the very thing I was needing. There was a moment where I knew I wanted this to last forever. I wanted to be here with the man who thought of me, giving me what I needed before I realized it, forever.

Then Knox moved again, and I felt the vibrator moving between us as well. It felt incredible, and my body, usually done after one orgasm, found a way to do it again, sending pleasure to the tips of my toes.

I cried out his name and one hand gripped my hip like a vice as he thrust in one last time.

My body was exhausted after *two* orgasms in one night, and I slumped over him.

"That was . . ." He trailed off.

"You better not say bad."

"Absolutely not, Ruth. I was going to say that was the best thing I'd ever had. But we're not done yet."

"What do you mean?"

"Because after we clean up, I believe I owe you a foot rub."

Knox

As Ruth slept next to me, my mind refused to let me drift off.

This always happened when I had an idea. Back in college, when I'd dreamed up the plan for the PATH system, I was up for nearly twenty-four hours straight. This could easily be one of those nights.

I didn't want to let her go, but I had too many ideas. I slowly rolled away from her and grabbed my iPad. I was up for hours, drawing out what I needed. When I was done, it was early in the morning, and my hand ached.

But I had a plan.

My first move was to call Preston.

"This better be good," he muttered when he answered. There was shuffling, and a man's voice in the background.

"Are you busy at three in the morning?"

"A man has needs."

"Oh, it's *that* kind of busy."

"Shut up." Preston sounded annoyed, as he always did when he was interrupted at night.

"Do you have a minute? I'm sending you something I want PATH to work on."

"Is this like the safety tech thing?"

"No, it's not that. This has nothing to do with cars."

"Then what is it?"

"I'm sending you the schematics right now."

He paused for a moment. "Are these . . . headphones?"

"Yes."

"This is a totally new market."

"I'm also sending off the quick plan I typed up. This is what I want to code them to be able to do."

There was silence, and then, "Damn it, Knox. This is good."

"Can you make a prototype?"

"You'll have to be available to the R&D team for questions. More so than you have been." I'd finally found another invention I was passionate about. While I loved the safety tech, this was a new level of interest.

"I can do that."

"We'll get working on it. Can I ask one question?"

"Sure."

"Where did you get this idea?"

I glanced in the direction of my bedroom, where the very inspiration slept.

"It came to me in a dream."

"Must have been some dream," Preston said. "How late are you going to be working on this?"

I glanced back at the bedroom, my arms already missing the feel of her in them. "A few hours. Then I'll get some sleep."

"You? Sleeping?"

"My bed is very comfortable."

Especially with Ruth in it.

CHAPTER EIGHTEEN

Ruth

"So, is there anything you want to tell me?" Jenny's voice was accusing.

I hadn't even had my second cup of office-brewed coffee yet. Admittedly, it wasn't as good as Knox's that he'd made for me before I left his house. He'd even bought my favorite creamer.

I'd stayed both Saturday night and the next day. I never once wanted to go back to my cold and empty apartment.

"About what?"

"About the fact that the company only got billed for *one* hotel room?"

Oh *fuck*. I forgot she was responsible for overseeing the company credit cards since she was assigned with ordering all of the executives' food.

"There was an issue with the rooms," I said.

"I figured. I also figured I should document that it was a double queen room, despite the fact that the receipt they emailed me definitely said it was not."

"Thank you," I said, my voice low.

"How was it?"

"Knox? He was great. The weather was terrible."

"I'm sorry, Knox was *great*? You've got to give me more than that."

My mind flashed to the way he held me. He was more than *great*. He was the man of my dreams.

"It was a very eye-opening night," I said. "That's all I can say in this office."

"Oh, yes!" Jenny said. "Finally, some good news after all the drama with your parents."

My shoulders slumped at the reminder of the boundary I'd set with them. "The weekly dinner is tonight."

"You've got this," she said. "You're a badass."

"Thank you. This shouldn't be too bad. I've only told them I don't want to talk about Knox."

"Maybe they'll do the right thing."

I thought of my conversation with Tom and Barry. None of us had high hopes. At least Jenny was trying to be positive. Someone needed to be.

"Maybe," I said. "Mind if I head off to answer some emails?"

"Not at all. I have to order lunch for Dave again anyway." She pretended to gag before she walked out of my office.

My inbox was probably overflowing with things I needed to look at, but I had no energy to look at them. I wanted to be in that bed in Atlanta, or tucked away in the comfort of Knox's house.

Shaking it off, I was determined to focus. He had dropped me off at my apartment early so I could get my car and change. It was before I usually got up, but he'd seemed more tired than I was. My bet was that he was sneaking away during the night for work. He was always back in the morning, but I knew what a workaholic would do to get in extra hours.

One of these days, I'd set some sort of trap to catch him in the act of leaving bed. Then it would be easier to drag him back into it.

I was pondering that idea as I forced myself to open my email, but the thought was immediately squashed by the first entry in my inbox.

Dave had sent me an interview time for the VP position, and it was scheduled for ten a.m.

And that was less than two hours away.

I cursed. The lack of time meant lack of preparation. Lack of preparation was not my strong suit.

I waited for my usual fire to make its way into me and force me to work. My own determination and refusal to fail was the perfect motivator.

But now? Now it failed me.

I ran my hand over my forehead, wondering why I cared so little. Sure, this was only because of my friendship with Knox, but it was still a promotion—a huge one.

But it was one I had to beg for.

It was no different than how I got this job. I'd begged for it too. And yet back then, I'd cared.

Now, I wondered if it would be worth it. I was already doing half the job, but I didn't feel invigorated by all the questions and issues that made their way to my inbox. Usually, I loved helping people. I loved being able to solve problems and prove I was the best.

But none of it mattered until I was known as Knox's friend.

I groaned as I grabbed my headphones from my purse. If focus wouldn't come to me, then I would force it. Maybe I was feeling off from the issues with my parents and from the storm two nights before. That had to be all this was.

I focused on preparing myself the best I could for the interview.

Just before ten, I felt marginally better about my chances of landing the promotion. I had concrete data of what I'd done. I had my employees' work survey scores—which all praised me—and I had an in with Knox.

Yet, I still felt a dread I couldn't understand. This was what I *wanted*. Just a few weeks ago, I would have been dying for this job.

And I had to force myself to go to the interview.

I shook it off, determined that it was only a fluke because of how my weekend had been. I'd feel much better once this was over and I was promoted.

Then, my phone buzzed with a text.

Mom: Reminder of dinner tonight. Come prepared to discuss work updates.

I felt a hint of relief. The dinner was about *work*. Not Knox. That gave me the tiniest bit of hope for what would come.

And that propelled me to go to my interview.

To: Knox Price
  From: Ruth Murray
  Subject: Availability

> *Are you in meetings ALL day today? Are you on some kind*
> *of project?*

  Worriedly, Ruth

  To: Ruth Murray
  From: Knox Price
  Subject: Availability

Yes, I am. It's definitely kept my attention. I'm sorry I've been so busy. We can meet over dinner if you want to catch up, especially since you had an interview today for the VP position.

Sincerely, Knox

To: Knox Price
From: Ruth Murray

I can't tonight. Family dinner, but we DO need to catch up. Same place as this weekend?

To: Ruth Murray
From: Knox Price

Of course. I'll see you there.

Excitedly, Knox

⚓

It had been a long day. My interview went remarkably well for how little time I had to prepare for it. Dave and Charles half listened, but the resigned, job-specific questions at the end told me they were considering me.

And while I was happy to have shown them exactly what I could do, there was no pride in my interview, no excitement for the promotion, or for the family dinner where I could tell everyone about it, even after Mom's reminder text.

The only thing that felt right was Knox, but I'd barely seen him all day. I didn't know what the hell Dave had him working on, but he'd been locked in his office with whatever it was.

As the day progressed, however, I was a little glad he was busy. My nerves had been getting worse, and I knew he'd read me like a book if he saw me in person. I had no doubt that he would have insisted he come to the dinner. While I loved his dedication to helping me out, my parents would never let me live it down.

As I pulled into my parents' driveway, my hands shook. I didn't have a good feeling about this dinner.

"Ruth," Mom said as she opened the front door. "Good to see you."

"You too," I replied, but I could feel my stomach tighten with defensiveness. I was reminded of the boundary I set.

"And how is Knox?" Her eyebrows raised expectantly.

"We aren't talking about him."

Her lips thinned, but she turned on her heel and walked away. My heart raced as I followed her in.

So far so good.

Barry was at the table. He looked as miserable as he usually did.

"Hey, Ruth," he said. "Ready for dinner?"

"No." I lowered my voice. "Do you wanna fake being sick and get out of here?"

"No," he said. "I'm fine with seeing this through. I can't let you hold your ground on your own."

Damn. He may have turned into a grump, but at least he was still kind. I had the urge to hug him, but my brothers and I hadn't hugged since the tornado.

"Where's Tom?"

"Talking business with Dad. Apparently, their four billion in revenue wasn't enough. They *still* are pushing to expand."

"Let me guess, Dad is saying lay out their problem and leave them begging for the solution." I mimicked his deep voice.

"The only thing people are begging for is a new company logo."

I snickered. "It's so bad. It looks like a penis, doesn't it?"

Barry chuckled, hiding his smile behind his hand. He'd always said that, but back when I was dying to be at Murray and Sons, I would stop him.

"Glad to see you've joined the dark side." He fist-bumped me.

Mom brought out the food, none of which looked prepared by her. I remembered when she used to bake us banana bread cake. It was the greatest thing I'd ever tasted.

Tom and Dad came into the room, and I caught the annoyed expression on my older brother's face. Had we always been this miserable?

"We'll figure this out," Dad said to Tom. "Someone will have to break somewhere. I need revenue up by twenty percent."

"Is Murray and Sons in danger of financial collapse or something?" I asked against my better judgment.

"Don't worry about it, Ruth." Dad's dismissal made me grit my teeth.

"Things are fine," Tom replied. His voice was low, and his frown told me he'd not had a good day.

"If we don't increase revenue, our only option is to cut benefits. The first thing to go is that stupid parental leave policy. I can't believe I let you talk me into it, Tom."

"Parental leave is a great thing, Dad," I countered. "Most companies that offer it have happier employees."

"I assume you care because you're having kids soon, then?" Dad asked as he sat at the table.

"Why would I be having kids right now? I'm not even married."

"That's not what I heard."

"We're not talking about Knox," I reminded, my voice flat.

"And *that* is why you're unmarried." Dad shook his head. "That attitude of yours."

"Unmarried? Since when do you care about my marital status?"

"Since you crossed over twenty-eight with no prospects in sight."

"Todd," my mother said lowly. "We agreed not to talk about this."

"She's almost thirty!"

"What are you saying?" Barry hissed, his eyebrows pulled low on his forehead. Any humor was gone from his face.

"I'm saying that your sister is nearly too old to have kids. She should be worried about that."

"I have more to worry about than children, Dad," I insisted.

He scoffed. "Not in my books."

"Todd," my mother pleaded, "we agreed to let her try to have a career."

"And what has she made of herself? She's refusing to talk about the one man who can make her into something, and she's a menial director of a shitty banking company."

"Oh, now you're bringing up my place of work? You didn't even know where I worked until recently."

"I don't care to." His voice was sharp. He turned his attention to dinner, evidently done with the conversation.

I was not.

"Why not? You wanted me to be successful."

He laughed humorlessly. "Your mother was the one who cared. I thought you'd get the hint when your application to Murray and Sons was thrown out the moment you applied."

"You knew I applied?"

"Of course. But it's Murray and *Sons*, Ruth. You're not a part of this. You never were."

"So, it was my gender?" I asked, standing as rage shot down my spine. "You turned me down because I'm a woman?"

"She deserved the same treatment as the boys," Mom said.

"No, she doesn't!" he snapped. "You wanted to name her after that stupid Supreme Court Justice because *you* thought she was equal to the boys. And now she's got it in her head that she can tell *us* what we can and can't talk about in our own house!"

"I have the right to set a boundary," I added.

"These boundaries are why your generation is soft."

"Soft?" Barry asked. "We were raised by you to *never* be soft."

"You boys were, but she was excluded from it all. Her only use is supporting the men who are making money. Your mother begged for me to let her try at it herself, but she's done nothing but make excuses."

"I am doing my *best*."

"And it would never be good enough."

"Todd!" Mom snapped, standing up as well. "You said she had time. She could be like her brothers!"

"You should have taught her how to be a respectable woman! I never wanted her to be this man-hating, evil feminist! I've heard enough of you for one night. Sit *down*, woman."

Mom's lips pursed, but she did as she was told.

He turned to me. "You too, Ruth."

"Fuck you."

Dad slammed his hand down. "You will do as I say!"

I met his gaze head-on.

"Why should I? You're more of a failure than I am. I believe you were a director at thirty, Dad. You didn't become a CEO until grandpa died and handed you the company. You didn't do shit to get where you are. Everything was handed to you."

His fists clenched and he screamed, "I will not tolerate this from you!"

Mom flinched away. I wondered how often this had been used on her.

"What are you going to do?" I asked. "You gonna scream? Slam things around? I'm not scared of you."

"And if you touch her," Barry added, "you'll have me to answer to."

"You two are the biggest disappointments in this family."

"Fuck this," I said. "I'm leaving."

"Excuse me?" he bellowed. "Ruth Murray, you do not get to leave—"

"I don't know if you know this," I said, spinning around, "but I'm a grown-ass woman. I don't listen to people like you."

I stormed out, completely forgetting about my brothers. As I got to the car, I considered going back to help them, but I couldn't make myself turn around.

There was a cascade of guilt.

God, what if all I was good for was homemaking? I had to fight my way through every wall at my job. My boss never respected me, and I was only a director at twenty-eight.

But then I shook it off. *No.* If there was one thing I was, it was stubborn. I wasn't going to let them see me upset. I'd cry about this in my apartment alone.

I never imagined I would know why Dad turned me down; I had assumed it was because I didn't have the required experience for the position and he was trying not to play favorites, but the real reason was far worse than I could have ever thought. On the drive home, I relived my childhood, thinking back to what was said to me by my parents.

I remembered Mom telling me to get my grades up, to be the best.

I remembered Dad saying it to my *brothers*, never me.

Fuck. It was obvious. He always saw me as inferior.

I pulled into my apartment complex, the full wave of my emotions hitting me. I walked inside, tears brimming my vision, and I lost it the moment the door shut.

I sobbed into pillows and threw them. I cursed how empty this stupid place felt, and how empty my life was because I had given up everything for Dad, who never saw me as anything other than a girl whose only possible contribution to society would be having children.

My anger had been replaced with pure, heavy sadness, a sadness I couldn't bear alone.

And the first person I called was Knox.

Knox

When I walked into my parents' house, it smelled deceptively good. Usually, when Mom cooked, it smelled more . . . *burnt*.

"Knox!" she called, coming around the corner with a smile. She pulled me into a warm hug, and I knew I was home. They'd called me over after I'd been locked in my office for more than eight hours. I knew Ruth was wondering what the hell I was doing, but I was busy with the PATH R&D team, working on the first prototype for the headphones.

I hated that I didn't get to talk to her, but at least we'd emailed. While she was busy with her parents, I decided to spend some time with my own.

"I'm making lasagna again," Mom said, pulling away.

"She's trying to, anyway." Dad walked up to greet me. He was freshly showered after a long day of work. "It's a new recipe."

In my mind, I was already making an order to an Italian place.

"You look good, kid," he said.

"You really do," Mom added. "How's Ruth?"

"Good." I left it at that.

"You're still seeing her, right? Not working too much to have a friend?"

My cheeks heated. "I didn't do my best today, but I'll make it up to her."

"I know how you are, Knox. You work far too much."

I wondered if she and Ruth would somehow gang up on me, forcing me to take a breather and live a little.

And they both were in Nashville—another thing making me want to stay.

"Don't lecture him too much, Lynn," Dad said. "Let him actually relax. Come sit with me. *Family Feud* is on."

I followed him to the living room while Mom returned to the kitchen. I sat on the old, well-loved couch, finally feeling my back loosen after a long day in my stiff office chair.

"Any ideas for takeout?" he muttered to me.

"We could always get a non-burnt lasagna," I replied, leaning deeply into the old cushions.

"It's *im-pasta-ble* for her to cook it right."

And there it was. The first pun of the evening.

"Okay!" she called. "There's only about an hour left." She sat on the couch beside me and smiled. "Oh, it's Steve Harvey. I love him."

I was able to listen to my parents with my full attention, something I'd struggled with until I'd returned to Nashville. There was so much here that was making things *better*.

Then my phone rang.

My first thought was that it was the R&D team with another question about the prototype. I'd told them all to go home and that we'd work on it more tomorrow, but several of them were just like me—difficult to pull away from a project in the middle of it.

I pulled out my phone, thinking of ways to politely tell them to fuck off, but I hesitated when I saw who it was.

Ruth.

I thought she was at dinner with her parents. Why was she calling me?

"I need to take this," I said as I stood. Was she at the house? Did she need me?

I stepped out onto the porch, feeling the hot summer air stick to my skin.

"Ruth?" I answered. "What's wrong?"

There was a pause. "I . . . I've had a bad night. Are you busy?"

"It doesn't matter. Is something wrong?"

"Y-yes." Her voice was thick and strained, as if she had been crying.

"What happened?"

"My dad and I got into a fight. A huge one."

"Did he hurt you?"

"Not physically. But it was bad. I-I don't think I can have a relationship with my parents anymore. Not after tonight."

"What did he say?"

"That he never cared about my success because I was born a girl."

"What the fuck?" I spat out. "What kind of 1950s bullshit is that?"

"It's his, I guess. I knew he was wrong, and I told him to go fuck himself, but it still hurt. I always thought if I proved myself, I could work at his company like Tom does. Guess that was never going to happen no matter what I achieved."

"Where are you?" If she was still at her parents', then I would have no problem going and telling her father exactly what I thought of his outdated views.

"At my apartment, but I don't want to be alone. Can I come to your house?"

"I'm at my parents' place."

"Oh, you're busy. Shit, I'm sorry for taking you away from—"

"You should come here."

"I don't want to intrude on family time."

"They won't mind." I knew Mom would fly off the handle if she heard even a hint of what Ruth's dad had said to her. She felt very strongly about emotional abuse from parents ever since she'd escaped from her own. It was the only thing she got angry about.

"But still—"

"You'll have fun. If you don't, I'll take you back to my place tonight."

"What if they hate me?" she asked quietly.

"They won't, and I highly doubt you won't like them. I'll text you their address. You don't need to be alone right now."

"Okay," she said. "Yeah, I'll come over then. But I'm a mess."

"Come as you are, not as who you think you should be."

"I think I can swing that. I'll be there soon."

After she hung up, I walked back into the living room, still fuming at what was said to her.

"Is everything okay?" Mom asked. "You look angry."

"My . . . friend had a bad night. Do you mind if she joins us?"

"She?" both of my parents asked at the same time.

I sighed, knowing my parents were going to have many questions, but it was worth it if Ruth wasn't sitting at her apartment alone, voice shaking like it had been on that call.

"Yes, she. It's Ruth."

"Oh my God! We finally get to meet her!"

"Does she like *Family Feud*?" Dad asked. "Oh, what else is there? *Jeopardy*?"

"I . . . I don't know," I replied. I wished I did.

In the twenty minutes it took Ruth to arrive, Dad had gotten out his pun book four times, and Mom had asked me a million questions about her. As they prepared for their surprise guest, I knew there was no way they wouldn't like her.

I walked outside to meet her, but stopped in place when I saw that her hair was down. She was wearing leggings and a T-shirt, which was the last thing I expected to see her in.

If this was her as a mess, I didn't care. I still found her stunning.

At the sight of me, she sighed. "Please tell me I don't look as bad as I feel."

Before I could answer, Mom ran out the front door. "Hi, honey!" she called. "It's so nice to meet you. Your hair is just *gorgeous*."

"Oh, thank you," Ruth replied, cheeks turning pink at the full force of a greeting from Mom. "I usually have it up."

"Why not show off something as beautiful as this? Now, everyone else Knox has brought home isn't exactly a huge fan of our house. So, if you want to go somewhere else, then let us know."

"Why would I judge anyone who's opening their home to me?" Ruth shook her head, then her eyes took in the outside of house. "Besides, there's nothing to judge. It's homey, just like a house should be."

Mom's head tilted, and I knew Ruth had made a fantastic first impression.

"I'm Lynn," she said instead of a hug. "Lynn Price. You should come inside and meet my husband."

She led Ruth inside.

I remembered Gia's expression when she walked in. Her eyes were wide and her lips narrowed as she tried to fake a smile.

Ruth's smile, however, was very real.

"Are these baby pictures?" she exclaimed, nearly running over to the wall.

"Of course," Mom said. "All of Knox. We tried for so long to have a baby that we didn't want to forget a moment once we had him."

"These are great." She turned to me. "You were a dorky-ass kid."

"I stand by it," I said, smiling over at her.

"It's too bad you didn't keep the glasses," she mused. "They were a good look on you."

"He got that fancy LASIK thing the moment he could, but he's going to ruin his eyes if he keeps working as much as he does." Mom crossed her arms and glared in my direction.

"She's one hundred percent right," Ruth added.

"Like you have room to talk," I interjected. "You work almost as much as I do."

"I have perfect vision, though. Always have." She stuck out her tongue at me.

Mom smiled widely at her, a smile I'd never seen directed at Gia.

"Benji!" she called. "Come meet this sweetheart in here."

Dad slowly got up and shuffled over.

"Nice to meet you," he said with a smile.

"Honey, we've met her before. She was at Knox's graduation."

"I don't call it a meeting unless I've shaken their hand." He held out his hand to her. "It is nice to see you again, Ruth. I heard you gave Knox a run from his money in high school."

"Did I?" she asked.

"He's never studied more."

"But now she tells me to stop working," I scoffed.

"I've matured."

"Well, welcome to our home," Dad continued. "What do you like? We can watch TV, play board games . . ."

"You don't have to change any of what you were doing because I'm here," she said. "I can be invisible."

"Where's the fun in that?" he asked. "We want to get to know you! Is that so bad?"

"I guess it's not," she replied, her voice quiet.

"Do you like puns and jokes?" A huge grin plastered itself across his face. "I have some good ones."

"Give me your best."

"What's the state flower?"

"I'm pretty sure it's the lilies . . . no wait, the iris?"

"It's a traffic cone. It pops up in the spring and disappears in the summer."

Ruth snickered, and then it turned into a full-on laugh that had her wiping at her eyes. "I needed that."

Dad's smile somehow got wider. This was the first person I'd brought home who actually laughed at his attempt at humor.

"That reminds me of one I heard in grade school. Have you heard that time flies like an arrow?" she asked. When he shook his head, she added, "But fruit flies like a banana."

Dad laughed so hard he almost fell over. "What about the two men who walked into a bar?"

"What about them?"

"They ended up in the ER. The third ducked."

Ruth laughed again, her face turning red.

"Are you happy, son?" Mom leaned into me. "Now there's two of them."

"I am."

Her smile was bright. "I can tell."

I was more than happy. Seeing Ruth smile made me remember that I no longer felt only my emotions, but hers too. Every laugh I mirrored, and when she cried, my eyes grew wet too.

I could see why Dad could never take it when Mom cried. A lot more things about their relationship made sense.

"Shoot," Mom said, running to the kitchen and pulling me out of my thoughts. "I forgot about the food."

Dad wiped at his eyes. "Takeout it is, then. How does pizza sound?"

The smell of burnt food hit my nose. "Way better than what Mom just burnt."

I opened my phone and started to pull up a menu.

"You have a great family," Ruth said after I'd placed the order. "I wish my dinner had gone half as well as this."

"They like you, you know."

"You think?"

"I haven't seen my dad laugh that hard in years."

"Is it bad that I sort of wish they were *my* family?"

"They could be."

She shook her head. "Nah, you're an only child. I'm sure you don't want to share them."

I wanted to share everything with her. I'd share every cent I'd earned, every invention I'd made, just to make sure she didn't feel like she had before she walked through these doors.

The idea should have been terrifying, but as I gazed into the smiling face of the most beautiful woman I'd ever seen, all I knew was that I would be hers until the day I died.

Chapter Nineteen

Ruth

I hadn't touched my phone in hours by the time I'd escaped Lynn Price's tight, warm hugs and gotten into my car. Knox had walked out with me, insisting that I go to his house rather than the silence of my apartment.

I was about to agree when I finally looked at my phone. All thoughts flew out the window when I saw I had a dozen messages. My eyes went wide as I scrolled through the countless texts from my brothers.

Tom: Sibling meeting. We're coming to your place, Ruth.

Tom: We've been here thirty minutes. Ruth, are you okay? This isn't like you.

Barry: Seriously. Now you even have ME worried.

Tom: I will hunt you down if you don't answer in ten minutes.

That was nine minutes ago. Shit.

I quickly texted back.

Ruth: I'm fine. We don't need a sibling meeting.

Tom: We, in fact, do. Where at you and why aren't you at your apartment?

"What's wrong?" Knox asked, walking over to stand close to me, as if he could protect me from whatever was on my phone.

I shook my head. "Nothing. My brothers are insisting we do a sibling meeting."

"If they're going to be like your father was, then don't go."

"They aren't. Well, at least Barry isn't. He was on my side at dinner."

"And your other brother?"

"Tom used to be just like my dad, but he's changed since he stopped drinking."

"Has he changed enough to not hurt you tonight?"

"I hope so."

"I'm going with you."

"You don't have to do this," I reminded him.

He smiled. "Because I will do anything I can for you."

"And why's that?"

"Because I *want* to."

When I saw Tom's old truck and Barry's newer car in my apartment's parking lot, my nerves grew. While I knew neither of them weren't on my side, I was worried that any sign of either of them defending Dad might make me lose it again.

And I refused to cry in front of my brothers.

"Are you okay?" Knox asked as he got out of his car.

"This might get messy," I said, taking a deep breath. "I apologize in advance for what you're about to see."

Knox looked at me before he grabbed my hand. "It's going to be okay."

When we walked in, my empty apartment was silent. If I couldn't see my brothers folded onto the couch in the living room, I wouldn't have even noticed they were there.

"I'm back," I said, and they turned. Their eyes landed on Knox.

"I still have . . . a lot of questions," Barry said.

"You can ask *one*." My heart raced at whatever thing Barry would pick.

"Does he know what happened tonight?"

"Yeah."

"It's bullshit," Knox added, crossing his arms.

"Wonderful," Barry muttered. "Now that's *two* celebrities who know our drama."

"Who's the other one?"

"Still can't say," Barry said. "One more question, then I promise I'm done. Are you two a . . . thing now?"

"Not publicly, considering he's my boss."

Tom blew out a breath. "That's a massive HR violation."

"Fuck HR. People are people," Barry said. "If she's happy, I'm happy."

"I'm happy too," Tom grumbled.

"Are you? I believe I heard you slam your hunk of junk's door ten times."

"It's an old truck. I have to slam it a few times to get the door to shut properly."

"What's the sibling meeting about?" I interrupted, not wanting to see Tom and Barry slip into a fight.

"We need to talk about what happened with Dad." Tom glanced over at Barry.

"I'm not apologizing for what I did," Barry said, crossing his arms.

"What did he do?"

"He punched Dad in the face when he tried to follow you."

"What?"

"Nice," Knox remarked.

"No, no," I snapped, glaring at them both. "Not nice. Why?"

"He said he wanted to knock some sense into you. So, I decided to do it to him first."

"He said *what*?" All the mirth was gone from Knox's voice.

"I regret bringing Knox now," I muttered. "But Barry, was punching him the best option?"

"It's what he deserved."

"He could press charges."

Tom shook his head. "He won't. He's going to be tied up with something else very soon."

"I don't think there is enough revenue in the world to make Dad not go after Barry," I said.

"It's not revenue," Tom replied. "It's a lawsuit that's making him take a leave of absence as CEO. I left the papers HR drafted on his desk tonight."

"You *what*?" Barry and I asked simultaneously.

"I like you, Tom," Knox added.

Barry stood. "What did he do to get put on leave?"

"He sexually harassed multiple women. I found the emails when digging in our archive system."

Barry and I could only stare.

"*You* found this? You went looking for it?" Barry's voice was quiet.

"I did. Ever since I stopped drinking and doing whatever he says, I've seen him do very illegal things. This is why I wanted us to wait a week. I needed to get everything together."

"Oh my God. You played a double agent." For the first time in my adult life, I felt like the little sister being tucked under her big brother's protective wings.

"He's not going to take this lying down," Tom said. "He has access to the greatest lawyers. I have a feeling he will find a way around it."

"So do I," Knox piped in. "I've made connections since I started PATH. Tell me what you need, and I'll find it."

Tom met Knox's eyes and nodded, a rare smile on his face.

"Mom is going to be pissed," I muttered.

"I don't know," Barry said. "She wasn't too happy about how Dad talked to you tonight."

I bit my lip, happy that in some way, our mom had tried to stand up for me for once.

"It doesn't change that she allowed it to get this far," Knox said. "For all three of you."

"I know," I said, sighing. "But I at least had hope that she could be even a tiny bit better."

Barry shook his head. Tom shrugged and said, "Dad has her exactly how he wants her, though."

"What if we never talk to her again? What if she's always on Dad's side?" I asked, feeling a weight on my chest.

"My mom had to cut off my grandfather for a similar reason." Knox's voice was soft.

"What?"

"He wasn't happy she married an electrician. She tried to make it work, but he never budged. She had to stop bending to try to be what he wanted."

"And if our mom does the same thing," Barry added, "then it's her choice."

I looked at my feet, thinking about the version of our mother that cared, the woman who baked for us on our birthdays, who cuddled up to us to read books at night, and tended to our wounds when we fell. I could only hope she hadn't been stamped out of existence entirely.

"So, I guess it goes without saying," Barry said quietly. "No more family dinners."

"No more of a lot of things."

Knox

As Ruth and her siblings realized the weight of what their parents had done to them, I stepped into the kitchen to get her something to drink.

And to take a breath.

I couldn't stand seeing her in pain. Even the slightest frown made me want to pull her to me and protect her from whatever may hurt her. It wasn't just an emotion, it was a compulsion.

"Mr. Price," a voice said. I turned to see Tom had walked into the kitchen with me. He spoke lowly, as if he didn't want Ruth to hear him.

"Call me Knox," I said. "Unless you piss me off."

"The goal isn't to. I just wanted to say that . . . I think you're good for my sister."

I raised an eyebrow. "Aren't you supposed to give me the shovel talk?"

He shook his head. "Ruth can fend for herself. I can tell she's comfortable with you. It takes a lot for her to be that way with anyone."

"I care about her."

He nodded. "She needs that." He glanced over his shoulder. "I've been a terrible brother to both of them. The weight of our father's expectations dragged me down, and they'll probably never trust me because I seemed too close to him."

"You never know."

"I do, though. Ruth holds grudges, and Barry . . . well, Barry does too. He's more like us than he likes to admit. But this isn't your problem to solve. I just . . . just take care of her, okay?"

I stared at him. His teeth were clenched, but I wondered if it was out of anger or if he was feeling an emotion he didn't want to feel.

"I was serious about my offer to help keep your father out of power, by the way." I grabbed a glass, filled it with water, and set it in front of him. "And not just for Ruth. I'm beginning to see that all of you need a friend."

"I don't want to take up your time with a problem that isn't yours."

"You're not taking my time. I'm offering it. Let's swap numbers. I'll help keep your asshole of a father away from the company."

He nodded, pulling out his phone to hand to me.

As I typed my number into his contacts, I added, "Also, I saw your truck when you pulled in. It's a classic."

"It's the first thing I bought. It's a death trap, but I can't bear to get rid of it."

"I'm working on something to add safety equipment to older cars. I could use someone to test it."

"I want to keep it original."

"It's an airbag mechanism. It only sits over the steering wheel column. It won't damage the car."

His lips twisted in thought. "I'll think about it, but I can't make any promises. I've been the only one who works on that car."

As many people do. I smiled and held out my hand. "That's fine. I'd be happy to only work with you on ruining your father's life."

One corner of his lip turned, and his hand met mine. "Now that I can agree to today."

I gave him one more nod, and then brought out another glass of water for Ruth. She was finally sitting on the couch. She took the drink from me and smiled.

"So," she started, smile dropping as she looked between her brothers. "Do I need to remind everyone that if you tell a single soul about me and Knox I will kill you?"

"I can keep a secret," Barry said. "After all, I've had Lila Wilde in my bar and no one's known."

At the name of the international pop singer, Ruth choked on her water. "Really? At your bar?"

"Yep."

Lila Wilde was a big name, even for me. Her writing prowess was second only to her dance moves on stage. She had the record for longest held note while dancing to her songs. She had a level of fame I could never want.

"But you guys can't tell anyone," he said.

We all nodded.

"Okay, so I trust Barry," Ruth said. "Tom? You're not going to rat me out, right?"

"I won't. I'll be too busy keeping Dad out of the company."

"So, we're good then." She let out a sigh of relief. "Sibling meeting over?"

"Yeah," Barry said, looking at the door. "I guess it is."

They said their sullen goodbyes before leaving. Ruth had walked them out and leaned her head against the door once it was shut.

I took a moment to text Tom my lawyer's contact information before I went to her.

"Are you okay?"

"I'm exhausted," she said, but she turned to face me. "Thank you for coming here with me, though."

"It's no problem. They weren't what I expected."

"They used to be different when we were kids. I guess my parents took their toll."

"For everything you guys have been through, I think it's remarkable that you guys can even stand to be in the same room together."

"It doesn't feel remarkable," she muttered. "I hate that every conversation is like the start of a fight."

"Give them some time. That's all you can do."

"I know." Her eyes met mine. "Can we get out of here now? Being in this apartment just makes me sad."

"Of course," I said, kissing her forehead.

Her smile finally returned after we walked into my house. We crawled into bed to watch a movie, and her head hit my shoulder within the first ten minutes. By the half-hour mark, she was sound asleep, curled into me.

I gazed at her sleeping profile, hair strewn about on the pillow, face half-tucked under the comforter, and she was relaxed for the first time that evening. I knew I couldn't let her go; I wanted this for a very long time, and now that I had it, almost nothing could keep me away.

I loved PATH, but I cared about her just as much. If she asked me to stay, I would. I'd be happy living out the rest of my life with her in my arms instead of my constant inventions in my hands.

CHAPTER TWENTY

Ruth

To Knox Price:

From: Ruth Murray

Subject: *eyes emoji*

> *Please find the link included in this email to a rare monstera*
> *plan. It might pique your interest.*

Seedsofthought.com/albinomonsteraRARE

Sincerely, Ruth Murray

To: Ruth Murray

From: Knox Price

*Subject: *eyes emoji**

I am out of floor space and do not need this.

(I ordered two.)

With no regrets, Knox Price

To: Knox Price
From: Ruth Murray

Happy to help.

ALSO with no regrets, Ruth

My family imploded once Dad was put on leave for harassment. Tom had been at the Murray and Sons office nonstop. Mom endlessly called Barry and me to see if we had anything to do with the turn of events, and I tried my best to keep my head down and let Tom handle it. Knox had already employed his own lawyers to keep Dad out of the office and told me to leave it to them to prove his guilt.

And he was doing a great job at that. He'd tried to enter the Murray and Sons corporate office three times, and yelled obscenities at anyone who stopped him. It wasn't a good look, yet his status as CEO on leave still stood. Knox told me it would take time to have him fully removed, but I wondered if he was using his connections to keep himself on board.

I tried to focus on work, but my personal life was hard to ignore. Often, I found myself itching to check in on Tom and see how he was weathering the latest events.

The more chaotic things became, the more time I wanted to spend with Knox. He was my storm cellar and being near him calmed my anxieties, even if our nights were me pacing back and forth telling him more and more about my past.

I hadn't told him his unintended role in it yet. One of these days, I would get around to that, but reliving how much I'd been compared to him, even to tell him, was not something I was ready to face.

All of this meant work was not on my mind. I'd completely forgotten about the VP job I had so desperately wanted for the last six months.

I was shocked when HR called to offer me the position.

What was worse was that I didn't even feel one ounce of pride. I accepted out of instinct, but I didn't feel great once I hung up the phone.

There was a part of me that wanted to run home and tell my parents all about it. Maybe if they heard what I'd done, they would finally be proud of me.

But the larger part wanted nothing to do with them.

The idea of taking on more work while I was also dealing with my personal life was not a fun one, but it wasn't as intense as it could have been had I not already been filling in for Caroline. I was still doing two jobs, considering there was no one who wanted to step into my old director role.

But I would get it done. Even at my lowest point of motivation, I couldn't sit still for long.

There was a knock at the door, and I looked up to see Jenny. She had a small smile on her face.

"I overheard the execs talking about it. I hear congratulations are in order."

"They are," I said. "At least they should be."

She leaned against the doorframe. "Not excited?"

I shrugged. "I fought so hard for this."

"And maybe all of that fighting led to resentment. It shouldn't have taken this long to give you the job. You more than deserve it. Someone very wise once told me that you can't stop negativity in the workplace once it starts."

"All of my career has been negativity."

"You don't have to take this, you know."

"I already accepted."

"I mean this company. You can find something else."

"I don't know if I can. I doubt there is something out there that isn't a step down from my new title."

Jenny glanced out the window, biting her lip. "Would you be mad if I said *I* had found something else?"

"Did you really?"

She nodded.

"When?"

"Just last week when I applied for the job." She looked at her feet. "It's at PATH."

"Wow," I said. "But that's in San Francisco."

"They're hiring for some remote positions in the area," she said. "They offered me the job this morning."

"Congratulations, Jenny."

"Are you angry with me?"

"Why would I be mad? PATH is a good company. Even their CEO isn't such a bad guy."

"Former CEO," she corrected.

I shrugged. "He'll always be tied to them."

"Which is why I was worried you'd think he stole me or something."

"Why?" I asked. "He's not the CEO currently and even if he were, he and I are on good terms now."

"I don't know. Maybe I'm worried this is too good to be true, like something has to be wrong. For a while, I didn't know what it could be, but then I thought you might hate me for leaving."

If I was being honest with myself, I was jealous. PATH was a good company, and I knew she would be treated well there.

I only wanted that for myself.

"Of course I wouldn't. I want what's best for you. Even if that's not here."

"We can meet for dinner, right?" Jenny asked. "We're still friends if we don't work together."

"Of *course*. Don't you want to be around for when my dad finally gets fired?"

Jenny smirked. "Obviously I do. Hearing about him simmering in a pot of his own mistakes is amazing."

"I'm not having dinner every week with my parents. How about we meet up instead?"

Her eyes lit up. "Yes!" She ran across my office to hug me. I was surprised, since the only person I usually touched was Knox, but I couldn't stop myself from giving her just as tight of a hug back.

"We're really friends now," she said. "I've wanted to hug you for so long."

"I'm not much of a hugger."

"You are now." Her arms squeezed around me even tighter. "Has anyone ever told you that you give the best damn hugs?"

Knox

"Jesus," Ruth muttered at the end of the day. "Who knew everyone would want to talk to the new VP?"

She was looking at her phone as we walked to our respective cars. As usual, we were heading to my house, but we still drove separately to avoid any unwanted attention.

"They can't help it. You're interesting to talk to."

"You flirt," she said, smiling over at me.

I glanced around, making sure no one was in the parking lot. We were extra careful not to talk to each other at work anymore, since neither of us were good at controlling our expressions. All of the communication about the app progress went through email to try to ensure we wouldn't be caught.

The next project was the fraud tracking system, but that had taken a back seat to my own invention that I was making with PATH. Most of the time I was in my office, I was working on that.

"They probably want to be sure I'm not going to fire every man in sight." She rolled her eyes. "Whatever. I'm done thinking about work right now. Let's talk weekend plans."

"First things first, food. Since we *both* forgot our lunches because we slept in . . ."

"Yeah, we *slept*."

I smiled over at her, thinking of our not-work-appropriate activities. "And the fact that we're both terrible at remembering to eat, how about I treat us to dinner?"

"I want to try to cook tonight," she said.

"I didn't think you cooked."

"I don't *yet*."

I mentally calculated all the ways this could go wrong. Then again, I was scarred by my mother's failed attempts at cooking, so my automatic assumption that this could be bad wasn't fair to her.

"Thanks for the vote of confidence," she said as she eyed my expression. "You're looking at me like I'm about to start a fire."

"Sorry," I said. "But you were there when we all tried my mother's lasagna."

"She just cooked it a little too long. Besides, the burnt bits kind of tasted good."

"I don't know if you should be cooking tonight if you think that's delicious."

"Maybe *you're* the one with bad taste. Besides, I'm trying to find my plant therapy."

"You can call it what it is, an addiction."

"But it makes you happy. And I love watching you water them, but I want my own thing. I bought a cookbook and everything. Please?" She pouted her lower lip.

Damn it. That one-word puppy dog expression was all it took.

"What are you thinking?"

"Let's start easy. How about pasta?"

"What do we need to make that?"

"We'll need to go to the store."

Two hours later, I was watching Ruth cook for the first time. But instead of a simple pasta dish, she was making the whole thing from scratch.

"So apparently 1:1 is the perfect ratio of semolina flour to regular flour for pasta." She was reading from her new cookbook as she poured flour into a measuring cup. I leaned against the counter, watching her from a distance.

It was late in the evening, but neither of us were going to sleep anytime soon. Ruth was determined to make the food, so much so that she requested we make a second stop to pick up a pasta press.

"Come here," she urged.

"If I do anything, I'll ruin the dinner. I inherited my mother's cooking skills."

She rolled her eyes and reached over to grab me. She handed me a wire whisk.

"Ruth," I warned.

"Oh, come on. Take the *whisk* with me."

A shocked chuckle escaped me. "You can't make a pun right now. I'm trying to warn you that I'm not good in the kitchen."

"Have you ever tried?"

"No."

"How do you know you're bad then? Cooking skills aren't genetic."

"There are still a lot of mysteries in genetic science."

"Let's solve one then." She dragged me by the arm into the kitchen. She handed me the whisk and told me to stir.

The first thing I did was stir too hard and a cloud of flour puffed into the air.

"Gently," she said. "You don't need to beat it up."

I tried to move more gently, and she turned to grab eggs.

"I'm going to make a well in the flour," she announced.

"A what?" I wasn't sure I heard her right.

"The cookbook says to make a well." She moved me out of the way and reached her hand into the bowl to form a dip in the flour. I watched with my eyebrows high, wondering what the point was.

She cracked open each egg and separated the white from the yolk, letting the yellow blob plop into the hole that she had created. It was fascinating to watch, both because she seemed like she was doing well and because I'd never seen Mom create anything like this in the kitchen. But then I remembered all the things that could still go wrong.

"I'll be thinking of my pizza order while you do this."

She looked up at me with that cute expression she used to get when I annoyed her. I was mesmerized by it for all of one second.

Then she flicked flour on my black shirt. "Wha—*Ruth*!"

"Talk shit. Get flicked."

Before I could reply, her attention was back on the food. She used a fork to fold the egg yolks into the flour until it started to combine into a rough, doughy shape. She pulled out the yellow flour ball and plopped it on the counter before she worked it with her hands to create a smooth form. I couldn't take my eyes off the process.

"Now to press it," she announced. "Go stir the sauce, please."

As she worked on the pasta, I carefully watched the pot of sauce she'd started, readying myself for the distinctive smell of burnt food. Surprisingly, giving it a few stirs now and again as it bubbled kept it from burning.

"It's pasta!" she exclaimed after pulling the first sheet of dough through the press.

"Color me impressed."

"Shut up and keep stirring the sauce."

"Bossy."

I did as she said, wondering how this would turn out. I hadn't been served a delicious homecooked meal . . . ever.

She instructed me to taste the sauce to see if it was to my liking. It tasted remarkably good, so she had me turn off the heat on the stove while she readied the boiling pot of salted water. This was the most activity my kitchen had ever seen.

The house smelled more and more delicious as the evening progressed. When it was all said and done, I was starving.

"This better be good," she said as she mixed the sauce and pasta.

"It smells amazing."

"Where was this confidence earlier?"

"I had to know that I wouldn't be eating burnt food. Again."

"*I've* never cooked you burnt food before."

"You've never cooked for me before."

"Really? I guess this is all for me, then."

My stomach growled, reminding me of my hunger. "Okay, you've cooked for me, and you seem amazing at it, just like you are with so many other things."

"Usually flattery doesn't work with me," she said. "But I'll let it slide this time."

She smiled and walked to the already-set dining room table.

"Ready?" she asked.

I sat, more than ready to eat, and she followed suit, but she didn't dig in like I expected her to. Instead, she was looking at me.

"What?" I asked.

"I want to see what you think." She leaned forward, eyes bright as she gestured for me to try.

I took one bite.

And it was delicious. It reminded me of the family-owned, hole-in-the-wall Italian restaurants I would frequent in San Francisco.

"Do you like it?"

"I do," I said.

She took a bite, humming thoughtfully. "Next time I'm adding more garlic." Her voice was low. "And maybe some . . . nutmeg."

"In pasta?"

"Don't question me. I'm getting the vibe that nutmeg would go good in this."

She looked so happy that it made me smile too. I could see us doing this every night.

If only she'd ask me to stay.

My chest clenched at the thought. If I stayed, I knew I'd miss PATH. I'd mourn it like a lost family member. But like death, in time, I would move forward. How could I not? I'd have her and she was worth risking everything for.

"What's wrong?" She frowned at me. "Is it the food? Did you find an undercooked noodle or something?"

"No," I said, shaking my head. "It's nothing."

"It doesn't seem like nothing."

How did I tell her how much I missed PATH, but also hated the life I'd built around it? How did I tell her that I wanted to stay with her so badly that I was okay with never going back, yet the grief of even the thought of it hit me like a wave. I wasn't leaving just yet, but it was coming. I was slowly starting to be involved in more and more with my company. Preston didn't want to be the acting CEO forever.

So, I had to start preparing myself now. And soon, her too.

The simple answer was that I didn't, because I had a feeling if she knew then she would never ask me to stay.

"I think I see what you mean," I said. "About the nutmeg. We should try it tomorrow."

Her eyes narrowed as if she knew my clumsy attempt to change the subject was a failed attempt to deflect from the truth.

"Yeah, we can try it."

I loosened, grateful she didn't push me this one time.

CHAPTER TWENTY-ONE

Ruth

He wasn't telling me something.

The unwelcome thought woke me up far too early the next morning. I sat with it, gazing at Knox's sheer curtains and how they swayed due to the ceiling fan.

I could tell it was big, whatever it was.

I didn't want to be suspicious, but I couldn't help it. Things felt almost *too* perfect.

My thoughts swirled, and I knew I would grow more upset the longer I laid in bed, thinking about it.

So, I went back to the kitchen.

I'd heard people baked when they were stressed. A recipe for scones had caught my eye when I flipped through the pages of the cookbook back when I'd bought it. It didn't look too difficult, either. Maybe it would take my mind off of things.

A quick trip to the store was all I needed.

Since I was still somewhat of a novice, cooking required a lot of focus. I had to read directions multiple times, measure things slowly to try and get everything right. After I put them into the oven, I worked on cleaning up the mess I'd made.

As I loaded the dishwasher, there was a knock at the door.

When I opened it, I saw a man I dimly recognized, but couldn't place his name.

"Uh, hi," I said. "Can I help you?"

"Ruth?" he asked.

I narrowed my eyes. "How do you know who I am?"

"I'm Preston." He held out one hand. "I'm Knox's business partner."

I loosened. "Preston. I know who you are. Was Knox expecting you?"

"No. This is a personal visit. I wanted to hand deliver something and catch up."

I wondered if what Preston had brought with him was something Knox knew about, and if that was what he didn't want to tell me about.

"What is that smell?" Preston asked, looking into the house. "Is Knox . . . cooking?"

"I'm the one cooking," I said. "It's only my second time making something but . . ."

"It's your second time cooking and it smells like *that*?"

The air was sweet with the scent of the orange zest I'd put in the dough. I didn't realize it would make the house smell so summery so quickly.

The timer went off on my phone. "I need to get that. You can come in, I guess."

I let him in to the foyer and went to pull the food out of the oven. Luckily, I'd had the forethought to make icing before Knox's unexpected guest arrived. I could throw that on them without too much distraction.

"Wow, there are plants everywhere."

"Yeah, Knox likes to live in a jungle," I said as I grabbed the icing. When I tried to drizzle it on the tops of the golden-brown scones, it immediately melted off and I deflated. Damn it. I must have forgotten a step.

"He told me he was into them, but this is way more than I expected."

"The greenery is nice," I said. "I've heard it makes people happier."

"I sure hope so," Preston replied. "Usually, he's stuck in his office working."

"Yeah. I cut him off after about ten hours."

"You do?"

"Yes. Otherwise, he'll run himself into the ground."

The door to Knox's bedroom opened, and he walked out, thankfully in clothes. He was yawning as he emerged but stuttered in his step when he saw his guest.

"Preston?"

"Surprise! I had a delivery." He set down the box he had been holding. "This is the prototype you requested."

Knox's eyes shifted over to me for a moment, but then they were on the box. "Thanks. I'd been waiting for this."

Was he hiding an invention from me? Was that it?

"So . . . plants," Preston started. "And someone is cooking in your kitchen."

"That is all Ruth's doing. As of last night."

"Keep that up and I'll take the scones I'm making back to my own apartment."

Knox frowned, his eyebrows low on his forehead. He looked genuinely offended.

"Is there any way that I could have one if I ask nicely?" Preston said.

"Sure. They're a little ugly, but I'm still new. As long as you're nice, you can have as many as you want."

"I love your new hobby," Knox said, walking toward the kitchen. "I'm just scarred from my mom's cooking."

"It's not *that* bad."

"I don't know how you can say that. You saw what she did to that poor lasagna."

"I'm not going to say anything negative about her after how sweet she was to me," I said as I plated the scones. Nerves hit me as I looked at them. They looked perfectly baked, the icing a little sloppy, but I wondered if I could have done something wrong. "I hope these are okay." I bit my lip.

"I'll gladly taste test," Preston said. "May I?"

I offered him one, adding, "You might want to blow on them first. They're hot."

He did as I said and then slowly took a small bite. A smile spread on his face. "Are you really sure this is your second time cooking? These are incredible."

"Really?" I asked, a big grin plastered on my lips.

"Okay, my turn," Knox said. He blew on it as well before popping a piece into his mouth. "Yeah, he's right. These are great. How did you get them so light and fluffy?"

"I followed the recipe," I said.

I finally grabbed one, wondering if they both were simply placating me.

But it *was* delicious. The icing was sweet, if you mopped it up from where it fell, and the dough was the perfect texture. I wondered what else I could bake in my free time. Knox walked over and kissed me on the cheek.

"I take back everything I said. Can I have a second one?"

"Kiss up," I said, but I handed him the second scone anyway.

I glanced at Preston who was watching us with a grin on his face. It was nice to see that Knox had a friend who seemed genuinely happy for him.

"So, did you really come all this way just to give me the prototype?" Knox asked.

"That and I wanted to see how my favorite inventor was doing. Nashville's been good for you. I'm glad your break is helping."

"I needed it."

"How do you feel about coming back as CEO?"

"Are you that tired of it already?"

"It's . . . something. But I said I'd do it until you felt better. What do you say? Are you ready to take back the reins of PATH?"

Knox didn't answer the question, and his eyes shot over to me.

That was when it hit me. He wasn't hiding an invention. He was hiding that he was always meant to go back to PATH someday.

And that was in San Francisco.

Stanford's app was doing well, and it would be easy for him to quit and return to PATH. He wouldn't be under a boss that he hated, and he would be at the helm of the company he loved.

But it would be across the country.

My heart sank. I could hear the conversation now.

I'll come visit, he'd say. *I still have the house here. We can still see each other.*

Damn it. I should have known he was going back. I shouldn't have gotten so attached, because now I didn't know if I could even put space in between us.

I wasn't built for long distance. I wanted to be with him all the time. After he'd held me during that stormy night, he'd become my person.

But I couldn't imagine leaving everything in order to follow him, either. I couldn't leave my brothers to fend off Dad. I couldn't leave Jenny or the town I'd known my entire life.

"Wait, did I say something wrong?" Preston asked.

"N-no," I said, feeling emotion claw its way up my throat. "I think I'll head out so you two can catch up. I need to go check on something at my apartment, anyway."

"Ruth, wait," Knox said.

But I shook my head. The last thing I wanted to do was cry in front of Preston. I threw on my shoes, even though I was still in my pajamas, knowing I needed to leave before he tried to stop me.

I'd made it outside before he did exactly that. "Ruth," he said. He grabbed my arm. "Don't leave. I know . . . I know what you're upset about."

"Just give me some time."

"Ask me to stay. Please, Ruth."

I stared at the car door, swallowing heavily as I thought about it. Him staying would mean I'd get to spend forever in this little house. We could buy plants and cook dinners and never have a problem in the world.

At least, I wouldn't.

But I knew his heart wouldn't be here.

I slowly turned to him. "No."

"Why not? I'd do it if you asked."

"Because you love PATH. And I care about you too much to tell you to stay away from something you love."

"I care about you too. We'll figure this out. I'm not going to push you aside to go back."

I slowly nodded. "And I'm not going to put you in a position to choose."

"Come back inside, please."

"I can't do that right now. I need to process this. And you have a guest."

"I can send him away," Knox said. "Whatever he wants to tell me, he can do it over the phone."

"No. He flew across the country to see you. It's fine." I pulled my arm out of his grip, giving him a forced smile. "I'll see you later."

And I made my escape before he could say anything else.

Knox

"Could you not have mentioned me going back to PATH?" I asked Preston the moment I came back inside. As much as I was glad to see him, I also wanted to strangle him.

"Sorry," he said. "I thought she knew."

I rubbed a hand over my face and let out an angry groan. "We hadn't talked about it yet. Moving back has been something I've been avoiding telling her."

"Moving back to San Francisco, you mean?"

"Of course. I'd need to in order to be the CEO. I know that."

"But San Francisco was the place you felt numb."

"And? It is what it is. Nashville was always meant to be temporary."

Preston looked around. "Didn't you buy this place?"

"I can keep it so I can come out to visit my parents."

"Seems like you were putting down roots."

"Do you want me back or not? I can't invent and be here. Making this prototype has been a nightmare without me physically being there in person to fix things; it's taken three times as long as it should've because of the distance. I need to be close to my team and I'm not the kind of guy to fly back and forth every night just because I can."

"But you were miserable."

I glared over at him. "I *know*. You don't need to tell me this. I'm still trying to figure out how to be two places at once."

"You could just be in one place."

"We've just established that I can't do that," I said.

"I'm trying to *hint* at something here, Knox."

"Can you stop hinting and just tell me? It's too early in the morning for this."

"Fine. I'll spoil it. We're thinking about moving PATH to Nashville. If you wanted to, of course. But judging by this," he gestured to my house, "I doubt you'll say no."

"What? Why?"

"Because you're happy here. But we also *need* you. So why not get the best of both worlds here in Nashville?"

"I can't ask that of my employees."

"You don't have to. We can offer them packages to move, or remote positions if they don't want to."

"But *you* hate Nashville."

"I hate my dad, but this city? I've missed it a little. I grew up here, after all."

"Wait, you hate your dad, but you sent me to work for him?"

Preston smiled. "Now *that* was the best part of my plan."

"Was it to put me at a company where I'd get arrested for stabbing the CEO?"

"No. It was Ruth."

I blinked. "Ruth?"

"Her mom sent you a letter. One of the administrative assistants gave it to me." He fished out a folded piece of paper out of his pocket and handed it over.

I glanced down at the paper in my hands. Handwriting that dimly reminded me of Ruth's was scribbled on the page. It was signed from Jolene Murray.

My eyes tried to read it, but I tore them away. Ruth deserved to see this first, especially with everything that was going on.

Besides, I was too shocked by my friend. I could only handle one earth-shattering realization at a time.

"It was a gamble, and you're within your rights to be mad that I didn't tell you the real reason I sent you back, but look at you now. You have a hobby. You have your family. And you got Ruth on top of it. You found yourself, Knox. That was all I wanted."

I finally looked at him. I *was* a little mad he sent me here to work for an asshole like Dave.

But the positives outweighed any anger I felt.

Preston was right. I was myself again, and the moment I went back to San Francisco, I would be heading down the same path. He'd solved the problem before I even knew what it was.

"Thank you," I said, my voice thick. "I can't tell you how much I appreciate you, Preston."

"Oh, shit. I didn't expect . . . whatever this is."

"This is gratitude, you emotionally stunted ass."

"So, you're not mad I pushed you to work for my dad?"

"I want to kick your ass for that, but that can wait. I'll get my revenge when you see my mom again and she makes you have another emotional breakthrough."

"Lynn is good at that. I'll prepare myself for when I move back here."

"If we do this, how quickly do you think we could get this up and running?"

"Fall," he said matter-of-factly.

"That soon? I need to tell Ruth about this."

"Hang on," he said. "Don't do that just yet."

"Why not?"

"I've done the research and made the phone calls because I figured you'd agree, but nothing is official yet. As the acting CEO, I have to ensure that it still confidential until we announce."

"Ruth isn't going to tell anyone."

"I'm sure that's true, but this will be a huge move. The last thing we need is people getting wind of it before we've secured an office."

I let out a long breath. Acquiring our first building had been a tumul-tuous experience. Once people knew we intended on making self-driving car technology, those who opposed the idea tried to make it impossible to find a suitable location. The few offices that had the right amount of space had office managers who didn't want that kind of press outside their doors. We wound up building our warehouse for that very reason.

After, I'd put strict confidentiality rules in place to ensure we wouldn't go through that again, ones I knew even I had to follow.

"With your blessing, I'll set up a meeting with a builder," Preston said. "If all goes well, I'll draw up a contract, and you can tell her once it's signed. Just let me get a place secured before we tell anyone outside of the company."

"Fine," I said. "I'll do it."

"I know this isn't what you want," he said, sighing.

"I hate my own rule."

"You did it for a reason. The last thing we need is her phone hacked because of her proximity to you and it getting out there."

It had happened to Preston before. Whoever had done it faced serious consequences, but it was still nerve-racking for both of us. I'd installed special protection on his phone, and I needed to do that to Ruth's too.

My to-do list only grew.

"Tell me about this office you have planned," I said, determined to focus on what Preston had up his sleeve instead of thinking about how badly I wanted to spill the secret to Ruth.

"Gladly," he said. "I think you'll love what I've come up with."

We sat at the table as he explained how he wanted to expand research and development. We'd make a large office and warehouse, both for building our newest cars and for the newer technology we'd been working on. It would be perfect since we wouldn't have to wait for shipping for prototypes from our current factory.

I lost myself in work, desperately trying to keep my mind on this new task in front of me. There were so many details to finalize, and it wouldn't be *that* long until I could share the news with Ruth. At least, that was what I kept telling myself.

It only slightly helped the guilt I felt.

CHAPTER TWENTY-TWO

Ruth

My hands shook as I knocked on Tom's door. It was late in the evening and I'd spent most of the day wallowing in my own misery. Eventually, I'd decided I wanted to see my older brother in a childlike hope that he would give me some sort of advice, but I was beginning to wonder if he'd even be home.

I never visited him enough to know.

"Ruth?" he asked as he opened the door. "What's wrong?"

"Are you busy?"

"My weekends are either filled with work or sitting at home doing nothing. But you didn't answer my question." He sounded annoyed. Maybe I shouldn't have come.

"I . . . I wanted advice," I said slowly. "Can you help your little sister out?"

I stared into his green eyes, forcing myself not to back down from his intensity. With the way his jaw was clenched, I expected him to kick me out.

Then he opened the door wider to let me in.

"Thanks," I said. "I know you're busy with the whole kicking Dad out of the company thing."

"I'll gladly take a distraction."

"Knox is going to go back to San Francisco. Maybe not now, but soon. He's going back to PATH."

"I'm not surprised, considering he's still working on inventions for them."

"Yeah, and PATH is on the other side of the country."

"Are you going with him?"

I shook my head.

"Oh," he said. "That would be hard, considering I'm pretty sure you're in love with him."

"You're not wrong. Isn't that stupid? Why the hell would I fall for someone who is leaving?"

"I don't know. I don't even know why you're here, Ruth. What am I supposed to tell you?"

"That it'll be okay? That I'll survive? Can you not be an emotionally constipated asshole for ten seconds and be a supportive big brother?" My voice cracked, and I realized my emotion was not all about Knox.

It was about Tom too.

I missed the boy who'd thrown his arms around Barry and me to protect us from the storm, but I wasn't sure the man who stood in front of me was that anymore.

With lips pursed, he stared at me like I was a stain on his white couch. I let out a long breath, trying in vain to stop any tears from falling before I could make a break for the door.

"I wish I could be that." His voice was quiet. When I slowly turned to look at him, his gaze was on his feet. "But I'm not about to make this about me, not when you're hurting. I only wish I knew the right thing to say to make it better. All I know is that I need to fix what Dad did. Then I'll have redeemed myself."

I shook my head. "That's not how this works."

"It is for me. He made me what I am today, and I want to be the one who ends him."

"Then what?"

"Then you and Barry can be free of his expectations. Especially you, Ruth."

"I don't need freedom right now. I need my brother."

"This is all I am. This is all Dad made me to be. I'm sorry I don't know how to be anything more."

I could only stare at him. When I thought of Tom, I thought of how successful he was, how he was the first at everything in our family.

Now I wondered if he was the most broken of us all.

"You can be more, Tom. You're not Dad."

"That's where I think you're wrong, Ruth. I was built to be Dad's shadow. And I'm nothing else." He walked to the door and opened it. "Go find Barry. He'll be far more helpful."

"And that's all he said," I said. I was in my car, hands still shaking as I recounted everything to Barry. I wasn't in any shape to drive, so I stayed in Tom's parking lot. "I'm worried about him."

"He's always cryptic. He'll bounce back like he always does."

"But what if he doesn't? What if he genuinely believes those things?"

"Then ruining Dad will be cathartic for him."

"We need to do something." My voice was tight with frustration.

"No, we don't. Us Murrays do things better alone."

"That's not true, Barry. We still need to stick together."

"Against Dad? Sure. But we don't even like each other beyond that. Once this is over, we'll all go on our merry little ways and be alone. Like we're meant to be."

"Damn it, Barry. You're not doing this to me too!"

"Doing what?"

"I'm not losing anyone else!" I snapped. Tears blurred my vision. "Knox is leaving. Tom kicked me out. And now *you're* trying to get rid of me? Am I such a terrible person? What did I do to deserve this?"

"A-are you crying?"

"Of fucking course I'm crying! Three people I love are all pushing me away, whether by leaving or just because they want nothing to do with me!" I leaned my forehead against the steering wheel. "What did I *do*, Barry? Whatever it was, I'm sorry. I just can't lose Mom, Dad and then you too. Please. Not like this."

The line was silent. I wondered if he'd hung up on me.

"I . . . I don't think you did anything, Ruth. Not with the intent to hurt me. I'm not trying to push you away, but we're not like this. We don't talk about our feelings or open up."

"And how is that working out for us?"

"Not well." His voice was quiet. "But I figured you guys wrote me off as the family screwup. You and Tom wanted to impress Dad so bad."

"But we never did."

"I know. Trust me, I do. But I got so used to being shunned for being different that I grew used to being alone, even when someone is reaching out."

"Are you okay, Barry?"

"No. Are you?"

"No."

"And I wish I knew what we were supposed to do about that, but I don't."

"I was hoping Tom did. I just wanted someone to tell me it was going to be okay. Just like I wanted someone to say they were proud of me."

"That's the thing about expectations. Once you have them, they're rarely met."

"Maybe you're right. I sometimes just think about Tom protecting us during that tornado. And I miss that version of him."

Barry was silent for a long moment, then he said, "I do too."

"But he's convinced he's too far gone, that his only purpose is ending Dad."

Barry let out a soft chuckle. "If you think about it in a certain light, it's his way of still protecting us."

My eyes watered again. "But what about after? I don't want us to drift apart." I tried to get a handle on my emotions. "I want us to talk about stuff that's not about Dad."

"There's not much to say."

"Please? Can we at least try?"

"I . . . guess we can, but I don't know where to start."

"We can start simple. How was your day, Barry? How is the bar?"

"It's fine. Everything is fine."

"But how is it fine?" I asked. "What did you do? Do you have a favorite employee? A favorite customer?"

Dead silence again, and I waited patiently for Barry to answer, even if he'd only shut me out.

But then he finally spoke. "I have this one bartender who dances as he serves drinks."

"What? And he wasn't there on the dance night?"

"He was sick that night. You should come back and see him in action."

"He sounds amazing."

"All of my employees are. God, they do so much to keep the place afloat."

"That's great."

"And the customers are too. I still can't believe how many people come here. So many women have told me it's the one place they feel safe. I don't take that lightly."

"You shouldn't. I'm so proud of you."

Barry coughed. "Is your goal to make me cry too?"

"No. I'm just being honest."

"You just said the words every Murray is dying to hear."

"But it's the truth," I said. "You've done well for yourself. I'm glad."

"I'm not the family rebel?"

"You say rebel like it's a bad thing. You own one of the hottest bars in Nashville."

He let out a sound dangerously close to a laugh. "Thanks, Ruth. I guess it's my turn to ask then. How was *your* day?"

"My boyfriend is going back to San Francisco, and I hate my job. So, it wasn't great."

"I'm sorry. Do you have enough saved up to quit?"

"I do, but it would kill my career. I still *like* working, just not for *this* boss. I need to make it through Knox leaving, and then . . . then I'll look."

"I'll lie and say you worked for me. I'd give you a good reference."

I laughed despite my sullen mood. "You'd talk to businesspeople for me? Who even are you, anyway?"

"Just a guy who cares about his big sister."

I made it through Monday and Tuesday like a zombie. I was present, but barely functioning. I texted Knox that I still needed to process, but now I was working through more than I knew what to do with. Not only was he leaving, but I had to figure out how to get Tom to not push me away.

And the new vice president role at Stanford. My days were filled with meetings as I still struggled to make my newest team members accept that I wasn't out for blood.

By the time evening rolled around, I was about ready to say fuck it all. I needed to see Knox. I slept more peacefully when I wasn't alone, and I hoped he felt the same way.

I bet he was still at work. He'd been working late all this week.

I was just about to turn my car around when my phone rang.

And it was the very person I wanted to hear from.

"Knox?" I answered, relieved. "I was hoping you'd call."

"Well, I'm sorry to disappoint," a southern voice said. I instantly knew it was Lynn. "But it's not Knox."

"Hi, Lynn." My heart was in my throat. "Please tell me you're not calling because Knox is in the hospital or something."

"No, it's nothing like that. I only took his phone to invite you to dinner. Preston has already left town, and I made extra since I hoped more would be here tonight. It's even *edible*."

Relief hit me, and then a warm feeling replaced it.

"I can come," I said. "As long as this isn't family time."

"It *is* family time, so you have to be there!"

"I'm not family."

"Anyone who laughs at Benji's jokes is family. Now get on over here! I'll make a seat for you."

My throat closed up, emotions swelling at being included.

But I fought them back, not wanting to cry again this week; I was tired of it. I wasn't even sure I had anything left in me. What I wanted to do was see Lynn, Benji, and Knox, even if he was going to be leaving soon.

Maybe distance wasn't what I needed. Maybe I needed to enjoy every second of it while it lasted.

Knox

"All right," Mom said, coming into the room. "I have invited my favorite guest."

She handed me my phone and I stared at her with a raised eyebrow. "What did you do?"

"I called Ruth, of course. I made extra for dinner, and *someone* let Preston go back to San Francisco without saying hello."

Preston had gone home after talking with the builder to work on drafting up the contract. Once it was signed, I could finally tell Ruth I was staying.

"What did she say?" I asked. "She and I had somewhat of a . . . fight."

"I could tell by that frown on your face," she said. "And she said yes."

I blinked. "Really? She said she needed space."

"Maybe she's done with all that. Or she'll ignore you and talk to us all night."

"I'd be fine with that," Dad piped in. "I can throw out more puns."

My chest tightened at the idea of seeing her. I knew that I couldn't take her being upset about me leaving. The moment she looked at me with those sad, green eyes, I'd break my own rule and tell her everything.

But I didn't get to find out. When Ruth pulled up, Mom darted out the door. I followed behind, but stayed on the porch to give her space.

"Ruth!" she greeted, giving her a tight hug.

Ruth smiled and returned it, accompanied with a soft, "Hi." She was still in her tight skirt and heels, and she towered over Mom.

"You look so pretty today!" Mom exclaimed. "I don't know how you walk so well in those heels."

"It took years of practice."

"Come in, come in! I made a new recipe for us to try and it turned out okay."

Mom walked inside, and Ruth followed her up until she got to the porch where I was. For a moment, she looked at me, biting her lip. I took in a shaky breath, wondering if I should simply blurt out the change in my plans.

But then she hugged me tightly, her warm body pressing against mine.

All thoughts flew out of my head when I realized her hands were shaking.

"Ruth, what's wrong?" I whispered.

"It's been a hell of a week," she said. "I missed you."

"I'm not going anywhere." I said it without thinking, but I knew that if she questioned me, I'd fold in an instant.

"It doesn't matter right now. You're here. That's what I care about." She squeezed me one last time before she tagged along with Mom. I was left staring after her.

After a moment of confusion, I walked inside too and I noticed Dad approaching Ruth.

"Ruth! So good to see you again."

"You too, Benji. Got any puns for me? I could use a good laugh right now."

"You know I do. What did one wall say to another?"

She tapped her chin, smiling despite her still shaky hands. "I don't know."

"I'll meet you at the corner."

Ruth laughed. "That's a good one. Oh! I looked one up myself. What do you call a sad strawberry?"

"Tell me," he demanded.

"A *blue* berry."

Dad cackled.

"You did this to us," I muttered to Mom.

"I saw that hug," she replied, smirking over at me. "I refuse to apologize."

"You shouldn't, even if we're listening to jokes and puns all night. It's good to have her here."

"That's what I thought."

"Is the food ready?" Dad asked. "It smells good for once."

"That's right! I'll bring it to the table."

We all shuffled away, gathering at the old oak dining room table.

"It's not burnt!" Mom announced proudly, setting the hot dish in the center of the table.

And to her credit, it wasn't.

"I got a new recipe book." She beamed.

"Is it the one that's for beginners?" Dad asked.

"Benji! Don't make me look bad."

"We all have to start somewhere," Ruth said, smiling. "I bet it's great."

Mom blushed. "You are too sweet."

She served each of us a plate of food, which was mostly cooked, and sat next to Dad. "Okay, now that we all have a homecooked meal for once, does anyone have any good news?"

I looked over at Ruth.

"What?" she asked.

"Your promotion," I urged.

"Oh, there was a promotion?" Mom's eyes brightened.

"It's not anything compared to what Knox has done," Ruth said quietly.

"Sweetheart, this isn't about Knox. What happened?"

"It's really nothing."

"I doubt it, considering you work as hard as he does," Dad added.

"Okay, fine. I'll tell you." She took a deep breath. "I was offered a VP position at Stanford."

"What?" Mom's jaw dropped. "That's amazing!"

"Seriously," Dad echoed. "Someone your age being a vice president? Incredible!"

"Knox had to basically get me the job, though."

"Nonsense. Did he do the work for you?" Mom asked.

"N-no. I did the work."

"Sounds like he just put in a good word for you." Mom beamed again. "*You* still earned the promotion, though."

"T-thank you," she said, swallowing hard. She blinked quickly, and I started to sense her emotions were rising.

I tried to stop Mom in order to pull Ruth to privacy, but nothing would stop Lynn Price when she was excited.

"Wow," she continued, clapping her hands. "I am so *proud* of you, dear."

Ruth froze, taking in a shaky breath as Mom's kind words hit her.

Then she started sobbing.

CHAPTER TWENTY-THREE

Ruth

As my tears fell without warning, I realized I was probably never going to be invited to a Price family dinner again.

But I couldn't stop. I'd dreamed of those words. I'd needed them my whole life.

And Lynn, who barely knew me, had said them with no hesitation.

It broke something in me.

I didn't do this. I didn't cry randomly at a dinner table. I was supposed to be Ruth the Ruthless, always fighting anyone who stood in my way.

But I couldn't be that person—not when the mother of my former rival had said what my own damn family could never.

Hands gripped my arms, and I bet Knox was trying to coax me to look at him. I couldn't. I needed to wait until Lynn and Benji shuffled out of the room before I let my tears show.

Words that had once been said to played back in my head.

What a weird girl, crying like that.

Couldn't she do that some other time?

Girls are so weak.

"Did I say something wrong?" Lynn asked sweetly, and horror dawned on me. She was the one with her hands on my arms, still being nice despite my weakness.

"N-no," I struggled to say. "I'm just crying because I'm weird. You can go laugh at me now if you want."

"Now why would I do that?" she asked.

Another person handed me a tissue, and I saw it was Knox. Across the table, Benji watched me without an ounce of judgment on his face.

But *I* was judging me.

"You said you were proud of me. It's not a reason for me to break down like this. Sure, my parents never once said it to me, but that's not *your* problem."

"Your parents never said they were proud of you?" she asked. "Well, that's just not right." Her voice shook, as if she were holding back something. Maybe it was the laugh I deserved.

"It's fine. I'm fine."

"It's okay if you're not," Benji added.

"You guys are *so* a-amazing. It makes sense why Knox turned out so perfect."

"But we're not talking about Knox," Lynn reminded. "We're talking about *you*."

I shook my head. "But he's your son. I'm just the woman you invited to dinner."

"That's not what you are," Knox said, a hint of warning in his voice.

"It is what I am. It's what I always was. *You* were the golden child to my parents. It wasn't Tom. It wasn't me. It was *you*. My parents loved you more than they ever did me. Anytime they talked to me, it was about how you were better. They were proud of you. Never of me."

"But . . . *you* are their child," Lynn protested.

"They didn't want children. They wanted trophies."

"Is that why you hated me?" Knox asked.

"I didn't hate *you*. I hated how much my parents loved you."

"They made you feel inferior," Lynn said softly.

"I *am* inferior. To him."

"No, you're not," Knox snapped. "Don't ever say that."

Lynn turned to her son, and then looked at Benji. They communicated almost telepathically.

"Come on, kid," Benji said, putting a hand on his son's shoulder. "You need to cool off for a minute."

"No, I need to make sure she knows—"

"Your mom's got this. Let's go."

Knox gritted his teeth, not willing to leave.

"C-can I have some water at least?" I asked.

Knox's shoulders fell. "Of course, Ruth." His voice was softer. Benji nodded at me and walked with him to the kitchen.

"I'm sorry," I said, still sniffling. "I didn't mean to cause a problem. Me and my brothers are just broken people."

"It gets better, dear," Lynn said.

"Does it?"

"It did for me." Lynn gave me a sad smile. "My parents hurt me too, sweetheart, and there was a time where I never felt like I would be whole again, but I was."

"How?"

"I made a family."

"I-I'm not ready for kids yet, I—"

"No, not like that. My friends became my family. Knox's aunt isn't related to him. She was my best friend, and she stepped up when I had no one."

Like Jenny had with me.

"Then I met Benji, who would move the stars themselves for me."

Like Knox would for me.

"And then his dad walked me down the aisle when mine wouldn't. He may not have raised me, but he was more of a father than anyone else was." Nothing formed in my mind. I didn't have a parental figure who'd stepped into my life yet. "And we may have only just met, but I could be that for you."

Lynn's smiling face broke through my thoughts and I blinked over at her.

"You don't have to be. I'm not related to you."

"I don't care if we're not related. I want to care about *you*, but only if you want me to."

I could see where Knox got his kindness.

"So, what does that mean?"

"It means you call me about anything. It can be about your day, your week. I can give you advice if you need it, or just a listening ear. Life can be lonely when your parents fail you, and I don't want that for anyone."

"What if Knox leaves? What if we break up?"

"If he leaves, then I can still be your friend. And if he's stupid enough to lose you, then that's his problem." She grabbed my hand and squeezed it. "I like you, Ruth, and I want to show you that not everyone is like your parents."

My eyes grew wet again. "This is so . . . *nice* of you."

"I once felt like you, Ruth. I was so angry, but then I decided that I would never make anyone else feel this way. It ends with me. And it ends with you. I already see that you're kinder than you were raised to be."

"If my dad were here, he'd say it's because I'm a girl. I'm soft."

"That sounds like a sad, insecure man to me."

"I think you're right. Benji is *way* nicer."

She wiped a stray tear from my face. "It's going to be okay, Ruth."

And there it was. The assurance I had needed. I slowly nodded and her hand stayed on my cheek. I leaned into the warm touch.

"Now, you look like you've had a bad week. Do you want to tell me what happened?"

I nodded again, taking in a shaky breath to tell her everything.

And she listened to every single word. Her eyes didn't stray from mine as I told her about Tom, about Barry, and how I was afraid we were broken forever.

And when I was done, she asked, "Do you want some advice?"

"Y-yes, please."

"Tom needs time, but with support he will come around. Barry sounds like he's receptive to connecting. You did an amazing thing talking to him like that. It's what you wanted from Tom, isn't it?"

I looked at my hands and nodded. My mind returning to the last person I hadn't mentioned that was on my mind. "I think Knox is going back to PATH in San Francisco."

Lynn's lips pressed together. "He can't stay away from his inventions long."

"I don't think I can handle him leaving."

"I know, but maybe things aren't set in stone. You might find that some things bend, even when we think they can't."

"I guess I'll have to see it to believe it."

"I have seen it in the way he looks at you. So, I believe it."

The sincerity in her voice was impossible to deny. She held out her arms, inviting me in for a hug. I leaned into her gratefully. Suddenly, I wasn't a twenty-eight-year-old woman crying in a stranger's house. I was a kid who needed a hug from a mom.

And I'd found one.

Knox

I tried to get the water, but I was too angry to even begin to see straight.

"Knox," Dad started placatingly.

"No," I said. "*No*. Don't try to calm me down. They compared her to me. I played into their hands by trying to beat her all the time in school and then teasing her for it."

"You were a kid, and you didn't know."

"Well, I do now, and I hope I never see her dad because I want to ruin his life in ways he hasn't even imagined yet."

Dad let out a long sigh.

"What?" I asked. "You can't tell me you didn't feel the way about grandpa."

"Of course I did, Knox."

"Then why do you look disappointed?"

"I'm not disappointed," he said. "But I need you to sit down. It's time for a life lesson."

I was too busy thinking of revenge for that.

"Knox," he said again. "Please sit down."

As much as I wanted to ignore him, I respected him far too much for that. I slowly sat, gritting my teeth. "You're not going to make me not hate him."

"That's not my goal. But I want to ask you something, son. What will going after her dad do for her?"

"It'll make sure he doesn't do it again."

"And how does that help her in this very moment?"

I opened my mouth, and then closed it. "I don't know."

"You know I have no love for your mom's father. I once punched him in the face for making her cry. And you know what? It pissed your mom off."

"Why? You were defending her."

"Because she was crying, and I wasn't there. I was too busy going after that man that I forgot about who he hurt. Is that what you want?"

"Of course not."

"She needs you comforting her, not you being angry about what happened to her."

My shoulders fell. "I know. I just . . ." I didn't know what to say.

"You love her. It makes sense that you want to protect her."

I stared at my father, trying to find the words to tell him that I felt like I was unable to love anyone, that it wasn't what I was programmed to do.

But the words never came out because he was *right*.

I loved her. I loved her so much I was willing to ruin a man I'd never met. I loved her so much that I was willing to let go of my company for good.

And I loved my parents. I loved Preston and PATH. Albeit in different ways, but love was love. Love was an emotion.

I *loved* so much. And for a man who felt numb only months ago, I felt like it was a miracle, brought on by my best friend's actions, my parent's warmth, and Ruth's ability to get me to stop working and *live*.

"I . . . do," I said. "I really love her. What do I even *do* about that?"

"You show her. You tell her. You enjoy every second you can."

"I-I didn't think I could even love, Dad. I thought I was doomed to only care about work."

"Now when did you start thinking like that?"

"It was always a thing I worried about. But it got worse after I left home."

Dad's eyebrows furrowed and a deep frown made its way on to his face.

"Why didn't you tell us?"

"I didn't want to worry you."

"We were worried about you anyway," he said. "We knew something was wrong, but you always said you were fine."

"I was numb. I felt nothing, and I didn't know what to do."

"There's therapy. There're hobbies."

"There's Ruth."

"Yes, there is. But unfortunately, love doesn't solve *all* problems. One day, you might feel that way again, but rest assured, your mother and I will be checking in on you more often, now that I know what's going on."

"And Ruth will join you. She already makes me stop working when she sees I've been doing it for too long."

Dad smiled. "I knew I liked her, and it wasn't just because of the puns and jokes. She's good for you."

"She is," I agreed. "Which is why I want nothing to hurt her."

"She's a human, Knox. It's going to happen."

"I know." I filled a glass of water I'd promised Ruth. "I'm going to be there for her. But I do feel the need to tell you I sent my lawyers against her dad already. He's on leave from his company for sexual harassment. I want to be sure he's never able to be in a position of power again."

Dad laughed. "Sounds like it's what he deserves. Just be there for her before you find your revenge."

"I think I can make that work," I said.

"That's my boy. Now go check on your girl. I'll give you a few minutes before I join in."

I nodded, walking back to the dining room.

Ruth was locked in a tight hug with Mom, but her tears were gone.

"Sorry," she said as she looked over at me. "I took your mom."

"Oh, don't you even worry about that," Mom said. "I'll give you a hug and tell you how proud I am of you anytime."

Ruth nodded, tightening her arms. She slowly pulled away.

"So, about this whole comparison thing . . ." I began.

"Oh, I know you want to kill my parents for that one."

"I do, but that's unrelated. You know there're plenty of things you can kick my ass at, right?"

"Name one thing."

"I can't walk in heels as well as you do."

"Wait," she asked. "Have you tried?"

"Once," Mom said, laughing. "He tried to grab groceries out of the car in my old heels. He tripped on the step and landed on his face."

A slow smile spread onto Ruth's face. "Oh, I wish I could have seen that."

"They were the only shoes around and you needed help!" I tried to defend myself.

"I could give you some pointers," Ruth said.

"See? You're also the queen of marketing. I don't know anything about that."

"That also might be true."

"Oh, and you can cook."

"She's also better at puns," Mom added.

"That's true too."

"I get the point," Ruth said. "Thank you for all the compliments. This was exactly what I needed."

Dad came back into the room, giving Ruth a kind smile.

"Benji," Ruth said, eying him warily. "I'm sorry for losing it."

"No, don't apologize," he said, shaking his head. "I'm not bothered at all."

"I just feel bad for hijacking dinner."

"It was either that or I would do it with dad jokes. We all need a good cry, Ruth. Let yourself be human."

"That's an important thing to remember," she said, nodding.

We all sat to finish our meals, and my parents did a great job keeping her engaged in everything. Mom told her all about fake Dolly Parton, and Dad told her about some of the houses he'd been in as an electrician. By the time we'd finished eating, she couldn't be seen without a full, beautiful smile.

We stayed late, talking about our lives. Ruth opened up about Dave, and we all traded stories about terrible bosses. The sky was fully dark by the time we were done talking.

I walked Ruth to her car, itching to ask her to come to my house.

"I am still so mortified that I fucking cried in there," she muttered the moment we were alone.

"It's fine. Preston cried in front of them too. Mom told him she loved him exactly the way he is and to never pretend to be something he's not. He immediately broke down."

"Wow. They really know what someone needs to hear."

"My mom wanted a big a family, but she only had me. She loves helping others."

"It's really sweet," she said. "I needed to talk to someone about these last couple of days anyway."

"What happened, other than you needing space?"

"It's my brothers. Tom is pushing me away and Barry tried to as well. That's why I was so sad. I now see how much we're all hurting."

"I don't know about Barry, but Tom said something interesting that evening in your apartment."

"What did he say?"

"That he'd fucked up too badly with you guys."

"He hasn't. I'd forgive him if he apologized."

"He needs time."

"That's what your mom said. I'm finally seeing it." A yawn escaped her, cutting off whatever she was about to say next. "Damn. I think I need sleep. Who knew crying would be so exhausting?"

"Emotions are always exhausting, I've found. Do you want to come home with me? I know you said you needed space, but I miss you. I'd sleep better if you were next to me."

"Does that line usually work?"

"I've only used it on you, so you tell me."

She pretended to think about it. "It's *kind* of working."

"I also bought a stand mixer for you to use when you cook."

She raised her eyebrows. "Really?"

"I've heard they're useful."

"Okay, now I'm definitely coming over. Your kitchen is way bigger than mine."

I grabbed her hand. "Then let's go home."

As I gazed at her face, I waited for her to correct me.

She never did.

"I'll follow you back," she said instead.

Excitement filled me at the thought of her spending the night again, even if we just slept.

When her car pulled into the driveway, I couldn't wait to bring her inside. She peeled off her heels the moment she walked in the door.

She admired the new mixer while I tried tugging her to the bedroom. "Come on. You said you were tired."

"But the mixer—"

"You need to rest and unwind. I have an idea."

She raised an eyebrow and followed me to the room. I sat her on the bed and rubbed her shoulders.

"Oh, that feels nice."

"You've been stressed."

"I have been, but this is helping."

I moved to her neck. Her muscles were tight, and I could tell she held all her stress there. I focused my attention on that area, kneading the tightness.

"This is just what I needed."

I continued to work on her shoulders, but then she started to lean on me, eyes closed.

"Ruth? Are you awake?"

"Barely," she muttered. Her eyes didn't open.

"Let's get ready for bed then."

She'd left a toothbrush and pajamas here when she'd vacated the premises so quickly, which had only made me miss her more while she was gone. Her stuff reminded me that she had a place here.

She dragged her feet to get ready for bed, but she finally let her hair down and brushed her teeth. When she laid down, she was so still that I thought she had already fallen asleep by the time I climbed in next to her.

But she rested her head on my shoulder the moment I joined her, hand around my waist, as if to keep me where she wanted me.

Little did she know, I wasn't going anywhere.

The previous nights, I'd laid awake missing her. I'd thrown myself into figuring out the new office while Preston was gone, just so I could tell her sooner.

I didn't know peace when she was gone, but now it was all I knew since she was back where she belonged.

I traced patterns onto the skin of her shoulder, unable to keep my hands off of her. I felt like a teenager with a crush drawing in a notebook.

Only I was an adult, and my paper was her.

I wrote my name. I wrote hers. And eventually, I wrote new one.

Her name and then my last one. It didn't technically exist yet, but I wanted it to eventually.

Ruth Price had a nice ring to it.

CHAPTER
TWENTY-FOUR

Ruth

When I woke up, I was calmer than I had been in days. Sunlight gently filtered in through the curtains, but the house was quiet in a way that my apartment never was.

I was laying on my side with Knox behind me, his body pressed against mine. My hand was under his, and I was surrounded by his scent.

I closed my eyes and drank it all in in a futile attempt to tattoo the moment into my memory. I wished time would stand still so I could stay here forever.

"Morning," Knox's hushed voice said. His lips pressed to my shoulder. "Did you sleep okay?"

"I slept great," I said. "Apparently, I'm not good at sleeping without you."

"You can sleep with me whenever you want," he said, his mouth moving against my skin.

I bit my tongue to keep from telling him that I couldn't do it when he was across the country from me. I didn't want to ruin such a perfect moment.

"I promise you that you don't need to worry about what it is you're worrying about," he said. "At least not when you're in my bed."

His lips had crept up my neck, and his words coupled with the soft press of his lips against my nape made me forget of all thoughts of the future.

His hand grasped my hip, pulling me closer to him. I could feel his hardness push against me, and my mind flashed to his hands on my skin. I'd gone far too long without him. Especially when everything had been so draining day after day.

Any remaining worry gave way to heat. I needed him again.

I rolled over to face him, slanting my mouth over his. His hands kept me pressed into him. His lips were firm on mine, moving like words he was desperate to say. I had a feeling there was a goodbye somewhere in there.

But I wouldn't think about that. I had him in the moment, and my body needed him—all of him.

"I fucking missed this," I said, moving my mouth away from his for only a moment.

"I did too," he said, advancing toward my neck.

My skin heated as I felt his mouth move against the sensitive skin under my throat. I tightened my hold on his shoulders.

His hand drifted up to my breast and he took only a moment to ask if it was okay before he cupped it in his hand. I couldn't help the stuttering sigh I let out at the contact.

"I want more, Knox."

"I'm happy to give you whatever you like."

Forever, I thought. *I want forever.*

But that wasn't in the cards. I would have to settle for this.

"Grab the—"

"I know," he said.

He grabbed my vibrator, something I'd left there. Masturbation was the last thing on my mind when I knew what an orgasm was like when it came from his hands.

I was wet already, and the feeling of the vibration was a relief I didn't know I'd needed. Words left my mind, and I was only able to let out a broken moan as he moved the device expertly to right where I needed it.

He moved the vibrator up and down, but what sent me over the edge was when he teased the tip of it into me.

Shockwaves echoed through my body and I lost myself in the sensation. I'd never come so fast before.

"Did you like that?" he whispered into my ear.

"I-I did."

"Good. Then I'll remember it for next time."

As my thoughts cleared, I realized I hadn't even touched him yet. It was a shame, considering it was one of my favorite things to do.

I trailed my hand to wrap around his length, moving up and down. I focused on that for a moment as the remains of my orgasmic high left my body.

"Ruth," he said, his voice rough. "If you keep doing that, then this will be over very soon."

My thighs clenched at the thought of not having him in me. "Do you have a condom?" I asked.

"I've figured out that I need to keep them around," he said, kissing me again before grabbing one.

Once the condom was rolled onto his ready cock, I pulled him on top of me. The tip of him pressed inside, sending a wave of pleasure through my entire body as a reminder of how I'd just came.

He moved slowly, and I knew he didn't want to hurt me, but I was more than ready for him.

"Fuck me, Knox. Hard." I locked my legs around him, pushing him farther into me.

"I'm going to ask you if you're sure one time," he choked out, "and if you say yes, I will lose all control."

"Yes," I said. "Please lose control."

He slammed into me then, pressing all the way in. Then he pulled out and did it again. I clenched around him, body humming in pleasure as he moved the exact way I wanted him to. This wasn't the time for gentle movements or going slow. This was passion, and I was lost in it.

"Fuck, yes," I gasped out, hands gripping the sheets.

He pounded into me, never slowing down for a second. My body was tight around him and I felt a warmth building inside of me.

Knox came with a muttered, "Fuck." His movements stilled, and I could feel myself loosen. That didn't feel like my usual orgasms, but it felt like something.

"Are you okay?" he asked. "Was I too rough?"

"No," I replied. "It just felt . . . different. Like I was building to something."

"Do you want me to keep moving?"

"No," I replied. "But maybe we can explore than next time."

Please let there be a next time, I wanted to add.

"Of course, Ruth," he said. "Anything you want."

I arrived at work after nine but couldn't find it in me to care.

I was the VP now. If Caroline could sleep in her office, I could arrive a little late.

But despite my little pep talk, anxiety hit me as I walked into the building. Everything was quiet, and not a soul was in sight.

It reminded me of the calm before the storm.

My fears were confirmed when I saw Jenny's face. Her eyes were wide, and she was waiting outside of the door.

I knew this wasn't going to be good news.

"What's going on?"

"They know."

"Who knows? About what?"

"Dave knows about you and Knox. We were called into a meeting asking if we knew any information."

My heart raced. "We haven't done anything. Not here, at least."

"I believe you, but they don't. You should prepare yourself. They might fire you both."

"Damn it," I said.

My phone buzzed with a notification and I made the mistake of checking it.

Tom: Did you want this getting out?

And it was a video of me going into Knox's house, and me leaving it the next morning.

I cursed. Of course they'd seen this, and now they were on a warpath. I never stopped to think that maybe I needed to be careful in a neighborhood like his.

But I should have.

The very next thing I saw was a notification from my work calendar for a meeting involving Knox and me.

"Fuck. *Fuck*."

"Yeah," Jenny said. "It's bad."

I took a moment to close my eyes. This could be the end of my career.

Jenny grabbed my shoulders, then she hugged me. "You don't deserve this."

"I know."

I went to open the door but froze. Fear turned into anger. I could claim discrimination if they fired me and not Knox, which I had a feeling was going to be the result of this meeting.

And I'd need proof of my that.

In a split-second decision, an idea hit me. I grabbed my phone again and opened the voice recorder.

"What are you doing?"

"Whatever bullshit Dave is about to try, he better be okay with everyone else hearing it."

A slow smile spread onto Jenny's face. "That's my girl."

Knox

I tapped my foot against the floor, waiting for Ruth to arrive. When I'd gotten the email for the meeting, titled only "Discussion," I knew something was wrong.

Dave was sitting at his desk. When I made eye contact with him, he was glaring.

Ruth walked in, lips pursed.

"You wanted to see me?" Her voice was breathy, and I saw she had her purse with her. Had she even gotten to her desk before they pulled her into this?

"It has come to our attention that you two are in a romantic relationship," Dave said matter-of-factly. His voice was level, depicting a calm I doubted he felt. He turned to Ruth. "You were photographed leaving his house one morning after entering the night before."

Damn it. Someone must have known who I was and where I lived. They must have really wanted to catch a story on me.

And they did.

"I accept responsibility for this," I said immediately. "As the one in the position of power—"

"Now, now, you don't need to worry. The best course of action is to let Ruth go and you stay."

My eyes narrowed. "That is illegal."

"*You* are the one who is needed around here."

"And I'm not?" Ruth asked.

"You should have known better," he said to her. "We told everyone no workplace relationships, and he is your *superior*."

"Which means *I* was the problem," I said.

"You were, but your name has done more for Stanford than anything she's done."

"She's kept your business afloat."

"She's just a loud woman who wants everything her way."

"So you're firing me for my relationship," Ruth cut in. "And he gets off with no consequences?"

"Which is, again, illegal," I added.

"If you two are going to be *difficult*," Dave stood, eyes on me, "then I could tell everyone what you did. I could say you were warned. I could describe how you *told* me to promote her, which I didn't want to. People will draw conclusions, Knox. They will know that you promised her a promotion, slept with her, and then tried to hide it. News like this will ruin you. So it's in your best interest to let her walk out this door and end whatever little entanglement you made the mistake of making."

"Hang on," Ruth said.

"No!" Dave yelled, slamming his hand on the desk. "I am tired of hearing you *talk*, Ruth. I am tired of seeing you waltz around this office like you own the place. This is the end of you. You're just a quick lay to him. He won't destroy his career for *you*."

"And that's where you're wrong." My voice echoed in the room. For once, I was louder than Dave, and that was saying something.

"Am I? It's your *career* or her."

"I choose her." The words slipped out like a hot knife through butter; they were the easiest words I'd ever said.

For a moment, no one dared to speak.

"W-wait," Ruth said. "No. Don't choose me."

"I'm going to," I said. "Go ahead and tell everyone everything. I don't care."

It would make things difficult, for sure. Preston would have to stay the CEO, and I would have to be sure to keep my name away from PATH. But in that moment, I didn't care. I loved my company, but I loved her more.

"You will be *eviscerated* by the media," Dave said. "You slept with her and got her a promotion—"

"That's not what happened. I told you to promote her because she *was* your best bet. And I did that *before* we were together. I made no decisions on her hiring because I wasn't even in her interview. *You* chose her."

"To keep *you* happy."

"Right, because you will never see that she is the reason this company has any standing in the banking industry."

"She will ruin you."

"She's not the one making the threat to. You are. So go ahead. Try me."

"You would ruin your reputation over Ruth Murray?"

"Yes. I would."

"You'll take my son's company down with you."

"You're the one making the threat, and besides, PATH will be fine. It's made a name for itself that doesn't hinge on me."

"But you'll be out of a job."

"I have more money than you can *dream* of. Ruin my reputation, Dave. I can promise you, I will still be more successful than you. To quote someone I care about very much, 'Do your worst.'"

Dave's face was tomato red. "Get. Out."

"Hang on," Ruth began.

"I will call security!" Dave yelled. I was sure the whole office heard him.

"Okay, fine," she said. "But for the record, I hope this place crashes and *burns*. You're a terrible boss, a terrible *person*, and your son deserves someone far better as a father figure. You're a disgrace."

"OUT!" Dave's voice got impossibly louder. I grabbed Ruth's arm. "Let's go."

She gritted her teeth and stormed out of Dave's office.

"She's right, you know," I said. "Preston *is* better than you."

I turned on my heel and left.

Amber was in the hall, talking in a hushed tone to Ruth as they hugged goodbye.

"Don't worry," Amber said. "We'll stall any media releases."

"Thank you," Ruth said. To me, she instructed, "Let's go."

"Fucking asshole," I muttered the moment we were in the parking lot.

"I want to kill him. No, I want to torture him in slow and painful ways."

"Preston is going to kill me for that," I said.

"Yeah, that wasn't very smart." She crossed her arms. "But it was very sweet. Thank you."

"You're welcome."

"We should fight this."

"How? It's going to look bad either way. Even if Amber stalls the release, it's going to be our word against his."

"More like our recording."

"What?"

She took out her phone, which had a voice recorder app open. She hit end and smiled at me. "I had a feeling that would be bad. So, I took a precaution."

"You . . . are the smartest and most beautiful woman on the planet."

"Thank you," she said, still grinning.

"We need to get this out before he does."

"We could call a press conference. People are dying for the story. The comments on the news articles have been wild. Any reporter would come to it and we could play the recording." Her face fell. "But you don't like public speaking, and no one knows who I am. Can Preston do it?"

"By the time we explain to him what happened, Dave might have the story out. Besides, he might react emotionally. His dad is involved, after all."

"Perfect, so we have no major name to use to get this story out."

"I'll do the press conference."

"Knox, no. I know what fears are like. I'm not asking you to do this."

"I said I'll do it. But only if you're with me. That's the only way."

"Are you sure?"

"As much as I can be. Let me call PATH's publicist."

CHAPTER TWENTY-FIVE

Ruth

I chewed on my nail as I watched reporters file in. Knox's publicist hadn't needed to do much work. A recluse inventor leading a press conference drew a huge crowd, especially now that he'd been seen with me.

In only twenty minutes, we were standing in a small room attached to a hotel. More reporters were there than I think either of us expected. I kept refreshing social media, but nothing was out from Stanford yet.

Thank God for Amber. If I was able to find another job anywhere, she'd be my first hire.

"Are you sure about this?" I asked him again. His was looking a little pale as he gazed out at the sea of reporters.

"No."

I tried to think of what I would need if I were in his position. My fear was still there, but the last storm I'd made it through. What had worked was *him*.

His support and his kindness.

I supposed I could try the same thing. I grabbed his hand, giving him a small smile.

"You've got this."

"I definitely don't."

"Even so, I'm here. Even if you cry like a baby."

He took a steady breath, but I could feel his hands shake. "No judging if I do."

"You've seen me crying over thunder and your mom being nice to me. We'd be even."

He kissed me once more before turning to the stage.

I walked out with him, keeping my hand in his. The people were *loud* as they yelled questions we weren't ready for, but I took a deep breath, determined to be here for him.

"G-good evening, everyone. Thanks for coming."

I bit my lip. It was definitely not the evening, but I was sure he knew that.

"You may hear news coming out of Stanford about me, news that isn't true. First and foremost, I want to announce my resignation from the company and explain what transpired."

"Who's the woman?" a bold reporter exclaimed. "Is that Ruth?"

"Yes, I'm Ruth. Now there will be no further questions until Knox is finished speaking," I said firmly, leaning into the microphone.

He took another unsteady breath. "I'd like to play a recording for you of what happened upon the news breaking of Ruth's and my relationship."

I grabbed my phone, playing the recording for everyone. I saw a few jaws drop. Hearing it again brought back all the pain I was hiding from the day. Soon, I would be crying in a pile on the floor over losing my job so publicly, but for now, I kept it together for Knox.

"This is one of the many sexist comments I've heard from Dave Stanford, the CEO of the company. It pains me to say this, since he is the father of a dear friend. But Ruth was always mistreated from day one. She only gained respect once *I* stepped in. She would have never been promoted, never been acknowledged, if I hadn't done anything. And that is wrong."

"But are you in a relationship?"

"Yes," he said firmly. "We are. And I acknowledge that I was in a higher position. We broke rules." His grip on my hand tightened. "I tried to stay away so she could grow professionally, but I wasn't able to."

"Did she lure you into the relationship to get the promotion?"

Knox glared. "She did not. The promotion was never a part of our relationship. I was never in her interview. I did not have the final say."

"Why tell us this?" another reporter asked. "You could have simply hidden it."

"Because Ruth is the love of my life. And I'm not interested in hiding anything to do with her, just like I will never let her be punished for something for my benefit. My plan is to always do right by her."

Holy. *Shit.*

My face burst into flame, and I was torn between kissing him and killing him for saying he loved me in this damn press conference.

Reporters started yelling over each other, but one question could be heard many times.

"Will you be returning to PATH?"

He held up a hand. When there was silence, he continued, "I will return to PATH as the CEO as long as this news does not damage the company. It was already something I was considering before this happened."

"What about Ruth?"

"She'll be coming with me."

And then my heart, which was soaring from the news that Knox loved me, plummeted.

I couldn't go with him. I didn't want to leave my life. I wanted to be near my brothers while they healed, so we could heal together. I wanted regular dinners with Jenny.

Knox glanced over and I could see how fast he was breathing. His speech was wearing on him. I pushed down what I was feeling so I could focus on him. We could talk about this later.

I gave him a reassuring smile and leaned into the microphone, saying that we would be wrapping up. He said a quick goodbye and then we left the stage, ignoring all the questions shouted at us.

"You did great," I said.

"They want more information," he said. "Give me your phone."

"Why?" I said, handing it to him.

"They might try to hack it," he said. "I'll add some security measures when we get home."

"I think you need take a breath."

He sighed, and for a second, I thought he would argue, but his shoulders lowered, letting the tension ease out of him via a deep exhale.

"Did we beat them to the announcement?" he asked.

"We did," I said. "I bet Dave's pissed."

"I don't ever want to think of that man again," he said firmly. "Let's go home."

Knox

"Dude, what the *fuck*?" Preston's voice was tight over the car speaker. "I turn my phone off for two hours only for you to be a top story because *you*, the man who hates public speaking, held a press conference?"

"He also admitted to being in a relationship with someone who was technically under him," Ruth added.

"I . . . I think I need to sit down. Wait, I'm already sitting. Maybe I need to lie down."

"I didn't have time to explain," I said.

"You know, Knox, usually your inventions are what surprises me. You've been on a roll lately."

"I know this is going to look bad," Knox said. "I know I broke rules and I'm sorry that it was all announced like this."

"I knew there was a risk to you working there," he said. "I just didn't think it would go down like *this*."

"Me either."

"Did they ever put the no relationship rule in writing?"

"Nothing at Stanford is in writing," Ruth replied. "It's all verbal."

"Perfect. We can fight this then. I need to do damage control. You're lucky I like you, Knox. And that I hate my dad."

"I'm sorry you came from him."

"Me too."

"There's one other thing in the press conference. It's about Ruth and PATH."

Ruth's eyes flew to mine.

"We can discuss that later. I need to go. Go calm down, both of you. It's been a busy day."

I said my goodbye and glanced over at Ruth.

"As much as I love sitting in your car to talk to Preston, I need to drive mine back to your place."

"Yeah, of course," I said. She bit her lip and then got out of the car. "Is everything okay?"

"Yep," she said. "Let's get back to your house. Then we can talk about . . . what you said in there."

Ruth walked away and I could make a solid guess and say she was talking about what I'd told everyone about her future employment.

I checked my email for a copy of the signed contract. Nothing so far, but I knew it was Preston's top priority.

I sent a quick text to him.

Knox: I blurted out that Ruth is coming to work at PATH. I've gotta tell her.

Preston: I just saw that. You've been breaking a lot of rules today.

Knox: I know. Sorry. I answered the question without thinking.

Preston: Tell her. This contract is going through smoothly. Just secure her phone.

I sighed.

"Let's get inside," I said after we pulled into the driveway. I watched to see if anyone was around, but thankfully no one dared to come near the house despite the news.

Her jaw was tight as she climbed out.

"We need to talk," she said the moment the front door shut behind us.

"Let me work on your phone. You take a breather. It's been a tough couple of days for you."

"Of course it has. I just got *fired*. I bet my mom is losing her shit right now."

I let out a long breath, thinking of the letter. I somehow had to think of a way to both tell her about that and that PATH was moving to Nashville.

But that would have to wait. I moved toward my office to work on her phone, but she stopped me with a hand on my chest.

"You sighed when I mentioned my mom. Why?"

"It's not the priority right now."

"No, but if it involves my mom, I want to know. Did she contact you or something?" Damn it. I hated how smart she was.

"How is that your first guess?"

"Because she's your biggest fan," she said. "And judging by the way you won't meet my eyes, I'm guessing I'm right."

"Okay, yes. You're right. Just let me—"

"When?"

"Before I came back."

"You knew?"

"Not until recently, I swear. There was a letter that Preston had seen. I didn't even read it."

"I want to."

"I need to—"

"My phone is fine," she said. "I don't talk to anyone about anything on there. Just show me the letter."

"Are you sure you're in the right mental state to see them?"

"I'm fine. What did my mom send you?"

I knew she wouldn't let this go. I went to the mail organizer that to pull out the letter. She looked near tears, and I had a terrible feeling this wasn't going to go well.

Ruth's hands shook, but she opened the envelope, and I watched her closely as her eyes glanced over the paper.

CHAPTER TWENTY–SIX

Ruth

Dear Knox Price,

I doubt you will read this, but it is worth a try. I am a massive fan of your work. You are one of the biggest inspirations of this generation. I hope my kids would see even a fraction of your success.

"It's fucking fan mail," I hissed.

"You don't have to read it then."

"I'm definitely reading this. Even if it's only to remember why I'm mad at her."

My eyes went back to the page and I traced my mother's handwriting.

To be honest with you, I'm not even sure if I should send this, but I've heard this is a good way to get emotions out. I can't very well tell this to my daughter, Ruth, because it's not her fault I've failed her as a mother.

I've failed at every turn, actually. I've married a man I'm too afraid to leave. I pushed my daughter to be just as good as her brothers, but when I look at her, I see the same resigned exhaustion that I see in the mirror every day. I hoped she would be the one to defy every expectation, that she would be the one to prove to the monster I married that she could *do what he thought she couldn't.*

But I worry that she will fall into the same trap I did.

You may be wondering why I am even telling you this, but you used to know my daughter, actually. You went to high school with her. If you do remember her, I bet you remember how much she tried to best you at every turn.

I always thought you and her could rule the world together if she would only admit her feelings for you. I used to wonder if perhaps you felt the same.

But you're famous now, and the opportunity is gone.

I need to leave Todd. I need to stand up for Ruth. But as time passes, I grow more and more afraid. I once hoped her spirit would inspire me, so I fostered her ferocity as much as I could.

Now I fear I've brought her down with me.

If you do read this, Knox, then come back for Ruth. I think leaving her here was a mistake. I know she doesn't deserve to be in the position I am, and I can't shake the feeling that the two of you could do great things together.

With much admiration, and a certain amount of delusion,

Jolene Murray

A tear dropped onto the page and it took me a minute to realize it was my own.

"Ruth?" Knox said softly. "Was it bad?"

"She cares," I said. "She asked you to come back for me."

His eyebrows knit in confusion and I wordlessly handed him the letter, unable to talk with the dangerous swirl of emotions building in my gut.

My brain unhelpfully conjured the sound of thunder to match my darkening mood.

"This is why Preston sent me here. It's how he knew about you."

"What?" I croaked.

"Preston didn't send me here to work for Dave. He told me it was *you*, that this letter made him think you were the key to fixing the numbness I found myself in, you and my family. Dave was just the excuse to get here. He was right."

"My *mom* did this. God, this is what I wanted from her, just an acknowledgment that I was a human being, but she didn't even do it to my face. I got what I wanted and I'm still mad."

"You can be mad. Has she reached out since you set the boundary with them?"

I shook my head.

"She has a reason for why she did what she did, but it hurt you. She still tried to make you meet expectations that were impossible. She compared you to me all the time."

"I *know*," I said. "Trust me, I know. I just wish things were different."

"Maybe they will be, but you need a break before we think about anything else."

"I can't take a break right now. I need to find a new job."

"You'll have a job at PATH."

"No, *no*. I can't take that."

"Why not?"

"I don't want a job just *given* to me."

And I didn't want to move across the country to get it, but saying that made it real. Once it was real, I had to acknowledge that we were doomed.

"Ruth, I want you to work for PATH, you'd be great at it—"

"I can't have you giving me anything."

"Even if you deserve it?"

"Not when you're the first choice!" I snapped "The only thing I *ever* won for myself in my whole life was being the damn valedictorian."

His jaw dropped open as if to speak, but he froze, and the same expression crossed his face as when he'd told me about the letter.

"Do you have *another* secret to tell me?"

"It's not something you need to hear right now."

"What is it?"

"Ruth, no."

"Tell me," I said, my voice firm. "Please."

"No. I'm not changing my mind about this."

"Fine. Then I'll figure it out." I paced the room as my mind worked overtime. "You tried to pay to have it taken from me."

His eyes stayed glued to my face. "You know I didn't have the money for that."

"You planned on taking it from me on stage."

"No, never."

"You actually won it and gave to me because—" My mind put the pieces together and horror dawned on me. *"Because you couldn't do the speech."*

His eyes shot to the floor, and I knew that I was right.

Mother. *Fucker.*

"It was ten years ago. It's not a huge deal."

"This is a joke, right?"

"It's not a—"

"If you tell me it's not a big deal one more time, I will lose it. *Please* tell me you're joking. I didn't even get valedictorian fair and square?"

"You *were* the valedictorian."

"I was the second choice! Like always!"

"Ruth, today has been a lot. I didn't want to tell you because you need a second to *breathe.*"

"I need to be good enough for once! God, why am I never enough?"

"You are enough, Ruth."

"No. No, I'm not. I've lost my job. My parents fucking hate me. And now I find out I wasn't even the valedictorian! You won *everything*!"

"Why is it even a competition?" he snapped. His eyes narrowed and I dimly realized this was the first time he was truly *mad* at me. "None of it matters. We don't need to compete for anything, and we shouldn't have had to then."

"My whole life has been a competition."

"But it's not *now*. Ruth, you're upset about today, and you have every right to be. About all of it." He stepped forward to touch me, but I moved back.

"Don't."

"*No.* This is not coming between us."

My mind conjured more thunder. I squeezed my eyes shut, hating my own brain. When I opened them, Knox was glancing outside.

"Son of a bitch," he muttered.

It must have been reporters.

"I need to go." I would face them if I had to.

"Ruth, do not leave this house."

"No! I need a minute to fucking *think*!" I turned away from him and heard the sounds of footsteps. Maybe he was finally walking away from me.

The thunder in my mind remained loud, insistent. I needed it to stop. I couldn't breathe. I turned for the door, only for *real* lightning to strike the tree across the street.

The thunder was *deafening*.

I screamed and crouched down in a huddle, covering my ears as I realized what Knox was cursing at.

The imaginary thunder wasn't in my head. It was a real fucking storm brewing.

The power flickered and the wind pummeled the branches of the trees surrounding Knox's house. I watched as they bent, thinking they could break at any second. When a familiar sound reached my ears, it hit me.

Nashville's tornado sirens were crying out.

Not a tornado. Please. Not today. Not on what was already the worst day of my life.

That siren haunted me as it echoed through my dreams. I heard it even when there was no threat of bad weather.

And now that the real one blared through every inch of the city, bounced around every corner of Knox's house, no other emotion beyond panic mattered. This was it. My worst fear was once again on my doorstep.

Knox

I caught Ruth as she sank to the floor, wrapping her in my arms as the reality of the situation hit her. I'd barely had time to grab the prototype for the headphones before the tornado siren went off.

I didn't care that we were in the middle of a fight. I didn't care about the damn update to her phone or anything else. She needed me, and I would always be there for her.

Dimly, I knew a tornado during her childhood was what started this fear. I remembered she mentioned panic attacks, and her breathing was already unsteady.

"Ruth," I said. "Let's get to the basement."

Her anger was gone, replaced with fear.

"It's a tornado," she said, catatonic. "It's happening again."

"We need to get to safety."

"I can't move."

"Then I'll carry you."

The last time she was in my arms like this, she fought it. Her body was tense and she leaned away, almost as if she wanted to jump *out* of my arms.

This time, she leaned in. She *burrowed* into me, as if she couldn't get close enough.

The basement wasn't completely underground, but there was one corner far enough away from the sole window on the exposed side.

After slowly descending the stairs, careful not to trip over anything, I tucked us into the corner. Ruth hadn't even noticed I'd brought the prototype with me and slipped them over her ears while I carried her, but I was glad I had.

The device was lacking the polish I wanted. Some of the wires were exposed, and the power button was hard to press. But they worked. I could see it in Ruth's expression.

"Wh-what?" Thunder struck again, and I watched her face carefully. She didn't react. "What are these?"

"Calibratable active noise-canceling headphones. Right now, they're blocking out thunder."

She stared. "Really?"

Another rumble shook the sky, but her eyes remained on me.

I let out a sigh of relief. All those hours making this had been worth it.

"You didn't hear it, did you?" I asked.

"I can hear the tornado siren, but not the thunder."

"It's not calibrated to that yet, but it can be. Does blocking out the thunder help?"

"Yes. I can *think*."

"Good. That's what they are for. Can you hear me okay?"

She nodded and reached up to feel them. Outside, lightning struck, and her eyes watched it. I heard the rumbling that followed. She didn't.

"When did you do this?" Her voice was small.

"It's what Preston delivered. I got the idea at the convention."

"You did this for *me*?"

"I will do *anything* for you."

She only stared at me. "Wh-what if I asked you not to go back to PATH?"

"You already know I would stay, but you don't need to worry about that."

"But I do. I can't move to California, Knox. I don't want to leave Nashville."

"You're not going to San Francisco."

"But *you* are, and I don't you to leave me."

"I'm not going either."

"If you're the CEO, you *have* to be there."

"Not if PATH is here," I said slowly, hoping she would connect the dots.

"What?"

"It's not official yet, and I wasn't supposed to tell you, but PATH is moving here. I'm not leaving you."

"You're really staying?"

"I am. I may need to go back to help with the move once I'm the CEO again, but it would only be for a few days at a time."

"Why couldn't you tell me?"

"The first time we tried to find an office, people made it difficult. You know how the general public felt about PATH when it first came out."

"They hated it."

"We had a hard time finding space, and when we did, people protested. We wanted a contract in place here before anyone would know."

"I wouldn't have told."

"But you might've mentioned it to a friend." He took out my phone. "That's why I need to update this. Preston got hacked once and we almost spilled company secrets."

"So, I was worried about nothing?"

"I'm sorry, Ruth," I said. "I didn't want to keep it from you."

"N-no, I get it. I don't even think I'm mad. I'm just so fucking relieved. Well, other than the tornado."

"I think we're fine." But I took out my phone to check. "The storm system looks to be passing."

She let out a sigh and slumped against the wall. "I should have taken that break when you told me to."

"I'm just glad that you're okay."

"Thank you," she said softly as her fingers caressed the headphones over her ears. "For everything."

"It was all worth it, Ruth. I should have never left Nashville to begin with. This place is where my parents are, where *you* are."

She smiled.

"I think it's my turn to tell you something, Knox." Her eyes steadily held mine. "I think I'm in love with you."

For a moment, I could only stare at her. My heart was beating too fast as I took in her words. *She loved me?* The world fell away. I didn't care about the storm, or the invention. It was only her.

"What a coincidence," I whispered as my thoughts returned to me, "because I think I'm in love with you too."

Ruth kissed me and I could feel the shakiness in her hands slow as the storm inside her dissipated, and the storm outside was quieting too.

We fitted together, even while sitting on the basement floor.

"I've loved you ever since I laid eyes on you," I said, moving my lips to her neck. "And I want to keep loving you for as long as I live."

"Even when I'm stubborn?" Her voice was breathy, but this time it wasn't from fear.

"Especially when you're stubborn." I swiped my tongue across her lower lip, and she let me in immediately. I wanted to never forget the taste of her. She was my favorite wine. My favorite food. Everything I loved.

I could try for the rest of my life to invent some way to tell her everything I felt about her, but even I knew it would be impossible.

I'd settle for pouring all of that into this kiss.

I hiked up her legs and pulled her closer to me. She let out a sound of surprise but leaned into it.

She leaned away and I only got a moment to admire her lips before she said, "Let's go upstairs. I need you."

And I could never turn her down. I wasted no time in getting us off the floor of the basement. Her lips were on mine again before we even hit the bed, but once we were near it, her hands were pulling off my shirt.

"Are you sure you're—"

"Yes," she said. "The man I love literally inventing a device to help me through my fear turns me on."

"Seeing you test my inventions turns *me* on. Or maybe it's just you."

I grabbed her hand, feeling no hint of the tremors the storm caused. I could tell by the brightness in her eyes that she was okay.

And all bets were off for me.

The rest of our clothes came off in a frenzy, and I was eager to get my hands on her warm skin. Her mouth's return to mine made my already interested member grow heavier.

I blindly reached for the device that helped her finish, and once it was in my hand, I couldn't wait to turn it on and subject her to the best form of torture.

But when I pressed the button, nothing happened.

I paused in kissing her, frowning at the vibrator.

"Oh no," she muttered. "Did I not charge it?"

"I guess not."

She groaned, but then shook her head. "It doesn't matter. I still want this. I don't have to come."

I shook my head. "I want to try."

"I haven't been able to orgasm without a vibrator in years."

"I'm a patient man."

"I don't think it'll be enjoyable for you."

"I love making you feel good. It can take as long as you need."

"What if I don't?"

"I just want to give it a shot."

She bit her lip but nodded. "Okay," she said. "I trust you."

I kissed her lips once more before the urge to kiss other parts of her were too strong to resist. I hadn't gone down on her before, mostly because she was insistent that she wouldn't be able to come that way, but the smell of her arousal was too tempting to resist.

She liked it rough, so that was exactly what I'd do for her.

I gave her center one exploratory swipe of my tongue.

And that was when I found my new favorite taste. I was unable to hold back, but I knew she liked it when I let go. I heard her gasp as I pressed into her delicious center.

Her fingers raked through my hair, pulling me in even deeper.

I took my time, enjoying every second that I got to taste her. Every moan I drew from her lips was like another dose of an intoxicating drug, spurring me to continue giving her attention in order to get a bigger high.

I buried one finger inside of her.

"Oh, *fuck*," she gasped. She moved my head exactly where she wanted it, and I was happy to give her what she needed. I lost track of time as I nipped, kissed, and sucked on her clit, all while my finger moved inside of her.

I could have stayed there forever, breathing in her addictive scent, but eventually, her breath grew faster, and her hips jerked against my face.

I continued my relentless assault and her body shook as I felt her clench around my finger. She screamed as she came, and I couldn't resist the smirk that graced my face as I gazed up at her.

"I can't believe it," she said, out of breath. "I haven't been able to come like that in . . ."

"You just needed the right kind of attention. You're a force of nature, Ruth. You need to be treated like one."

"I both love and hate that you're right. Get a condom, Knox. I'm not finished with you."

After grabbing a condom and putting it on, I slanted my mouth over hers only once before she flipped me over, settling on top of me.

Ruth's ample breasts were on full display and my eyes could only focus on how she moved as she lined herself up, bringing her entrance to the tip of my hard length.

I was desperate to feel her tightness around me, but I managed to whisper out, "Go slow if you need to."

"You said I like it fast and rough," she said, pressing her hips down and fully sliding me into her.

"Fuck," I groaned as I felt her take me in. When I looked up at her, her eyes were half lidded. I couldn't wait any longer, and I jerked up my hips, pushing even deeper into her. Her hands came to grip my shoulders, nails digging in to my skin.

"Fast and rough, right?" I said, slamming back into her. Her head dropped back in pleasure as I thrust up into her with strength I didn't know I had.

"Yes," she said, her thighs clenching around my hips. "Yes, like that!"

As I slammed into her, I felt myself build toward something intense. She was tight around me, just as she had been the last time I'd fucked her.

"Harder," she muttered, nails digging deeper into my skin.

"Then we're going to need to move," I said, pulling out of her.

"Where do you want me?" she asked right before I rolled her over onto her stomach. She was bent over, hair everywhere, and I paused for only a second to admire the literal art that was in front of me.

She moaned when I pressed into her again, but I made sure to pull all the way out before slamming in again. Her hands gripped the sheets, just like she had the last time she said she was building to something.

It was work to not come just from the sight alone, but I knew she needed time.

And I was rewarded for that.

After only a few minutes of this new position, she was moaning and pressing back into me. I sped up, hoping to give her more of what she needed.

"Oh, *fuck*," she yelled. "Yes!"

I felt her tighten around me like a vice as she came again with a broken moan. I wasn't able to hold back any longer, and I came harder than I had ever in my life. My vision went white and my entire body felt like it was on fire in the best way.

"Holy shit," she said, her voice breathy. "That was *two*."

"I fucking love you," I said, tracing the skin of her hip with my hands.

"I love you too," she said, turning to smile at me, but her eyes caught on the red marks on my skin. "Sorry if I was too rough."

"You? Never. I like you as you are."

The corner of her lip turned upward and a pretty blush painted her cheeks.

The wind outside still blew angrily, but I couldn't care less. The world may have been in chaos from the storm, and our careers forever changed, but I had her.

And that was all that mattered.

CHAPTER TWENTY-SEVEN

Ruth

As I stood in front of Preston in his comfortable, colorful office in the San Francisco headquarters, I knew why he was the face of PATH. He was charismatic and smooth as he talked business, which was a far cry from the slightly dorky man I'd met at Knox's doorstep.

"You're very impressive, Ruth," he said, and I frowned. I sensed a *but* coming. "But we are still doing damage control from the fallout of Stanford's response to the backlash. We have to tread carefully."

"I understand."

Knox's name was in everyone's mouths. The timing of my promotion plus the photographs of us together *were* suspicious, but no one could deny the misogyny in the recording I had played.

"PATH is a very forward-thinking company. You would be an incredible asset to the team, but giving you a position, especially considering your relationship, is something we have to be careful with."

"Okay. So it's a no, then?"

"It would be foolish to turn you down. I just need to justify the risk to the other executives. Knox usually threatens them into submission. I want to take a gentler path."

"So, what do you want me to do?"

"Show me what you can bring to the table for PATH. Find a marketing angle we haven't considered. Propose an outrageous scheme that will boost profits. If you do that, then I can convince the board of directors to take this risk."

"To hire me as . . . as what?"

"I have a couple of job openings that I know of. It depends on what I can angle for."

"Okay. How long do I have?"

"Two weeks."

I nodded, mind spinning with things I could try to do. I needed to get to a computer to see their current marketing campaign. Maybe I could come up with something to improve on.

"Oh, and one more thing?" Preston asked.

I turned to him.

"Try your best to get Knox to let you prove yourself. I'm sure his method would be to bypass everything I want to do, but it will still look bad. Trust me when I say that I have a reason I'm asking this of you."

"Got it."

"I have confidence that you *will* get the job, though."

"I'll do my best."

I said goodbye and slowly walked downstairs. Knox was, of course, waiting. He was talking to someone that had to be an employee because he looked happy to see them.

But when he saw me, he walked over immediately.

"How did it go?"

"It's a maybe."

"Seriously?" Knox said flatly. "A maybe isn't good enough." He turned to head upstairs, but I stopped him.

"He has good reasons. A maybe is not a no. I need to prove myself. Just give me a minute to think, okay?"

"Are you okay with thinking as we head back? People know I'm here and I can see the photographers lining up."

I glanced outside, groaning when I saw the hordes with cameras. Knox grabbed my hand and we beelined to our temporary car borrowed from PATH.

As we rode to the airport, I racked my brain on what to present to Preston. A simple marketing plan, even if effective, didn't seem good enough.

My thoughts were abruptly cut off, however, by a semitruck swerving into our lane. The car reacted quickly, moving us out of the way.

"Damn it," Knox said, his hands on the wheel in case he needed to take over. "This is why PATH needs to assist drivers."

I glanced over at the truck, only to blink when I saw my last name on the back of it. The company had only barely reached this side of the country, but there were a few trucks on the road. I was grateful for it, because my brain finally started to formulate an idea.

And it might have been one of my best.

Twenty-four hours later, I'd had one conversation with Tom and a meeting was confirmed with Murray and Sons. As I walked up to the building I always wanted to work at, my heart raced, but I knew I had something.

"Are you ready?" he asked as he met me in the hallway.

"As ready as I can be. I think this will go over well."

"Don't get your hopes up too high. Dad is here."

"Can he even do that? He's on leave."

"I may have said it was *you* presenting."

I glared at him.

"I'm sorry. I had to. Other senior management wanted to know."

"It's fine," I muttered.

"Is it?"

"I would have liked more preparation for seeing him again after he told me I was always meant to be a housewife, but it's not your fault. I'm here on business. It's not personal."

"It is to him."

"Then I'll exploit that. I have no problem making him look bad."

"He was wrong about you, you know."

I did know, but hearing that from my big brother was nice. I smiled over at him.

"Thank you for saying that."

"Do you have a backup if this doesn't work?"

"Of course. I've got this."

He acknowledged me with a nod and then opened the door to the conference room. It felt a little like walking into a shark tank, but after being at Stanford for so long, it was practically normal to me.

My father had a thing for flashy offices. There were floor-to-ceiling windows overlooking the skyline. The table stretched the length of the meeting room and my heels clacked against the marble floor. The room was filled with people who were dressed in their nicest suits. In a strange way, their piercing gazes made me feel right at home.

"Hello, everyone," I greeted, donning a brave smile.

"Ruth," Dad said, his tone soft but cruel at the same time. "I know why you're here."

"I assure you that you're wrong."

"You're doing this to prove that you're worth more than a housewife. I'm here to tell you there is *nothing* you can do to prove me wrong."

One of the men laughed.

"I'm sorry, *sir*, but I'm not here to discuss my personal life. This is *business*. Are you ready to begin?"

Dad blinked and the screen changed to my PowerPoint.

"Thank you, Tom." I nodded to him. "I'm here to discuss the interest in a project to increase revenue for this company. I am no stranger to the fact that competition in this sector is high, and all companies are dying to have an edge. It's my understanding that those are hard to find."

Lay out their problems, Dad would say.

"Murray and Sons has bought five other companies this year, and the current method of gaining competitive edge is by sheer size. Yet, revenue for those purchases isn't increasing, leading other companies to question if they should allow buyout. It's a very tough problem to solve."

"And I am guessing you have a solution?" Dad said lowly. "You're using my method, after all."

"I am. I'm sure you all have heard I have a connection with the CEO of PATH. Their revenue speaks for itself."

"Of course it does." Dad rolled his eyes. "But they've come to us before. Their requests were too high."

"They wanted you not to lay off truckers or dock their pay," I retorted. "That was their only request."

"I'm not a fan of keeping on employees who do *nothing*. Nor am I okay with paying them the same amount when they have less to do."

"Let's discuss what you'd gain from this deal, shall we?" I changed the slide. Behind me showed a graph. "Here are the revenues of the company that PATH partnered with for taxi services. They got the tech, kept their drivers, kept the same pay, and look at what happened to their profits."

I pointed to a sharp increase in the graph.

"People trusted the driver. The driver trusted the tech. But I also want to show you the insurance interest in self-driving technologies. Eighteen-wheelers are large and can cause serious damage if in an accident. PATH technology is preferred by insurances because of its open-source language. People can read it to see exactly what happened in a crash."

"We've heard all this before, Ruth. We aren't changing our—"

I continued to talk over him. "Here are the projected numbers that you would save on insurance. I've already contacted four insurance agencies that PATH works with. These are their estimates." A few people's jaws dropped. It was a *very* low rate compared to what most companies paid.

Five people started writing frantically.

"But we do not have the investment power to buy a whole new fleet of vehicles," Dad said quickly, as if trying to stop the interest from catching fire.

"PATH retrofits existing vehicles, meaning that you don't have to buy a whole new fleet. I believe Murray and Sons has about ten thousand trucks at its disposal. To implement self-driving vehicles, you would have to pay upwards of ten million for that many new trucks. You would only have to buy the PATH package. And if you keep your drivers on staff, PATH might be willing to negotiate a lower offer."

"So, we would be saving money there too?" someone asked.

"I have a proposed business interest plan I want to present to them. Since I've grown up hearing about this industry and also worked in marketing for the last few years, I can ensure both companies get exactly what they want."

There. I'd done it. I'd used my Dad's method.

In the back of the room, Tom nodded, obviously impressed.

"We would be paying people to do nothing, Ruth. I refuse."

"PATH is not licensed to have no drivers in the car."

"Then we'd cut their pay," he added.

"Drivers still have things to do. PATH's tech can't yet select loads that will be a viable business opportunity. You *tried* to automate that three years ago and it failed. The truck drivers have managed that, as well as facilitating the loading and unloading of the vehicles. PATH also clearly states an alert adult must be present at the wheel at all times. They will still be working the same hours."

Dad narrowed his eyes. "We will hold firm, Ruth. We will not be taking this deal."

A few people glared at him.

"That's fine. I was prepared to offer this to multiple other companies. I was hoping you'd want first movers' advantage since you've been so concerned with raising revenue."

I smiled as I added in my own little method.

Say fuck them and go for another company when they say no.

"You're going to offer this to other logistics companies?" a man on my right asked.

"Oh, yes. I have a meeting in two hours with one. I believe you've heard of Adams Trucking."

Whispers broke out. That was their biggest competitor.

"Can we add something to the interest form that stops other companies from hearing this proposal?"

"That's already added. Whoever signs first has exclusivity unless the deal falls through."

"No, no," Dad said. "We are *not* considering it."

"The numbers don't lie, Todd. This is the deal we've been looking for."

"I said *no*."

"May I remind you that *I* am the acting CEO," Tom said, stepping in. "And I will be the first to sign the papers."

"Yes," the sole woman in the room said. "Todd is on leave. We don't need his permission."

I smiled innocently at Dad, who tried and failed to get everyone back on his side.

I knew these kinds of people. They followed the money, and I'd managed to get them the perfect deal.

When they all lined up to sign the interest paperwork, I knew I'd won.

Judging by the glare from Dad, he knew too.

"You should check your email," I said on a video call to Preston an hour later. "I've sent you a business proposal for PATH and Murray and Sons Logistics."

"Murray? Any relation?"

"Yes, but it doesn't change the terms of the deal. Nothing is legally binding, but it is notarized to be a certificate of interest in working with PATH."

I saw Preston focus on the screen where the interest form was displayed. His jaw dropped once he opened the file.

"Is this an agreement to work with a massive trucking company on self-driving eighteen-wheelers?"

"With the promise of not laying off or decreasing the drivers' pay, yes."

"You got them to agree?"

"The logistics industry is having a revenue problem. I spoke to them in terms they needed to hear."

"Murray and Sons is one of the biggest companies in the south. Their CEO refused to work with us."

"There's been a change of leadership, someone I can work with far better."

"This . . . this is huge. We would be breaking into a new market, one we've tried to for years."

"Is that impressive enough for you?"

"Ruth, I would have said yes if you told me you were planning to go viral on TikTok. I expected more, yes, but not . . . *this*."

"It's just an interest form."

"Which is more than we ever had before. You definitely have a job with us. And now I know which one."

"Don't you have to get it approved?"

"I did. The other executives were open to it if you came up with something satisfactory. This is revolutionary, Ruth."

"So, what's the job?" I asked. "Manager? Director?" I'd hate to take a step down in my career, but I hated being unemployed more.

"No," he said. "I can't have you as a director or manager with Knox as a CEO. It's too risky considering the public news of your relationship."

"But you said I had a job."

"You do. As the chief operation officer of PATH."

It was my jaw's turn to drop. "Is that . . . an executive position?"

"Yes, it is. We're creating the position for you. You won't report to Knox, either. You'll report to the board of directors like he does. You will have to disclose your relationship to HR, though. They know, but having it in writing is better than not."

"I can't be an executive. I have no experience."

"You just opened the door for a multimillion-dollar deal for us. I feel completely confident in giving you this role. Everyone else did too."

"I-I don't know what to say."

"I hope you accept."

"I accept. Of course I accept, I just . . ."

"I have a feeling you're used to not getting rewarded for hard work. That's not how this company operates."

"Y-you're right."

"I think you'll fit in just fine," Preston said with an unwavering smile. "But there is one rule I just implemented."

"What's that?"

"Forty-hour work weeks. I expect both you and Knox to follow it. Or I will kill you both once I move to Nashville."

"Even for management?"

"Especially for management. I'm not having Knox burn out again."

"I respect that. You have yourself a deal," I said. "But can I ask for one quick thing?"

"What is it?"

"How soon can you get me a company email?"

"Almost instantly, why?"

"I have a very important email to send."

Knox

When Preston called me, I was lamenting the fact that Ruth was busy doing whatever task he'd set out for her, and wondering why the hell he had sent her on whatever mission she was on to give her a job.

"You're ready to be the CEO again, right?" Preston asked.

"You're not even going to say hello after you sent my girlfriend on a wild goose chase?"

"I was hoping you weren't mad about that."

"I am *very* mad about it."

"It all worked out, okay? A few people wanted to be sure this wasn't purely a nepotism hire."

"Was it Mike who said that? He wouldn't have done it to my face."

"Mike was worried about our public image. We just needed her to show us what she was capable of."

"And how did she do?"

"She blew us out of the water."

A smile crossed my face.

"But I didn't call about Ruth. I called about business."

"I have some updates on the headphones if that's what it is."

"No, this is *way* bigger. We need your brain."

"What is it?"

"We made some headway into the trucking business."

"Without truckers getting fired or having their pay cut?"

"Yes. We have a signed letter of interest from one of the biggest companies in the industry. There is a clause where they won't lay off any truckers in relation to the deal."

"What company is this?"

"Murray and Sons."

That was when it hit me.

"Ruth did this, didn't she?"

"I don't know how, but yes. She did. We need that office open in Nashville immediately. We're going to be having a lot of meetings with Murray and Sons and I want her leading it."

"She better have a title that justifies that."

"I think you'll be happy with what I found. Work with her to get it open. I'll be in town by fall, and another executive will work in that office too."

My mind was full of things I needed to do, but I was far more excited about it than I had been for anything at Stanford.

I said goodbye to Preston, ready to get to work. I logged into my PATH email, eager to tell my employees that I was back, but something stopped me.

It was an email from an executive, but it had a very familiar name.

To: Knox Price
  From: Ruth Murray
  Subject: Introductions

        Hello, Mr. Price,

        I wanted to formally introduce myself. I am Ruth Murray,
        the newest Chief Operations Officer of PATH. I look forward
        to working very closely with you. Please find this Chuck E.
        Cheese gift card as a token of my excitement.

        Attachments: HR relationship disclosure file, and a gift
        card.

All thoughts of work gone, I closed my laptop.

Fucking Preston. He'd hired her as an executive, which was a bold move. It meant she was on the same level as me, and if she reported to the board of directors, then it also meant I had no power over her.

Now I knew why she needed to prove herself.

I heard a knock at the door, and I opened it. I glowered at a very smug Ruth. She had her phone out and took a photo the moment the door opened.

"Oh, your *face*!" she exclaimed. "I bet I looked the same way when Preston offered me the job."

"I hate you," I muttered.

"Do you?"

"No. I love you, but you got me this time. Do you think it's against the rules for me to kiss the newest hire?"

"I think we can make that work."

As I brought Ruth in for a kiss, I was hit with a happiness I never thought I could feel. I had her, my home, my parents, and now she worked for a company I could guarantee would treat her right. I'd gone from feeling nothing to having everything I could ever want. And I couldn't regret a single thing about it.

EPILOGUE

Ruth

Three Months Later

"That might be the hottest thing you've ever done." Knox leaned against the desk of my newest office.

"What—yelling at Mike for trying to suggest we hire unpaid interns?"

"Yes. Your passion is alluring."

He leaned in for a kiss, but I stopped him.

"I am not up for getting caught in this office again," I said. "Preston was *so* mad."

"Preston is always mad when we're a couple."

I rolled my eyes. "Wait until we get home. I'll make it worth your while."

He glanced at his watch. "So, we're going home at three, right?"

"Sure. I've worked late a lot this week. Preston will lecture us *again* if we go over forty hours."

While I was good at stopping Knox from working too much, I easily fell into the old habit of staying late. So much so that Preston routinely lurked the halls trying to catch us.

"Right," he said, smiling. "We could probably leave now if you wanted to, unless you still have a lot of work to do."

"My late nights did me a favor. I'm not too busy today. Well, work wise, I'm not busy. I still need to get the ingredients for the cake Lynn and I are making. I need to cancel the lease for the apartment I never stay at and . . ." I sighed and pulled a letter from my desk. "I need to decide if I'm sending this or not."

What was in my hand was a letter I'd drafted to send back to Mom. Her handwritten one to Knox had a permanent place in my mind. I was sympathetic to her feeling trapped with Dad but also unwilling to let her control my career.

"You don't have to."

"I do want her to know she has options." The lawyer's card I'd attached was the main one. "But I don't want things to go back to how they were."

Lynn had told me that I could do both. I could give Mom an out by connecting her with a lawyer, but make it clear that her expectations of my career were not allowed to be discussed.

Some nights, I laid awake racked with guilt as I imagined what Dad must have put her through, especially after he no longer had a company to run. Tom's and Knox's lawyers had managed to keep him out of power, even if he was still fighting it.

I bit my lip, opening the letter to read it once more.

Mom,

I've seen the letter you sent to Knox, and while I wished you would have said it to me, it was also good to know you care about me for more than what I've accomplished in my career.

But this isn't about me.

Attached is a business card to a well-respected divorce lawyer. You don't deserve to be treated as you are, and I know Tom, Barry, and I miss the old you. Who Dad has forced you to be is not you who have to be.

I know I'm not aware of how difficult it has been for you, but I can do one thing. If you meet with the lawyer whose card I've attached, I'll cover the costs of the divorce. I have enough saved up.

If you do decide to leave, I'd be open to discussing what our relationship could look like going forward, but I won't be talking to Dad. I'm sorry, but he's hurt us too many times.

Respectfully, Ruth

Knox's hand rested on my shoulder.

"I'm going to send it," I told him. "And I'll deal with whatever choice she makes."

He leaned over to kiss my hair but was interrupted with a knock on the door.

Preston popped his head in, but he'd covered his eyes with a hand. "*Please* tell me you two are decent."

I gratefully accepted the distraction from the heavy topic. I put on a smile as I placed the letter back in the drawer.

Knox rolled his eyes. "We're not doing anything inappropriate, Preston."

He peeked and then removed his hand completely. "Okay, good. I never know with you two."

"Neither of us want another lecture," I replied exasperatedly.

"Really? I have some good ones prepared. Next time I want to do the disappointed Dad stare and say 'how dare you' while shaking my head."

"What do you need?" I asked, trying not to laugh at Preston's imagined lecture. "You better not be here to give me a major project. I was finally about to do as you demand and leave early."

"It's not a big project, but I need you to talk with Tom. He's not been responding to emails."

"Really?"

"Yeah, and it's been a few days. We need him on top of this considering your Dad is still trying to undermine the project."

I frowned, worry tightening my shoulders. "I'll drop by his place on the way home. If he's not there, then I'll go by the office. I have some other errands to run, anyway."

"Thank you," he said. "That's my main concern. Everything else seems under control."

"Do you have plans?" Knox asked. "Ruth wants to do a big cookout this weekend. We're inviting her friend and Mom instructed me to invite you."

"You didn't invite me because you wanted me there?"

"I do want you there, but Mom *really* wants you to come. She hasn't seen you since you moved back."

"I'm afraid she's going to unlock some unprocessed trauma again."

"No trauma unlocking this weekend," I said. "We're going to either play Monopoly or Uno."

"Are you two *really* going to play some of the most relationship-ruining games ever?"

"It's a test of our commitment," Knox said. "Especially if I win."

"We've played it before. But Lynn and Benji usually get left behind when it's just the four of us."

"Ah, so we're the buffer."

"Kind of. We also want to have dinner with you."

"Fine, I'll join. I don't have any other plans since I blocked my dad."

"I'm still sorry you had to," I said.

"It's fine. It's his fault anyways. Backing people into a corner is never a good idea and ignoring me when I said I didn't want to talk about it only sealed the deal. Now if you'll excuse me, I need to get to another meeting. I've heard Ruth pissed off Mike by telling him no again."

"It was deserved," I protested.

"Probably so. The guy is great with numbers but terrible with decisions." Preston shook his head and walked to his own office.

"Let me wrap up a couple of things here, and then we'll go home."

"I'll work on the trucking equipment then."

"I'm telling Preston too. He will come stop you if you go over."

"Yeah, I know," he said. "I'll try not to get too lost in work."

I gave him a kiss before I got back to work, which was so much easier to do now that I actually liked my job and who I worked for.

Working at PATH was probably the greatest decision I'd ever made. Knox and I had a very similar idea of how an office should run, so we rarely butted heads on operations of the newest working space. Preston was more than happy to let go of the reins and let Knox lead.

And I'd like to think we were doing a good job. So far, ten people from Stanford had transferred over. My former employer's reputation had sunk to new lows, especially when the rest of my marketing team abandoned ship.

The new office was worlds better than Stanford's. People were only required to come in if they needed to. But if they did, they weren't working within tan walls with no decor. It was a nice office with free snacks and coffee. About half of the people wanted to come in and some did far better working from home. Knox and I both were happy to let people work in whatever way suited them.

While I didn't have too much of a hand in marketing, the team was still under me, and I'd taken to mentoring Jimmy. Even if PATH's products marketed themselves, Jimmy and I managed a few campaigns that had people even more interested in the business.

But my main focus had to be the official deal with Murray and Sons. Tom had been reasonable to work with, which made his absence worrying.

After my meeting with Jimmy was over, my mind was on my family. I left the moment I could, eager to drop off the letter and nearly desperate to know what was going on with Tom.

My worst fear was that he'd returned to drinking.

Once the letter was sent, I drove to his apartment which was where he would be if he was drunk. He never once got shit-faced in the office, and if he was going back on his sobriety, he'd try to hide it.

I honestly hoped he would be at work, so at least I knew he wasn't drinking, but my heart sank when I saw his old truck parked in its usual spot.

I was definitely going to need to talk to Lynn about what to do. She'd been dying to try to help Tom in some way to realize that he wasn't too far gone for forgiveness and growth, but he'd been stubborn about it.

Barry and I were the only ones regularly talking about non-work things. Tom and I had only discussed the business deal.

I took a deep breath, preparing myself for seeing Tom as his old self, drunk and angry. Then I went to knock on the door.

For a moment, he didn't answer.

"I have a key," I yelled. "I will come in, so you better have pants on."

The door opened after that.

"What?" he answered, his voice tighter than usual. "I'm out of office today."

I took a long look at him. He was still in his work shirt, but it wasn't unbuttoned like it used to be when he would drink. He didn't smell like alcohol, but when I peered into his apartment, I saw a glass bottle on the counter.

"I'm not drunk," he said, following my line of sight. "Yet."

"What's wrong?" I asked.

"Nothing you need to worry about."

I rolled my eyes and I shouldered past him to get into the apartment. I grabbed the bottle and poured it down the sink.

"Ruth!" he snapped.

"No. You need to talk about the problem rather than drinking. You can trust me, Tom."

"It's not your problem."

"No, it's not. But you're my brother, and you need to get it through your thick skull that I am here to *help* you. Now stop stalling and tell me what has you upset."

"Ruth," he began.

"Tom," I said back. "I care about you."

"You won't after this."

"Why not?"

"Because it's bad, Ruth."

"Like Dad level bad?"

"Honestly? Yes."

"What did you do?"

"You remember my college days, right?"

"We all do. You never spent a weekend not partying. Between the drinking and women, I'm surprised you didn't get yourself in trouble."

"I did get into trouble, Ruth." He ran his hands through his hair, a nervous action I hadn't seen in years. "I ran into someone the other day. Someone I used to know. Someone I had . . . a *night* with twelve years ago."

"And?" I asked slowly.

"And she has a son, Ruth. One who looks to be twelve years old, with green eyes and dark hair."

COMING SOON…

The Murrays' story will continue with Tom in Man of Action—Coming in 2024! Pre-order it <u>on Amazon!</u>

LOOKING FOR ANOTHER READ?

Check out these other books by Elle!

Contractual Obligations

When Lily is offered a ticket out of the career and life she hates, she takes it. Even if it means signing a contract to marry the attractive but aloof Sebastian Miller for five years.

Her job is simple: play the happy house wife in person and on social media and she will get awarded a million dollars of her inheritance. That money is more than enough for her to start a life on her own and away from her controlling parents. It should be easy.

But four years in, she's more than ready to be done with this marriage. She's pretty sure her husband hates her, and she longs for the freedom the end of their contract will bring—a freedom that is threatened when she's called to meet Sebastian's father, the orchestrator of this whole sham. She worries he will try to extend their contractual marriage.

What he does is worse.

Forced to move across the country due to a promotion for Sebastian is her worst nightmare, but her only choice is to pretend to be fine.

She prepares for the last year of their marriage to be more cold indifference, but being stuck in a new city shows a sweeter side of Sebastian that Lily never thought possible. Gone is the indifferent man she knows and in his place is the kind and patient man of her dreams.

But their clock is ticking—only one year of their marriage remains. Will they find love or will contractual obligations get in the way?

Failure to Thrive

Riley Emerson is probably the last person anyone would expect to be a nanny. For starters, her life has fallen apart. Her boyfriend just cheated on her. She lives with her mom, and she might have a drinking problem.

But Oliver Brian is desperate. His daughter, Zoe, has refused to go to sleep for anyone else in four years and with his career Oliver can't always be there for her. Riley is only supposed to watch Zoe for one night, but somehow she gets Zoe to bed on her own. He's so shocked that he offers her a job on the spot.

Riley needs the money, and Oliver needs the time for himself. It's a match made in Heaven... until feelings get involved.

Under Any Conditions

What happens after the happily ever after?

Riley and Oliver are finally together. Things should be perfect, but Riley struggles with the ghosts of her past while Oliver finds himself trapped in a workplace legal battle, which puts him face-to-face with someone he'd rather forget.

While Riley wonders if she isn't good enough, Oliver knows she's the one for him, but they have a lot of work to do if they want to figure out how to merge their very different lives into one. Does love persevere under any conditions? Or will it crumble under the weight of someone's past?

To Make Matters Worse

Violet Moore is not having a good week.

It starts with a fight between her and Charlie Davis—the usual bane of her existence—and ends with a drink thrown on her. Then, she somehow agrees to be *fake friends* with the same man to ensure her best friend's wedding goes off without a hitch. And last but certainly not least, her apartment collapses, and the only person with an open room is Charlie himself.

Violet isn't sure what's going to be worse: the wedding or her living situation.

There are few people that are more confusing than Violet Moore.

Charlie has never understood her, but the quick-witted, five-foot-three schoolteacher has a huge grudge against him. Why? He has no clue. He's not proud of his immature spats with his former college friend turned enemy, but he can never seem to stop himself—not when it's her he's fighting with. He's content to get this wedding and their fake friendship over with so they can go back to their normal fighting lifestyle.

Then he finds her crying and needing a place to stay, and it changes all of his plans. Feelings he had long since buried rush to the surface, and he finds himself unable to stop thinking about the beautiful, but confusing, Violet Moore.

They haven't agreed on anything in six years, but can one wedding, a ruined apartment, and being stuck in one house somehow bring them together?

THANK YOU

Words cannot say how much gratitude I feel for all of my readers. I wrote the first draft of this novel when I had no idea that I would be a full-time author within a year and finished it right before I left my day job permanently. Writing has been my dream since I was a little girl, and each story I tell has a little piece of me in it, especially this novel.

For all of my friends who have listened to me vent as I was coming to leave my job, thank you. I needed your kind words and support. For my husband, who singlehandedly ran our home while I was working a demanding day job and writing when I could, thank you. You may not be much of a reader, but your investment of time made this possible. I owe you so much.

And finally, I want to thank those who made this book what it is. Kasey, your edits always are on point, and I am so glad we work together. Allie, thank you for designing not only this book cover, but also my logo and website. Though we met in a less than ideal situation, it was all worth it because I met you!

Made in United States
Orlando, FL
19 January 2024

42697430R00204